Grace Wynne-Jones was born and brought up in Ireland and has also lived in Africa, the US and England. She has a deep interest in psychology, spirituality and healing and she also loves to celebrate the strangeness and wonders of ordinary life and love. She has frequently been praised for the warm belly-laugh humour and tender poignancy in her writing and has been described as 'a novelist who tells the truth about the human heart'.

Her feature articles have appeared in many magazines and national papers in Ireland and in England and her radio play *Ebb Tide* was broadcast on RTE 1. Her short stories have been published in magazines in Ireland, England and Australia, and have also been broadcast on RTE and BBC Radio 4. She is the author of four critically acclaimed novels: *Ordinary Miracles*, *Wise Follies*, *Ready Or Not?* and *The Truth Club*. Some of her fiction has also been translated into German, Russian and Indonesian. She has written and broadcast many radio talks and is also the producer and presenter of two forthcoming radio documentaries. She has been included in the book *Sunday Miscellany A Selection From 2004 – 2006* (New Island). She also contributed to the travel book *Travelling Light* (Tivoli).

Please visit her website for more information:

www.gracewynnejones.com

For Maura

ACKNOWLEDGMENTS

A big thank you goes to my agent Lisa Eveleigh for all her support, encouragement and help with this book. Loads of thanks also go to Hazel Cushion and Bob Cushion of the wonderful Accent Press and to Joelle Brindley for the lovely jacket artwork. I also send my brother Patrick Wynne-Jones a big printed hug for his kindness and understanding.

Thanks too go to Eve Dolphin, Leo Rutherford, Richard Offutt, Julie Turner, Philip Casey, Lin Kirk, Gwynnie, Leo Rutherford, Liz, John, Joe Keveny, John Cantwell and Karen Ward, Alison Walsh, Tana Eilis French, the Ulster Bank and the friendly folks at Teignmouth Library, and to Alberto Villoldo for his inspiring teachings about healing and Shamanism. Love and light is sent to my various 'helpers' and to the characters in this novel who taught me so much. I also thank my lovely relatives and pals in the U.K. and Ireland and U.S.A. for being so supportive. My dear friend and former neighbour, Maura Egan, passed away in 2004. She was a wonderful woman who will be sorely missed by her family and many friends in Little Bray. I so enjoyed our chats and cups of tea and I was so grateful for her kindness.

PRAISE FOR *THE TRUTH CLUB:*

'...Grace Wynne-Jones has written an entertaining, intelligent and genuinely funny story...this is a great read, especially for commuters...guaranteed to shorten any journey.' THE IRISH TIMES

'It ('The Truth Club') manages to achieve something that most chick 'lit' doesn't. It makes you want to read past the half-way point. And most unusually, you even find yourself wanting to read right to the end, as opposed to finishing it out of a sense of tidiness, as you would the last biscuit on the plate...there are shades of an intense Anne Tyler novel about it, especially in Sally's intimate assessment of her relationship with her husband, which is mature and insightful...If 'The Truth Club' were a dessert, it would be a tiramisu: multi-layered, and definitely substantial, with some surprising elements to it. Ultimately satisfying...' EVENING HERALD

'The terrain of 'The Truth Club'...is the fragility of the human heart, the conflicting loyalties that relationships bring, the choices that we make or simply fail to....a delicate exploration of being human.' THE IRISH EXAMINER

'...a novel which by turns had me laughing (aloud) entranced and, by the end a little bit wiser than I was at the beginning. In 'The Truth Club' Grace Wynne-Jones has produced a book in which the eclectic characters almost leap from the pages...the book also contains a perfect man, Nathaniel, who 'almost always' says the right thing...' IRELAND ON SUNDAY

'In the latest crop of chick-lit beach reads...Grace Wynne-Jones comes out top with her quirky new novel 'The Truth Club'. Her characterisation is always amusing and the plot is delivered with warmth and a healthy sense of the ridiculous...it's Ms Wynne-Jones's cutesy sense of humour that makes this book so tasty.' THE SUNDAY INDEPENDENT

'It is a tour de force.' KATIE FFORDE

Chapter One

SOMETHING WEIRD HAPPENED YESTERDAY when I was talking
to my sister April on the phone. She said, 'I wonder what
happened to Great-Aunt DeeDee.'

I said, 'I thought she was dead.'

'Oh, no,' April replied. 'She went missing. Just left home,
when she was in her early twenties, and told no one where she
was going. No one's heard from her since.' Then April
added something that was entirely typical of her. She said,
'You *know* that, Sally. For God's sake, where have you been
for the last thirty-five years?' She was asking where I've been all
my life, since I am thirty-five, though I'm often told I look
younger. That's one of the things I cling to – that people say I
look younger. I don't see it myself. When I look in the mirror I
see honey-coloured hair, brown eyes, highish cheekbones, and
wrinkles and crow's-feet and grey hairs.

'Of course I've *heard* of DeeDee,' I said. 'But only a few
times. Nobody ever seems to talk about her.'

'Well, they wouldn't, would they?' April said. 'After
what she did.'

'What did she do?'

'I don't know, but I get the impression people are really
pissed off with her.'

'How do you know all this?' I demanded. I'm the one who
is supposed to be privy to the family secrets.

'I've known it for *years,*' April replied, without going
into detail. 'Look, could you tell Aunt Marie I can't get to her
big do? I can't believe she expects me to fly over from
California for a finger buffet. I have my own life.'

She knew, of course, that I wasn't going to say this verbatim
to Aunt Marie. She knew I would find a way to be more
tactful. Aunt Marie, who is my mother's sister, feels she needs
to corral family members every few years and frog-march them
into some sort of intimacy. Somehow we all fit into Aunt

1

Marie's front room, though it's quite a squeeze. I usually end up saying, 'Oh, really? How interesting!' to the various younger relatives who are involved in important-sounding courses. I seem to come from a family that has a great involvement in further education. Then, of course, there are the ones who are methodically working their way up the Civil Service; they sound impressive too, especially the ones who have to make regular trips to Brussels. And there's a cluster of lovely bright young women who have married nice decent men and are having children or expecting them, and are teachers or social workers or aromatherapists.

I'd absorb more of what they were telling me if I weren't so fixated on trying to make a good impression myself. In some ways these gatherings feel like school reunions, at which we check up on one another and measure one another's achievements. But in another way they are nothing like school reunions, which are softened by genuine affection and curiosity and giggles about daft things in the past. Many of the people in Aunt Marie's front room are almost strangers. It says a lot for the force of her character that we show up at all. We are not the sort of large extended family that gathers for the fun of it. It's not that we don't like each other; it's just that we have other things to do, and other people to do them with.

I am beginning to dread Marie's next big get-together, because my separation from Diarmuid is bound to crop up in conversations, and there is no way I can make that sound impressive. At the last gathering I had just met him, and my parents must have mentioned it to someone, because suddenly the room was buzzing with the news that 'Sally has found a man!' Naturally I had found men before, but people had never got quite so excited about it. I suppose it was because I was over thirty and they felt I had better get a move on in the marriage stakes.

They were, of course, thrilled when I walked down the aisle. They gave me things like alarm clocks that make tea, and hostess trolleys, which are all now carefully stored in the smart suburban house that Diarmuid and I bought together and where he still lives. The main thing I seem to have gained from my marriage is a very comfortable orange sofa that's too big for my small sitting-room. I enjoy lying on it when I watch TV.

My phone conversation with my sister ended when she said she had to go to a meeting. April was ringing from an office in San Francisco. She is twenty-four and she has started to look Californian – I know this from the very occasional photos she sends our parents; she hasn't come back to Ireland since she left three years ago. Her hair is sun-bleached blonde, her skin is golden-brown and her small snub nose looks cuter than ever. Her smile still has that steely, determined look to it, but her teeth are whiter. She has also acquired that wiry, lean look people get when they jog regularly and visit the gym and do Pilates. I have, naturally, not told her that I force myself to get exercise by occasionally walking an imaginary dog called Felix along a nearby beach. She is an important person in real estate, or it could be banking; it's hard to keep track of her career. Not too long ago she was involved in the vacation industry. April is a young hotshot manager, so her skills are easily transferable.

I, on the other hand, am a freelance journalist who has somehow ended up specialising in interior decoration and pets, with the occasional article on refugees and other worthy social issues. Since my separation, I also sometimes interview people who write self-help books and grill them on the secrets of a contented marriage. I make a kind of living from it, but freelance journalists aren't that well paid; and the big thrill of seeing my name in the paper above articles about bathroom tiling has, to tell the truth, sort of waned. Another thing is that loads of people want to be freelance journalists, because it's supposed to be so interesting, so you can't afford to be too bolshie with editors, because there's a horde of young eager beavers who would be more than willing to replace you. In an ideal world, April would regularly say, 'Oh, I wish my job was as interesting as yours,' but she doesn't. She has her own lovely sea-view condominium, a sports car and loads of handsome men taking her out for sushi. She is happy – and I keep feeling she shouldn't be, because she never seems to want to talk about anything that really matters. Come to think of it, my parents are rather like that too.

The conversation about DeeDee was typical. Even though April said she wondered what happened to DeeDee, she didn't really want to go into details, ponder who DeeDee was and why she left; according to her, things are as they are, and it's pointless analysing them. Sometimes I envy her blithe indifference, but most of the time it just makes me feel lonely, so it's just as well I hardly ever talk to her. If you start talking about feelings to April, she always finds a way to make you feel foolish. When I tried to talk to her about the break-up of my marriage, for example, she said, 'Oh, well, these things happen sometimes. You'll find someone else. Go and have a facial. That always cheers me up.' I think she was trying to be kind.

DeeDee has been popping into my mind ever since my conversation with April. This is rather inconvenient, because I'm currently trying to write an article about bathroom accessories. Also, every so often I ask myself *why* I am writing about bathroom accessories when I have no real interest in the subject. Four years ago the editor of *The Sunday Lunch,* Ned Wainwright, said he wanted more articles for the 'Home' section, and I said, 'Oh, what kind?' with a big fake-interested smile. Freelance journalists can't afford to be too fussy. I didn't think I'd end up with a column – which, of course, was wonderful; *is* wonderful. I need the regular income, to pay for my mortgage and those extra little luxuries such as food, electricity and clothes. It's just that, quite a lot of the time, I wish I were involved in something else. This happened with my marriage, too. I'm beginning to wonder if it's a 'psychological pattern'. Perhaps I'll always have these dreams of elsewhere. Maybe I've inherited some of DeeDee's feckless genes.

As I said, since my break-up with Diarmuid I have interviewed a number of authors of self-help psychology books. Some of them say that people who aren't compatible should part, and some of them say that people who aren't compatible

4

should work out why they aren't compatible and try to make some appropriate changes; then, apparently, they may find they are far more compatible than they thought. Sadly, none of them offer advice on husbands who suddenly become obsessed with mice.

That's what happened with Diarmuid. He's a carpentry teacher, and he wanted to be able to teach biology too; so he started this biology course, and the mice thing just took off. We hardly ever saw each other because he was so busy studying mice. Sometimes he brought them home for the weekend, and gradually they moved in permanently. I started to feel sorry for them. It's not that I like mice all that much, but I hated seeing them in that cage. So one night, after a row and too much wine and wild, romantic music, I set them free in the tool shed. Diarmuid and I parted shortly after that. If we get divorced, I suppose the mice may be mentioned as a third party. He managed to lure them back using mature cheddar cheese. I still feel a bit angry with those mice. I feel, deep down, that they should have made a run for it.

When I left, I told Diarmuid I needed time to think things over. I didn't quite know what I was going to be thinking about, but it sounded like the sort of thing a woman bolting out the front door with a large cream suitcase should say. I liked the dramatic exit, but the whole effect was watered down somewhat because I had to keep returning for things like my hair-dryer and my jumpers and my transistor radio. And, naturally, Diarmuid and I got chatting, and I ended up hugging him because he was sad; I was sad myself, which is why I let him kiss me and run his hands tenderly through my hair. He kept saying he was sorry about the mice, which I noticed were still in the spare room and looking pretty contented despite their lack of freedom. He even said he'd get rid of them, but I said we could talk about that another time. Because what I was realising was that, even if Diarmuid made lots of 'appropriate changes' to help our 'compatibility', I still wasn't sure I'd want to go back to him.

We separated over half a year ago, and I'm not any clearer

5

about whether I should go back to him. I'm not even sure why I feel like this, because I'm thirty-five and old enough to know I'm not going to find the perfect man and he is such a decent, loving guy. I sometimes feel I don't miss him enough. But I miss the home we bought together. It's an ordinary suburban house, but it's detached and in a leafy area, and it has a big garden with nice shrubs and trees and scented plants. We wanted to move to the country after we had our two kids, but for the time being we were happy to live in a house near the Dublin mountains. We could see the countryside through our bedroom window. The main bedroom has an en-suite bathroom. I bought lovely thick white towels. The carpets still have a new, bouncy feel to them. Diarmuid now shares our home with a tenant called Barry, who's Australian and keeps wanting to have barbecues.

I suppose I'd miss my marital home more if I hadn't owned a house already. I bought this little cottage in my late twenties, before house prices became astronomical. I couldn't afford to buy it now. Even though it only has one bedroom and the orange sofa takes up a lot of the sitting-room, it's beside the sea and fairly close to central Dublin. When Diarmuid and I got married, we decided it was a good idea to keep my cottage and rent it out. We couldn't have shared it, because it's so 'cosy' – as the estate agents put it – that two people can barely fit in the kitchen.

When I left my marital home with my large cream suitcase, I think part of me must have been aware that the current tenants were due to leave in three weeks, though I didn't know I was being quite so practical. I stayed with my friend Erika until the cottage was free again. She's a good person to be sad with. We watched loads of DVDs and ate chocolate biscuits, and I took very long baths.

The kindest way to describe this cottage would be 'shabby but sweet'. The outside is painted Mediterranean blue, and it has big twinkly windows that overlook the sea. That's why I bought it: I wanted to look out at the sea and see it change colour. I wanted that vastness, that unbuilt space. It's a bit like living next to a golf course, only nicer.

I look out the window at the sea while I try to decide whether to encourage readers to 'experiment' and personally decorate some of their bathroom tiles. It's a sunny, blustery May afternoon; the sea is bouncing around, and the foliage on one of Dublin's sturdy palm trees is waving in the breeze beside the beach. My neighbour's wind-chimes are tinkling, and this is the sort of moment when I wish I owned a cat. I could pick it up and cuddle it and find the favourite spot behind its ears.

Tea. I need a cup of Earl Grey. I get up and pad, shoeless – I am wearing a pair of thick, soft pink socks – to the kitchen. When the tea is made and in my favourite wide-rimmed cream cup – a present from my extremely successful friend Fiona, who regularly visits Paris to discuss software – I decide to phone Aunt Marie. I want to ask her about DeeDee.

After I have told Marie that April won't be flying back from California to feel uncomfortable in her front room, I say, with studied nonchalance, 'Marie, you know Great-Aunt DeeDee…'

This is met with silence: a strange, hissing silence. I feel like I have lifted a seashell to my ear. 'Hello?' I say, wondering if she's still on the line.

'What do you want to know about her?' Marie says brusquely.

'Well, I was just… just wondering if anyone knows what happened to her.'

'Of course they don't,' Marie replies, as if this is a blatantly idiotic question.

'Has anyone tried to find out?' I persist.

I hear a deep intake of breath. Then Marie says, 'Sorry, Sally, I have to go. I have a lasagne in the oven.'

'But –'

Marie sighs sharply. 'I don't know what happened to DeeDee. No one does. We don't talk about her any more.'

'Why?'

'Because there's no point. She's gone,' Marie says flatly.

7

'Thanks for your call, dear. Bye.' She hangs up the phone.

This is unusual. Marie is far from perfect, but she's not usually rude. What on earth happened to DeeDee? And why doesn't Marie share my curiosity? Perhaps DeeDee was just a feckless, uncaring, horrible person. Maybe that's why no one misses her.

I go to the kitchen and fetch a chocolate biscuit, then head reluctantly back to my article about bathroom accessories. It seems that DeeDee will remain a mystery – for the moment, anyway. I'll have to ask Mum about her. Perhaps she'll be more forthcoming.

I start to type frantically, because someone might pop by for tea at any moment. My friend Erika says I should have been a geisha. Even Diarmuid regularly drops in for Earl Grey and almond cookies. We never mention the mice, naturally. When he's sitting on our sofa – it is still *our* sofa, since we bought it together – I can't help noticing that he's a handsome man with great biceps and lovely broad shoulders. And his stomach is so flat and toned. I know I'm describing him as though he were a horse or something, but one of Diarmuid's attractions is that he has a great body, and he's very good in bed. Come to think of it, I really miss that too.

He's not tall – about five foot ten – and he's kind of stocky, but in a nice way; it's muscle, not fat. His bum is firm and looks great in jeans. His face is well proportioned, and he has a strong jawline and thick black eyebrows to go with his wavy dark hair. His eyes always seem a bit distant, but maybe it's because deep down he's quite shy. When he gets up to leave, I always feel a pang of regret. Just for a moment I forget how lonely I was with him; all our differences seem so small, compared to his big strong arms around me.

When Diarmuid leaves, I always want someone to phone or drop by and show me I'm happy to be single, but they never do. It's suddenly like a desert. Of course, at times like this you know you could ring someone yourself, but you also know they'll probably be in the middle of something – they'll be in the supermarket or a meeting, or changing a nappy, or really preoccupied and unusually abrupt. That's the weird thing about life: sometimes you can hardly get a moment to yourself, and sometimes you're forgotten. When you ache with all your heart for a certain person to call you – when that call would make all the difference – they probably won't phone till three days later, when you have five people in the sitting-room and the neighbour's cat has just pooped on the carpet. It's just something you have to get used to. Tough titties, as my friend Fiona would say.

Fiona isn't very sentimental, even though she's sensitive – and not just about herself. My friend Erika, however, is sentimental. She is also a floating secretary. This doesn't mean she spends her time decorously poised above Dublin with a shorthand notepad; it means that, when various large corporations need temporary help for a variety of reasons, she's one of the people they call upon. And they call upon her a lot – which is just as well, because she doesn't make much money from her papier-mâché cats. She loves making and painting them – each one has his or her very own personality – but they take quite a while to get 'just right', and people don't pay all that much for them. In an ideal world, Erika could stay at home with her mashed-paper animals and not have to find her way intrepidly to her desk. Sometimes she makes it sounds like Arctic exploration. Apparently the floors in many modern office blocks are almost identical and devoid of distinguishing features; her landmarks are things like red storage-boxes and water-coolers and photocopiers. Sometimes she even leaves little 'You are here' notes for herself.

Erika is small and blonde and has a sweet, turned-up nose and a slightly dazed expression, which is extremely attractive to men. Especially to someone called Alex. Alex is why Erika is on the phone right now. I was just typing, 'These zebra-patterned soap dishes are available from…' when she called.

'Alex said he doesn't want to leave his wife,' she says. 'Not yet, anyway. Because she may leave him first, and that would be so much easier.'

'Oh.'

'His wife is getting very friendly with her yoga teacher. They even go out for herbal tea after classes.'

'I see.'

'He told me yesterday. We only met for half an hour because Alex had to collect his daughter from her tai chi class.'

'Oh, dear.'

'I didn't mind.' Erika suddenly sounds brave and adamant. 'I had things to do myself. I... I had two marmalade-coloured cats to finish – a bride and groom. I'm making them as a wedding present for Fiona's cousin.'

'Oh. Good.' And it is good. Erika adores making bride and groom cats; she loves painting on the tuxedos and long white dresses. The thing is, hardly any shops seem to want them. Most of them are sold to people she knows.

'I've just read an article about how important it is to have your own life,' Erika says. 'Even if you meet your soulmate, you need to have your own life.'

'Yes,' I say, knowing that at any minute she is going to try to quote Kahlil Gibran.

'As Kahlil Gibran wrote, "The olive and the... the..."' There is a long pause. 'I've forgotten what exactly, but anyway, they don't grow in each other's shade.' Erika hasn't got a great memory for quotations and jokes; when she's telling one of the five jokes she knows, she usually gets to the punch line way before she's mentioned any of the details that would make it funny. Diarmuid thinks she is a bit daft, but in a nice way that he doesn't quite get but can tolerate. And Erika has never really told me what she thinks of Diarmuid, which probably means she isn't that keen on him.

She is certainly very keen on Alex. I saw him once. He was in a bookshop, signing copies of his latest self-help offering. At this point I should probably mention that Alex writes hugely popular books about having healthy relationships. He was very tanned and earnest-looking and fairly muscular around the shoulders; his blue-grey eyes seemed kind and tired, but you could see how they might blaze with raw passion. I didn't buy

10

the book. I just looked at him sniffily and walked by. I wanted him to see I knew he was a fraud – just like I am. He writes books about having wonderful relationships, and I write articles about having a wonderful home.

'I feel such a fraud!' Is Erika telepathic? 'I keep telling Alex I don't mind waiting. I keep telling him that I understand, that I want almost nothing from him. But I do! I… I want us to go to the supermarket together. I want to watch DVDs with him and… and eat crisps. I… I want to *kiss his eyelashes.'*

I don't know what to say to this. Even though I've had quite a sobering romantic career, this is not a longing I have had to deal with. Maybe I should have wanted to kiss Diarmuid's eyelashes. Maybe that's what is missing.

'Oh, Sally, I'm sorry.' Erika sighs forlornly. 'I shouldn't be going on like this. I should be asking you about Diarmuid.'

'I'm very glad you're not,' I say. 'If you did, I wouldn't know what to say.'

There is a long pause. Then Erika says, 'Alex said something else. He said he loved me but he thought it might be best if we didn't meet again. Ever.'

'Oh, dear.'

'Alex says he thinks we're all heated up, and if we get together we'll burst into flames and that will be it.' Erika's voice sounds distant and lonely, as though it's coming from the bottom of the sea. 'I said I understood.' She is sobbing now. 'I said he was right. And… and then Alex said he wasn't so sure. Maybe he was wrong. Maybe we both need the combustion. Maybe we both need our lives to be totally different.'

I hold my breath. *Totally different.* The words seem to tug at my heart.

'So then I had to be the one who was strong, and I said that lives don't become totally different just like that. It takes patience and planning and probably years of therapy.'

I suddenly want to disagree, but I don't. I suddenly think that maybe you can reach a point of desperation when things have to change; that maybe you *can* take a big leap

11

and end up somewhere different, even if you're not quite sure how you got there.

'So how did you leave it, then?'

'He said he'll be in town on Thursday.'

'He wants to meet you?'

'Yes,' she sighs. 'Yes, I suppose he does.'

'And are you going to meet him?'

'I don't know. I want to. I feel like... like maybe the whole thing can teach me something.'

Erika is forever thinking that things can teach her something. She thinks that life is one great big university, and that when she understands love better none of this stuff will bother her any more. But Alex has done relationship courses and he's got relationship certificates, and it hasn't made any difference.

After Erika hangs up, I get back to the article. I tell people to decorate their tiles with enamel paint, and I virtually order them to collect shells and make collages. I add that their shower curtains must be 'boisterous' and their bath mats 'sensuous'. As for flooring, I mention exotic stone slates that need to be imported from Hyderabad. So many people go on, these days, about how to make your house nicer. But it seems to me that they – and I include myself in the bunch – don't talk much about how to make a *home*.

Somehow the word 'home' always reminds me of the house we had when I was little – the old, shabby one where the cushions were faded and the carpets were frayed, and dust motes danced in the light. There was a curved drive and tall trees and a big lazy lawn that never got mowed enough. That was how we lived. We all sort of pottered around, and Dad practised his cello and went off and gave concerts every so often. Sometimes pets died, and I was inconsolable – the world was virtually torn from me when I laid guinea pigs and dogs and hamsters in their final resting-places; but most of the time I was happy, and I didn't even know it.

The doorbell rings. I consider ignoring it. Somehow I have to make time to finish this article *and* visit my great-aunt Aggie, who is old and frail and weird these days, living in a nursing home and convinced that her room is full of sheep.

I decide to ignore the doorbell. I just don't have time to answer it. But I do creep over to the window and peep out between the curtains.

It's Diarmuid – and he's seen me. He's waving and smiling and looking rather pleased with himself. I assume this is because he's carrying a large bunch of flowers, and they clearly weren't bought in a garage. They are beautiful, and they are swathed in soft pink paper, with a ribbon round them.

I open the door and let him in.

Chapter Two

I'VE PUT DIARMUID'S FLOWERS in a large glass vase, and they're on the mantelpiece. They are clearly expensive, because they include blossoms that look as though they belong in Hawaii.

'Thank you so much, Diarmuid,' I say again, as I hand him a blue mug of Earl Grey and put a plate of almond biscuits on the coffee table.

'You're welcome,' he says. His 'welcome' has a slight American twang to it, because he spent five years working as a builder in Brooklyn. That's one of the things we have in common: we've both lived in America. My family moved to California when I was nine and returned to Dublin when I was twelve. Diarmuid went to New York when he was twenty-one; he has loads of cousins out there. Sometimes he talks as though the Bronx is just down the road.

'They really are lovely.' I have already thanked him five times.

Diarmuid smiles at me with obvious pleasure. One of the advantages of separating from Diarmuid is that he is being kind and attentive again – only I wonder how long it would last if I went back to him. Because it wasn't just the mice that made me storm out of the house with my cream suitcase. I was also furious because he had forgotten our first wedding anniversary. There wasn't even a card. He had also taken to going out with friends to the pub, after his biology lectures, and returning home late without so much as a phone call. He just didn't seem like the Diarmuid I had married. When I asked him if he still loved me, he said, 'Well, I'm here, aren't I?' which to be frank didn't offer me much reassurance. Then he held me close and said that the romantic part of love was just the icing. The cake, the nutritious part, was working as a team and building a home together. A family. He explained that he was doing the biology course for us, because he wanted to earn more money, so that we wouldn't have to delay having children for too long and I could, if I wanted, give up journalism for a while and be a stay-at-home parent. And what I wanted to say, but didn't say, was that I wanted more of the icing. I felt I was entitled to it. This cake he was talking about didn't sound all that appetising.

'You'll feel differently when we have kids,' he kept saying, but I'm not the sort of person who wants to use kids to keep me with someone. Diarmuid is very keen to be a parent – in fact, I sometimes wonder if that's the main reason he married me – and he still thinks that a 'kid' would be the answer. That is why, despite our differences, he sometimes tries to get me into bed. He tries to get me to sit beside him on the orange sofa so that he'll have easy access to the ultra-sensitive blissful spots just behind my ears. He knows that, once he really got into gear, he could make me forget little details like condoms. I think he must have a diagram of all my erogenous areas. I have never met a man who could press the right buttons quite so fast.

The argument that made me bolt was about spermicidal cream. One of the many dismaying aspects of my marriage is that some of the crucial details sound almost farcical. Diarmuid found some spermicidal cream in a drawer and asked me why I had it, and I sort of mumbled and stuttered and said, 'Oh… goodness… do I still have that?' And then I blushed, and he said, 'You've been using this, haven't you?' And I said, 'Well, maybe just… just *occasionally,*' and he hit the roof. Because, although we had never discussed it in detail, Diarmuid had formed the impression that we were 'trying to start a family'. And I felt we should get to know each other better before we went straight into teething and nappies and leaky breasts. I wanted more of that icing.

That's why I frequently used a diaphragm. I'd dart into the bathroom and attempt to insert the thing without it springing from my hands and bouncing against the wall.

'What are you doing in there?' he'd call out as he lay in our double bed, erect and waiting.

'Oh… just washing,' I'd shout back.

That's how he formed the impression that I was, perhaps, over-fastidious about hygiene – though he's pretty fastidious too. He is not the sort of man who says, 'Let's just do it now, on the kitchen table.' He has a little wash too, and gargles with mouthwash; then he sprays himself with an aftershave called Ocean. Sometimes I wanted to say that it would be nice just to smell him – that it was all becoming a little too sanitised.

'You lied to me!' That's what Diarmuid shouted when he found the cream – and then the diaphragm – at the back of the drawer.

'No, I didn't! We never discussed it!' I screamed back.

This did not mollify him. As far as he was concerned, we had come to an agreement. He was so enraged that he turned on his heel and left the bedroom. That's another thing I've discovered about Diarmuid: when he is bulging with anger, he doesn't want to talk about it. And I desperately needed to talk about it. I needed to talk about all sorts of things. I felt I might burst with frustration.

'You lied to me too!' I yelled down to the sitting room. And, because he didn't ask me what I meant – he had just turned on the television – I added, 'You're not the person I married. I don't know you. I don't know what we're doing together.'

Silence. There was just the sound of an English voice discussing some team's chances in the Premiership. That's when I started packing. I have never packed so fast in my life.

I rang Fiona on my mobile and asked her to come and collect me; despite my fury, I could hardly drive off in Diarmuid's car. When the doorbell rang I almost ran down the stairs, despite the heavy suitcase. And that's how I ended up staying at Erika's flat until the tenants had left my cottage.

But Diarmuid and I are, naturally, not going to talk about any of that now. At this moment, Diarmuid is telling me that he's just been giving Charlene a driving lesson. Charlene is a colleague of his – she teaches remedial English at the same school where he teaches woodwork – and any time he mentions her, he adds carefully that she is 'just a friend' and that her boyfriend tried to teach her to drive but got too impatient; and she needs to be able to drive, because she is divorced and has a son who's got interested in swimming, karate and football. I believe him. Diarmuid is the kind of man who does that sort of thing. He thinks people should help each other out.

What we are doing is 'keeping the lines of communication open'. That's what the marriage counsellor told us to do. We only visited her once, and I wish she had added something about Diarmuid phoning before he turned up, but she didn't. Diarmuid visits at least once a week, and he always tells me he is only dropping by for a moment and he hopes he hasn't called at an inconvenient time. In fact, he has just said this, and I'm wondering if I should mention the article on bathroom accessories and my visit to Aunt Aggie. It's 5.30 p.m. and I said I'd e-mail the article by the end of the day; this could be construed as meaning 11.55 p.m., but I think that would be stretching the point a little.

'So, Sally, how are you?' Diarmuid asks. I feel like replying that not much has changed since we spoke on the phone last night; I haven't, for instance, suddenly decided to be an airline pilot.

I look him straight in the eye. 'Diarmuid, it's lovely to see you,' I say, which of course doesn't really answer his question. I take a deep breath. 'It's just that… I'm a bit late with an article. I was just trying to finish it.'

Diarmuid looks at me long and hard.

'They're real sticklers for deadlines at *The Sunday Lunch,*' I continue, apologetically, because I have begun to feel extremely guilty. I am very good at guilt. It's been my devoted companion since I left my marriage.

'That's a pity,' Diarmuid replies. 'I wanted to take you out for dinner.'

This, of course, is the ideal time to mention that if you want to take someone out to dinner it would be wise to give her advance notice. But I don't say this. What I say is, 'Oh, that would have been lovely.'

'It could still be lovely.' Diarmuid smiles. 'I can wait here until you've finished the article, and then we can head off. There's a new Thai place in Donnybrook I think you'd like.'

'That's very kind of you, Diarmuid,' I say. I have been repeating this sentence at regular intervals for months now, because Diarmuid *is* being kind – almost unreasonably kind. It frequently occurs to me that he should be far more pissed-off. 'It's just that I've promised to visit Aunt Aggie.'

Diarmuid clenches his jaw. 'Couldn't you visit her tomorrow?'

'Yes, I suppose I could,' I agree. 'But I'd have to phone her, and she'd be disappointed.'

There is a silence, in which I am sure Diarmuid is thinking that I've just admitted something crucial and unflattering: I have just admitted that a woman who thinks her room is full of sheep is more important to me than my own husband, the man I promised to love for ever.

'And then we could go to a film,' Diarmuid remarks.

'What?' For the first time in this conversation, I frown at him.

'After dinner, we could go to a film… if you want.'

I can't think about films and dinner, because I'm thinking about Aunt Aggie. How she'll say, 'Oh, well, dear… come when you can.' How her voice will trail off sadly, despite her attempts to sound as though it doesn't matter. Despite the sheep who have moved into her bedroom, it is still possible to have fairly normal conversations with her sometimes. I love her. I've always loved her. She's been my ally and my friend for thirty-five years. I spent countless hours at her house when I was younger. She seemed to relish my company; she always made time for me. Now I need to make time for her. She won't be around that much longer. Diarmuid should know that.

'Have another biscuit.' I shove the plate towards him, a little too roughly; it almost falls off the table, but he grabs it in time.

'Are you going to phone her, then?' he enquires. 'I should probably ring the restaurant and book us a table.'

I look out the window at the sea moving around, going with the flow of things… changing. Then I turn towards my husband and, without knowing what I am about to say, tell him, 'No.'

Diarmuid is clearly shocked. Ever since I left him, I've treated him with great civility and slight subservience. It seemed the least I could do for him, in the circumstances.

What I have come to realise is that this 'time to think' I have asked for is, in fact, something I should have asked for before I married. But, the minute the engagement was announced, I somehow got completely caught up in the wedding and the dress and the cake and the violin players. I fretted for days about who should sit beside whom at the top table, when I should have been asking myself if I truly loved Diarmuid – loved him enough to make these big promises to him. Because he is a good man, despite the mice. He is the kind of man many women would be happy to marry. I know this because I went out with a bunch of right bastards before I met him. I can hardly count the number of times I've been dumped by men who seemed so nice and sensitive at first. This is one of the many reasons I should run to Diarmuid right now and cling to him like a limpet. But, for some reason I still can't quite explain to myself, I don't.

The 'No' silences us both, and I begin to wonder if I should make him more tea. But, since this is clearly not doing much to keep the lines of communication open, I decide to venture onto the topic of advance notification.

'The thing is, Diarmuid,' I begin slowly, 'I'd *love* to go to dinner and a film with you… it's just that I've made other plans.'

Diarmuid reaches for a biscuit and chomps it solemnly. They're his favourite brand. I buy them for him specially.

'You see, the thing is' – I know I'm saying 'the thing is' too often – 'it would really help if you phoned beforehand. Then… then I wouldn't make other arrangements.'

'But you said you wanted me to be more spontaneous,' he says, too quickly.

'Yes, but that was when we… we were sharing the same house.' I decide not to mention all the evenings he spent closeted with the mice and his textbooks in the spare room.

'I didn't realise you had such a busy social diary, Sally.' There is a distinct edge to Diarmuid's voice, and his eyes have narrowed. And I suddenly know what all this is about. These impromptu visits aren't just him being spontaneous; they are a way of checking up on me. He wants to know if I'm seeing someone else.

'I'm not seeing someone else.'

'I never said you were.'

'But you think I might be.'

'I never said that.'

'You never said it, but you suspect it. You don't trust me.'

His jaw is clenched again, and he's tapping a finger on the arm of the sofa. 'I don't know what to suspect any more,' he says. 'Since you ran away, I just don't know what to think about you.'

Diarmuid has never said I 'ran away' before. I shudder. It makes me sound like DeeDee – and I don't want to be like DeeDee. I don't want to break people's hearts without caring, without even an explanation.

'I didn't run away, Diarmuid,' I say. 'I just needed time to think.'

'About what?' he demands, and I can hear the hidden anger. I suddenly realise what an effort it must be for him to come here and be so nice and civil.

'To think about us. About what it all means.'

He stands up. 'Marriage isn't a philosophy course, Sally.' He doesn't even try to hide his weariness. 'Sometimes I think your sister is right: you analyse things too much. If people love each other, they just love each other.' He sticks his hands deep in the pockets of his jeans.

I feel like crying. He knows how I feel about April. He knows that what he just said will hurt me. I don't want him to leave like this. I want him to keep wanting me.

I say something I know I shouldn't. 'I do love you,

20

Diarmuid.' It's so easy to say those words; so seductive. 'It's just that…'

He turns away from me. This love I'm talking about no longer impresses him. I almost race to the phone to ring Aunt Aggie, like he wants me to. But his expression is so hard and aloof that it seems pointless trying to soften him. He wants to know why I left him and if I'm going to come back; he wants an explanation, and I can't give him one.

'Tomorrow, Diarmuid… let's go to that dinner and film tomorrow. I'd love that.'

'I've got a lecture.'

'The night after that, then.'

'I'll phone you tomorrow and we can discuss it,' he says coldly.

Oh, dear. I just know that now he'll really get into this advance notice thing; he might just possibly bring around a wall chart. I look anxiously out the window as he gets into his old maroon Ford Fiesta. Diarmuid's patience is wearing thin. I simply must make up my mind about our marriage soon.

I return to my advice about how people can transform their bathrooms – not that I really care what they do to their bathrooms. They could all go out and buy tin tubs and I wouldn't care.

At last it's ready, and I press the 'Send' button and stretch my arms and lean back in my chair. The ceiling needs to be repainted. There are so many things in this house that need to be repainted or replaced or grouted. I wish builders used less technical words. Talking to them is like trying to explain things to a computer help desk. I just don't know most of the terminology. Maybe love is like that too. Maybe you have to learn a whole new language.

I grab a quick supper – watercress and salami, with some tomatoes and low-fat cheese; I feel very virtuous as I race out the door. I feel rather less virtuous after I am lured into the newsagent's and buy myself a KitKat. I wonder if I should buy one for Aunt Aggie too, but I buy her mints instead. She's very fond of mints.

21

As I wait for the bus, I think of Alex's wife. I wonder if she knows that her husband has got quite so fond of Erika. Maybe she's turned to her yoga teacher for solace. Then I think of all the poor women who find their husbands are being unfaithful, and wonder how I could care so much about Diarmuid's mice and the spermicidal cream and his spurious spontaneity. All husbands and wives must disagree sometimes. Surely the trick is to learn to talk it out.

Sometimes, when you're waiting at a bus stop, you get this feeling that the bus may never arrive and that you may be left standing there for ever. I get that feeling now, so I distract myself by thinking about DeeDee. I begin to wonder if DeeDee ran off with another man's wife. Maybe that's why no one in the family wants to speak about her. And maybe they're right. Maybe she is best forgotten. As I begin to eat one of Aggie's mints, I decide to forget DeeDee as well. After all this time, it would be impossible to find her.

I remember Diarmuid's expression as he left the house. Yes, we really will have to visit that marriage counsellor again. As soon as possible.

Chapter Three

'I WANT YOU TO find DeeDee.' These are the first words Aunt
Aggie says to me – or seems to say to me; I must
have misheard her. I pull up a chair and sit beside her bed.

'I want you to find DeeDee,' she repeats, her big brown
eyes shining. 'I must see her.'

'Why do you want me to find DeeDee?' I can't believe that
Aggie is talking about her lost sister – especially now, just
when I've begun to wonder about DeeDee myself. I sit on the
edge of my seat, clutching my handbag, and wait for Aggie's
answer. I haven't even taken off my navy linen jacket.

Aggie lies back on her plumped-up pillows. 'Get those
sheep out of here. They're pissing all over the carpet.'

I make vague shooing gestures. Then I say, 'Do you think
DeeDee is still in Ireland? Where do you think I should
look for her?'

Aggie looks at me sternly, so I stand up and wave my arms
about. This is the routine required whenever the sheep get a bit
too boisterous. Then I sit down again and say, 'If you want me
to find DeeDee, you'll have to tell me more about her.' I take
Aggie's hand and squeeze it gently.

'Rio de Janeiro,' Aggie says. 'She often said she wanted to
go there.'

'Oh.' This is a little farther than I had imagined.

'And hats… she loved hats.' Aggie's eyes are too bright. She
is going to cry at any moment.

'Anything else?' I coax.

'Marble cake. She liked that too.' I know about the marble
cake. As far as I remember, Aggie has only mentioned
DeeDee once before. She had baked a marble cake, and the
words just slipped out: 'This was DeeDee's favourite.' Then
she stared into the distance, and Mum and Marie said the cake
was delicious. I was fifteen and said the cake was delicious too.
At the time I was in love with a boy called Roy Bailey, who

was the first decent French kisser I had encountered. Absent relatives were of absolutely no interest to me. I'm surprised I even remember these meagre details.

'She told no one where she was going. She just left us. Without even a note.' Tiny tears are trickling down Aggie's cheeks.

I know I can't press her more on the subject. She won't be with us for much longer. Every time I visit her, I feel I might be saying goodbye. She's actually my great-aunt, my grandfather's sister. Eighty-nine is a good age, of course; but I can't get used to the idea of Aggie not being around any more.

'I brought you some mints.' I hand them to her, and she smiles wanly. She is just lying back on her pillows and staring into the distance. Saying DeeDee's name seems to have exhausted her. Perhaps she won't mention her again. I wonder if I should start talking about Diarmuid and my happy marriage. That always cheers her up.

But Aggie has closed her eyes and appears to be dozing. I look around. It's a very plain room. The curtains are faded aubergine and the carpet is navy. I am sitting on a fake leather armchair the colour of over-boiled cabbage.

'I don't know where they come from,' she murmurs.

'Who?'

'The sheep, of course.' She sighs. I try not to sigh myself. Every time I visit Aggie the sheep turn up. In fact, according to her they're here all the time. Sometimes they get on her bed and try to eat her duvet. She feels sorry for them because they'd be happier in a field. I've tried to tell her there are no sheep, but it makes no difference.

She closes her eyes again, so I just sit beside her. I'm not here out of duty. I do a lot of things mainly out of duty, but this isn't one of them. In these silences, while Aggie is dozing and the nurses are laughing about something and the thick smell of stew is drifting from the kitchen, I remember what it was like when we could have proper conversations. How I loved visiting her rambling old house. How her dog, Scamp, used to throw himself on top of me as soon as I was in the hallway, with its gumboots and sensible coats and dog leads. Aggie always had something in her hand – a geranium cutting or a recipe book or a garden trowel. She would lower her head and peer at me warmly over her glasses, and then we would go into her untidy, cheerful kitchen and she would make us both some tea and give me some freshly baked cake. There was an enveloping sense of welcome and warmth. It was the same whether I was eight or thirty. I'd help her in the garden, and when we were tired she'd make pancakes and we'd watch TV – maybe an afternoon Western. What I knew most about her was that she loved me. 'If I'd ever had a daughter, Sally, I'd have wanted her to be like you,' she once told me. It was the biggest compliment I'd ever received in my life.

Aggie was the happiest person at my wedding. She was beaming – glowing, almost. She always wanted me to settle down and start a family. She didn't have children herself. She married Great-Uncle Joseph in her mid-forties, though she had known him for years – it must have been the longest engagement in history. I've never quite understood why they didn't marry earlier, since she has often said she would have liked to have children, but naturally this isn't something I mention – especially now, since Joseph is dead, and so are many of the people who attended their wedding. I remember the wedding photos: Joseph and Aggie standing together outside the church with Aggie's parents. They were all beaming, of course; beaming so much it looked like they might burst…

I remember my wedding to Diarmuid, and sigh. It was on the wedding day that my doubts started. I thought they came later, after the mice, but I suddenly remember that as I was about to walk up the aisle I had this really strong feeling that I still had time to make a run for it. But then I got caught up in all the excitement again. My doubts evaporated. I truly thought they had gone for ever.

What makes people feel alone, when they so clearly aren't – when they're surrounded by friends and relatives and husbands? Maybe there is another kind of alone, the kind that your soul feels when it longs for a kindred spirit – someone who understands. Someone who knows what it feels like. Someone whose eyes meet yours across a crowded room.

That's the person I talk about when I tell Aggie about my happy marriage to Diarmuid. I talk about how I sometimes look up to find him watching me, tenderly. How we walk along the beach and make squiggly marks on the sand with our bare feet. I talk about how we sometimes laugh at nothing; how he teases me when I get 'too serious'; how we munch bowls of corn chips and watch really stupid television programmes. I tell her how, on our honeymoon, we drank too much champagne one night and decided to skinny-dip in the pool at midnight. I describe how warm the water was against our naked skin.

Only when I talk like this I'm not describing Diarmuid. I wanted Diarmuid to skinny-dip in the pool on our honeymoon, but he wouldn't. Even though it was in the wee small hours, he was sure that someone from Dublin would see us – probably someone who knew his mother.

I don't tell Aggie this, of course. She really likes this other Diarmuid, the one I make up. The one who tenderly traced his fingers over my naked skin by a blossom-scented pool. The one who kissed me under the golden, star-filled sky.

'Sally...'

'Yes, Aunt Aggie?'

'Sally, that thing that happened with your parents... It wasn't your fault.' Aggie is looking at me like a bird. She is thin-faced; her mouth was once full and soft, but now it's a sort of crevice. Her wispy grey hair still has its curls. They lie limply on her forehead.

'Sally, I'm talking to you.'

I look down. That's the thing I can't stand about visiting Aggie these days: she says things like this. She reminds me of stuff I don't want to remember. She seems to have formed opinions about certain things, and they leap out of her suddenly. It's as if part of her has travelled ahead, seen the big picture. But I don't want to see the big picture. I don't want to know what was my fault and what wasn't. I just want to sit with her and love her while I can.

'Thank you, Aggie.' I say it because I know she thinks I'll be pleased to hear her pardon. Her amnesty. Her exoneration.

'It's true.' She studies me earnestly. She looks as though she expects me to keep talking. Her scrawny hands clasp the top of the duvet. They look so sweet and sad and lost, somehow, on the bright-orange fabric. Why did she have to mention something I try so hard to forget?

Mum gave birth to April around the time we discovered she'd been having an affair with one of Dad's best friends. He was called Al, and, like Dad, he was a musician. They played in the same orchestra when we lived in California. Al played the oboe and Dad played the cello.

I'm the one who discovered the affair, actually. I was on my way home, and I was wearing loads of mascara. I'd been playing make-up with a pal called Astrid; this involved sneaking into her parents' room and trying on her mum's eyeshadow and lipstick and eyeliner. I decided to walk home along a lonely dirt track, because I wanted to look for raccoons. Instead, I saw a couple kissing in a parked car. I was interested in the techniques of kissing, so I had a closer look. That's when I realised the woman was my mother.

I just stood there, and she must have felt me watching; she looked up. I ran home, my mascara streaming in black lines down my face because of the tears, and phoned Astrid. I tried to make my voice a whisper, but I was so upset I didn't hear Dad coming into the room. He was barefoot. I think he listened closely *because* I was almost whispering. He'd been sort of watchful and suspicious for months.

When I saw him and got off the phone, he just looked at me blankly. I felt that his face should be contorted in misery, that he should cry and wail, but all he said was, 'What's that stuff on your face, Sally? Go and wash it off immediately.'

There was a terrible row that night, and the night after and the one after that. They probably would have been more dramatic if Mum hadn't been pregnant. As it was, Dad shouted for a bit and then just left the house, and Mum used to go up to her room and cry. I'd hear her sobbing as I stood outside the door. Sometimes I went in and offered to brush her hair; she always used to like that before, but now she had this distant, miserable look on her face as she said, 'Thanks, darling,' and patted my arm.

April sprang into the world a week later, and we all had a good look at her as soon as she was cleaned up. Frankly, for more than a year she could have been anybody's baby; it was only when she was going on two that her nose began to look like Dad's, and we could see that her eyebrows had a similar configuration and her smile was almost identical. Deep down, I think it must have affected her. Few babies have been stared at quite so hard or so cautiously. She developed the technique of staring back just as intensely. 'So what?' her big baby eyes seemed to be saying. 'This is your problem, not mine.'

Somehow Mum and Dad worked it out and stayed together. Only it wasn't like before. Sometimes you could see they really wanted to be somewhere else. They went out a lot. Dad spent hours hiking in the dry brown Californian hills. Mum went over to her friend Veronica's a lot, with April, and sat on the wooden deck beside the wind-chimes and the hummingbird-feeders. She always came back with puffy eyes, walking slowly. I used to make them cups of tea when they got back from wherever they'd gone to. Mum liked Earl Grey, not too strong and not too weak, with a splash of milk and half a spoon of sugar. Dad liked ordinary tea with no sugar and lots of milk.

Diarmuid takes his with half a spoon of sugar. Since then I have had a mental database about how people like their tea.

'Marie's going to have another of her big family get-togethers in September,' I tell Aggie, mainly just for something to say. Then I wish I hadn't mentioned it, because Aggie actually likes Marie's gatherings and I doubt if she'll be able to attend this one. It's still months away – it's only May now; Aggie mightn't even be here. I must get off the subject.

I'm about to mention that Diarmuid wants to take me to a Thai restaurant when Aggie says, 'Marie who?'

I look at her sadly. 'Aunt Marie. She's… she's married to Bob.'

'Oh, yes, of course,' Aggie says. 'Poor dear Marie. Always asking questions, always wanting to know exactly what one's plans are. As if life's like that. As if one always knows exactly what one wants.'

I stare at Aggie. When she is with it, she is as bright as a button. That's it, exactly: Marie always wants to know the details. If you're separated, she wants to know why, and where you plan to live, and if there's a financial settlement, and what's happened to her wedding present (a frightful set of table-mats that has to be retrieved from the attic any time she visits). One of these days I think she may ask me for a five-year plan.

'Aggie…' I draw the chair closer and touch her cheek softly. 'Aggie, I love you. I always have. You understand things. You understand me.' I stare at her dear, familiar face. It looks like someone has been at it with a chisel – whittling away the curves, diminishing the features, making deep lines just for effect.

She hasn't heard. She's staring at the wall; she does that when she's tired. It's time to go. I lean forwards and kiss her.

'Are you going?' She looks towards me, wide-eyed.

'Yes.'

'Say you'll try to find DeeDee for me.'

I look at her warily.

'Say it… please…' Aggie is leaning towards me earnestly. I'm afraid she'll fall out of the bed.

'I… suppose I could do some… research,' I mumble.

She leans back. 'Oh, good. Thank you.' She clasps my hand. 'Thank you so much.'

I suspect that on my next visit she will have forgotten all about this conversation. I certainly hope so, because knowing that someone likes hats and Rio de Janeiro and marble cake isn't quite enough to establish her exact location. DeeDee may not even be alive – and, if she is, she may not want to be found. I store the whole thing in the 'too difficult' file and start the

29

ritual I always go through before I leave Aggie's room. I make shooing noises towards a corner cupboard, like a shepherd directing my flock. 'Go on, sheep,' I say. 'Go on towards the field. It's bedtime.' As I get nearer to the cupboard, I pretend to open a gate. 'That's right, on you go – out into the field.' I clap to get them going faster.

Aunt Aggie watches. 'Bye, Sally, dear,' she says. 'Give my love to Diarmuid. I'm so glad you found yourself such a nice, sensible young man.'

I kiss her softly on the cheek, and then I leave, with the word 'sensible' ringing in my ears. Diarmuid *is* sensible. He knows what he wants. He knows who he is. And he wants me to be sensible, too – sensible in his terms, the only ones he understands. That's one of the things I find most difficult about my husband: he doesn't see how different people can be. Maybe that's why he likes mice so much. They seldom vary in their desire for cheese.

I creep out of Aggie's room, and suddenly I don't know what to do with all these feelings inside me, popping like popcorn. I don't know how to do this. I don't know how to lose her. I walk down the corridor, past the sitting-room and its blaring television; the group of residents sitting there, waiting for the stew and the relatives that might just visit. I open the front door and crunch down the gravel path. The winding road to the bus stop is familiar now, and even it is tinged with grief.

What, in truth, is there to keep me in Dublin after Aggie is gone? Of course, Diarmuid and I may get back together; but if we remain apart, it might be nice to move somewhere new, with no associations to remind me of my failed marriage. I might even go back to California...

Just for a moment I feel a burst of lightness in my heart, a blaze of excitement. My step quickens; and then it slows again, as I realise there is no way I can go back to California. I have a life here in Dublin. People expect things of me. I have a job, and parents who aren't getting any younger; I have friends and a mortgage. I can't be like DeeDee and turn my back on it all. I could never just leave without even writing a note. I already

30

nearly hate her and the heartbreak she has caused.

It looks like it might rain. I start to walk more quickly. I want to get home so I can curl up under the duvet with a nice big mug of hot chocolate and watch the telly. That's one of the nice things about being alone: I don't have to bargain with Diarmuid about whether to watch one of my favourite American sitcoms or one of his sports programmes.

My mobile phone rings, and I grab it from my pocket. It could be Diarmuid. I want to talk to him and apologise. I really want to keep the lines of communication open.

'Hi, how are you?' Fiona says cheerfully. Fiona is my oldest friend and a cheerful sort of person. Even if she didn't own a big tasteful house and have a silver sports car and a garden pond full of koi carp, she would probably be happy. And she is even happier now that she and Zak are expecting their first baby.

'Hi there, Fiona!' I raise my voice an octave. When I compare my life to Fiona's, I can't help thinking that she seems to know how to be Fiona O'Driscoll so much better than I know how to be Sally Adams. I've known her since secondary school, and she's always had this sort of glow and buzz about her. It's almost impossible not to like her; but, now that she's even happier than ever and I'm frequently far from ecstatic, I have not been seeking out her company. But Fiona is the kind of person who keeps in touch with her friends, especially friends who have recently separated from almost-brand-new husbands – I've only been married to Diarmuid for a year, eight months and four days.

'Look, why don't you come round for a nice big glass of wine?' Fiona says. 'I know you need a bit of cheering up after visiting Aggie.'

'How do you know I've just visited Aggie?' I enquire, wondering if all the people I know are suddenly becoming telepathic.

'You always visit Aggie on Tuesday evenings between seven and half-eight,' Fiona laughs. 'It's part of the Sally Adams schedule!'

I frown. Fiona has clearly decided I'm a stickler for routine just because I like to keep Tuesday evenings – and sometimes Thursday evenings and Sunday afternoons – free for Aggie. I hesitate before replying. Do I really feel up to visiting Fiona's exquisite house and drinking wine out of one of her huge billowy hand-blown glasses?

'Sally? Sally, are you still there?' Fiona says. 'I'll come and collect you if you like. Where are you?'

'I'm getting on a bus,' I reply. In fact, the bus nearly sailed by as if it were in a Formula One race, and I had to stick my arm out and jump up and down to get the driver's attention. 'Thanks so much, Fiona. That glass of wine sounds great. I should be with you in…' At this point I drop the phone, because I have been attempting to extract the *exact* fare from my purse and the driver has been glowering at me. I toss some coins at him and bend to retrieve my phone before he stampedes off again. Even though I scurry, the bus lurches off dramatically and I am flung into a seat and sit there scowling. Do drivers do that on purpose? And why have I said 'Yes' to Fiona, when what I really want to do is just go home? Sometimes I really envy April's ability to say 'No' without the slightest trace of doubt or guilt. If I were living in San Francisco, I bet I'd feel I had to fly home for Marie's big do. I am the dutiful daughter, the one who turns up and phones and remembers people's birthdays. That's why everyone finds it so hard to believe I left Diarmuid. I am just not the sort of person who does that kind of thing.

The only people who don't seem to be surprised are Fiona and Erika. Before I got married, I sometimes saw them huddled together in earnest conversations, and I knew they were discussing me because they always said things like 'So you use *five* carrots' when I joined them. Erika and Fiona are not the type of women who sit around discussing casseroles. I assumed they were talking about wedding presents; but now I suspect they were wondering how to tell me they didn't think Diarmuid and I were suited. Looking back, I can see they gave me little hints, like, 'They say a sense of humour is crucial for a healthy relationship; I could never be with a man who didn't make me laugh.' Diarmuid is a rather serious person, but I didn't mind, because life is a serious business. You can't just go around laughing at everything. There are decisions to be made, practicalities to be attended to. You have to know what's important.

Fiona's large cream house overlooks a well-maintained, tree-lined square in Monkstown, which is an old and grand and very attractive Dublin suburb. As the bus bumps its way along, I think that, if I were Fiona, I wouldn't be on this bus; I would have walked, because of my firm commitment to regular exercise. I also think that, if I were Fiona, I wouldn't be wearing jeans with a zip that opens up stealthily every time I sit down and a pink cotton jumper with a small rip underneath the right arm. If I were Fiona, I would still be happily married, because I would have thought about it all long and carefully, before, not after, the wedding. She and Zak even went to a marriage counsellor *before* they said, 'I do.'

Fiona's first question to me as I walk through her front door is, 'Would you like some lasagne? It's delicious. We got it from that swanky new deli. The chef is Italian.'

I naturally say yes, because I am now in comfort-food territory. Any time I'm with Fiona, I eat far more than I should, while she pecks at salad and radishes. She and Zak never have large portions, which is why they haven't finished the lasagne and greedy plump little Sally has been called upon to finish it. I was nine stone when I married, and now I'm ten.

As I consume Fiona's lasagne, my eyes are drawn to her large, luxuriant stomach, which is not caused by chocolate biscuits and crackers covered in hummus. There is a baby in there.

'Sally?' Fiona smiles. 'Why are you looking at me like that?'

'I'm thinking about that lovely little baby that's in your stomach.' I smile back. 'And I'm thinking you'll make a great mother because you know how to love people.' As I say this, I feel lighter. When I'm not comparing myself to Fiona, but just appreciating her, I feel more like her. I feel like I've been let in

33

on some secret.

She laughs. 'I wish I were as sure about that as you are,' she says. Fiona has a lovely, deeply playful laugh. This is not, of course, the only lovely thing about her. Her blaze of red-blonde hair frames a soft, thoughtful and extremely pretty oval face. It is the sort of face that manages to be an unexpected combination of qualities. Her nose, for example, hints at steely determination, while her full lips regularly curl up into a playful, stunning smile that reveals even, pristine white teeth. Her eyes are grey-blue and watchful, because she notices things. She is wearing a beautiful, voluminous woven shirt with buttons in unusual places, including the elbows. Fiona has those sorts of clothes – clothes that aren't generally available in ordinary shops.

Fiona gives me one of her looks. 'Sally, I hate to bring the subject up, but have you thought any more about…'

I know she is referring to Diarmuid. 'No… I mean, sort of.'

Fiona nods, and I know she wants me to talk about Diarmuid. If I were Fiona and had left my husband, I would be talking about it and getting advice and support and perhaps even crying. Because Fiona doesn't just know how to be happy; she knows how to be sad. She cries at funerals and she cries at poignant films. She cried buckets when Alfie Armitage went off with Naomi O'Sullivan at that dance when we were fifteen; she was heartbroken for a week, until she met that French exchange student who was the first person to feel inside her bra. When Fiona has been dumped, she has been known to *howl*. Maybe that's why she gets over it so quickly.

But, now that she's met Zak, her love life seems to be verging on the idyllic. And the thing is, he's not even handsome. He's bald and has rather small eyes and a plumpish nose. His mouth is too big; when he smiles, it virtually takes over the lower part of his face. But there is something about him – a confidence, an aura of strength and wisdom. His body is compact and muscular and his movements are lithe and agile, like a dancer's. I wouldn't have looked at him twice, so that's another impressive thing about Fiona: she looked at Zak twice

34

and saw he was special. And he is special. He is very kind and thoughtful and sweet and funny. He and Fiona look after each other. Sometimes they feed each other chocolate ice-cream in bed. Somehow I wish she hadn't told me that little detail.

Zak isn't with us this evening because, after he had his lasagne, he went to the pub with some friends. He isn't the sort of man who *prefers* being at the pub with his friends; but when the baby is born he won't see his friends so often, so he wants to have some quality time with them now. He is an accountant, but that simply seems to make the whole profession more glamorous. And Fiona is something very important in software. Sometimes she even gives talks at conferences in London and Paris and Rome.

We sit in silence while Fiona clearly hopes I will say more about Diarmuid. Eventually she says, 'Would you like some chocolate cake? It's home-baked. I got it from the deli too.'

I look at her warily.

'It's got cream in it, so it has to be eaten soon,' Fiona coaxes.

'Oh, all right, then.' I grin at her. Then I add, and I am not entirely joking, 'Sometimes I think you're trying to fatten me up, Fiona. I'm going to be like a woman in a Rubens painting if I go on like this.'

Fiona smiles serenely and pads, barefooted, to her gleaming kitchen. It has a maple floor and an Aga cooker that she actually understands. I don't understand my cooker. It does things I don't need it to, and sometimes it makes strange noises.

'I always find a nice chocolate cake cheers me up when I'm worried,' Fiona says, as she hands me a large slice on a hand-decorated ceramic plate.

I'm about to protest that this is nonsense, but then I realise that Fiona does comfort-eat sometimes. I have seen her. But she never gains an extra pound. For a moment I feel like throwing myself on the hand-woven Persian carpet in outrage.

'Sally, I know this really good therapist who –'

'Look, Fiona, I can't *afford* to see a therapist right now,' I snap, my mouth full of creamy calories. 'I have to write imploring letters to the bank manager about my overdraft as it is. You wouldn't believe the things I say to him about cash flow.'

'Make it a priority,' Fiona says. 'It *is* a priority. I'd lend you the money.'

I take another bite of cake and chomp it thoughtfully. 'Maybe. I don't know. I'll think about it.' But what I'm thinking is that I've tried therapy, and I just ended up talking about things that happened *years* ago when I was a kid in California and it looked like my parents were about to divorce. I can't see how talking about my parents is going to help me decide about Diarmuid.

'Not all therapists get you to talk for ages about the past,' Fiona tells me. 'At least talk to me, Sally. You're unhappy. I can see it.'

This would be the ideal moment to cry. I *should* cry. I want to, but I somehow can't. I don't feel I deserve to cry, because this situation with Diarmuid is entirely of my own making. He is the one who deserves to cry. He is the one who has been left to share a house with Barbecue Barry. He is the one who has to eat alone tonight because I wouldn't alter my arrangements.

Instead I sigh, deeply and dramatically.

'What are you sighing about?'

'About Diarmuid. About how unfair I've been to him. Sometimes I wish he'd been able to marry Becky.'

'Who's Becky?' Fiona leans forward.

'A girl he loved. They met when he was fourteen and she was twelve. They went out for five whole years.'

'And where is she now?'

'In New Zealand. Her family moved there. She and Diarmuid kept in contact for a while, and then she got engaged to a guy over there. It broke Diarmuid's heart – I'm sure it did, though he hardly ever speaks about it. His mother says they were an ideal couple.'

'Diarmuid's mother sounds like a right old bag,' Fiona snorts, and I do not disagree.

'She's never really liked me,' I say, through cake. I am now on my second helping. The icing is a kind of creamy chocolate fudge and extremely tasty. 'She even has a silver-framed photo of Becky in the sitting-room. She's in a canoe, looking all outdoorsy and cute. Diarmuid's mother calls her "the daughter I never had".'

'That's outrageous!' Fiona splutters. 'You're her daughter-in-law. She could be a bit more… *tactful*.'

I know she is right to be annoyed. Diarmuid's mother, Madge, has never treated me as though I belong in her family. Any time I'm in a room with her, she greets me, talks for a few moments and moves on to someone else. Diarmuid has to keep reminding her to introduce me to their friends and relatives. When he does, she exclaims, 'Oh, yes, of course – this is Sally. Diarmuid's…' And there is always a small pause before she adds, 'Wife.' I've often asked Diarmuid to have a word with her about it, but he hasn't done it yet. He's really worried about hurting her feelings, because apparently she is very 'sensitive' and doesn't mean to be rude, so I 'shouldn't take it personally'. I don't really believe him, because I haven't noticed her being like that with anyone else.

I'm amazed at how much I've tolerated Madge's behaviour. Maybe it's because, deep down, I think she's right. Becky is the person Diarmuid should have married.

And I think he knows it too.

Chapter Four

I AM STARING AT the aquamarine curtains in Diarmuid's bedroom. I think of it as Diarmuid's bedroom even though it is still, theoretically, ours. I took ages choosing those curtains. I wanted them to be textured and soft, and they are. They are also lined in thick cream cotton. It's expensive lining, because I wanted the curtains to last and not get bleached by sunlight. Everything in this room was chosen with such care and such concern about its durability – apart from the man sleeping beside me. I rushed into my marriage, because I thought no one else half decent would want me, and I was scared of being alone.

Diarmuid must have felt that way too. He still does. He as much as admitted it just ten minutes ago, before he fell into what seems to be a restive sleep: he twitches every so often, and his face does not hold that childlike softness of forgetting. 'You can't believe how lonely I've been.' That's what he muttered, just before his head deepened on the pillow. 'I need someone to hold... someone to love.' And then his eyes closed and he drifted away from me. I wish I knew where he's gone. I wish I knew so much more about him than I do.

I am still in a daze. I can't believe what has just happened. There is something dreadful and lovely about it. Just for a while, when I walked into this room again, I felt such relief that he had made my mind up for me, that all the indecision was over. And now I don't know what I'm feeling any more. All I know is that I may be pregnant. I do not carry my diaphragm around in my handbag. And I know I must have chosen this, because I let it happen.. I must have wanted *something* to happen to help me make my mind up about my marriage.

This week my visit to Aggie was unexceptional, until she started to say that the sheep were now floating. I didn't know what to say to that, so I started to make up a story about how Diarmuid and I had gone into town for lunch last Sunday. I told her it had been sunny enough to sit outside; we'd eaten pasta and drunk fruity red wine, followed by wonderfully frothy cappuccinos. And we'd talked for ages about all sorts of things – our dreams, our hopes, and some of those scary feelings you think no one will understand. Only Diarmuid had understood. I told Aggie that what was so great about him was that we could talk about anything together; and when I got too serious he knew how to lighten things up, make me laugh. I was happy as I spoke about this Sunday lunch, until I remembered it was just something I'd made up. And then my heart filled with this incredible yearning, and I thought, *If only what I was saying were true.* Because the man I was describing wasn't Diarmuid. Diarmuid doesn't know how to be that open. Any time I almost get him to tell me more about himself, his deep secret self, this closed look comes over his face and he changes the subject.

And I suddenly knew the pain I feel when this happens isn't a new pain. It's an old pain, one that I've felt with April and my parents. And so – in a weird, wrong way – it sometimes feels right, because it's familiar. But I also knew that, deep down, I hoped that Diarmuid would prove to be the exception and that we would somehow find a way to reach each other and break down the barriers. That we would discover a new, open kind of love, a more real kind of love. One that I was desperate to believe in.

As Aggie went on about the floating sheep, I felt pangs of despair. She was the one who had offered me glimpses of this bigger kind of love, and now she was talking nonsense. I was about to do my usual ritual of shooing the sheep into the field when she said, 'No, leave them. It's nice to have them here.' And then this radiant look came over her face, and she said, 'They're so, so *beautiful.*'

I didn't ask her why the sheep were so beautiful. I just couldn't face talking to her any more at that moment. I leaned forwards and kissed her; and she said, very softly, 'DeeDee can help you, Sally. You're so alike. So very similar.' I just looked at her and squeezed her arm. Then I left the room.

After that weird conversation, I was pleased when Diarmuid just happened to be driving by when I was waiting for a bus. I welcomed the distraction, because I had started thinking about DeeDee again. I didn't want to be similar to her. I began to wonder if Aggie was just being sly when she said those things. Maybe she thought that saying DeeDee could help me would make me want to look for her.

'Hi there, Sally!' Diarmuid actually managed to make it seem like he was driving past just by chance, though now I know he must have watched me walking down the road. 'Would you like a lift home?'

I accepted because I knew I could be waiting at the bus stop for half an hour. In fact, Diarmuid's 'lift' was very welcome – until I realised he wasn't driving me to my cottage. He was driving me to 'our' house.

'Diarmuid,' I said, very calmly and evenly. 'Where exactly are we going?'

'I'm driving you home,' he said. 'To your real home. This thing has gone on far too long.'

I just sat there, numb with disbelief. This wasn't like him. But then, so many things didn't seem like him these days. Sometimes he seemed like one of those paper samples of paint – the colour always looks so different when you actually get it on a wall.

'Everyone says I've been too patient with you,' he continued. The word 'everyone' seemed to boom reproachfully. 'If we're going to save our marriage, we at least have to be under the same roof.'

We drove on in silence. I felt I should put up some kind of fight, but I didn't know what to say. He pressed one of the gleaming buttons on the radio, and the Corrs started singing 'I Would Love To Love You', which seemed very insensitive of them: even though it's a lovely song, I didn't want to love Diarmuid like he loved me. His view of love seemed entirely different from mine. I glowered at Diarmuid and he smiled at me, and the Corrs sang about this love we had; and somehow the song became just about me and Diarmuid, and how great it would be if all these barriers between us could come crashing down and disappear.

For some reason, I suddenly remembered my mother's voice – the hushed tone, the genuine concern: 'Do you think Sally will ever find someone?' I'd come over for Sunday lunch; afterwards, when I was supposed to be watching television, I had got up to make myself a cup of tea and heard my parents talking in the kitchen. I stood stock-still in the corridor and waited for my father's reply.

'I don't know,' he said. 'Sometimes I worry that she's turning into the kind of woman who's got some idea in her head about her ideal man.' There was the sound of clinking crockery. They were washing up. 'I really hope she isn't ignoring the decent, good, unglamorous men who could love her. Sally needs love.'

'We all need love,' my mother said rather brusquely. And I knew the conversation had become about them, so they would immediately start discussing something else. On this occasion it had been whether they should put the leftover chicken in the freezer.

I roused myself from this reverie and said sharply to Diarmuid, 'I want to go back to my cottage.' I said it far too late. We were virtually in 'our' driveway.

'Let's talk about that over dinner,' he said. 'I've got us some beef with black bean sauce and green peppers – oh, yes, and extra garlic.' He smiled; I always ask for extra garlic with this particular dish.

He's trying to lure me back with food, just like he did with the mice, I thought. But I was suddenly very hungry.

When the car was parked, Diarmuid came around and opened my door for me. Then he held out his hand and virtually pulled me from the car.

Diarmuid held my hand as he unlocked the front door, and he held my hand as he led me upstairs to 'our' bedroom with its view of the Dublin mountains. He held my hand as we sat down on the bed. Then he kissed that ultra-sensitive spot behind my ear and started to undress me. And, just as I was thinking that I

41

must call a taxi immediately, he poured me a large glass of red wine – he had an open bottle and glasses on the bedside table. He handed the glass to me and I gulped it down like lemonade. 'Just hold me, Diarmuid,' I said. 'I just want you to hold me.' The wine was already going to my head. I must be the cheapest drunk in Ireland. I wanted, needed, someone to comfort me; and that person was Diarmuid, even though he was the reason I needed comfort in the first place.

But of course we didn't just lie together chastely. After a few minutes, he had somehow managed to remove all my clothes and his own. He got on top of me and kissed my lips, my breasts, my hair; his breath was ragged with emotion. And then he was suddenly inside me. Sex with Diarmuid is usually tender at first, but this time it was hard and urgent, raw with intensity; the bed bounced so much I thought we might take off into the air. He didn't bother to press the right buttons this time. This wasn't about reaching out to me; it was about something else. I looked into his eyes, and then I looked away. There was more anger in them than love.

Something in me pulled back and just watched us, pounding against each other on the bed we had chosen together. Why shouldn't he be angry, and why shouldn't he use sex to prove that I was still his wife? Sex can be so many things. It doesn't have to be tender.

But I needed it to be tender. I closed my eyes as the thrusting became more intense and he groaned and shuddered and just lay there for a moment. I couldn't look at him. I just wanted him to be off me. I had never felt so lonely in my life.

That's why small tears gathered in the corners of my eyes. I tried to blink them away, but Diarmuid must have seen them.

'Oh, Sally, what is it now?' he asked. He sounded frustrated. Weary.

'It's nothing.' I managed a smile. 'It's just that all this has been a bit... you know... unexpected.'

He touched my cheek tenderly. 'Do you want me to go down and heat up dinner in the microwave?'

'No. Let's wait.' I couldn't tell him I was no longer hungry.

And then he said those things about how much he had missed me, and fell asleep.

I get up carefully from the bed. I start to gather my clothes, which are strewn on the floor. I want to leave, but I don't want Diarmuid to wake up and find me gone. I want to explain to him that, if I come back to live in this house, it needs to be my decision.

I start to snoop around the room, like Diarmuid snoops around mine. I expect to find biology textbooks and magazines about cars, and I do. I also find an empty box of Turkish Delight, which makes me smile: Turkish Delight is one of Diarmuid's few guilty passions. I am about to go downstairs and make myself a cup of tea when I see what looks like a handwritten letter poking out from his brown leather Filofax, which is on a chair next to his navy-blue boxer shorts. I shouldn't look at the letter. Of course I shouldn't look at it. It's a woman's writing. It must be.

Diarmuid stirs. I think he's about to wake up, but instead he turns over, his back to me. I reach for the letter. It's probably from Charlene, thanking him for the driving lessons. I almost put the letter down; but there is something about the round, enthusiastic handwriting that makes me read it.

'Dear Diarmuid, it was so lovely to see you after all these years. You haven't changed. I know I must have, even though you say I haven't.'

Diarmuid moves again and makes those queer sucking sounds he sometimes makes when he's waking up. I turn the letter over. I haven't time to read it all; I just want to know who it's from. Probably one of his cousins in New York.

Only it isn't.

'Do let's try to keep in touch. Now that I'm back in Dublin, maybe we could meet for lunch again sometime.' I look at the bottom of the page. The letter is signed, 'Love, Becky.'

Chapter Five

'HE'S SEEING BECKY.'

'Who's Becky?'

'I've told you about her, Erika,' I say into my mobile, somewhat impatiently. I'm striding along a road towards my parents' house, panting slightly. 'She's the girl... the woman he dated for five years. The one who left for New Zealand.'

'Oh, yes... just a moment. There's a call.' Erika is working as a temporary receptionist. At this minute she's saying, 'International Holdings,' to someone, though she doesn't know why the holdings are international or what the company actually does with them.

'Sorry about that.' She comes back on the line. 'The calls come in here in bunches.'

'He says he only met her once for lunch and she's planning to go back to New Zealand soon. He says they're just friends now.'

'Well...' Erika hesitates. 'Well, that's not too bad, is it? Maybe he's telling the truth.'

'I don't know... there was a funny look on his face when he said it.'

'Sorry. Just a moment.' She takes another call.

'I slept with him,' I say, as soon as Erika is back on the line. Knowing that she may disappear at any moment means I have to get to the headlines fast.

'*What?* Was this after you found out about Becky?'

'No, before it. I found a letter from her in the bedroom.'

'I see. Oh, dear.' Erika no longer sounds quite so reassuring. 'How did you leave it, then?'

'I told him he was one to talk.' I almost spit the words into the phone.

'Talk about what?'

'Talk about not seeing other people. He kept checking up on me, but he was the one who was seeing someone else.'

'For lunch,' Erika points out. Even though I don't think she particularly likes Diarmuid, she has a fair-minded streak that can, at times, be extremely annoying.

'*Anything* can happen over lunch.' My voice rises with emotion. 'People can fall in love again over lunch. He's always loved her – she's the woman he wanted to marry, only she got engaged to someone in New Zealand, though she didn't marry the guy in the end. His mother even has a photo of her in the sitting-room. She's in a canoe.'

'Calm down, Sally,' Erika says. 'He married you, didn't he? Yes, put it over there. Where do I have to sign for it?' I assume she is now talking to someone who has delivered something.

'Erika?' I say, after about thirty seconds. 'Are you still there?'

'Yes,' she sighs. 'Sorry about that. As I was saying, you mustn't jump to conclusions. Anyway, what if he does still sort of like this woman? It wouldn't be all that bad, would it? I mean... to be absolutely honest, Sally, you don't seem all that thrilled about being married to him.'

'I need time to think about it!' I exclaim indignantly. 'That's all. I haven't been seeing other people. So I told him that maybe, given the circumstances, he should take the opportunity to have a little think about things too.'

'I suppose that's only fair,' Erika says. She disappears to take another call.

As I wait, I wish Erika realised that sometimes I want her to be unfair. I want her to take my side and call Diarmuid a stupid bollocks – even though he isn't, of course. It would be so much easier if he were.

'He said he didn't need time to think about things,' I gabble, when Erika gets back on the line. 'But then he said he would if I insisted, because we need to make a decision about the house.'

'The horse?'

'The *house*. For God's sake, Erika, why would we be making a decision about a horse? We don't own one.'

'You're speaking so fast I can hardly keep up with you.'

'I can't stand it. He wouldn't talk about Becky at all, apart from saying they were just friends. He doesn't talk to me, not properly. There's always been this distant look in his eyes – even on the day we married.'

'It's not gone yet.'

'What… what's not gone?' I demand impatiently.

'The post. Someone just asked me about it.'

'So now this decision seems to be about whether to sell the house, when what I want to talk about is… is whether or not we love each other.'

'Men aren't very good at talking about emotions, are they?' Erika sighs. 'That's why Alex is so special. He doesn't mind talking about emotions.'

I almost mention my worries about being pregnant, but I decide not to. I'm expecting my period soon, so I suppose it's kind of unlikely – but I'd say Diarmuid's sperm are a pretty determined bunch. 'Thanks for talking to me, Erika,' I say. 'I'm sorry for interrupting you at work.'

'I *love* being interrupted at work,' Erika says. 'Do you want to call round this evening?'

'That would be lovely.' I sigh. 'But I'm meeting Fiona. We're going for one of her hikes through the hills.'

'Oh, dear God,' Erika groans. 'Is it going to be a ten-miler?'

'No. She's promised we'll take it gently. She's going to give birth soon, after all.'

'Oh, of course,' Erika says. 'I hope she doesn't do it halfway up a mountain.'

The thought of being an untrained midwife on some craggy promontory briefly distracts me from my worries about Diarmuid. 'Bye, Erika. Talk to you soon.'

'Byeee, sweetie,' Erika says. Before she hangs up I hear the unmistakable sound of her cramming a chocolate biscuit into her mouth. Sitting at a reception desk, any reception desk, makes Erika want to eat lots of biscuits. She's got very good at tucking them into her cheek, like a hamster, when she has to answer the phone.

I turn into a tree-lined, middle-class suburban street and head towards my parents' home. It has the tidiest exterior of all the houses, because my parents have made convenience a priority: the lawn at the front has been replaced by concrete, and the round flowerbed is liberally scattered with fetching brown, white and pale-orange stones – there are a few plants as well, but the stones are the main feature and naturally do not require watering. Near the front door there is a small and rather polite evergreen tree, which will never, apparently, grow too tall or require much pruning or fertiliser.

'Hi, Sally!' Mum calls out as I open the door – I still have my own key. She has a phone stuck to her ear, which is not unusual. 'I've just made some coffee.' She gestures towards the kitchen. My mother has become a coffee drinker in recent years; she grinds it herself and has a number of special blends in white ceramic jars. She is a small, trim woman prone to darting, eager movements. When she was younger she was pretty in an unexceptional, standard sort of way; now she is what Diarmuid calls 'handsome' and I call 'well maintained'. Her hair colour, for example, varies regularly because she likes to 'experiment with highlights', and she is permanently tanned due to some very expensive cream that also protects her skin from ultraviolet rays.

I wander towards the kitchen, which is very tidy and extremely fitted – there are, for example, no stray jars of honey hanging around attracting ants, as there are in my kitchen. What I find is Aunt Marie guiltily helping herself to a chocolate chip cookie. My parents are rather like Fiona in that they regularly acquire seductive foodstuffs and then get guests to eat them. Without the guests, a packet of high-grade chocolate chip cookies could last them a whole month.

'Oh, hello, dear,' Marie says, trying to eat the biscuit as fast as possible. She claims to be on an almost constant diet. 'How nice to see you.'

I say that it's nice to see her too, even though I wish she wasn't here. I want to go up to the attic and look for the music box Aggie gave to me and April. She bought it in Switzerland, when she and Joseph were on holiday. I don't know why it's suddenly become so important to me, but I don't like the idea that I may never see it again.

'What mug would you like?' Marie is opening one of the tidy cabinets. This is something we agree on: we both believe that coffee or tea tastes better if it's in a mug that has a pleasing colour and shape.

'I think they're pretty much all the same, aren't they?' All of my parents' mugs are blue. They don't want to be bothered with choosing between different colours and patterns.

'Oh, no. I got them this nice orange one,' Marie says.

It is indeed a very nice, bright tangerine colour, and there are small golden stars around the rim. It isn't the type of mug I would have expected Marie to buy – which is just another reminder that people are rarely quite the way you think they are. They have secrets, hidden parts: things that even they themselves sometimes don't know are there.

'That would be lovely.' I smile. 'It's a very nice mug.'

'I'm sorry I can't find the honey,' Marie says, as she places a steaming mug of tea before me. 'You like honey in your tea, don't you?' She pours in some milk – just the right amount. I smile at her gratefully.

Marie is a curious mixture of things I admire and things I deeply dislike. She is plump and has a bossy side, which retreats and advances or sometimes just hangs around waiting. Because of this, you never know which particular Marie you are dealing with. On some days, you can see she is doing her very best to listen and only give advice if she is asked for it. This, however, is not in her true nature.

Her true nature, when unleashed, says, 'So, dear, how are things between you and Diarmuid?'

I know I should expect this, but it is always a surprise, because no one else in the family asks me about Diarmuid. I think they just don't know what to say.

'Oh, grand,' I say grimly. 'We're in frequent communication.'

'But I just don't understand it, dear. Why aren't you living

48

in the same house? What *happened?*' She is cradling her blue mug. 'Did he hit you?'

'Of course not.' I shudder.

'Or have an affair?'

'Not that I know of.'

'Was he a secret gambler? Or…' She lowers her voice and looks around furtively. 'Or did he have some… dreadful sexual deviances?'

I shake my head. Marie is like a terrier when she wants to find a reason. In Marie's world, women do not just leave their husbands on a whim – especially not women like me. I've always been the responsible one. April was the one who stole lipstick and jeans and records from shops, as a teenager; she was the one who came home drunk and argued about wanting to have a tattoo. I was the good girl. I still want to be the good girl – only I'm not any more. I can see it in people's eyes.

Marie is still waiting for some sort of reply, so I say, 'It's complicated. It's not that I'm avoiding your question; it's just that… well, it's all very complicated.'

'But *why* is it complicated?' Marie leans forward. 'None of us understand it.'

I think guiltily of my relatives in their finery outside the church. The wedding was on a sunny day. Erika and Fiona were bridesmaids, and Erika ran like an Olympic sprinter when I threw my bouquet. She didn't catch it. It was caught by a cousin whose name I keep forgetting; what I do remember about her is that she has a post-graduate degree in business studies and, at Marie's last family gathering, informed me that she planned to work in personnel. I assume she'll tell me all about it at the next gathering in September. And I may have to tell her that I am separated and pregnant and that my crisp addiction has returned. My crisp addiction always resurfaces at Marie's parties; I grab whole handfuls of them and stuff them into my mouth. Sometimes I wish these cousins weren't quite so well adjusted. If only one of them could become a lesbian, or start a degree and then leave it because of an unsuitable man…

49

Pregnant. The impact of the possibility suddenly hits me. Maybe it wouldn't be all that bad if I was. It would supply some sort of answer – give my life the direction it so clearly needs. I suppose it is possible to get pregnant even if you're expecting your period – which should, by rights, have already started. I place my hand gently on my stomach. All that bingeing at Fiona's has given it a noticeable bulge.

Marie is staring at me. There was a time when I thought I had to answer her questions, but now I know there are some questions you can't answer. She is getting frustrated; there is annoyance in the way she sweeps some bread-crumbs from the table. She's probably under orders from the family to prise these details out of me. I know I am a frequent topic of conversation; I have even learned that Uncle Bob, Marie's husband, refers to me as 'the Bolting Bride'.

Marie's cloyingly sweet body-spray is wafting towards me. Some of her determination must be drifting in the air too, because I take a deep breath and say, 'Marie, sorry to bring this up again, but why does no one want to talk about Great-Aunt DeeDee?'

She just sits there, motionless. 'We don't talk about her, Sally,' she says in a steely voice. 'I thought I'd made that clear.'

'But *why?*' I lean forward, like Marie did herself. 'I just don't understand it.'

Marie's bright little eyes get the distant look that Diarmuid has perfected. She starts to fiddle with the zip on her yellow tracksuit, pulling it up and down distractedly.

' *Why?*'

'Oh, stop asking me that.' Her voice is hollow, and her face has that slightly melting look about it that happens when someone just might cry.

'OK. I'm sorry.' I pat her hand. 'It's just that Aggie says she wants to see her. She virtually begged me to find her.'

'That poor woman! She doesn't know what she's saying any more. Her memory must have almost gone.'

'No, it hasn't,' I say. 'She remembers lots of things. She

even remembers...' I'm about to say that Aggie remembers my mother's affair in California, but this is another thing we are not supposed to mention.

Marie stands up abruptly and goes to wash her mug, running it brusquely under the tap. 'Look, Sally, if Aggie was herself she wouldn't want to see DeeDee ever again. She only wants to see her now because she's forgotten.'

'Forgotten *what?*' I'm almost jumping up and down on my chair with curiosity.

'That DeeDee broke her heart.' Marie grabs a tea towel and starts to dry the mug roughly. 'So please don't ask me any more about that woman. It's just too painful.' She appears to be addressing a geranium on the windowsill. Then she turns round sharply, as though expecting me to remonstrate. 'That's all I'm going to say on the matter.'

At that moment Mum comes into the kitchen. 'Hi, dear!' she beams. 'Sorry I was so long. The tennis club is having a charity dance and we were discussing the prizes for the raffle.' She bends to kiss me on the cheek. 'Will you stay for dinner?'

'I'd love to,' I say, 'only I'm going hillwalking with Fiona.' I am buzzing with questions about DeeDee, but I realise that it will be impossible to lure Marie back onto the subject.

'Hillwalking!' Mum exclaims. 'Good for you. There's nothing like getting out into that fresh country air.'

As I listen to Mum and Marie having a mild argument about the therapeutic benefits of gardening, I wonder how DeeDee broke Aggie's heart. Was it because she disappeared without a trace... or was it something else? And surely they should be more worried about what happened to her? The fact that they aren't implies that they know more than they are letting on about where she may have gone. I also wonder whether not talking about DeeDee has made it easier for the family to avoid other uncomfortable subjects.

If I'm pregnant, they'll probably avoid talking about that, too. Instead they'll buy me things – baby clothes, special skin cream for stretch marks, attractive blouses that are somehow supposed to make me feel I have not lost my womanly allure.

They won't want to know what I'm feeling. And when I try to tell Aggie about it all, she'll say, 'Oh, look, there's another floating sheep!'

I help myself to another calorie-loaded cookie. I ask Marie if she wants one, and she says, 'Oh, no, dear,' as though she has never touched a cookie in her life.

'Do you mind if I have a quick look in the attic?' I say.

'Go ahead. What are you looking for?' Mum enquires.

'That music box, the one Aggie gave me and April. I think Aggie would like to see it again.'

'Heaven knows where it's got to.' Mum sighs. 'I don't think it's in the attic, but have a look if you want.'

I go upstairs and negotiate the narrow, rickety ladder that leads to the attic. It's fastened to the ceiling and you have to pull it down. The dust makes me sneeze. I push open the old, unpainted door and fumble around for the light switch.

I look around, expecting to find boxes and sentimental objects my parents aren't quite sure what to do with; only they aren't there. The attic is almost empty, apart from a jumble of sports equipment – badminton racquets, croquet hoops, a riding hat. There is also an old lagging jacket my father keeps planning to put on the hot-water cylinder. There are no old teddy bears, none of the stuff one should find in a place like this. I remember now: my parents did a major clear-out when they moved to this house three years ago. It's as though, in some way, they've been trying to erase the past.

A large beach ball catches my eye, and I smile. At least I recognise that. Dad and April and I used to kick it around on the beach while Mum read books about lone sea voyages. She claimed to find them 'restful'. She devoured books about travel when we were younger. She loved nothing better than finding out how someone had spent a year with the Bedouins or met jungle tribes who had remained free from the trappings of modern life. I spot one of those books: it's about a woman anthropologist who studied the 'native ways' of the Aborigines. I pick it up and blow the dust off the jacket.

When I open it, I find a small red notebook cradled in the

centre. The paper is frayed and old, and the big, bold writing is in faded blue ink. I open it. 'Marble Cake,' I read. It must be one of Aggie's recipe books. I skim through it and see the ingredients for Vietnamese Chicken, and Sweet Potato Casserole with Lentils. Aggie must have been more adventurous in her cuisine when she was younger. I tuck it into the pocket of my jeans. Maybe I should read it out to her; maybe it will help her remember who she was – who she is. She's drifting away from us, and I must find ways to call her back. If only I could find the music box.

I start to hunt. Under a big crocheted blanket I find the hummingbird feeder we had up in the big eucalyptus tree in our garden in California, and an old Sierra Club calendar full of pictures of American nature at its most photogenic. My mother has also kept a pair of very old leather sandals. She always used to wear bright-red nail varnish on her toes back then, and long, full cotton skirts.

It's not here. I realise this after half an hour. The music box has gone. I take a deep breath and prepare to go downstairs. Then my mobile phone rings. I take it from my pocket. It's probably Fiona reminding me to wear good thick boots for our hike.

'Sally?' It's Diarmuid. He sounds as if he's been drinking. 'Sally, are you there?'

'Yes.' I stare at a cobweb.

'I won't see Becky again if you don't want me to. We're just friends, but if you don't want me to see her again I won't.'

I look at the hummingbird feeder. Hummingbirds fly huge distances every year on their annual migrations. They looked so beautiful in the garden, iridescent and small and full of life.

'Sally, did you hear me?'

'Yes.'

'Is that all you have to say?'

'I'm sorry, Diarmuid. I'm in an attic.' I don't know why I should use this as an excuse. 'That's very… good to hear. But if you want to see her, you should. I wouldn't want to stop you.' What I mean is that if he still loves her I want to know it

53

now, not later.

'I don't want to see her.'

'Really?' My heart lightens.

'I want to see you.'

I smile with relief. 'I want to see you too.'

'Becky isn't even in Dublin any more.'

'Oh. Has she gone back to New Zealand?'

'No, she's in Galway with her new boyfriend.'

I wonder if Diarmuid can hear me smile.

'I can't meet up for a few days, I'm afraid,' he continues. 'I promised Mum I'd help her with some tiling in the bathroom. I'll phone you.'

After the call, I realise something. I realise that Diarmuid is getting used to being alone. He's not just waiting around for me to make up my mind. He has his own life and his own plans – and that's just how it should be. I have changed the way he loves me, diluted it by all this questioning.

He has learned to live without me. I can hear it in his voice.

Chapter Six

FIONA AND I ARE walking briskly along a pier; she changed her mind about trekking through the hills, thank goodness. It is a bright June evening – the same bright June evening on which Diarmuid said he wouldn't see Becky again, and I realised I wasn't pregnant.

My period arrived after Diarmuid's phone call. I didn't know if I was happy or sad until I found myself sobbing in my parents' toilet. The tears arrived before I knew why I was crying. But, as I felt the tight twist of fear loosen inside my heart, I realised I was relieved. It didn't seem like the right time. It wouldn't have been the right kind of answer. But what would be? Had I even been asking the right questions?

I managed not to be lured into Fiona's house before we started this walk. She wanted to show me some new baby clothes, but I knew I would end up eating leftover cheesecake or moussaka, so I said we should meet at the pier. This would have been a good solution if an ice-cream van hadn't been located directly beside me as I waited – and I had to wait a quarter of an hour, because Fiona was late. People were queuing, walking past me licking the creamy cones, and it seemed to me suddenly that ice-cream was one of life's compensations. Buying one was seizing the day. Everyone died eventually, and perhaps one of the things they'd regret was all the ice-creams they hadn't bought. I virtually ran up to the van and ordered a large cone with a piece of chocolate flake stuck into it. Then I ate it as if I'd never had an ice-cream in my life.

When Fiona arrived, she looked unusually untidy. There was actually a small tomato stain on the front of her turquoise sweatshirt, and her hair was tied back with a shoelace. She looked like she had had the baby already and had succumbed to the tender, exhausting chaos. 'I don't think I'll be able to walk very far,' she mumbled. 'I'm so bloody tired. And it's so *hot!'*

It wasn't all that hot, actually, but naturally I didn't say this. 'Are you sure you really want to go for a walk?' I asked.

'Of course I do,' she said, somewhat brusquely. Then she added, 'Look, when the baby is born, don't go on about whether it looks more like me or Zak. I hate that kind of stuff.'

'OK,' I said slowly. Fiona can be a bit grumpy, very occasionally, but this was a whole new level. She was scowling furiously.

'So let's start this walk, shall we?' she announced, striding ahead of me. 'And don't get pissed off if I suddenly have to pee.'

She was in such a foul mood that I expected her to pee in the middle of the promenade if she felt like it. It must be the hormones.

'I hate it when people start comparing noses and eyebrows,' Fiona hissed. 'A baby is just a baby. He or she doesn't have to look like anyone in particular.'

'Yes, indeed,' I agreed, deciding to let her get on with it. I also decided not to tell her about the dream I had last night, in which I was giving birth myself. I was panting and groaning and heaving, and sweat was coming off me in buckets. At last it was over. 'What is it?' I asked Diarmuid, flushed with exhilaration. 'Is it a boy or a girl?' He held my hand tenderly, his eyes brimming with tears of joy. 'Oh, Sally, darling, it's a mouse. A beautiful white boy mouse.' And the weird thing was, I wasn't even that surprised.

'They always say the baby has someone's smile,' Fiona continued. 'I hate that too. The baby has his *own* smile. The baby is an individual.'

'Indeed,' I agreed. All this was reminding me rather too clearly of April's arrival and how we all gawped at her.

'I've told Erika she has to stop this thing with Alex,' Fiona is now telling me. She's sitting on a bench and panting. Her legs are sprawled out in front of her. She is making absolutely no attempt at decorum.

'It's hard to know what to say to her,' I sigh, sitting down beside her.

'No, it isn't,' Fiona snaps. 'She's being idiotic. He'll never leave his wife. They never do.'

'But they behave as if they might,' I say. 'And he does seem to have a lot of the… the qualities she's been looking for.'

'I won't talk about him any more when she phones,' Fiona says. 'I simply won't encourage it.'

I look at some chewing gum on the ground. I thought pregnancy was supposed to make women placid. What's happened to the sweet, understanding Fiona – the Fiona who knows that people can want all sorts of things they shouldn't?

She gets up, arduously, and places a hand on her back. We set off on our walk again. It seems to me Fiona shouldn't be walking; she should be at home, watching something silly and escapist on the television. Maybe she sometimes takes this self-discipline stuff just a bit too far. I assume she'll get round to my marriage at any moment. Heaven knows what she'll say, but it is unlikely to be flattering. If Diarmuid were to be as bolshie as Fiona's being just now, I'd find it far harder to forgive. Why do we expect so much more from lovers and husbands than from friends?

The pier is suddenly full of brisk walkers, people who do this kind of thing regularly and at a certain time; people who know the benefits of sea air and exercise. Dublin's proximity to the sea is one of its greatest comforts, especially now that the city has got so sleek and modern and uppity. There is still this space where things are as they have always been; this great expanse of water, with the tall, striped towers of the Pigeon House in the distance. We rely on so many things to remain unchanged, but so few of them do. We so often base our lives on things that are bound to alter.

Fiona sits down on one of the benches again and says, 'I think I'll just take a breather.' She is puffing and panting. I smile at her. Suddenly I hope with all my heart that her baby is healthy and bonny and doesn't drive her demented by screeching at all hours of the night. I feel protective of her. I wonder what I would do if she started her contractions here, now, on this pier. I would probably mutter something about deep breaths while I summoned help. Just for a moment, I feel a small surge of panic.

This subsides when Fiona gets up again and we resume our walk. She seems unusually preoccupied this evening. I almost ask her what's on her mind, but another look at her face tells me she isn't quite ready to speak about it, whatever it is. It's probably normal worries, worries that anyone who is expecting a baby might have. Any minute now the calming baby hormones will kick in again, and she'll be serene and smiling and glowing.

A young couple walks past us. They are so close together, pressed against each other's bodies. His arm is around her back protectively. She has a daisy chain in her hair. She is laughing, and he is watching, drinking in the look and the smell of her – the shape of her mouth, the goofy, incomparable sweetness of her gummy teeth. She is everything to him in that moment. The diamond on her finger sparkles.

I cannot bear to watch them. It is petty and miserly of me to turn away; but it's just that I've never had that. I've never had that closeness with anyone. I don't even know how it's done. How can people become so unselfconscious – lost to everyone except each other, sealed so blissfully in that sweetness? It's what I always wanted most, and what I grew to know I'd never find.

And the thing is, I never knew I wanted this icing so much until I married Diarmuid. It loosened something inside me – all the dreams I thought I'd tucked away and sensibly forgotten. I will have to forget them again somehow. I must find a way. Because then I will be the Sally I knew again, and not this bewildered stranger.

Fiona seems to be gulping. I look at her with consternation. We're not even near a bench. 'What is it, Fiona?' I take her arm.

'Oh, Sally…' Her eyes are wide and plaintive. 'Did I make you marry Diarmuid?'

'Why on earth would you say that?' I exclaim. 'Of course you didn't!'

'But you caught the bouquet at my wedding. I wanted you to catch it. I threw it in your direction.'

'Erika made a grab for it too.' I smile. 'This is nonsense, Fiona. Surely you must see that.'

'But you felt left behind when I married Zak. I know you did. You said, "All our friends are married now, apart from me and Erika." You sounded so lonely. That's why I said I was sure you'd meet someone soon – and you did. I planted the idea in your head.'

'Stop it, Fiona,' I scold. 'My marriage is not your responsibility. Believe it or not, I made the decision myself.'

'Really?'

'Yes, really.' I pat her back. We are approaching another bench. 'Let's sit down for a while,' I coax. 'And then let's go to your house. I bet you have some scrumptious moussaka or chocolate cake just waiting to be devoured.'

Fiona clutches her stomach and rocks back and forth in her seat. *Oh dear God, maybe she's about to give birth.* I imagine myself shouting, 'Push!' in the middle of Dun Laoghaire pier and ordering people to go off and boil water and fetch blankets.

'What is it?' I ask warily. 'Is it… the baby?'

'Yes.'

'Oh.' I gulp. 'Well… try to breathe deeply. And –'

'Oh, no, I don't mean in that way.' She smiles wanly. 'I mean in… another way.'

'OK…' I say slowly. 'What other way?'

She looks at me. Her eyes are wide and stricken, terrified. 'I have to tell someone. I just have to tell someone.'

'Tell me, then!' I am almost airborne with consternation.

'Oh, Sally, this… this isn't Zak's baby.'

Tears are coursing down her cheeks.

Chapter Seven

'THIS PAVLOVA IS ABSOLUTELY delicious.' This is the first thing I say to Zak as he comes into his own plush sitting-room. 'I love sweet things. Diarmuid prefers savouries.' As I say this, I realise it pretty well sums up my marriage.

Fiona is studying me anxiously, from a large, round cane chair. It has a huge plump cushion and many people, including myself, have been known to fall asleep on it after over-indulging at dinner parties, but Fiona is almost too alert. Her whole face is tense, and her smile is far too wide and rigid. We have just returned from our walk, though the last half-hour of it was spent with me comforting Fiona while she howled on a bench on the pier.

I feel the secret is crawling over us all like bees. I fear that at any minute I'll shout, 'Ouch!' and Zak will ask me what's wrong, and I will blurt out that Fiona became pregnant in a fertility clinic in the United States when she was at that conference about databases. I'll say that I realise Fiona should have told him this, and that she would have, only she didn't want to upset him by telling him he had slow sperm – not the type that can suddenly get a move on and stop dawdling, like he thinks, but *really* slow sperm. And then I will say that I know she was wrong and beg him to forgive her. 'Because it's amazing the things people don't tell each other, Zak,' I will add. 'We're a very strange species. I have a great-aunt who seems to have disappeared entirely, and no one even wants to discuss her.'

I don't say this, however. What I say is, 'Do you know what I learned the other day? I learned that mice share ninety-nine per cent of their genetic sequence with humans. Can you believe that?'

Zak smiles at me. 'Yes, I heard that too. That's why they're so useful in research.'

I must get off the subject of genes. I can't believe how

Freudian that remark was. I hardly ever discuss mice. Why am I talking about them now?

'I let them loose in the tool shed.' What on earth has got into me? I'm still gabbling on about them.

'What?' Zak enquires, reaching out to pat Fiona tenderly on the shoulder.

'Diarmuid's mice.' I take a gulp of wine. 'He spent so much time with them. He was helping one of his lecturers with research that wasn't even on his course. I don't know exactly what the research was, but he gave different ones different food, and he had to look at them regularly and make notes. I think it was something about nutrition and ageing...'

Zak and Fiona are both looking at me slightly warily.

'Some of them certainly seemed more springy than others,' I gabble. Since when do I use words like 'springy'?

'That's interesting,' Zak says. 'The whole area of nutrition and health really needs more research.'

'But all these food scares are really infuriating,' Fiona says. 'I mean, we end up guzzling stuff that we're told is good for us – and then, more often than not, someone comes along and says we shouldn't eat too much of it because it's loaded with pesticides or metals or drugs.'

'That's why most of the stuff we buy is organic,' Zak says. 'Especially now.' He gazes lovingly at Fiona's stomach.

I feel a surge of panic. If he starts talking about the baby, I might just burst into tears. 'He lured them back,' I gabble. 'All he had to do was leave some cheese in the cage and they all wandered back into it. They put up no fight whatsoever.'

'Well, I suppose they'd got used to the comfort,' Zak comments. 'It can't be easy being a mouse, especially a wild mouse. I don't even know what they eat. I suppose they get seeds and things, and leftovers.'

There is a long pause. Then he says, 'I'm going to make hot chocolate. Would you like some more pavlova, Sally?'

'No. I'd better go,' I say. 'I think I'm a bit drunk, actually. This wine seems to have gone straight to my head.'

'It always does that.' Fiona smiles.

'Yes… yes, I know,' I sigh. 'I'm the cheapest drunk in Ireland.'

But, as Fiona and Zak head into the kitchen to make hot chocolate, I don't attempt to prise myself from the embrace of their deep, seductive sofa. Because I am suddenly realising that, if I weren't the cheapest drunk in Ireland, I would probably never have married Diarmuid.

I encountered Diarmuid at a party given by a woman called Gladys, whom I'd met at an evening class about restoring antiques. Gladys and I both joined the class hoping it would be full of hunky men with tool-belts, but it wasn't; it was full of women hoping to meet hunky men with tool-belts. I don't know why we were so surprised. At the end of the term Gladys decided to have a party, and I went along to it – rather reluctantly, because there was a good film on the telly. I had reached the point of singledom where I never expected to meet a half-decent single man again.

I'm shy at parties, and not a great talker, so I tend to end up chatting to people I know, or helping with the washing up, or handing out sausage rolls. But Gladys was determined we would all have a good time, and she was virtually pouring the red wine down us forcibly. So by the time I reached Diarmuid, who was sort of cowering in a corner by a cheese plant – he's shy at parties too – I stuck a plate of Ritz crackers loaded with egg swirls under his nose and said, 'Hi there, beautiful stranger!'

It wasn't that I thought Diarmuid was stunningly handsome, though he is attractive. I just liked the idea of saying that particular sentence to someone. I was feeling skittish and feckless, and I kept bumping into people and saying, 'Oops!' and then giggling. Gladys's Chilean wine must have been industrial strength.

Diarmuid gulped when I called him 'beautiful'. Then he took one of the crackers and looked at me dubiously. I could see he thought I was a brazen and completely un-shy sort of woman, and he wasn't entirely sure what to say.

Because he was saying nothing and everyone in the room

now had a Ritz cracker with egg swirl, I asked him how he had met Gladys, and he said she was a friend of his brother's. Then he asked me how I had met Gladys, and I explained about the evening class. I told him the main thing I'd learned was that life is too short to attempt to re-upholster your own armchair.

'I know quite a bit about re-upholstery,' Diarmuid mumbled bravely. He was knocking back the wine himself and seemed to have formed the impression that I was not about to bite him. 'Actually, I teach carpentry.'

'So you own a tool-belt!' I shrieked with delight. I was now extremely sozzled. 'Gladys...' I shouted across the room. 'I've found Tool-Belt Man!'

'Go for it, honey!' Gladys yelled back. 'Ask him where he keeps his drill.'

Gladys and I snorted with mirth, and a number of other female antique-restorers also giggled and stared at Diarmuid. It is much to his credit that he didn't walk off at that point. He just smiled shyly and said, 'So what do you do?'

'I'm a journalist,' I said. 'I write lots of stupid articles about any old thing at all.'

'I don't believe that,' Diarmuid said. 'I bet your articles are very interesting.'

And that's when Gladys came round with the big plates of spaghetti bolognese, and I sobered up enough to realise that I was talking to a single man who really seemed quite *nice*. He took my phone number; I didn't think he'd call, but he did, the very next day. We had a pizza and went to a film that Saturday, and that's how it started. And the really stupid thing is that, if Diarmuid had been someone I really fancied like crazy – someone I thought was sex on legs – I probably wouldn't even have offered him an egg-whirled Ritz cracker. Even the wine wouldn't have got rid of my embarrassment. But, because I had no particular feelings about him, I waltzed up to him brazenly and behaved as though I had been instantly attracted to him.

He still believes I was, in fact, and I have never denied it. Actually, I've encouraged him to retain this impression.

Because Diarmuid doesn't have a very high opinion of himself when it comes to women. He told me that he never made the first move because he was scared of being rejected. I did the very thing he was waiting for. I told him he was beautiful. And, even though it was a rather odd thing to say to a stranger at a party, it gave him the courage to ask me out and eventually marry me. Of course, he must have fancied me too; but I'm sure Diarmuid has fancied piles of women at parties and never even spoken to them. He was waiting for reassurance that he wasn't going to make an arse of himself – and I gave it to him with one chance remark.

And the stupidest thing of all is that it's a sentence I wanted to say to someone else at a party before, but didn't. Though Diarmuid is attractive, I would never call him beautiful. Beautiful is a big, extravagant word. To call a man beautiful implies that, in one glance, you have seen a sweetness of spirit – something that transcends other desirable attributes, such as a nice body or luxuriant hair or a wide, kind smile – something that speaks directly to your heart. And you can't understand how this has happened, how someone has become so precious to you in an instant; how, in some ridiculous golden way, he seems like part of the home you've been searching for.

I never even talked to the Beautiful Stranger I saw at the other party, so for all I know he could have been a right bollocks. And this incident seems typical of the way I live my life. I've always gone for the simplest choices – the ones that are most convenient and don't make waves or cause controversy.

'You look deep in thought,' Zak says, handing me a mug of hot chocolate – he and Fiona use their cappuccino machine to make a nice thick froth. 'You didn't even notice me. What were you thinking about?'

He smiles, that ridiculously wide smile. It should make him ugly, but it doesn't. There's a goodness about Zak that radiates from his smile, and from his small, deep-set eyes. It's even in his hands; they are broad, and the fingers are long and sensitive. Sometimes I love him myself, in a sort of detached way; I don't want him for myself, but I'm glad he's there to make me and everyone else feel warmer. Softer. Accepted. He is comfortable in his own skin; he is trusting and kind and almost obsessive about telling the truth. 'How can we really know people if they lie to us?' I remember he said that once, shortly after he and Fiona married. 'Even small white lies erode something. They're disrespectful.'

I decide not to tell Zak I was distracting myself from his slow sperm by tracing the provenance of my marriage. 'Actually, I was wondering about sofas,' I reply. 'There are too many designs and colours to choose from these days.'

Zak just sits there, as if he's waiting for me to tell him something else – as if, in some way, he already suspects a secret. Fiona is looking at him and then at me. I wish I could make everything right for them. I wish life wasn't so bloody complicated.

'I'd better go,' I say, as I finish the frothy chocolate.

'It's late. I'll drive you,' Zak says.

Fiona and I exchange careful glances.

'Go on,' she says, smiling. 'You look tired.' The placid hormones seem to have kicked in again. She looks serene and calm.

Zak appears to have got a new car. People who care about cars expect you to notice these things. 'What a lovely car!' I say to him. 'What lovely comfortable seats.'

He tells me what the car is. He talks about its special features and presses some buttons to illustrate technical details. 'My goodness, Zak,' I say, while he goes on about its advantages as a family vehicle.

What I'm really thinking about is the Beautiful Stranger – the man I thought I had erased from my memory. I haven't thought about him since I married Diarmuid – and it's just as well, because I found out he got married five months after I saw him at the party. But now, as Zak talks about cooling systems and hydraulics, it's as if the Beautiful Stranger has returned to me. I remember how we exchanged those long, heated glances, stared at each other with longing – surely it was longing – and then looked away. My feelings for him are so foolish. I can't believe I still remember it all in such detail. I even found out his name. It's Nathaniel. Shortly after his marriage he moved to New York. I will probably never meet him again.

I tumble out of the car gratefully as soon as I reach the cottage. 'Thanks, Zak, that was really good of you,' I say. This isn't a time to offer him a cup of tea. Even though I'm determined to keep Fiona's secret, something might slip out. When I push the car door closed, it slams dramatically. 'Sorry about that!' I smile, leaning into the open window. 'It's a beautiful car, Zak. Thanks so much for the lift.'

He smiles back and says, 'You're welcome.' Then he drives off happily. He's very smiley these days; he says the thought of the new baby makes him all soppy. I love that he's the kind of man who can be soppy. I fear for him. If only I could protect him and Fiona – and of course poor Erika, with her demented passion for Alex.

I used to feel that way about my parents, too, when I was little. I wanted to turn back time so that they could love each other like they used to. I wanted to rewrite history so that when Mum met Al, the man who became her lover, she just looked at him and walked off quickly in the other direction. I wanted her to see that she didn't need someone else. She had Dad and me. She had our lovely, rambling old house in the hills outside San Francisco. She had the big fat chocolate cookies I used to bake for us all; the laughter when I ran into the lawn sprinkler on those baking summer days.

Most of all, I wanted her to know that she had been happy before she met Al. But then sometimes I got to thinking that maybe she hadn't been happy, and we just hadn't noticed. So I lived with the feeling that one day Dad and I would wake up and find her gone. Gone without even a goodbye.

The minute I'm inside my cottage I decide to make myself a cup of tea, but when I'm walking to the kitchen I knock over my handbag. The notebook I found in my parents' attic falls onto the floor, and a photograph spills out of it. It must have been tucked away at the back.

I pick up the photo. It's a black-and-white picture of a woman smiling at the camera, a big, beaming smile. The photo is faded, but her smile isn't. She's a big-framed, attractive woman, the kind who isn't fat but will never look slender. She looks elegant, though you can see that she might walk in a sturdy, substantial fashion, her wide hips swaying under her low-cut cotton dress. She has a brave face – you can see it in her firm jawline and her strong eyebrows, the straight look in her eyes – and she has had to be braver than she expected. She is smiling even though she is sad. I don't know how I know this, but I do. She has longings she can't speak about; longings she feels no one will understand.

I get a queasy feeling in my stomach as I turn the picture over. I see the old gum and small, torn bits of paper: it was once in a photograph album, but it was removed. And in tidy black pencil on the back, someone has written, 'DeeDee'.

Chapter Eight

'WE COULD LIVE TOGETHER in a camper van,' Erika is informing me. 'Lots of people live in camper vans.'

'You and me?' I enquire. 'Because, to be quite frank, I'm not sure I'm that keen on the idea.'

I am talking into my mobile phone and walking along Grafton Street. I'm going to a reception organised by a woman called Greta, who has done lots of favours for me in the past, such as sending me on freebie furniture-related trips to Italy and London. Greta has her own PR company and is military and motherly, and frequently rather fierce.

'Not you and me!' Erika splutters. 'I'm talking about me and Alex. If he leaves his wife, he'll need somewhere to live... Yes, it's Thursday.' For a moment I wonder why Erika is telling me this; then I realise she must still be the receptionist at International Holdings. The staff there keep asking her the most basic questions. It's as if they regress to infancy as soon as they approach her desk.

'Couldn't he live in your flat?' I enquire.

'No, of course he couldn't!' she says, as if the suggestion is idiotic. 'It can't look as if he's just gone from one woman to another.'

'But that's what would have happened, isn't it?'

'Not really,' she says firmly. 'If he leaves his wife, it's because they don't love each other. He wouldn't even have looked at me if he was satisfied with his marriage.'

'Why couldn't he just rent a house?'

'Because if we had a camper van, we could go on trips,' Erika replies. 'Alex loves the idea of us going on trips in our little home – staying in Provence and Tuscany, falling asleep to the sound of the waves on a Wexford beach. He'd like to spend at least part of the summer travelling. He could bring his laptop along; he doesn't really need an office. Of course, sometimes he'd bring the kids along and I'd stay behind. It's only fair… Four thirty-five.'

I assume that someone has just asked her the time. At least I'm not late for the reception; it doesn't start until five.

'So you'd keep your flat?' I ask.

'Oh, yes,' Erika says. 'Though I'd have to get someone to share it with me, to help pay the rent while I'm away with Alex.'

'But you only have one bedroom.'

'I could use the utilities room. It's quite cosy.'

Erika's utilities room is mainly taken up with a washing machine, but I decide not to mention this. There is an excitement in her voice, a real exhilaration. She disappears to take a series of calls. I see a woman wheeling a pram and feel a surge of anxiety. What will Fiona do if Zak discovers their impending baby isn't his? It will be awful keeping such a big secret. I've already been rehearsing what to say when I peer into the cot.

Erika comes back on the line and starts telling me about the different kinds of camper vans you can buy. She's been looking it all up on the Internet. She has a computer on her desk. When people approach she has to hit 'Minimise', so she can give the impression that she is deeply, if temporarily, committed to International Holdings. The other day she pressed the wrong button and somehow ended up with a screen that blared, 'Single and sexy? Visit our chat room for fun, no strings attached!' just as a man called Jon was about to ask her what month it was.

'Sally? Sally, are you still there?' Erika is saying. Though I haven't really been listening to her, I presume she wants me to comment on which sort of camper van might be preferable. I must get off the subject.

'So… you and Alex have discussed all this?'

'Oh, yes,' Erika says. 'He'll rent a house later on, in the autumn. Divorce is very expensive; living in a camper van for a while would save him loads of money. And then he could sell it again if he wanted to.'

'Well… I suppose it could be quite practical,' I say. Then I add cautiously, 'But are you sure he really wants to leave his wife, Erika? So many of them sound as though they want to, then don't do it.'

'Of course he does!' she virtually shouts. 'I can't even believe you're saying that.'

I decide not to apologise. Erika needs to realise that what I've said is not that outlandish.

'Anyway, his wife may leave him first,' Erika declares defensively. 'She's spending more and more time with her yoga teacher.'

'How do you know?'

'I sometimes follow them.'

'What?'

'I sometimes follow them after class. They go to a park and talk.'

I'm not quite sure how to reply to the news that Erika stalks Alex's wife, so it's just as well that someone comes to her desk and asks her to type a letter. 'I hope you don't mind,' I hear a deep, hesitant voice saying. 'It would be a great help. It's not that long. Thanks, Erika. I hope you can read my handwriting.' From the sound of his tentative tone, I suspect that this is Lionel, one of Erika's more junior bosses, who doesn't have his own secretary. She has told me about him. He virtually cringes any time he has to ask her to do anything; it's as if he doesn't realise she is actually employed to do things like type letters.

'Don't worry, Lionel, you have the best handwriting in the building,' Erika says in a motherly tone. Lionel is probably blushing to the roots of his hair. I must find out if he's married, because I suspect he has a major crush on Erika. She keeps finding chocolate biscuits on her desk, and I bet they're from him.

As Erika gets on with her letter, I push my way down Grafton Street to the sound of buskers playing violins, guitars and trombones. The street is packed with shiny, manicured people with designer shopping bags. Shouldn't some of them be in offices? The building I'm heading for is down one of these side-streets. A very modern new store is showcasing 'top young design talent'. According to the swanky press release, the whole ground floor will be full of lamps with complex surfaces and flowing organic shapes, edgy twenty-first-century silver and sensually therapeutic textiles. The overall effect will be 'amusing, intimate, ironic and intriguing'. Greta certainly knows how to talk things up.

I'm on the right street and I'm early, so I decide to go into an Italian café and have a cappuccino. Van Morrison is playing in the big, slightly shaded interior; I get my cappuccino and sit on a lemon-coloured armchair by the window.

There are moments in my life when I feel perfectly contented, and this is one of them. The secret of happiness is to count your blessings and notice what you have, instead of what's missing; and I have so many reasons to be grateful.

I stir my cappuccino and watch the thick whorls covered in chocolate powder. Becky is probably back in New Zealand by now, anyway. She was only over for a visit. I must cook Diarmuid a lovely meal – big fat steaks and broccoli and chips, his favourite – and get in a big box of Turkish Delight. I can't believe how patient and understanding he's been. It's high time I appreciated him more. I was so *relieved* to marry him. I don't know why I've allowed myself to have these doubts. Being single was so lonely.

Out of nowhere I think of Nathaniel, the beautiful blue-eyed stranger, but this time I don't feel a pang of regret. He's just a nice memory that floats back into my head every so often.

My mobile rings just as I'm lifting the cup to my lips. Feck it, anyway. Sometimes I wonder if it really is an advantage to be quite so accessible. I consider leaving it in my bag, but I realise it could be Diarmuid. I really want to speak to Diarmuid. He hasn't phoned for days because he's studying for exams. I hope he does well.

'Sally, you have to stop asking Marie about DeeDee.' It isn't Diarmuid; it's April. She feels no need to build up to a subject gradually.

'How do you know I've been asking her about DeeDee?' I

frown. I also sit up straight and clench an armrest.

'She told me when she rang yesterday. She was wondering whether she should change the date of the party so I could be there, but I told her I was fully booked up for the whole of September. I told her there were weddings and very important meetings and, of course, the conference.'

'I see.' April is a very good liar. She does it with real conviction.

'Anyway, I got into her good books by saying I'd tell you to stop asking her about DeeDee. She brought it up because she knows I agree with her about things like that. There's no point poking around in the past.'

'But this is the present,' I say, trying to keep the irritation from my voice. 'If DeeDee's alive, we could meet her *now*.'

'Why should we want to?' April asks, and for a moment I almost agree with her. Her minimalist view of life sometimes seems like a restful contrast to my own.

'Aggie wants to meet her before she...' I can't bear to say 'dies', so I say, 'It's understandable, isn't it – wanting to see your sister again?'

April doesn't answer that. There are times when we talk when I could burst into tears. Instead she says, 'So how are you, anyway? Are you dating again?'

'What on earth are you talking about?' I splutter. 'Of course I'm not dating again. I'm *married.*'

'I think you should date again. It would get you out of yourself.' April has clearly formed the opinion that I am an introspective, miserable person who spends her spare time hunting for music boxes in attics.

'Look, I don't want to date anyone, OK?' I say fiercely. 'I'll probably go back to Diarmuid, but if I stay single, I... I want to keep loads of cats and... spend the weekends haring around the countryside on my mountain bike.' I hope this extravagant declaration will silence her.

It doesn't. She just laughs and says, 'Oh, you are funny sometimes.'

'I mean it!' I spit.

'Oh, come on. You're not a mountain-bike type of person,' she giggles. 'Anyway, I'd better go; I've got a meeting. Talk to you soon.' The line goes dead.

I sit there for a while in a sort of trance. Sometimes April's phone calls feel like ambushes. They make me say strange things. No wonder she thinks I'm not a mountain-bike kind of person; she was too small to remember that there was a time when I wanted a mountain bike with all my soul. My best friend Astrid had one. It was about freedom and adventure. A mountain bike seemed like a window to a whole new world. The Wild West is still wild, despite its veneer of civility, and I was wild too – wild in my heart.

But Mum and Dad just didn't like the idea of the mountain bike. They didn't want their well-behaved, pigtailed daughter taking off for dry brown hills and lumbering over tough, dusty terrain. What if I got stranded someplace with a flat tyre or something else that had to be fixed? Bikes could be quite temperamental. And a young girl shouldn't be out in the wilds on her own, anyway; an adult should be present. I pleaded and pleaded, but they wouldn't budge. It did make them think I should have a hobby, so they decided I should take piano lessons, which I hated.

But years later, when April said she wanted a mountain bike, things were different. We were back in Ireland, my parents had managed not to divorce and April appeared to be a full genetic member of the family; so, in the grand scheme of things, a mountain bike didn't seem such a big deal. She got one. It was hardly even discussed. She took off on her bike and then came back on it, and we began to see her as a rugged, outdoorsy person who took risks and had adventures. And maybe people would have seen me that way, too, if I'd got my mountain bike; but I didn't.

And now I'm lost. I've left the café immersed in these memories, and I must have walked straight past the building where the reception is being held. The street numbers don't seem to follow any logical pattern; even the landmarks Greta mentioned don't seem to exist. Time has fast-forwarded to five-twenty in what seems like three minutes. Greta will be angry, because all her favours come at a price: I am virtually under orders to attend this reception and walk around looking fascinated and making careful notes while interviewing 'top young designers'.

Maybe I should just go somewhere else. Sit by the pond in St Stephen's Green and dream…

But of course I can't. What am I thinking? I go into a newsagent's and ask them where the store is; it's just down the road, apparently, on the left. How can I have missed it? I race out. Beads of perspiration are gathering on my forehead. There it is – of course it is. I dart through the huge glass door.

I scan the room. I don't see *The Sunday Lunch*'s photographer. That will disappoint Greta. She seems to think I can boss the pictures editor around and demand that he include certain photographs in the paper, but I simply don't have that kind of clout. I grab a glass of sparkling water. I mustn't have any wine. I must stay sober and focused. I must dart around the room like a blue-arsed fly, looking fascinated.

I take a deep breath and am about to launch myself into the throng when I see him. He is standing by the big rosewood drinks table – the man I somehow know, although I have never even spoken to him. Nathaniel, the beautiful blue-eyed stranger.

Chapter Nine

I STARE AT THE Beautiful Stranger as though he were a famous sculpture in a Florence art gallery. I gawp like an American tourist who has never been to Europe before and finds it all fascinating. I want to reach out and touch him, trace the beautiful dark curve of his eyelashes. I've never seen eyelashes like that before, so long and thick, above such clear blue eyes.

'Sally, you made it!' Greta swoops down on me. 'What happened to you? There are so many people I want you to meet.' She looks more tall and muscular than ever, and her long black hair is tied up in a chignon. She's wearing a bat-winged silk thing that she probably painted herself.

Greta grabs my arm and hauls me over to a small, wiry man who appears to be wearing white cotton pyjamas. 'This is Tobias Armitage.' She beams at us both. 'Sally just loves your sofas, Tobias. She's from *The Sunday Lunch*.' In Greta's world, people don't just like sofas, they *love* them. It's her way of bolstering the artistic temperaments of her clients.

Tobias looks at me and I look at Tobias. I've never heard of his sofas, but this is a mere technical detail. Tobias clearly sees this as a chance for sofa fame and grabs it with his unusually hairy hands. The hairs are dark and long, and I find myself looking at them for far longer than is polite. I can't seem to focus on what he's saying.

I keep glancing over at Nathaniel to see if he's still there; I almost expect him to disappear like a mirage. *What's he doing here?* I think. *I thought he'd gone to live in New York.*

According to Tobias, one of the high points of anybody's life is choosing a sofa – preferably one of *his* sofas. 'These days, people want more from a sofa than just a place to sit,' he tells me in his nasal voice. He also has nose hair. 'In many ways, a sofa is a new member of the family.'

Nathaniel is leaning languidly against a large and very

75

minimal wardrobe, eating a sausage roll. He looks relaxed and laconic. I notice this even though I am scribbling furiously in my notebook, noting that Tobias likes the colours anthracite, 'donkey', burgundy and oatmeal. He believes it is worth paying that bit extra for built-in stain-resistant fabric protection. Sofas are his life.

I must ring Diarmuid. I must ring him right now and tell him to take me away from here. I need counselling. I need someone to hypnotise me out of these ridiculous feelings I have for this man. Nathaniel is all icing and no cake, I'm sure of it. I am not the sort of person this happens to. It doesn't happen to anyone.

And then I remember I am wrong. It does happen to some people. It happened to my parents. My father saw my mother across a crowded room after a concert, and that was it. He loved her high, gleeful laugh, her irreverence. He said there was a golden buzz in the air around her; even across the room, he could feel it. He used to talk about that night a lot when I was little. I knew the story as well as 'Cinderella' and 'Goldilocks and the Three Bears'. I loved that story; and then he stopped telling it. You can't tell that kind of story with a broken heart.

I want to run away. I can't stay in this room with Nathaniel. He may look over at any moment, and I may swoon with longing into Tobias's big hairy arms. Tobias also has tufts of hair growing out of his ears.

'Try to obtain a fabric swatch before making a decision,' Tobias is saying. 'Especially if you're matching your sofa to an existing colour scheme.'

Tobias's sofas are driving me crazy. I feel antsy and itchy, like when I was a kid and wanted to hare off into the hills on my mountain bike.

'Thank you so much, Tobias; that was really… interesting. I'd better go off now and…'

'I understand, Sally. Places to go, people to see.' He smiles jauntily. There are even long dark hairs peeping over the top of his open shirt. He must look like a gorilla in bed.

I really want a huge glass of wine. And a cigarette. I used to smoke with Erika, when we were sitting around at social events realising that we would never meet anything close to a soulmate. As we were smoking our cigarettes, we often said we wished we were lesbians, because Dublin seemed so full of interesting, warm-hearted women who kept meeting each other when they were supposed to be meeting interesting, warm-hearted men. Deep down, we began to prefer women in many ways (though not in bed); women just seemed *nicer*. I even felt that way when I married Diarmuid.

But I don't feel like that when I look at Nathaniel. He's reminding me of all the stupid longings I thought I'd ditched. My poor father must have felt just like this when he saw my mother, and look what happened to him. Maybe I should just go over to Nathaniel and say something incredibly rude. That would put an end to it.

I stand behind a large potted palm tree and watch him like a detective. He's just as I remember him from that party long ago. He is tall and lanky, and the top two buttons of his white cotton shirt are open; as far as I can tell, he is not troubled by excessive body hair. His fringe flops boyishly over his high, solemn forehead. He is steady and sure, and he's talking to a young woman with a purple fringe. The rest of her hair is dark and shiny and tied back in a chignon. She's called Eloise. I know this because I interviewed her some months ago about her cabinets. She just *loves* her cabinets. And that passion makes her eyes glow; that passion transforms her. I need a passion like that, something I really love doing. It would change everything; I know it would. How is it that some people find their passion so easily and others don't even have one?

I want to be Eloise. I want to be standing opposite Nathaniel chatting away casually. I don't want to feel this shy, this vulnerable. I'm married. And Nathaniel is married too. Why do I keep forgetting that? I feel I'm radiating so much lust that everyone must notice it. That's all it is – plain lust. I think longingly of Diarmuid and the restful hours we've spent discussing whether we should build a conservatory.

Diarmuid knows the real Sally. He married her. I must find her again, for him and for myself.

And they've put on *Riverdance*. We're all supposed to love *Riverdance* – it's part of that jolly, hoppy, raring-to-go Irish thing – but I need something more relaxing and enigmatic, a saxophone, a flute. Sometimes I get tired of how fascinated we are by what it means to be Irish. I think I'll scream if we have another referendum. The world is a big place. DeeDee knew that – I don't know how I know this, but I do. And I somehow know she'd understand what I'm feeling right now. That sound in the distance, that lure to another life that always seems better than the one you've got.

I grab a glass of wine. I don't care, I must have one, even if I am the cheapest drunk in Ireland. Maybe I'm on something. Maybe someone has slipped love mushrooms into the sushi.

And Nathaniel has seen me. He's looking at me just like he did last time, dragging me far out to sea with his deep blue stare. He's the man I should hit over the head with a loofah, not poor innocent sofa-obsessed Tobias. It's rude to stare. I should march up to Nathaniel and tell him that. He's a married man; he should know better. Maybe he does this all the time.

Greta introduces me to a man called Larry, who is apparently one of the evening's most important guests, because he buys bundles of stuff from young Irish designers and has some very important connections. I mumble something. Nathaniel is still talking to Eloise. She has one of those small, bright faces that virtually glow, and her big brown eyes belong to some innocent, adorable creature, a deer or a puppy. She practically pinned me to the wall at another reception because she wanted to tell me about her cabinets. I could never grab someone like that and demand that they listen to me, but Eloise is incredibly ambitious; she knows what she wants, and she just goes for it and doesn't care who gets in her way. Maybe I should be more like Eloise. Maybe that's what's wrong with my life.

This is unbearable. Every time I look at Nathaniel, he looks at me and doesn't even smile. Eloise looks over at me too, and glowers. She looks as if she'd like to bite me. This is clearly some kind of test, sent to make me realise how much I want to be married to Diarmuid. I must try to phone Diarmuid as soon as Larry is off helping himself to another plate of Irish stew.

Larry has large breasts. I know I shouldn't be dwelling on this sort of detail, but the fact is, he does. Maybe it's something to do with the contraceptive hormones that get into the water supply. I bet Diarmuid would have an interesting opinion on Larry's breasts, now that he's studying biology. Maybe I should mention it to him when I phone him. The wine has clearly gone to my head.

Larry is Irish-American. He's fat and balding, and he made his millions from feminine hygiene – I haven't been able to bring myself to ask him the details. He 'just loves' Ireland, the golf and the food and the sunsets and the sweet Irish air… What he means is that he loves the rich Ireland, the insulated one where everybody is nice because you are paying them such big bucks. There is a greedy, acquisitive glint in his eyes. He is the male equivalent of Eloise, though of course not nearly so attractive. They even have the same high, pert breasts.

Greta is watching us carefully and smiling. She's obviously pleased that I'm being so polite to her VIP guest. She darted over and gave me another press release a moment ago. I haven't even looked at it. It's probably about those disgusting table-mats she's been raving about. They look like matted sheep droppings.

Larry wants to take me out to dinner tonight. He says I have a lovely accent and remind him of some French actress.

'Larry, I'd… I'd love to, but I'm married,' I say.

'Oh, Sally, I'm not suggesting anything… you know…' He waves a bulky arm vaguely. 'I don't have any friends in Dublin, except Greta. I just want a bit of company and an early night.' I almost believe him.

Larry starts telling me how glad he is that Greta introduced us, because it can be really lonely being on your own in a foreign city, even though Dublin doesn't really feel foreign, Dublin always feels like home… Oh, feck it; it's beginning to look like

I'll have to have this meal with him. Greta has done me so many favours, and she is looking at us so hopefully.

'That meal sounds... lovely,' I say to Larry. 'But I'd better go to the toilet – I mean restroom – first.'

'Fine. Take as long as you want,' Larry says, as if I somehow need his permission. I decide that if he tries any hanky-panky I'll squirt him in the face with my aerosol deodorant.

I head grimly to the ladies'. As I push my way through gorgeous, happening top young designers and their acolytes, I don't look for Nathaniel. I haven't even thought about him for ten whole minutes. The whole effect seems to have worn off; it was like the brief high one gets from eating too much sugar. He's not standing by the rosewood drinks table any more. He must have left, and I'll probably never see him again. Oh, the relief of it!

I don't touch up my make-up in the ladies'. I just have a pee and dial Diarmuid's number. I'm going to tell him I want to cook him steak and chips and hand-feed him Turkish Delight tomorrow. That should cheer up his studying. But, when I dial, a recorded voice says Diarmuid's phone is out of range. How can that be? Where is he? Maybe he's giving Charlene a driving lesson. I'll try to ring him again in an hour.

I stuff my press releases into my bag and set my face into a grim, determined expression. Then I sweep out of the ladies' into the low-lit corridor.

'Let's go.' He darts from behind a column and whispers the words in my ear. Goodness, Larry is getting a bit too enthusiastic. There are people I should thank and say goodbye to, and I need to ask that woman who makes those mosaic lampshades to email me some photos. I don't even glance at him. I look straight ahead. 'Look, Larry, there are a few things I need to do before –'

'I'm not Larry.'

'What?' I turn on my heel, astonished.

'I'm Nathaniel.'

I can't speak. I'm just staring at him. It can't be, but it is.

Chapter Ten

'WHERE?' I SAY TO Nathaniel. 'Where do you want us to go?' I'm behaving as if this happens to me all the time.

'Let's just get out of here.'

It's a dream; it must be. They definitely put something in the sushi. I gulp and lean against the wall.

'Are you all right?'

I don't answer. I want to run away and hide somewhere. Things like this don't happen to me. They might have happened to the Sally who wanted a mountain bike, but not to the Sally I am now. Nothing has prepared me for this situation.

'You're trembling.' Nathaniel touches my arm; his hand feels warm and strong. I flinch. 'Relax.' He smiles. 'You don't have to have dinner with Larry. I've come to rescue you.'

This is when I should say that I don't want to be rescued, that I *want* to have dinner with Larry because it will please Greta. But I don't say anything.

'If we don't move fast, Larry will come out here and find you,' he grins. He's acting as if this is all a laugh, but it's actually dreadfully serious. I don't just leave important Irish-Americans in the lurch after I've promised to have dinner with them. I keep my promises… I think of my marriage; well, not all my promises, perhaps, but most of them. My sense of duty is widely known and appreciated.

'You're looking very worried, Sally.' His eyes are bright and teasing.

'How do you know my name?' I demand indignantly. This is good. This is more like the old Sally. She would tell Nathaniel, very calmly and politely, that she is a married woman and her husband doesn't like her running away from receptions with total strangers.

Dear God, I think, as I clasp my handbag to my chest. *Maybe this is what happened to DeeDee.* Maybe she was living a perfectly ordinary decent life until some stranger said, 'Let's go,' and she went and never came back. Maybe she was *abducted.*

Nathaniel doesn't tell me how he knows my name, and I decide not to press the issue. 'I don't do this kind of thing,' I tell him primly. 'I'm sorry. You clearly think I'm another sort of woman.'

'We don't have time to discuss that.' He grabs my arm.

I grab it back. 'How do you know I agreed to have dinner with Larry, anyway?'

'He just told me in the men's toilet. He said he'd found himself a lovely Irish colleen. He was dousing himself with aftershave. He said you'd gone to "pretty yourself up"; that's how I knew I'd find you here.'

'We're just going to dinner,' I say. 'He says he wants an early night.'

'And you believed him?' Nathaniel is studying me with amusement.

'Yes.'

'Then it's just as well I turned up when I did.'

I glare furiously into his bright-blue eyes. 'What are you implying?'

'I'm implying that your dinner with Larry might not be quite as innocent as you think.'

'That's for me to find out, isn't it?' I snap. 'I don't need your interference. I… I could spray him in the face with my deodorant if I needed to.'

'I think you should welcome my interference.' Nathaniel leans languidly against the wall. 'After all, it may save you the bother of spending the evening spanking Larry's rather large bottom in some five-star hotel.'

I almost fall over with outrage. 'I would *never* spank Larry's bottom!' I shout. Tobias the sofa designer happens to be passing by just as I declare this, and he gives me a rather lecherous smile. 'Why would you even suggest that?' I splutter. 'Do I *look* like the kind of woman who goes around doing that kind of thing?'

'No, you don't. You look very sweet and lovely.'

I get a strange fizzy feeling in my stomach.

'But Larry always asks his dinner dates to spank him. His wife won't do it, so he approaches nice understanding strangers at parties when he's abroad. He tells them that being spanked is the only way he can obtain any kind of sexual relief. It's amazing how many of them oblige, after a slap-up meal and four bottles of vintage wine.'

I am blushing to the roots of my easi-meche highlights. 'That's not true. Larry isn't like that,' I protest, trying to salvage some meagre dignity. Anyway, Nathaniel looks just the type who might make this sort of nonsense up for a joke. I don't know how I could have thought he was sweet and soulful.

'I think I'm in a position to know more about Larry than you do,' Nathaniel replies firmly.

'Oh, you've spanked his bottom, have you?' I say. 'I'm sorry, I didn't know you were speaking from first-hand experience.'

Nathaniel blithely overlooks this remark. 'Look, I lived in New York up until a few months ago. I know people Larry knows. He's got quite a reputation.'

Oh, God… maybe it's true. Oh, the humiliation of it. How has my life become this odd? And why did Larry choose me? Do I look like the biggest sucker in the room? I lower my head miserably.

Nathaniel touches my arm. This time I don't flinch. 'Look, he only chose you because you're so pretty. But we've got to go. He really will come out and start looking for you soon.'

'Where's the gents' toilet? That's where you last saw him, isn't it?' I'm starting to panic. It's as if I expect Larry to appear with a big stick and demand that I spank him right there and then.

'Yes. It's to the right and through the…'

'I don't want directions to it, I just want to know if it's *near* here,' I gabble. 'You're right: I'd better go. Bye.' I dash away from Nathaniel down the dimly lit corridor, yank open a door and find myself in a cleaning cupboard, surrounded by mops.

'It's the other way.' Nathaniel is standing behind me.

'What?' I glower.

'The exit. I'll show you. If we go this way, we don't have to go anywhere near the reception.'

'This store only opened last week. How do you know so much about it?' I demand. Everything about him is starting to irritate me.

'I've been helping Greta with this Young Irish Talent thing. She's my cousin.'

'Ah, yes,' I say. 'I should have known.'

As I race after him down another corridor, I want him to ask how I should have known, so I can tell him he is even more bossy and opinionated than Greta is. But he doesn't say anything. He just yanks open a door beside a cement staircase. 'Freedom!' he exclaims, as we find ourselves in a small and rather grimy side-street.

Good. Now I can get away from him. 'Well, I suppose it's goodbye, then,' I say stonily, proffering my hand to make the whole transaction as formal as possible.

'Since I deprived you of a meal with Larry, I think I should buy you one myself,' Nathaniel says. 'Come on. I know a fabulous place. You'd love it.'

How on earth do you know what I like and what I don't? I think. *The cheek of you and your presumptions!*

'You look like you could do with a really nice Chinese meal, Sally Adams.' He is standing far too close.

'I'm married.' I decide to just announce it.

'Yes, I know you are, and so am I... and so, of course, is Larry.' He smiles. Does he take *anything* seriously?

'We shouldn't even be *talking* like this,' I say frostily.

'Why didn't you talk to me before?' His eyes have darkened. He's serious now. 'Why didn't you talk to me at that party, years ago?'

'Why didn't you talk to me?' I counter.

'I wanted to, but when I came over to your side of the room you'd dashed off. Someone told me you had gone home. You were in such a rush you even left your coat.'

I take a deep breath. This is indeed true. Now I wish I had talked to him. I would have seen he wasn't a beautiful stranger, after all. He was just a great big handsome eejit.

'I'm going now,' I say firmly. 'And I assume you're going, too – going home to your wife.'

'I can't go home to her. She's having a torrid affair with a transvestite from the Bronx.'

I don't know what to say to that, so I just say, 'Oh,' and turn on my heel and leave.

I'm almost back on Grafton Street when my mobile rings. 'Sally?' It's Marie, and she's sounding very imperious. 'I've decided I have to tell you something.'

'What?' I demand. If she wants me to apply for another job on *Road Haulage Weekly,* I may well scream right in her ear.

'DeeDee's dead.'

I stop in my tracks. *'What?'*

'She's dead. I should have told you that.'

I lean against a wall. I can't speak for a moment. I look at a plastic bag dancing in the wind. 'How… how did she die?'

'I don't know. Some woman phoned me from Rio de Janeiro, fifteen years ago, to tell me she was dead. I was the only relative listed in DeeDee's address book – we used to be very close when I was a child – and this woman thought I should know.'

I don't say anything, so Marie adds, 'So now you know. I suppose I should have told you before. I didn't want to upset you, but then you kept going on about wanting to find her… I haven't told anyone else, Sally – as I've said, I think DeeDee is best forgotten – so let's keep it between ourselves.'

'Yes,' I say. 'Thank you for… for telling me the truth. Bye.'

I feel winded. Dazed. Surely this can't be true. I stare numbly at the pavement. I don't know why I'm so upset about someone I never met; but I feel I *should* have met her, I should have learned her story. Tears are coursing down my cheeks, stupid tears for a total stranger – a woman who just walked out on everyone; a woman who shouldn't be missed.

I am so lost in my grief that I scarcely notice Nathaniel has caught up with me.

'What is it? What was that phone call about?'

I don't reply.

He lowers his face towards mine. 'My car is in the next street. Please let me buy you a meal. You can't go home like that.' He sounds so concerned, so tender.

I should say no. I should go home. I should call Diarmuid. But he wouldn't understand; he would be comforting and kind, but he wouldn't really get it. He would remind me that I didn't really know DeeDee, that she wasn't part of my life. But she was – she *is,* in some way I can't even explain to myself. I need someone to talk to. I have needed it for so long.

Nathaniel offers me a paper hanky. I do not protest as he gently takes my hand.

Chapter Eleven

THE LATE-EVENING SUN is scorching. I put my hand to my forehead to shield my eyes from the glare. It wasn't this hot when I went into the reception, or when I came out of it; the heat seems to have arrived suddenly from nowhere.

Nathaniel's hand is warm too, warm and strong; I can almost feel the blood pulsing through his veins. He is leading me down a series of back streets I have never seen before, narrow alleys full of refuse sacks and the sweet, acrid scent of decay. The doors we pass are fire exits. Scrawny stray cats dart away from us as we approach. The tall buildings at each side shield us from the sun, and there is a blazing brilliance in the gaps. I wonder, vaguely, how long we will be walking – half an hour, ten minutes? I don't speak.

'Here it is.' Nathaniel lets go of my hand and approaches a battered blue car.

It's a very old car. I even know the make: it's a 2CV Citroën. I recall a long-ago student-exchange holiday in a Paris suburb: I was trying to improve my French, and ancient 2CVs seemed to be everywhere, driven by young, laughing tearaways smoking Gauloises.

'Sorry it's such a mess.' Nathaniel smiles as he yanks open a door, which doesn't appear to be locked. He starts to shove piles of paper and magazines to the back seat, which contains a large and very dirty cushion covered in dog hair. 'I'm a messy sort of person, I'm afraid.' He smiles at me, and for the first time he looks bashful. 'My apartment looks like a hurricane's hit it, and my office looks like some modern-art installation called "Chaos".'

I must look alarmed, because he laughs. 'I am exaggerating, just slightly. I'm determined to get more organised. I've been throwing piles of stuff away, and buying sleek coloured files in stationery shops.'

I consider asking him what he does, but I'm facing

the challenge of getting into his ancient car. I will, apparently, have to slide over to the passenger seat from the driver's seat; Nathaniel informs me that the passenger door does open from the inside, but sometimes it almost falls off with the effort. I feel muddled and strange. The fact that his car is almost impossible to get into seems oddly appropriate. I haven't got into a car like this in years. All my friends have sensible, shiny cars that purr and hum and glide. Every single one of them looks the same to me.

I twist and squirm my way into the passenger seat and thank Jesus that I am wearing trousers. If I were wearing a skirt, it would probably be up past my thighs.

'They're not very comfortable seats, I'm afraid,' Nathaniel says as he climbs in after me. 'And the suspension is bolloxed... but I love this car, which is just as well, because I can't afford a new one.' He yanks a lever and the canvas roof rolls back.

I sit there numbly. Then new plump tears start to fall down my cheeks.

Nathaniel looks at me keenly and starts the engine. 'It's a weird little place,' he remarks, 'but the food is great.'

'What?' The word seems to rise from my stomach. 'What are you talking about?'

'The Chinese restaurant. And it's cheap. Don't be put off by the scowls.'

'The what?'

'Henry, the owner, scowls at everyone. But his eyes are friendly. He's a great big teddy bear pretending to be a tiger.'

I feel panicky suddenly. I don't do this kind of thing. 'I think I should get out.' My voice is quivery.

'And they do really great imported beer.' The car is chugging forwards erratically, as though it's complaining about being woken from a pleasant slumber. 'She'll heat up in a minute.' Nathaniel pats the dashboard affectionately. 'You'll feel better when you're having some fat spring rolls. They do great spring rolls.'

I look at him dubiously.

'And then you can tell me why you're so sad.'

'You can let me out at the corner,' I say. 'I can get a bus home from the quays.'

'What was that phone call about?'

'Do the brakes in this car actually work?' I have to ask. We're going quite fast now, and this car may well be held together with Blu-Tack.

'Don't you ever answer a question, Sally Adams?' He looks at me with gentle reproach.

'Don't you ever listen?' I glower.

'Wow, your scowl looked just like Henry's then.' Nathaniel smiles. 'I'm a very good listener, actually. For seven whole years I did almost nothing else.'

I might as well accept it: I have no idea what's going on, except that I am apparently going to have dinner with this man. So I might as well try to find out something about him. 'Who did you listen to?' I enquire.

'People talking about how sad they were, and how lost and frightened and hopeless they felt…' He smiles at me cheerfully. 'It was like being a bank manager.'

I don't say anything.

'Actually, I was a social worker. I wanted to be a really good social worker.'

'And were you?' I'm getting used to the clanking sounds now. The car seems to be talking to us. It's probably telling us we should have got a bus.

'No, I think I was a fake social worker – a good fake social worker.' He is peering at street signs. 'Have you ever felt like a fake, Sally? Like you're getting away with stuff, but at any moment everybody will see through you?'

I gulp.

'Thought so,' he laughs. 'Has anyone ever told you that you have the most adorable frown? Your nose even crinkles.'

I decide not to feel flattered. 'Are you still a social worker?'

'No. I left when I realised I was just as fucked up as most of my clients – more, in some ways, because I was pretending not to be fucked up. It's a kind of deal: I pretended to be sorted so

89

that my clients could think they were talking to someone wise. People like that idea.'

The sun is blazing through the open roof and my hair is blowing in every direction. It will look like a haystack when I get out of the car.

'And I did offer them a lot of excellent practical suggestions about dealing with life – most of which I naturally don't follow myself,' Nathaniel continues, almost absent-mindedly. He is leaning over the steering-wheel as though looking for a turn-off.

'So... you're not wise.' I can't help being curious about him. He really is one of the oddest men I've ever met.

'No, not more than most, but I know how to look it. I know what to say and how to nod my head. I know how to look really calm and talk about the importance of seeing the bigger picture. That's what lots of people need to be reminded of – that there's a bigger picture.' There is now a slight smell of petrol in the car. 'And I got to know some useful theories and techniques. So, if I'm going to be fair to myself, I think I did help some people. I got some nice thank-you cards, anyway. But when Ziggy – that's my wife – started having her affair, I was a shambles. I couldn't listen to anyone. She and I were meant to be for ever and ever, and all that sort of thing... You know the story.'

The car jerks onto a main road. Where on earth are we going?

'There's a smell of petrol.'

'I know.' Nathaniel sighs. 'It's something to do with some tube or something. I had the garage look at it; they didn't seem too worried.'

I think of Diarmuid. He would know the name of the tube, and he would have got it fixed – although there is no way he would be driving a car like this to start with. This all seems very juvenile and *messy*. I should demand that Nathaniel stop the car now. We appear to be heading for Howth, which is some distance from the city centre. Are we really going to a Chinese restaurant? I think of the can of deodorant in my handbag.

90

'So was that call from your husband, telling you he'd found himself a transvestite too?' Nathaniel enquires, glancing at me.

'Oh, for God's sake!' I exclaim. 'Diarmuid isn't like that.'

'Or your lover? Was it your lover saying he'd decided to emigrate to Costa Rica and be a go-go dancer?'

'Of course not,' I snap. 'I don't have a lover. And, if I did, he wouldn't be that sort of person.'

'So you've thought about what sort of person he might be?' His eyes twinkle.

'No, of course I haven't. I'm *married.*'

'Yes, I know, but you aren't living with… Diarmuid, isn't it?' I stiffen.

'How do you know that?'

'Greta told me. Apparently news of your sudden departure from your marriage has been buzzing around the interior-decoration world… Would you like some chocolate? I think it's in that side pocket.'

'I don't want any chocolate at the moment, thank you.'

'Well, I do.'

I sigh, delve into a mass of papers and sweet wrappers and take out a fistful of street maps. One of them is of Manhattan. Beneath them is a very soft lump of chocolate, which is leaking out of the silver paper. Some of it gets onto my fingers.

'Do you have a tissue?' I look at Nathaniel frostily.

'No, I don't think I do… You used up the last one, remember?' I remember all too clearly – the big, helpless tears after hearing about DeeDee. The disbelief.

He smiles at me. 'Lick it off.'

I obey reluctantly. 'It's virtually liquid,' I mumble, pointing at the molten chocolate. I have placed it on the dashboard on top of an old ice-cream wrapper.

'I suppose we'll just have to leave it there for a while. It's getting cooler.'

It doesn't seem to be getting any cooler to me. I feel that at any moment we may combust.

'My separation from Diarmuid is only temporary,' I mumble. 'We just had some things we needed to sort out.'

'And now you have?'

We're careering along a coastal road. The sea looks flat and calm. 'Yes... I mean, sort of. It's... it's complicated.'

He doesn't say anything.

'Someone died. That's what the phone call was about. A great-aunt I never knew died in Rio de Janeiro. She was called DeeDee.'

'Oh. I'm sorry to hear that.' He reaches out and touches my arm. My skin absorbs his touch thirstily. Is it possible to have lonely skin?

'I almost wondered if I should go to Rio and try to find her, but of course now I don't need to.' I fiddle with a button on my pink blouse. 'I feel I should have met her. That's why I was crying. It was silly.'

'No, it wasn't silly,' Nathaniel says. 'It was important – it *is* important.' The words feel like a caress.

'She wasn't a good person,' I say slowly. 'She just left everyone – disappeared one day, without even telling anyone where she was going.'

'And sometimes you'd like to do that too?' He throws me a bright, piercing glance.

'Of course not!' I cry indignantly. 'How can you say that?'

'I think most people feel that way sometimes. To be honest, I think everyone has a bit of DeeDee in them.'

For some reason I think of the countless times I returned to our rambling old house in the hills outside San Francisco wondering if my mother would be there or if her wardrobe would be empty, her toothbrush gone. I even imagined the house without the smell of the light, flowery perfume she always wore.

'But some people stay.' It comes out as a whisper, almost a sigh. 'They stay even though they wanted to go.'

He says nothing, just waits.

'My mother stayed.' Why am I telling this to a stranger? 'She had an affair when we were living in California. She really loved him. She's never been the same since. She used to be so bright and happy, but now something's gone from her; she keeps herself busy and cheerful, but she's hardened inside.' I stare out the window. 'Even her mugs are all the same colour.'

We drive on in silence. Diarmuid would have asked why I mentioned the mugs – he would have wanted to get to the bottom of it, found out why it seemed important; and I would have had to tell him it was just something I said without thinking, a sideways sentence, not one you could understand from standing directly in front of it. But I wouldn't have said that, because I would have had to explain that too. And those were – are – the moments in which I feel lonely even though Diarmuid is there.

We haven't talked for minutes. 'Why do you keep a map of Manhattan in your car?' I ask eventually.

'Because I miss it. Jesus, I thought it was closer than this.'

'Manhattan?'

'Yes, Sally. I thought Manhattan was just down the road...' He looks at me with tender impatience. 'No, of course not. The Chinese restaurant. I think it's quite possible that it's receding. Maybe we'll be travelling towards it for the rest of our lives.'

For a weird, stupid moment I think that wouldn't be such a bad thing – travelling along the coastline in this bumpy old car, talking about anything at all.

'Do you miss California?' We are stopped at traffic lights again. Dublin traffic has multiplied in recent years.

'Yes,' I say. 'I mean, I did. I missed it ferociously.' The heat must be loosening me, making me say the first thing that comes into my head. 'When we got back to Dublin, it seemed to rain for years. I couldn't believe how much it rained.' I prod the chocolate; it does seem to be solidifying slightly. 'I missed the hummingbirds and the brown hills and the freedom. I missed the Wild West.'

He looks at me.

'It still has frontier-type people who aren't... you know... so set in their ways. And I suppose I missed the angels, too.'

'The *angels?*'

'Yes. I used to believe in them, but then I stopped. It seemed silly. Astrid – my best friend in California – believed in them. She had pictures of them all over her bedroom. I didn't know anyone in Dublin like that.'

'I believe in angels,' Nathaniel says. 'I mean, I like the idea of believing in angels. I don't see why I shouldn't, if I want to. After all, absence of evidence is not evidence of absence.' He is peering down side roads, muttering under his breath.

'What do you miss about Manhattan?'

'I miss the person I thought I was going to be there,' he says matter-of-factly. 'I was going to be someone happily married, maybe with kids, a successful social worker. I wasn't going to be the kind of person who spent his life looking for a Chinese restaurant.'

'Why do you exaggerate so much?' I can't help smiling.

'I enjoy it. Tell me more about DeeDee.'

'All I know is that she liked marble cake and hats and Rio de Janeiro.'

'Sounds like my kind of woman.'

I smile; then, as I glance across at the other side of the road, I stiffen.

Is that *Diarmuid?* It looks like his car, and it certainly looks like him... It *is* Diarmuid! And he might look over at any moment. I duck my head so that it's almost crammed against the gearbox. Prickles of fear dart around me like fireflies.

'What are you doing, Sally?' Nathaniel enquires. 'Have you lost something?'

'My husband,' is all I can manage to mutter. 'In the car across the road.'

'Which one?'

'The Ford Fiesta. Oh, God, do you think he saw me?'

'Would it matter if he had?'

'Of course it would!' I splutter. 'He'd jump to conclusions.'

'And you could explain that this was entirely innocent,' Nathaniel says calmly. 'Which it is.' Somehow I can't entirely agree.

I raise my head and peer through the bottom of the passenger window. If only the lights would change. Diarmuid is frowning, glancing at his watch. He looks preoccupied; he doesn't look like a man who thinks he has just seen his wife with her lover. Maybe he hasn't seen me. Of course he hasn't. But… but what is he doing on this side of Dublin?

The lights change, and the car grunts and lurches forwards. Nathaniel pats my arm. 'He's gone.'

I straighten cautiously and breathe a sigh of relief. 'I should go home.'

'But we haven't eaten.'

'I can eat at home.'

'But it wouldn't be as nice.'

'Seeing Diarmuid like that… it's frightened me. The coincidence of it.'

'Dublin is a small place.'

'Not that small.' I fidget agitatedly with my wedding ring. Maybe Becky lives on this side of Dublin. Maybe… no. I mustn't think about Becky. He could have just been visiting his parents. They live out in the countryside past Howth.

'Are you all right?' Nathaniel glances at me keenly.

I nod.

'We're nearly at the restaurant. It's on this road… Oh, buggery bollocks *feck!*'

'What?'

'The restaurant isn't open.'

'Are you sure?'

'I think that "Closed" sign on the door is meant to be a hint.' We both peer at what seems to be a shabby, forgotten hut wedged between a grocery store and a garage.

'This is terrible,' Nathaniel says. 'I don't think I can bear the disappointment.'

We both sit there glumly.

'I know!' Nathaniel suddenly exclaims. 'We'll go to Bull Island instead. We'll get takeaway spring rolls and stuff, and look at the birds and the sunset.' He must sense my alarm, because he adds, 'Don't worry – I won't even try to kiss you.'

'OK,' I say, because I am extremely hungry. 'But I want chips too.'

'Fine, you can have chips… chips and chocolate.' He

reaches for the chocolate on the dashboard. It's almost solid now; he breaks off a slab and hands it to me. I munch it. We sit for some time without speaking.

'I suppose we'd better go, then, hadn't we?' I say eventually. 'Are there any Chinese takeaways around here?'

'Of course there are. There are Chinese takeaways everywhere. They probably even have them on the moon.'

'We should ask someone where the nearest one is.'

Nathaniel looks at me reluctantly.

'Oh, no – you're not that sort of man, are you?' I sigh.

'What sort of man?'

'The sort who can't bear to ask people for directions.'

'Not any more!' He jumps out of the car and stops the first pedestrian he sees, an elderly woman with a poodle and a Harrods shopping bag. 'Since you are clearly a woman of taste,' he says to her, 'I was wondering if you could tell me where to find a Chinese takeway. The best one in the area.'

The poodle is smelling his brown loafers. It looks like it might cock its leg and pee on them at any minute. 'Stop that, Binky!' the woman says commandingly.

'Nice Binky,' Nathaniel says. 'Good Binky.' Binky snarls and bares his teeth, and Nathaniel backs away from him cautiously.

'A Chinese takeaway…' The woman frowns. 'It could be at the end of the road, to the right, take the next left and then go past the roundabout. Or maybe that's a beauty salon now.' She stops and peers into the distance.

'Thanks.' Nathaniel smiles.

'It could have moved.'

'It doesn't matter. Thanks anyway. You've been very helpful.'

'It has a big sign over it.'

'That's great. Bye, Binky.' He jumps into the car as Binky lunges towards his leg.

The woman peers into the car. 'You could ask at the erotic lingerie shop down there. They stay open past eight.'

'Great. We really appreciate your assistance.' Nathaniel

96

starts up the engine and waves at her. 'Dear God,' he says, as we drive off. We are speeding past the erotic lingerie shop when he adds, 'I can't remember any of her directions, can you?'

'There was a roundabout.'

'Yes, I remember the roundabout, and something about left and right – but I don't think I've got them in the proper sequence.'

'It could be a beauty parlour anyway.'

'Indeed.' We drive on, scanning the buildings.

'I've been to Rio de Janeiro, like that great-aunt of yours,' Nathaniel says, as we approach a takeaway of some sort. 'I lived there for a year. I taught English.'

The words land softly, almost inevitably. They sound sweet and strange, and for some reason I am not at all surprised.

'I can tell you about it while we eat our…' He peers at the takeaway. 'Our fish and chips – sorry, it doesn't seem to be Chinese.' He parks the car. 'I can tell you what DeeDee would have seen – the sights, the smells, the colours. It's an amazing place.' I am suddenly excited about the prospect of eating fish and chips and talking about DeeDee's home.

But my mobile rings just as we're going into the takeaway. I glance at it. 'Oh, feck – it's Diarmuid.'

'Sally…' His voice squawks and hisses, and there are buzzing sounds. 'Sally? Are you there?'

'Yes. Yes, I am. What is it, Diarmuid?' I put on my lines-of-communication voice.

'Sally, I need to see you. Now.' He sounds very upset.

Chapter Twelve

DIARMUID HAS SEEN ME with Nathaniel. He must have. Why else would he be so insistent that we meet now? He must have seen us when we were stopped at those traffic lights. Or – oh, God – maybe he's been following me! He's been suspicious that I'm seeing someone else, and now he'll think he has the proof.

The rushed journey back to central Dublin in Nathaniel's car was far from comfortable; the car jerked and spluttered, and the clanging noise got so loud I thought some crucial part was about to fall off. We didn't even have time to get our fish and chips, but I'm not hungry any more. When Nathaniel dropped me off at the top of Grafton Street, I had to repeat the whole business of sliding over the seats. And when I got out I realised that a big blob of chocolate was decorating the front of my fancy pink blouse.

Deep breaths. I must remember to take deep breaths. I've agreed to meet Diarmuid in a nearby pub, and it's good that I have to walk there; it gives me a bit of time to think about what to tell him. Nathaniel said I should just tell the truth, but that's clearly nonsense: the truth is sometimes too far-fetched to be believable, and Diarmuid would find the whole thing highly suspicious. I need some sensible excuse, something more in keeping with the Sally he knows and married.

I'm so busy thinking about excuses that I suddenly notice I am not actually walking to the pub at all; I'm walking to the bus stop at the bottom of Grafton Street, the one that takes me to my cottage. *I could just get on the bus,* I think. *I could just get on the bus and go home, and not meet Diarmuid at all.*

What am I thinking? Of course I must meet Diarmuid. I take a deep breath and set off back towards the pub. Why on earth am I feeling so guilty? It's not as if Diarmuid drove by and saw Nathaniel and me kissing…

Just for the briefest of moments, the image of Mum and her

lover in that car comes back to me. Why on earth am I behaving as though I've been having an affair too? I don't complain when Diarmuid drives around with Charlene, so why should Diarmuid reprimand me if I decide to go for a meal with someone I met at the reception?

That's it – of course! I'll tell him Nathaniel is a gay sofa designer who's heartbroken because his lover has left him for a transvestite from Rio de Janeiro! That's more like it. I feel more cheerful as I approach the pub. I may even entertain him by telling him about Nathaniel's excess body hair and breasts.

The pub is packed. We agreed to meet upstairs, in the room with sofas and soft seats, and Diarmuid is already sitting in our favourite corner. He has a pint of Guinness in front of him, and he looks lost and forlorn. I wasn't expecting him to look so sad. I thought he'd be angry. He doesn't even see me looking at him.

I flee the room and dive into the ladies'. How could I have thought Diarmuid would believe my lie about Nathaniel being gay? He must have been watching us from across the road. He must have seen how easy we are in each other's company – the quick intense glances, the extraordinary familiarity. But I'll have to use that excuse anyway, because I haven't time to come up with another one. I take out my deodorant and squirt under my arms. I splash some water on my face and dry it with toilet paper. Then I spend at least three minutes trying to find my lipstick.

I prepare a bright smile as I re-enter the room.

'Hello, Diarmuid!'

He looks up slowly. His eyes are dull and doleful.

I lean forwards to kiss him on the cheek. 'So how are you?' I say brightly. 'How's the studying going?'

He doesn't reply.

'I've just been to a reception,' I gabble 'I… I met this really weird gay sofa designer…'

Diarmuid reaches out and takes my hand. I've never seen him like this before. He's behaving as if he wants to break something to me softly. Oh dear God, maybe he's finally run out of patience. I must have crisps. Immediately. 'Do they have crisps here?'

'Oh, yes, of course. I'll get them now,' Diarmuid mumbles. 'What would you like to drink?'

'Red wine… as usual,' I say. Why is he asking me this? Why is he behaving as though he doesn't know me?

He gets up and walks dejectedly to the bar, orders my wine and crisps and comes back to me. He takes my hand again and looks into my eyes. 'Oh, Sally, I'm sorry,' he says. 'I'm so very sorry.'

'About… what?' I ask. But I already know. He wants a divorce. He's seen Becky again. That's why we haven't met for so long; it's not the studying or Charlene's driving lessons or his mother's tiling. He's grown tired of waiting for me – and he's always loved Becky more, anyway. That's why he's contrite when by rights he should be angry about seeing me with Nathaniel. But that must have only confirmed his opinion that our marriage is over. He's not even jealous, because he's realised he married me when in his heart he wanted to marry someone else.

'Can you forgive me?' he asks. He doesn't even have to mention the word 'divorce'. He must know that I know what he's thinking.

Small tears are forming in the corners of my eyes. 'Well… I did leave you, Diarmuid,' I mumble. 'You have every reason to have… reservations.'

'But I said I was going to make more of an effort.'

'You have been,' I say. 'You've been very sweet and understanding. It's me who –'

'But I've been so involved in my studies. I told you I was going to take you to that Thai restaurant weeks ago.'

'Yes, and you wanted to take me there that evening I was seeing Aggie,' I remind him. 'And I was the one who wasn't available.'

'I can't believe I forgot. I didn't even return your last phone call.'

'Look, Diarmuid, please stop worrying about the restaurant,' I say firmly. This is so typical of us: talking about an exotic meal we haven't had, instead of about our marriage and why it's ending.

'I'm not talking about the restaurant.' Diarmuid looks at me keenly. 'You know what I'm talking about... don't you?'

I sip my wine.

'Our anniversary.' There is an edge to his voice now. 'I forgot our anniversary.'

'But it...it isn't our anniversary,' I stutter.

And then Diarmuid does something that is totally unlike him. He raises his hand and bashes it down on the table. Our drinks jump, and drops of Guinness and wine leap out of the glasses. People look at us and then look away. Someone laughs.

'It's the anniversary of our *engagement.*' He is leaning towards me, virtually hissing. 'You said we should always celebrate the anniversary of our engagement – remember?'

I do remember, now that he's reminded me. But I said that when I was the other Sally, the Sally who cared about lining her bedroom curtains. I take a deep breath. I don't like this Diarmuid who bashed his hand down on the table, frightening me and sending wine splashing all over the front of my pink blouse. This is not the Diarmuid I married.

'I... I said that before the mice.' It's a cheap shot, but I have to defend myself somehow. 'I said it before the arguments about spermicide cream and... and finding out you'd met Becky for lunch.'

He starts to dab up the wine and Guinness with a paper napkin, very carefully – too carefully.

'And I said it before you forgot our first wedding anniversary,' I say. 'And... and the mice.'

'You've already mentioned the mice,' Diarmuid replies coldly. 'And, if you remember, you also said it before you bolted out of our house without an explanation.'

'I *did* have an explanation – a sort of explanation, anyway – only you wouldn't *listen* to it!' I shout. A number of people

101

are openly listening to our interchange, as if they're watching the telly.

'It wasn't a proper explanation,' Diarmuid says, pushing his chair back. Then he adds gruffly, 'More wine?'

I nod and dig my fingernails into my palms. If I had a loofah, I would definitely use it on him. This is pointless. I should just get up and go.

'You only say it wasn't a proper explanation because you didn't understand it,' I say as soon as he returns. 'You don't understand me, Diarmuid. You never have.'

'And you don't understand me,' he says, gulping his Guinness.

I take a large swig of wine and shove a fistful of crisps into my mouth.

'Why should we celebrate our engagement, anyway?' I demand. I'm a bit drunk already; if only he'd phoned *after* I'd eaten the fish and chips! 'We're living in separate houses... and your mother hates me.' I hiccup.

'No, she doesn't.'

'Well, she doesn't like me, anyway. She makes that clear.' I think of the photo of Becky on her side cabinet. 'You don't care when she's rude to me.'

'Of course I would,' he counters. 'But she isn't rude to you.'

'Yes, she is, but you don't notice. You don't care about my feelings.'

'Of course I do... but do you care about mine?'

'Yes, of course I care about your feelings,' I snap. Then we both just sit there, drinking and scowling, like an old married couple who never got around to leaving each other and can no longer bear to talk about it.

'We'd better go, anyway,' Diarmuid says at last.

'Where to?'

'That Thai restaurant. I booked a table just before you arrived.'

'I don't want to go out to dinner with you, Diarmuid.'

'And I don't particularly want to go to dinner with you at

this moment, Sally,' he says flatly. 'But I'm hungry. I assume you are too.'

And that's how we end up driving to a swanky new restaurant in Donnybrook. I expect the Corrs to come on the radio, but they don't; it's classical music, resigned and rather sad. We both bathe in its melancholy. I still don't know if Diarmuid saw me with Nathaniel, but it seems that he didn't. I wonder what made him suddenly remember our anniversary when he was driving back to town from... from where? I feel I should ask where he's been, but if I do, he'll ask me what I was doing on the Howth Road. *So this is how a marriage ends,* I think. *With a sigh and a slap-up meal.*

It is a very nice restaurant, large and uncluttered, with candles on the white tablecloths. The seats are cushioned and comfortable, and Eastern music tinkles cheerfully in the background. We order our food and then we eat it. We barely talk. We barely look at each other. It's like being alone – alone in a room, though you know someone else is in the house.

'You're looking very pretty this evening,' Diarmuid suddenly tells me, as we try to work out what they've put in the pudding. It's very strange – both sour and sweet, and not unpleasant.

'And you're looking handsome yourself,' I reply, because I'm keeping the lines of communication open, and because he is. I am also grateful that he isn't sulking. I hated him an hour ago, but now he just seems deeply puzzling. 'This is a lovely meal,' I add. 'Thank you, Diarmuid. It was a very kind thought.'

'I'm sorry I lost my temper earlier. I don't know what came over me.' He pours me some more wine. He isn't drinking much himself, because he's driving. I gaze at his strong jawline, his thick black eyebrows and wavy dark hair. His eyes seem less distant in the candlelight, and his smile is broader and more playful. 'It was ridiculous, getting so angry because you forgot the anniversary. I mean, who remembers an engagement anniversary?'

'You do, Diarmuid,' I say. 'And I should have. I made such

a fuss about your forgetting our wedding anniversary, it's no wonder you thought I'd be waiting around for you to take me out somewhere.'

'Why do we have these silly arguments, Sally?' He looks lost. Scared. 'I'm not like this with other people.'

'Neither am I.' I sigh, remembering the crazy night I let his mice loose in the tool shed.

'We like each other, don't we?' He takes my hand. 'Sometimes we behave as if we don't even like each other.'

'Oh, Diarmuid… of course we like each other.' I cradle his hand in mine and stroke his fingers. He looks rugged and kind, just like a Tool-Belt Man should look. When he gets up to go to the toilet I watch his departing back with a detached sort of appreciation, noticing the firmness of him, the trim, sexy look of his bottom in the faded blue jeans.

When he returns, I decide to cheer him up. I try to entertain him by telling him about Larry and his breasts, and how he wanted me to spank him, and how I said I couldn't because I was married to a very nice man called Diarmuid who never asked me to do such things.

'Can you believe that?' I laugh. 'Wanting a total stranger to spank you!'

Diarmuid just stares at me, so I look down at my pudding and wonder if I should have talked about something else. Maybe Diarmuid thinks this is the kind of conversation I have at receptions.

I feel his foot rubbing my ankle under the table. Then he leans forwards and stretches out his hand towards my left breast. 'Diarmuid!' I splutter, through a mouthful of strange pudding.

'What's that on your blouse?' His eyes have darkened.

'Wine and… and chocolate.' Am I actually blushing? One could get chocolate on oneself anywhere.

'I have chocolate cake at home. A lovely big chocolate cake.' He is holding my left hand now, holding the ring finger, twisting the ring round and round. 'A cake with lots of icing.'

He remembers! The thought comes to me like a kiss. *He*

remembers that I said I wanted more icing... Maybe this is how you save a marriage, I think. *Maybe you just go home and eat chocolate cake and stop talking about mice and diaphragms.*

There is a warmth between us now, a kind of wary and weary affection. We drink our coffees and leave the restaurant swiftly. As I get into Diarmuid's car, I know I will not be spending the night in my cosy, and sometimes very lonely, little cottage.

Chapter Thirteen

I AM NAKED AND lying next to my husband in our big double bed. He's snoring slightly; he's turned away from me, towards the wall. Our lovemaking, after we ate the cake, was tender, almost apologetic. We didn't rip our clothes off. For a while we just lay on the bed like two bewildered children, clinging to each other, not knowing what to make of all this.

This is another new Diarmuid – vulnerable, needing me to caress him, to find the special places; needing me to say, 'Yes. Yes, I want you,' before I lifted myself onto him and made love to him gently. He stared into my eyes as though trying to see the map of me, trying to pinpoint the place where our love got lost.

And I wanted with all my heart to heal this thing I've done to him, this thing that has made him doubt himself. I want him to know our arguments are about our differences, not about who is wrong or right. I want him to know that it's OK that he no longer trusts me; I wouldn't trust him either, if he had left like I did. I desperately want him to be happy again, with or without me.

I inch out of the bed, not wanting to wake him. My clothes are piled neatly on a chair. I take them into the bathroom and dress. Then I pad downstairs, hoping that Barry has gone out somewhere. Barry had eaten half of the cake by the time we got to it. He's a big brown man who chugs through life with almost unnatural cheer; he surfs and drinks huge quantities of beer, and brings home cheerful, sporty women who seem to have no particular expectations of him. I've only been to one of his barbecues. He and some mates started playing around with the garden hosepipe and thought it would be fun to drench us. I ended up going home in one of Diarmuid's sweatshirts.

Barry has gone. I breathe a sigh of relief as I set about making tea and toast and pouring out the breakfast cereal. It's nearly ten o'clock – and I told Aggie I'd visit her this morning…

My mobile rings. It's in my handbag, on an armchair in the sitting-room. I race towards it, in case the sound disturbs Diarmuid. I yank it out in a mild panic – maybe it's Fiona, saying she's gone into labour – but I don't recognise the number.

'Hello.'

'Hello there, Sally Adams.' It's Nathaniel.

'What is it?' I lower my voice and go back to the kitchen. I close the door so that the sound won't travel upstairs.

'How did it go?'

'What?'

'Meeting Diarmuid.'

'I'm in his – I mean, our – house now,' I whisper. 'How did you get my number, anyway?'

'I asked Greta. You left something in my car.'

'What?'

'A notebook. It must have fallen out of your bag. It appears to be full of recipes. And there's a photo; it says "DeeDee" on the back. There's something about her eyes that –'

I think I hear a creak on the stairs. 'Look, Nathaniel, I can't have this conversation now.'

'– that reminds me of you…'

I switch off the phone and lean against a sideboard. The kitchen is capacious and fitted and well designed; it's a very organised room, and perhaps if I look at it for long enough I'll feel organised too. I will know where to store these strange bits of myself that keep leaking out. I will know what to throw away and what to keep.

'Morning.' Diarmuid walks into the room sleepily, wearing a white T-shirt and a pair of dark blue boxer shorts. 'Were you on the phone? I heard you talking.'

'Yes. It was… someone ringing about… about table-mats.'

'On a Saturday?' He rubs his eyes sleepily. 'Their enthusiasm for household accessories clearly knows no bounds.'

'I wanted to bring you up breakfast.'

'Come here.'

He wraps his arms around me. The softness of sleep is still in him; it feels cosy. Nice.

'I have to shower and go soon.' He releases me and wanders over to get a mug.

'Why?'

'I promised Charlene I'd give her a driving lesson.' He looks at me carefully.

'Shouldn't you be studying?' I sound like my mother used to.

'I studied last night,' he says. 'Before we met up in the pub.'

I gaze at him. 'Last night?'

'Yes.' He spoons some instant coffee into his mug, then pours in some boiling water. Diarmuid doesn't take milk with his coffee, and he just takes half a spoon of sugar. I place a spoon and a sugar bowl on the table.

Is he lying to me? He really looks as if he is telling the truth. But I definitely saw him at those traffic lights. He was even wearing the same wine-coloured shirt that he wore to the pub.

I turn away from him, towards the toast. 'Do you want marmalade?'

'Just a skim of it.' He is sitting at the table, scratching an elbow and yawning, and just for a moment I feel like throwing the toast at him. Can I believe anything he says any more? Has he ever really been honest with me? I should ask him, but I'm not sure I could handle his reply.

'DeeDee's dead.' I have to say it; I don't know why.

'Who?'

'That great-aunt I told you about.'

'Oh, yes – the one who just disappeared.'

'I felt very sad when I heard. It's silly, isn't it? I never even met her.'

'She was a relative. That's only natural,' Diarmuid says. 'You come from a close family.' I don't know how Diarmuid has formed this impression, but I don't contradict him. 'At least now you don't have to worry about trying to find her. Who told you?'

'Marie. Someone phoned her from Rio de Janeiro.'

'Is that where she landed up, then?' He is drinking his coffee. Somehow the expression 'landed up' doesn't sound right for DeeDee. There's an arbitrariness about it that is entirely inappropriate. 'She always wanted to go to Rio de Janeiro,' I say.

'So you've learned more about her, have you?'

'Yes,' I say, but I don't add that I have only found out she liked marble cakes and hats.

'Poor woman.' Diarmuid munches his toast.

'I'm not entirely sure she was a "poor woman", Diarmuid. I think she may have actually led a very interesting life.'

'Completely cut off from her own country and her family, her oldest friends – running away like that...' Diarmuid looks out the window. 'It isn't natural.'

'Maybe it felt natural to DeeDee,' I say. 'Some things may feel unnatural to you, Diarmuid, but entirely natural to someone else.'

'Fine. Fine; have it your way.' He gets up from the table. 'I don't want to have an argument about this, Sally. Thanks for the toast.' He goes upstairs. I hear the sound of the shower while I wander around the kitchen washing things and wiping them. I even sweep the floor.

'Do you want a lift anywhere?' Diarmuid calls down to me.

'Yes, please. I said I'd go and visit Aggie.'

'Fine. I can drop you off.' He says it brightly, breezily; there's no suggestion that I might stay here, even just for the weekend.

He has asked me to come back so many times already; maybe he's got tired of asking. Maybe he's waiting for me to say I want to. But, if I do, he's the one who may say he needs time to think about it. Because our marriage hasn't been on hold, like I thought it was. It's been changing – becoming something else.

I must ask him where he was last night, I think. Maybe it's quite innocent. He probably just felt guilty about not studying.

Or maybe he *was* studying, at his parents' house: his mother loves spoiling him, and Barry plays his rock CDs very loudly... If it had been an important lie, Diarmuid would have gone pink and stumbled over the words. Of course he would have.

I take out my mobile phone and see that someone has sent me a text message.

'If you want your notebook and the photo back – and I assume you probably do – then phone this number. I'll leave them somewhere for you, so we don't have to meet if you'd prefer not to. N.'

But I want to meet Nathaniel again. I want him to tell me about Rio de Janeiro. I want to get into his crazy old car. I want to know that, in this lonely old world, I'm not as alone as I think I am. I want him to tell me what he saw in DeeDee's eyes.

Chapter Fourteen

IT'S RAINING, PISSING DOWN in buckets, as Diarmuid and I leave the house. We scurry to his car. I have borrowed one of his jumpers; it hangs on me like a brown tent.

'They say it may ease up in the afternoon,' says Diarmuid, who tends to listen to weather forecasts. He is sitting beside me, solid and preoccupied, and seems very far away.

'Good,' I reply, wondering where the other Diarmuid has gone to, the one who needed me to hold him and caress him – the Diarmuid who was thoughtful enough to use a condom.

'I know you don't feel like starting a family in... in these circumstances,' he said tenderly, taking the packet out of the small cabinet beside the bed. It was a new packet. I was, of course, immensely grateful and surprised, because Diarmuid has always said he dislikes condoms. But now he seems to be able to use them without peering at them reluctantly and swearing and asking me to help him 'get the thing on'. Where did he learn this expertise?

No. I mustn't think these things. If I do, everything he does will seem suspicious. All men know how to put on condoms if they really need to.

I gaze out the window. 'Isn't it a lovely view?'

'Yes,' Diarmuid says, fiddling with some button on his car.

'We could almost be in the countryside,' I say, gazing at the small white cottages that hug the nearby mountains. We pass a huge beech tree; the leaves seem heavy and plump with rain.

'How's Aggie these days?' Diarmuid enquires, almost absent-mindedly.

'Oh... pretty much the same.' I decide not to mention the floating sheep.

'Will you tell her about DeeDee?'

'No. There's no need to.'

'Yes, I suppose you're right.'

We swing onto a larger road, away from the mountains. I feel a sudden yearning for the mountains, for some vast, daunting space. 'I've been wondering if I should visit her grave.' The sentence pops into my head and I just say it, like I would have to Nathaniel.

'Whose grave?'

'DeeDee's, of course.'

'Oh, for God's sake, Sally, can't you just forget her?' Diarmuid's voice is hard, infuriated. 'She's dead. Surely that's the end of it.' His voice softens. 'I'm sorry to be so blunt about it, but it's the truth.'

I decide not to argue. Truth is a strange thing, perhaps more flexible than we suspect. In a way he's right about DeeDee, and in a way he's wrong. And if he could see this, we could talk about so much else; we could explore the soft, forgiving places in between these delicate certainties.

'Barry may be moving out in a few months. He's thinking of going back to Australia.' Diarmuid glances at me quickly.

'Oh.' I tighten my grip on my handbag.

'I was wondering if we... if I should build a... a sort of one-roomed cottage at the bottom of the garden, instead of a conservatory. I think I might be able to get planning permission.'

'Yes,' I say slowly. 'Yes, why not? That would be nice.'

'I'd be building it for you,' he says quickly. 'If you come back, you could use it as an office. A... a place of your own.'

'Oh.' I gulp.

'I think you're right: we shouldn't start a family unless we're more sure about this whole marriage thing.' *This whole marriage thing.* Diarmuid doesn't say things like that. 'We're going to have to talk about all this properly soon, you know. My family have been pestering me with questions about us. They'd really like to see some kind of resolution.'

But it's our marriage, Diarmuid, I want to scream. *Why do we care so much about what other people think of us?*

'And of course we'll have to make some kind of decision

112

about the house – about whether we should keep it.'

So we're back to that again. Maybe we don't need a marriage counsellor at all. Just a good estate agent.

'I'm sorry to bring all this up now, when you're about to see Aggie.' His eyes crinkle kindly. 'Last night... the second half of it... was lovely.' He reaches out for my hand.

'Yes, it was.' I smile. There seem to be at least five Diarmuids, and I wish I knew which one married me.

'I miss you,' he says, but not the way he used to. The gap is smaller; the space is being filled with other things.

'And I miss you too,' I say, because it feels like I should – and because I sometimes do. But more often I ache for the idea I had of him.

Diarmuid stops the car on the winding road beside the nursing home. From the outside it just looks like a rather large suburban house. I wish it was. I wish Aggie's dog Scamp could rush towards me and plaster me with kisses as soon as she opens the door; I wish she would come to meet me with a geranium cutting in her hand and a cake just out of the oven. She is in a place where, though they take her pulse several times a day, they don't know the heart of her.

But when I get to her room, she is sitting up cheerfully. 'Sally!' she exclaims. 'Have a mint toffee. Marie just brought me some.'

I pull the boiled-cabbage-coloured chair to the side of the bed and dip my fingers into the plastic bag.

'I've been thinking about DeeDee.' Aggie's eyes are bright, excited. 'She says parts of us are like the back yard, and parts of us are like the Serengeti or... or Canada. It's a very individual thing, this mixture. Everyone has their own. What she means is that parts of us are small and parts of us are big... and I suppose there must be some medium-sized stuff in there too.'

She's talking as if DeeDee has just popped out to get a bar of chocolate. I feel like shaking her, shouting, 'DeeDee's dead,' to shut her up.

'How are the sheep?' I ask. 'Are they still floating?'

'Oh, they're not sheep, dear.' Aggie smiles at me indulgently. 'They're angels. Big white angels. I saw their wings the other night.' She chuckles. *'Sheep,* Sally? Sheep don't float.'

I allow myself to be gently reprimanded. Angels? Poor Aggie. 'DeeDee will love the angels,' Aggie says. 'I'll bake her some marble cake and we'll all have tea on the lawn.'

'That'll be nice,' I say, in this new voice I've learned lately – a sort of caring, professional voice, slightly detached. 'Would you like me to plump up those pillows for you?'

She shakes her head.

'Diarmuid drove me here to see you,' I tell her.

Aunt Aggie is crumpling a paper handkerchief in her hand. Her face suddenly looks sad. 'June, it was. Hot, too – a proper summer day. DeeDee was there and everyone was happy. Laughing on the family lawn.'

'Diarmuid and I had a takeaway meal on Bull Island last night,' I say. 'It was lovely – watching the sunset, laughing, getting away from it all…'

Aggie is completely lost in her memories. 'Tilly and Bruno were there, and your great-grandma, Clarice.'

I sense an opportunity to distract her. 'Grandma Tilly was your sister, isn't that right?' She always loves to explain the family tree.

'Yes. And she married Bruno, who was your grandfather. Of course, you know that.' She straightens a crease on her duvet. 'I wonder if DeeDee ever married. We'll find out when she visits. She might even bring her husband with her.'

'What was Great-Grandma Clarice's husband called?'

'Jethro. He was my father.'

'Of course.' I knew this already, but listing the names seems to calm her.

'He was a stern man in many ways,' Aggie says dreamily. 'He used to have awful arguments with DeeDee about her hats.'

I know I shouldn't encourage Aggie to talk about her lost sister, but my curiosity gets the better of me. 'Why?' I draw my chair closer.

'He said they were too big. Too extravagant and colourful. Sometimes they blew off in the wind.' She chuckles to herself at the memory. 'Mum used to argue with her too.'

'About what?'

'About being late. She was late for almost everything – sometimes it was just a few minutes, but she was never bang on time. Mum used to say she'd be late for her own funeral.' I look down at the floor.

'She and Tilly, your grandma, had disagreements as well. DeeDee had very strong opinions.'

'About what?'

'About life. She thought Tilly didn't think enough about life and feelings and love. She said she never wanted to discuss things properly.'

I twist a paper handkerchief around my fingers. 'Would you like me to open the window a bit? The heating is very warm, isn't it?'

'That day on the lawn, DeeDee was saying she wanted to be an actress. We all laughed. She did, too. She was forever saying she wanted to be this or that – an opera singer, a nurse… a nun, even.' Aggie smoothes the duvet again. 'That's what we were laughing at. Not at her wanting to be an actress, but…' She stares at me earnestly. 'But at the way she kept changing her mind.'

'Yes. Yes, of course,' I say. 'It must have been –'

'DeeDee always behaved as if her life might start off properly at any moment,' Aggie interrupts. 'As though she was only filling in time until it did. A number of nice young men wanted to marry her, but she didn't want them. She was waiting for some grand passion. She said an ordinary marriage would trap her; she wouldn't be able to stand it.'

The paper handkerchief is fraying in my hands. Hearing these things is dreadful and fascinating and almost unbearably sad – because Aggie thinks DeeDee may walk in here any day now, but I know she won't.

'She used to say that what she needed was someone she

115

could *really* talk to.'

I get up. 'Excuse me. I have to go to the toilet.' I flee the room and walk down the lino-covered corridor; I stand by the window and stare at the yellow summer roses blowing in the breeze. I take deep breaths. I don't have to stay here much longer. She'll stop talking about DeeDee when I get back. I'll get her onto the angels.

'She was working in that fancy hat shop,' Aggie says as soon as I return to her room, 'and every day she'd go to the same café for lunch and meet Alistair.'

'Alistair?' Despite myself, I am drawn into the conversation again. Every new detail about DeeDee seems shiny and strange, and some of them are preposterously familiar.

'Yes. He was the one who kept giving her those fancy ideas. He worked in the theatre; he was a costume designer or something. That's why he kept coming into the shop. He was married.'

'Oh.'

'She didn't love him.' Aunt Aggie answers my unspoken question. 'But she loved the world he suggested. More like the movies... you know, where things could change suddenly. Where you might find yourself in the south of France because some fancy film director liked your smile.' She sighs. 'DeeDee wanted more than ordinariness. She hated all the repetition, the way the bus to work always took the same route. Laundry. Remembering to buy things to eat.'

I find myself smiling, but then I notice there are some tears at the corners of Aggie's eyes. 'That's why we shouldn't have laughed that day,' she says. 'That day on the lawn... But she was so much younger than us, and she looked so pretty.'

I don't quite get the logic of this last sentence.

'What she can't have known was that we were laughing because we loved her. It wasn't like a joke... but... a celebration.' Aunt Aggie's face is creased with regret. 'She left us soon afterwards.'

'But she was laughing too, you said.'

'Yes, but it wasn't real laughter. It couldn't have been, in the circumstances.'

'What circumstances?' I say quickly, sensing a secret.

Aggie glances at me quickly, sharply. 'I don't want to go into that now, dear. We don't talk about that.' She looks fierce and frightened.

I feel like screaming, *Why don't we talk about it?* But I don't. Maybe I can prise it out of her another time. Or maybe someone else will tell me. I recall Marie's words in my parents' kitchen about DeeDee breaking Aggie's heart.

'DeeDee didn't feel loved, you see, even though she was. That happens to some people, Sally.' Aggie is looking at me carefully. 'They're loved, but they don't feel it. Something's happened to the part of them that would know it.'

Suddenly I can't stand talking about DeeDee any longer. The room is incredibly hot. I get up and open a window. I look at my watch: it's past lunchtime, and I said I'd meet Erika and go to a film.

'When will you find her?' Aunt Aggie's voice is pleading, desperate. 'I need to see her. I need her to know I love her.'

I stare at the floor. If I'm not careful, I will cry.

'I'm sure she knows you love her,' I say brightly. 'Of course she does, Aggie.'

'No, she doesn't. I didn't make it clear at all. Not afterwards.'

'After what?' I say gently. Aggie just stares blankly at my face. 'What if...' I look at her guardedly. 'What if I find her, but she's far away and doesn't feel up to the long journey to Dublin? I could get her address. You could send her a letter.'

'It wouldn't be the same,' Aggie says flatly. 'I need to see her. I'd go to her instead.'

I don't tell her that this is crazy. I can't tell her so many things now.

'I'd very much like to find DeeDee for you, Aggie.' It's a neutral, friendly thing to say. It seems to be enough. I smile at her, and she smiles back.

117

Chapter Fifteen

ERIKA AND I ARE walking along a leafy path in St Stephen's Green; the rain has gone and it's a nice, bright Saturday afternoon.

'Could you please slow down a bit, Sally?' Erika pants. 'You're almost running.'

'Aggie wants to eat cake with DeeDee on a lawn,' I say agitatedly. 'But DeeDee's dead, and I haven't the heart to tell her.'

'DeeDee's *dead?*' Erika says. 'You never told me that.'

'It happened yesterday. An awful lot of things happened yesterday.' I see a bench by the pond and slump onto it exhaustedly.

'She died yesterday?' Erika sits down beside me.

'Oh, no – no, I *heard* about it yesterday. Aunt Marie phoned to say she'd died in Rio de Janeiro fifteen years ago.'

'Oh, dear,' Erika says. 'I'm so sorry.'

'I shouldn't care, really. I never even met her.' I stare at the ducks diving in the pond. They look so cheerful and perky. 'It's just that Aggie is desperate to see DeeDee again. She keeps begging me to find her. I don't think she could deal with the news that DeeDee is replenishing the soil somewhere in South America.'

'That's just her body,' Erika says firmly. 'The soul lives on. She may even be listening to us right now. She's... she's probably smiling at you with great love and compassion.'

'Look, Erika, you know my feelings on that stuff,' I say sharply. 'When people die, that's the end of it; that's what I believe, anyway. But please don't let's talk about it now.'

Erika maintains a distinctly mutinous silence.

'I hope I don't start sobbing hysterically at Aggie's funeral,' I mutter. 'I didn't cry at Grandma Tilly's or Grandpa Bruno's, but I cried like an Oscar winner at Mary's and at Brian's.'

'I'm sorry, I don't think I've ever heard you mention these

people before,' Erika says, somewhat puzzled.

'They were distant cousins. Marie herded us all together to pay our last respects.'

'Good old Marie.'

'Why are you calling her good old Marie?' I demand. 'She's very bossy and opinionated.'

'Yes, but she cares about you all, doesn't she?' Erika says, with that awful fairness of hers. 'In her own clumsy, weird way, she really does care.'

'Yes, and sometimes I wish she didn't,' I snap. 'Marie's caring is very uncomfortable. It's only June, and I'm already worrying about that stupid family gathering of hers in September. I feel it's some sort of deadline.'

'What do you mean?'

'I feel like the whole thing with Diarmuid has to be sorted out by August, so that I'll know what to say to everyone.'

'About what?'

'About why I left him, and why I went back – or…. or didn't. It has to sound like I thought it through.'

'I don't understand.' Erika is attempting to make a daisy chain. 'It's not some sort of exam, is it?'

'Yes, it is. That's exactly what it is.' I sigh forlornly. 'We all sort of check up on each other while we eat Marie's soggy lemon meringue pie. And all the younger cousins are so well adjusted.' I am beginning to feel a mighty longing for a packet of crisps. 'Not one of them is a lesbian or divorced… not one of them even s*mokes.'*

'I don't believe that,' Erika says. She now has a daisy chain on her head. 'I don't believe they're all perfect. They can't be.'

'DeeDee seems to have been my only weird relative,' I say sadly. 'I know I shouldn't care what the others think, but I do. They were all so thrilled when I married Diarmuid. They gave us such nice presents.'

'Let's go to a café,' Erika says. 'Let's go to a café and talk about all this over custard-filled doughnuts.'

She starts to march determinedly in the direction

119

of Grafton Street and Bewley's. I follow her dejectedly. 'Chips,' she says. 'I need chips, too. I'm ravenous.' When Erika gets hungry, she needs to tuck in right there and then. Her daisy chain has fallen off; I pick it up and throw it onto the grass.

'Maybe I should start some sort of evening course,' I say, as we pass Laura Ashley. A number of my female cousins turn up at Marie's get-togethers in Laura Ashley dresses. They look so fresh and pretty, you expect to see morning dew on their tanned cheeks. 'A lot of my cousins seem to be doing courses. I could talk about that instead of about Diarmuid.'

'What kind of course?' Erika asks, sidestepping a trombone player. The street seems to be full of people playing instruments or plaiting things into people's hair or selling *The Big Issue*.

'I don't know – maybe something to do with psychology, or computers, or... or business management. It needs to be something impressive.'

'You should only do a course if you want to,' Erika says firmly. Her nose is already twitching; we're almost at Bewley's, and she can smell freshly ground coffee half a mile away. 'And it should be about something you actually find interesting.' It's good of her to be encouraging; she has already witnessed my half-hearted attempts to learn pottery, yoga, furniture restoration and how to be a contented wife – not to mention the slightly demented time when I thought I might be a wind-surfer.

'I slept with Diarmuid yesterday,' I say, when we've got our food and found a table. The words lunge out of me.

She manages to stop stuffing chips into her mouth for a moment and looks at me sympathetically. 'Was it... all right?'

'Yes.' I take a large bite of doughnut. 'It was just fine. It's the least I can do for him.' Then I add quickly, 'It's not as if it's a chore. I do sort of enjoy it.'

'Only sort of?' Erika fixes me with her soft hazel eyes. Her curly blonde hair is tumbling around her shoulders today. She

120

usually ties it back.

I gulp my Earl Grey. 'I know it sounds ridiculous, Erika, but those mice really affected our sex life. It's never been quite the same since. Diarmuid is a really good lover, but... but I really began to think he cared more about them than about me.'

'Oh, poor Sally!' Erika must be really interested: she has forgotten about her sausage.

'He spent hours with them in the spare room. He even had names for some of them – Snowy and Babs and Frank. Those were his favourites. He used to talk to them a lot.'

'About what?' Erika is clearly fascinated. She has even stopped looking around for the nearest bottle of tomato ketchup.

'About all sorts of things,' I say. 'One night I heard him say, "So, Snowy, how was your day? Life's a funny old business, isn't it? Come here and let Uncle Diarmuid give you a nice cuddle." He hadn't even asked me what my day was like; he'd just said, "Hi, Sally, I'm home," and bounded upstairs.'

'God,' Erika sighs.

'Babs was the shyest. Sometimes I heard Diarmuid telling her that she was a really beautiful mouse and needed to realise it. He used to tell her she had the cutest little pink nose in the world. He never said anything like that to me.'

Erika kindly doesn't point out that perhaps I wouldn't have been too pleased to be told I had a cute little pink nose. 'Men!' she says grimly. 'Bloody men. I don't know why we put up with them.' I know she isn't including Alex in this generalisation.

'The only proper conversation I ever had with his mother was about Diarmuid's love of animals,' I say. 'She told me he's always had a pet. Then she said she used to think Diarmuid loved animals more than people, until he met Becky.'

'Bloody Becky!' Erika almost snarls. 'That mother of his sounds like a right old walrus.'

I feel like defending walruses, but I polish off my doughnut instead. As I start to fiddle with some grains of sugar on the table, I decide not to mention that Diarmuid may have lied to me about his whereabouts last night. It would mean explaining about Nathaniel, and I don't know what I'd say.

'At least you're having sex,' Erika comments. 'I've almost forgotten how it's done. Alex and I don't even kiss properly. It's like we're relatives.' She sighs dramatically and crams the last of the chips into her mouth.

'But I thought you said…'

'Yes, I know, I said he was going to leave his wife – or *wanted* to. But he's just bought a tent. They're all going camping next week.'

'Well, that's hardly a renewal of their vows, is it?'

'I don't think you could camp with someone you didn't at least like,' Erika says. 'All that rain and discomfort, and boiling kettles over sodden wood, and… going into those shops and buying those awful fiddly special saucepans.'

This is, of course, not the time to mention that some people actually *like* camping. 'They're probably doing it for the kids,' I say. 'Kids love camping.' Alex has two children, a boy and a girl. 'Anyway, while he's away you can get on with the cats.'

'No one wants my cats,' Erika says. 'Only my friends buy them, and they all have them now.'

'That's not true! It's just about finding the right market.' I wonder if I can sneak yet another mention of Erika's cats into my interior decoration column. I add cheerfully, 'I need another of your cats, anyway.'

'Why?' Erika's eyes brighten, just slightly.

'For Fiona. I want a cat to celebrate her new baby, when she eventually has it.'

'What kind of cat?' Erika looks distinctly happier.

'A baby cat… a kitten. I'll leave the details up to you.'

'I'd better wait until she has the baby,' Erika says, getting quite excited. 'I'll need to know whether it's a boy or a girl cat.'

'Yes… yes, of course. She'll be thrilled.'

'Did I tell you I've started doing massage to make a bit of extra money?' Erika asks, as she swigs down the last of her coffee. 'I only do it occasionally. The staff at International Holdings get very tense sometimes.'

I gawp at her.

'I put up a little flier in the canteen, next to the poster that says "Come Swim with Dolphins".'

'What does the flier say?' I ask carefully. It would be just like Erika to end up with a bunch of massage clients who got the wrong idea entirely.

'Don't worry,' she laughs. 'I've made it clear I'm not offering sexual relief or whatever they call it. It's purely therapeutic. Lionel was my first client.'

'Lionel… he's the shy one who gets all embarrassed when he asks you to type letters, isn't he?' I ask hopefully.

'Yes. He only let me at his feet, but I'm hoping to get to his back any day now, after his head. I'll get him to strip off gradually.'

A man at a nearby table looks over at us with undisguised interest.

'Where do you do this?'

'In my flat.'

Oh, God, I think. *I hope these people don't start asking her to spank their bottoms or…* I silently begin to list some other sexual deviations I might mention to her.

'Don't worry,' Erika says. 'I know what you're thinking. You think I'm not trained to do massage, but I did an evening course ages ago. When I was working for Gregory.'

Just the name makes me want to growl. Erika spent eight years organising Gregory's office – he was something very important in metals – and being in love with him. Gregory was at least single, and he pretended to love Erika, but he also found time to love at least three other women in his spare time. Erika thought Gregory was far too good for her – which is why, I assume, she went on a massage course: so that she could pleasure him more thoroughly.

'OK, OK – I admit it,' she sighs, seeing my expression. 'I went on the course because of Gregory. I didn't tell you about it because I knew you'd guess I was doing it for him.' I don't comment. 'But now it's coming in really useful. I found the notes I made and I've read some more books on the subject. I'm not an *expert,* of course, but I know the basics. I don't charge that much, and people seem to find it comforting. I really enjoy it.'

'Good,' I say. 'That's really good, Erika.' Maybe I should mention the spanking business later.

In some ways, it's amazing that Erika has fallen so madly in love with Alex. She's had plenty of romantic disappointments; but when we were younger, love was just part of her life, and even if it ended it returned in a flash and hardly gave her time to wash her hair. She cried and drank too much wine and was disappointed for a few days, and then there was someone else. Gregory changed that. He was The One – the big slippery slug. He got into her corners with his silence and into her heart with his stares. Being unhappy with him was better than being happy with the others. He was Home. He was the one who Knew and Saw. He was suddenly living in County Kilkenny with a woman called Sabine. After Gregory, we really didn't think she'd open her heart to another human being ever again; she seemed to have transferred all her passion to her cats. So all this business with Alex would be wonderful – if only he was single.

We sit for at least three minutes without speaking. We cradle our mugs in the easy manner of old friends and look around us. Bewley's café is, as usual, very busy, and many of the staff and customers appear to be foreigners. I like this: it makes me feel I'm abroad, and I would very much like to be abroad, especially now. I think of Rio de Janeiro and DeeDee.

Erika starts to put sugar sachets into her bag. 'What are you doing?' I ask.

'They keep on running out of sugar in the office kitchen. Lionel likes some with his tea.'

'You've become rather fond of Lionel, haven't you?' I smile.

'No, of course not!' Erika says indignantly. 'He's far too…' I wonder if she's about to say 'nice'. 'He's far too embarrassed.'

'About what?'

'About everything. I could hardly get him to take off his socks for his foot massage.'

'He sounds very nice to me.'

'I wonder when Fiona's going to have her baby,' Erika says, when she's finished with the sugar sachets. 'Maybe she'll just get bigger and bigger. Maybe it will pop out in twenty years as a perfectly formed second-hand-car salesman.' She giggles. She still hasn't quite forgiven Fiona for saying she shouldn't see Alex.

'I doubt that Fiona's child will ever be a second-hand-car salesman.' I wish I could tell her the truth about the baby's parentage. I've even been having dreams about it, in which I keep saying, 'I've never seen a baby who looks so much like... a baby. Isn't it amazing how like a baby it looks?'

'Oh, yes, I know. Fiona's baby will probably be a quantum physicist by the time it's three.' Erika sighs. 'And we'll all have to sit round her koi pond while she tells us that it will be starting at Oxford as soon as it's out of nappies.'

'This isn't an easy time for Fiona,' I say slowly. 'She may look very self-contained and... perfect, but she has worries just like everyone else.'

'Yes, I know – I'm being a bitch,' Erika says. 'I'm sorry. I love her. Of course I do. She's so kind and beautiful and clever and generous.'

'And organised,' I add.

'Yes,' Erika says. 'What does she actually do in software?'

'I don't know, but she's frightfully good at it.'

Erika stares dreamily around the café. A sort of golden glow surrounds the people cosily reading papers or chatting. The smell of coffee wafts pungently around the room. Bewley's isn't your average café. It is old and knows itself. It is a good place to dream in, surrounded by people and talk and cakes. I think of Nathaniel, the feel of him sitting next to me, the beautiful stupid nonsense he talked; the look of his hand on the steering-wheel, the play of muscles on his arm when he threw the magazines and papers onto the back seat.

'What about the one with the nanny who falls in love with a shepherd in Tuscany? Or the one where that actor, the fellow with the big lips, almost marries that young actress for a bet?' Erika is trying to remember what films are on in town. We want to go to an early show, but naturally we don't have a paper we can refer to. She glances at her watch. 'It's nearly half past five. The film's probably started.' She grabs her jacket and bag and two large shopping bags; Erika does not know the meaning of travelling light.

'What film?'

'I don't know, but we're probably late for it,' she answers, bustling towards the exit. 'And then we'll have to see something else we don't like as much.'

We virtually run towards O'Connell Street. The streets are crowded with shoppers heading home with their purchases. Then, as we pass a kebab shop, Erika shouts, 'Wait!'

'What is it?'

'It's him… it's Gus!' Erika whispers excitedly. 'In the fast-food place!'

'Who's Gus?'

'Ingrid's yoga teacher.'

'Who's Ingrid?'

'Alex's wife, of course.' Erika darts over to a newsstand and buys a newspaper. She slinks behind a lamppost and peers over the top of the paper.

'Why are we staring at a man eating a kebab, Erika?' I demand. 'We could be watching a film. A really good film.'

'That we don't even know the name of,' Erika hisses. 'I need to see what he's up to. I need to see if… if some woman joins him.'

'Why? I mean, what if Gus is seeing other women? What difference will that make?'

'I need to know, that's all,' Erika says. 'If he's seeing other women, he probably won't run off with Ingrid.'

'And why is it so important that he should run off with Ingrid?' I sort of know the answer already, but I feel I need a proper explanation, especially now that chunks of tomato are landing on Gus's sweatshirt. It's almost impossible to eat a doner kebab with any sort of decorum. Gus has his blue yoga mat propped upright by his chair. He is wearing a beret and sandals and has the slightly gaunt, though extremely fit, look of someone who doesn't spend sufficient time eating cream buns in front of the telly.

'Because it would be so much simpler,' Erika hisses. 'If Alex runs off with me, it would really compromise his career. He writes books about trust and fidelity and working on marriages and being *responsible*. People just don't expect him to run off in a camper van with another woman.'

'It probably wouldn't matter,' I say, mainly to curtail this daft obsession. 'He could write a book about love after love instead. It could be a whole new market. It would be for people who found they couldn't live up to their romantic ideals. It could be all about the importance of forgiveness and...'

'Oh, Sally, please...' Erika looks decidedly pissed off. 'Just shut up about it, OK?'

'Let's just go see that film,' I say desperately.

'Which film?'

'Any film. The one about the big slug that tries to eat Los Angeles.' I squint. 'Look, it's on in that cinema over there. People are queuing for tickets.'

'I don't want to see a film about a slug,' Erika mutters.

'Look, it's late. We can't be too picky,' I say, exasperated. Erika is peering at Gus through a small hole she has made in her *Evening Herald*.

'He's having chips and Diet Coke, too.'

'Erika, I'm sorry, but I'm going to go soon,' I say. 'I don't want to spend the whole evening watching a yoga teacher dribbling mayonnaise down his front. You may find it riveting, but it just doesn't float my boat.'

Erika is still peering through the hole in the newspaper. 'Oh, look, there's a man joining him. He's leaning over him... He's...' She gulps.

I look over. 'He's collecting his tray, Erika. Get a grip.'

'Do you think Gus is gay?' Erika asks, clearly agonised. 'He might be. I hadn't thought of that.'

'Yes, he probably is, if he let someone clear his tray.' I sigh. 'That's a tell-tale sign. I'm going now.'

'OK, OK,' Erika says reluctantly. 'I'm coming too. You'd think a yoga teacher would have a better diet.'

'The slug film could be fun,' I say. 'The queue isn't long now.'

'I need some chocolate. If I'm going to watch a film about slugs, I have to have chocolate.'

I get chocolate-coated peanuts and Erika gets Maltesers, and we each buy a packet of fruit gums, because it is a known fact that if only one person buys a packet of sweets she will spend the first half of the film trying to get the other person to eat it.

'I wish we were going to see a romantic film,' Erika says mutinously as we leave the shop. She already has four Maltesers in her mouth.

'I bet there's some romance in the slug film,' I say. 'I bet some man saves a woman from being eaten.' And then I stop.

Nathaniel is in the queue. And he's standing beside Eloise, the cabinet-maker he was talking to at the reception – beautiful bossy Eloise with the purple fringe and big Bambi eyes. They are laughing, and his hand is on her elbow. I turn sharply away before they can see me. I can't face meeting him – not like this, not when he's with her. My breath catches in my throat. This is ridiculous. I hardly know him.

'Sally! Sally, where are you going?' Erika grabs my sleeve as I start to walk away.

'I can't go to that film, Erika. I'm sorry. I've changed my mind about it.'

'Why?' she almost shouts. 'You're the one who suggested it.'

'I've seen someone – someone I don't want to meet. I can't talk about it here.' I'm walking quickly away from the cinema, towards O'Connell Bridge.

'Who is it?' she puffs.

'It's… it's someone called Nathaniel.'

Erika studies my face swiftly, keenly. I don't know what she sees, but she stops tugging at my sleeve. 'OK, we'll do something else.'

'Maybe we could find another film.' I look at her guiltily. 'I don't know why I felt we had to go into the first cinema we saw. I think I was just desperate to get you away from Gus.'

'We'll rent a DVD and go back to my flat.' She smiles. 'That slug film sounded awful anyway.'

'Are you sure you don't mind?'

'Of course not.' Erika threads her arm under my elbow. 'When did you meet this Nathaniel?'

'Yesterday,' I sigh. 'I did tell you it was a very busy day.'

Chapter Sixteen

'HE SOUNDS NICE,' ERIKA says, after I've told her about how Nathaniel saved me from Larry. 'He sounds nice and kind and fun.'

'Yes, he is,' I agree, 'but he's also very odd and stubborn. And his car looks as if he found it in a skip. I really thought it was going to disintegrate on the Howth Road.'

Erika laughs.

'He left his wife because she was having an affair with a transvestite.'

'This gets more and more intriguing,' Erika says, bright-eyed.

'And he's got an extremely beautiful girlfriend called Eloise.'

'Oh, dear.' Erika frowns.

'He's Greta's cousin.' I shudder slightly. 'She'll probably be furious with me for running out on Larry.'

'Any sensible woman would have run out on Larry.'

'But I'm not a sensible woman.' I sigh. 'I was before I married Diarmuid, but marriage has done something to me. I've… I've started leaking.'

'Leaking?' Erika leans forward. We are surrounded by at least twenty papier-mâché cats at various stages of completion, and they all seem to be staring at me too.

'Yes. These strange new bits of me keep sort of seeping out. I keep thinking that maybe I don't have to do things I clearly *should* do. Yesterday, when I was going to that reception, I thought for a moment that I could just keep on walking, walking across Dublin, and never go to it at all.'

'That's understandable,' Erika says. 'Receptions can be a right pain in the arse.'

'Yes, but it's part of my *job* to turn up at these things and look interested.' I stare at a bright-pink table Erika made from wooden fruit-boxes. 'And then, when I was supposed to meet Diarmuid, I found myself walking to the bus stop; I actually had to *make* myself turn back and go to the pub.'

'Well, you must have wondered why he needed to see you quite so urgently,' Erika says soothingly.

I look at her guiltily. 'Sometimes, late at night, I even find myself thinking I don't have to go to Marie's big do in September. I could just say I have to attend a conference or something, like April.' Erika starts sniffing the air. 'And then I went off with Nathaniel like that – a man I don't even *know*...'

'Oh, *feck* – the pizza!' Erika jumps up from her chair and races into the kitchen. 'Oh, good... it's just a bit singed.'

I have never eaten a non-singed pizza cooked by Erika, so I can't pretend to be that surprised. 'Do you need some help?' I call.

'No, I've just got to cut some of the brown bits off.'

As Erika attends to this task, I stare at her lemon-coloured walls and turquoise bookshelves. When she has a paintbrush in her hand she gets a bit carried away. The midnight-blue sofa came from a warehouse that sells charity furniture; it's very squishy and soft, and she has scattered it with brightly coloured Indian cushions and a large teddy called Wilfred who always looks slightly depressed. The place is awash with 'alternative' things and books about how to love yourself more and connect with your guardian angels. Bloody Alex's books about how to have a contented relationship are, naturally, on prominent display.

'Sorry about that,' Erika says, when she returns with two large plates.

'It looks delicious,' I say, even though there isn't that much pizza left now that the singed bits have been removed.

'Maybe I should get some rice cakes... you know, to bulk it up a bit.'

'Oh, no, Erika – this is lovely.' I am not a great fan of Erika's rice cakes.

'We both need to have more fun,' Erika announces, as she opens a large bottle of red wine. 'We've become terribly earnest and worried. Nathaniel has the right attitude.'

'I hardly know what kind of attitude he has, Erika,' I say. 'I barely know him.'

'Yes, but he's light-hearted and playful. We should be more like that.'

I take a bite of pizza. 'Maybe he's only like that because he's crazed with grief about his marriage.'

'It doesn't sound like it,' Erika says. 'Not if he's already found himself a girlfriend.' She goes over to the stereo, and soon salsa music is cavorting wildly around her flat, making me feel jiggly and excited. It's the kind of music DeeDee would have heard in Rio. As I gulp another glass of wine and surrender to inebriation, I think of the fascinating life she must have led – not necessarily an easy one, but a life full of colour and variety. She probably danced and sang in sultry late-night cafés. She probably kissed her dark and handsome Latin lovers under the stars. Maybe they even swam naked in the sea, tossing off their clothes and rushing into the waves, laughing.

Erika must sense my thoughts, because she suddenly says that the problem with our lives is that we don't dance or sing enough. She adds that we also need to go to churches where they sing gospel music.

'And we need to go to New York, too,' she says, as she opens another bottle. 'We need to go to New York and shop for shoes.'

I laugh. I like this new Erika and Sally she's inventing, though neither of us is a shoe person. It's Fiona who has rows of shoes neatly arranged in her walk-in wardrobe... poor Fiona. I feel a stab of anxiety.

'Sailing,' Erika suddenly announces. 'We could go sailing, too. We need to get out and be more adventurous.'

I look at her doubtfully.

'Or photography. I'd really love to do more photography.'

I don't comment on this either, because I'm remembering the time Erika got Fiona and me to pose for hours at that funfair. She'd borrowed Fiona's fancy camera and was very excited. We posed beside the coloured carousel horses; we laughed gaily and smiled while eating candy floss. We even got the hunky young man in charge of the dodgems to photograph us all on the bouncy castle. They would have been really nice pictures if Erika had remembered to put the film in.

'Horse-riding,' I find myself declaring. 'That's it! We both really like horses.'

'But we mightn't like riding them,' Erika observes.

'I think we'd enjoy it,' I say. 'We need to get out in the country more. We need to get back to nature.'

'Not on big horses, though.'

'No,' I agree. 'Friendly horses that are just the right size.'

'And we must really *do* it,' Erika says. She's chomping on some taco shells; they're the closest thing to crisps that she had in the house. 'We mustn't just *talk* about it. We must ring a stable and book. If we want our lives to change, we have to be more proactive.'

She gets up to get more tacos and almost falls over the huge cheese plant by the bay window. She is slurring her words a bit, and heaven knows what I sound like. I find myself thinking fondly of April. April is proactive. She does things that actually change her circumstances, instead of complaining about them.

And then, I don't know why, I suddenly find myself thinking of Nathaniel again. I think of the map of Manhattan and the melted chocolate. I think of the beautiful dark curve of his eyelashes. In fact, I'm about to mention Nathaniel's eyelashes to Erika when the phone rings.

It's Zak, to say that Fiona has had a beautiful baby girl.

Chapter Seventeen

FIONA IS SITTING UP in her double bed. It is a vast four-poster, and she looks lost and fragile under the sky-blue satin coverlet. Her face looks puffy and drawn with tiredness, but her smile is serene and spreads across her face. Her baby is in a cot beside her, almost hidden by a soft pink blanket.

'Oh, Fiona,' Erika and I whisper, overcome by the moment. We move slowly towards the cot, somehow not wanting to disturb the room's stillness, the quiet after seven hours of labour. Fiona is still dazed by the force of it, the determination of this little creature to find her way into the world.

Fiona leans over and gently pulls back the blanket so we can see the baby's face – her tiny nose, the delicate line of her eyelashes; the rosebud mouth that sucks at something suddenly and then purses again. And she has hair. Dark-brown hair.

'Oh, Fiona…' Erika's breath catches with emotion. 'She's *gorgeous*.'

'Yes, she is,' I say. 'She is absolutely beautiful.'

'She's been crying for the last hour,' Fiona says. 'I couldn't get her to settle and I don't think she was hungry.'

'She looks very peaceful now,' Erika remarks, lowering her voice. 'Yes,' Fiona agrees, staring into the cot with something close to amazement.

'How are you, Fiona?' I say.

'Knackered, but at least I'm home.'

'Was it… all right?' Erika asks, obviously in awe of the whole situation.

'No, it was awful.' Fiona sighs. 'It was excruciating. I yelled for drugs.'

'When did it happen?'

'In the middle of Friday night.' Fiona smiles like a veteran. 'They scoot you out of that place as fast as they can, and that

134

was fine by me. I... we... got back here this morning.' She looks at us apologetically. 'I told Zak not to phone everyone the minute she'd popped out. I just couldn't do the beaming, happy, just-given-birth-thing right away.'

Erika and I sit down on the side of the bed.

'I felt like I was giving birth to a giraffe,' Fiona says. We both pat her hand. 'I thought it would never be over – all those people prodding and poking at me. It was so *undignified*.' She manages to look both indignant and cheerful. 'I'll never do it again.'

I, naturally, do not say that this is just as well, given Zak's slow-sperm situation.

Fiona shifts awkwardly. 'My breasts are leaking... I feel like I'm a cow or something.' She is clearly not the sort of mother who goes on about the miracle of birth. But she looks happy – incredibly tired and happy.

'Zak was great. He stayed with me the whole time. I think he went into labour too; the sweat was pouring off him. He didn't ring the family until it was all over. I didn't want Mum there, fussing about. She would have yelled at the midwife, I know she would. I yelled at her myself.'

'What did you say?' I ask.

'I said, "Push yourself, you big eejit!"'

'That's our girl,' says Erika.

Fiona looks into the cot again. 'Poor little Milly. You're tired too.'

She has a name. Milly. Erika and I didn't dare ask, because Fiona has come up with about a hundred and fifty names over the past nine months; there was a point when she said she was just going to call the child Maurice, regardless of its gender.

'She looks like a Milly,' Erika says.

'She does,' I agree. 'And Milly is a beautiful name.' I'm glad Zak is downstairs in the kitchen with Fiona's mother. I've congratulated him and hugged him, but I'm scared he'll somehow see the secret on my face. At least the baby doesn't have any particularly distinguishing features – not yet, anyway; for example, it doesn't seem to be partly Puerto

Rican. I assume Fiona had some say in the sperm donor's background, but what if they got the labels mixed up at the clinic? I find myself staring cautiously into the cot again. I am staring at Milly like I used to stare at April.

'She's eight pounds four ounces,' Fiona says. 'They checked her all over. I don't think anything's missing, thank God.' She starts going into details about baby things – how it took Milly a while to suckle properly, how her eyes can't focus properly yet, the awful temptation to keep checking on her to make sure she's breathing. How small she is, how incredibly small and opinionated.

'I got you a present,' Erika says, handing Fiona a rose-coloured parcel. 'It's Tranquillity bath oil.' For some reason, Erika often tells people what a present is before they've opened it. I think she somehow wants to protect them from disappointment, in case they were expecting the keys to a Tuscan villa or something.

Fiona removes the paper. 'Oh, how lovely! Thank you, sweetie.' She leans forward to kiss Erika and winces slightly.

I hand her a pink bag and she peers into it. 'And I got you one of Erika's specially prepared aromatherapy mixtures,' I say. 'And a teddy.'

'It's got the ingredients on the side of the bottle,' Erika says. 'There's –'

'Fabulous!' Fiona interrupts, knowing that Erika is about to go into detail about the properties of the different oils.

'You'll be getting more presents later,' Erika says. 'This is just for starters.' She leans into the cot and sniffs. 'Oh, I love the smell of babies. She's just so *adorable*.'

I know exactly what Erika means, so I don't sniff Milly myself. There is something about the smell of a baby that makes you want one of your very own as soon as possible.

'You should have smelt her an hour and a half ago.' Fiona smiles. 'Zak's getting very good at changing nappies. He was scared to hold her at first. She's so weensy, isn't she? Neither of us quite knew what to do with her.'

I look at her. She's talking as if Milly is Zak's baby. Maybe she's even convinced herself. She probably has to. And he *is* the father; of course he is, in the way that matters. He will love Milly with all his heart.

'When is the nanny starting?' Erika asks.

'The day after tomorrow. When Mum leaves.' Fiona has always made it clear that she did not plan to do this whole baby thing without paid help. She and Zak can afford it, and she plans to go back to her high-flying software job in a few months.

'What's she like?' Erika enquires.

'Very experienced with babies.'

That's good,' Erika says, looking at Milly again in wonderment. 'There's so much to know about babies, isn't there? It would be so much easier if they could speak.'

'Here's your tea.' Zak arrives in the room with a loaded tray and some huge shortbread and chocolate cookies. He's beaming from ear to ear. He'll probably be dealing with visitors all day, Fiona has so many friends. The room is already crammed with flowers.

'Thank you, darling.' Fiona and Zak exchange one of their love-loaded looks.

'I'm making lunch,' Zak says, looking at me and Erika. 'Would you like to stay? You'd be most welcome.'

'Oh, thank you, but no. Another time. We'll leave you to.... to...' I want to say 'adjust', but it sounds a bit too accurate. 'We'll leave you to enjoy Milly. We'll visit again soon.'

We leave after the tea and biscuits. I ate three. My diet can start properly tomorrow; after all, a friend has just given birth. Before we leave, Zak shows us Milly's room. We've seen it before, but now it's even more gorgeous. I stare at the multicoloured mermaid mobile, the heap of soft new toys; there's a rainbow mural by the window, and the turquoise curtains are covered in white unicorns. There's a white wooden wardrobe with pink hearts painted on it. 'I painted them myself,' Zak says when he sees me looking at it. I smile at him, but I avoid his eyes.

We walk towards the train station, past the grand old

137

houses and the lush grassy squares, lost in our thoughts. At last Erika says, 'Sally, if someone asked you to go camping, would you go?'

Oh, God, she's started to obsess about Alex and his camping holiday with his family again. Milly probably started it. Erika yearns to have a baby – and she particularly yearns to have a baby with Alex.

'I don't know, Erika. Lots of people go camping. It's not my preferred form of holiday, but ... but I suppose if I had a husband and kids and they wanted to go camping, I'd go too.' As soon as I've said this, I realise I do have a husband, but Erika doesn't seem to notice my absentmindedness.

'You'd go reluctantly?'

'Yes,' I say. 'In Ireland, anyway. It would be different if it was somewhere hotter.'

'Alex doesn't sound reluctant. They're going to County Galway.'

'That's a lovely part of the country,' I say. 'And he's probably not reluctant because he wants to spend some quality time with his children. Even if Ingrid runs off with Gus, or he runs off with you, his kids will always be part of his life. You said yourself he wanted to take them off in that camper van… if he gets one.' This whole Alex saga is beginning to sound more and more ridiculous.

'Yes,' Erika agrees. 'You're right. I'm being very selfish. I'd hate him not to spend time with his kids. Sometimes I wish Ingrid and I could both have him, on… on a sort of timeshare agreement.'

I don't comment. The truth is, I hope Alex will stay with his wife and family and Erika will find someone else, but if I say this to her she will probably burst into tears. All this is so unlike her; she's usually so sensitive about people's feelings and dreads hurting anyone, but her obsession with Alex has somehow made her forget this. I hate talking about him, wondering whether he'll leave or stay. It's too reminiscent of what happened with my mother and Al, and it reminds me of the promises I made to Diarmuid in that lovely old church, surrounded by our beaming relatives…

'I must phone Diarmuid,' I say, taking out my mobile. 'I have to wish him luck on his biology exams. They're tomorrow. He'll be at home studying.' But there's no ringing tone. The caller is 'out of range'.

I frown and put the phone back in my bag. Why should I expect Diarmuid to be at home on a sunny Sunday afternoon? Maybe he's gone for a hike in the countryside to clear his head.

'The wonderful thing about Zak is that he's always there for Fiona,' Erika says dreamily. 'That's what I want. Someone who's there for me.'

'But people can't always be there for others,' I say quickly. Even though I know she's thinking of Alex and his highly inconvenient marriage, I somehow feel that I'm defending Diarmuid. 'I mean, they might *want* to, but they might be busy. They… they might have other commitments.'

'But Zak would make time for Fiona if it was really important,' Erika says. 'He'd make her the priority.'

I can't really argue with that one. 'Yes,' I agree. 'Yes, I suppose he would.'

We part at the train station, because I want to walk for a while – I really need to take more exercise and walk off all those biscuits; Diarmuid hasn't mentioned the extra stone I've put on since I left him, but that's only because he's tactful – and Erika needs to get back to the flat quickly. She has a massage client. 'It's Lionel again,' she sighs. 'He wants his ankles to be looser.'

'*What?*'

'He says he has tight ankles. I'm sure the rest of him is tight, too, only he won't even take his shirt off.'

'Be patient with him.' I smile encouragingly. 'He might have all sorts of hidden depths.'

'No, I think he probably has hidden shallows. But at least he says he wants one of the cats.'

'Well, then, he's clearly a man of taste.'

'But he wants a football cat. In the Arsenal colours.' Erika has gone right off all forms of football since Gregory, who was a football fanatic.

'Think of it as branching out,' I say. 'I mean, even though you don't particularly like football' – this is a vast understatement – 'football cats might be a lucrative new market.'

She looks at me dubiously, and then the train arrives. We wave goodbye to each other and I start to walk determinedly along the coastal road.

I find myself thinking of Milly. Diarmuid is right: it would be lovely to have a sweet little baby – not immediately, perhaps, but before too long. I can't put it off indefinitely. And I like the idea of that little office in the garden, too. It would be nice to have that space, that privacy.

I walk along briskly, breathing in the crisp, tangy sea air. I recall the conversation I had with Erika last night – the bits I can remember – about horse-riding and gospel music and going to New York for shoes. It is suddenly clear to me that the problem with my marriage is that I expected Diarmuid to make my life more interesting and fulfilling, when I should have been doing something about it myself.

I smile to myself as I gaze out at the sea – the wind-surfers scudding along near the shore, the yachts in the distance, the poor water skier who keeps falling over. *I must bake some marble cake for Aggie.* The thought comes to me out of nowhere. She'd like that – and it was DeeDee's favourite. I'd be baking it for DeeDee too.

I must get the notebook back. It has Aggie's marble cake recipe in it. I stop and text Nathaniel. I tell him that he's right: I do want the notebook back. If he drops it off at Greta's, I'll collect it.

I feel a strange heaviness as I send the message to him. Is it because I saw him with Eloise? Surely not, when I'm thinking of going back to Diarmuid any day now.

This is all perfectly natural, I tell myself as I trudge onwards. The sky has clouded over, and the road is crowded with sleek, snarling, impatient cars. All married women must meet men they find attractive. I'm sure Diarmuid meets loads of women he finds attractive, and I bet he's almost relieved he doesn't have to do anything about it. That's one of the advantages of being married: it's tidier. You've made up your mind about who you want to be with.

I think of Fiona and Zak. There's an advertisement for marriage, if ever there was one – even if Milly's parentage has rather complicated matters. They work hard at their love. They don't give up because of minor irritations. They must have arguments, but Fiona doesn't storm out of the house. They talk it out; they have learned how to talk to each other.

And I must learn how to talk to Diarmuid and get him to talk to me – not just about the house and what we should have for supper; I want to know him, really know him. And once he gets used to it, I'm sure he won't mind.

The wind's getting stronger and my hair is blowing about wildly, just like it did in the car with Nathaniel – his stupid open-topped car that makes those strange noises. How can he love it so much? Even the radio just makes hissing noises. I wonder what Eloise makes of it...

Eloise... It's crazy, but I suddenly hate the thought of her in Nathaniel's car, sliding over the driver's seat, waiting while he dumps all those magazines into the back. Helping him to forget his broken heart, teaching him how to love again, how to love her – love her with all of himself, because that's the way he is.

Oh, bugger it anyway: I don't feel like walking all the way home. I'll leave that sort of stuff for marathon runners and Fiona. I reach a bus stop and stand by it. *But I don't have to go home,* I suddenly think. *I could walk to Dun Laoghaire and get the ferry to Holyhead...*

I'm doing it again! What is happening to me? I don't even *want* to go to Holyhead. If I'm going to think these crazy thoughts, I should at least choose somewhere more tempting, Rome or California – or Rio de Janeiro...

My mobile phone rings. I almost leave it, but at the last minute I grab it and lift it to my ear. It's my mother. She sounds a bit out of breath; her voice is high and unnatural. 'Sally, dear...'

'Hi, Mum.'

'I thought I should phone you ... but I'm only going to tell you this if you promise not to worry.'

Oh dear God, it's April. She's going to say that April has reverted to her old habits and started stealing from shops and getting tattoos and drinking cider in parks. I was the one who used to check up on her; who's checking up on her now, out there in California?

'What is it?' I am twitching with anxiety. 'Tell me!'

'It's all under control.' Mum is trying to sound calm. 'They're searching for her now. They'll probably find her any minute. She can't have gone far.'

'Who?' I am jumping up and down. 'Is it April? Has April run off with someone she met in a singles bar?'

Mum takes a deep breath. 'It's Aggie. She's gone missing from the home – they went into her room after lunch and couldn't find her. The door must have been off the latch. She's gone. She's disappeared.'

Chapter Eighteen

WHERE COULD SHE BE? Mum keeps saying not to worry, they'll find her any minute, but Dad and the people from the nursing home and the police have been searching for over an hour already. How can she have gone far? She only totters very short distances with her walking frame, and that's on a good day. She hasn't used that frame for weeks. Most of the time she's just been lying on the bed, propped up with pillows.

Could someone have taken her? I stare at the cars careering by. Who would want an eighty-nine-year-old woman who thinks angels are flying around her room? They've already been to her old home – it's the most obvious place to look, and it's nearby – and they've searched the roads that lead to it. They've rung up the local taxi companies to check if anyone has had a very frail and opinionated old lady as a passenger – an old lady wearing a smart navy raincoat over her nightgown. She may still be wearing her slippers. She can't have gone far. Of course she can't have.

But what if someone took pity on her and stopped his car and drove her somewhere – somewhere she and DeeDee used to go? That's it: she's gone to find DeeDee. I get an awful lurching sensation in the pit of my stomach.

'I don't know where DeeDee used to live,' Mum says briskly, when I ask her.

'Ask Marie,' I plead. 'Is she there?'

'Yes.'

'Well, ask her. She'll know.'

I hear a whispered conversation.

'She doesn't know either.' Mum sounds even more irritated. 'Apparently DeeDee left home and went to some flat in Ballsbridge before she... she went off. We don't know where the flat was.'

'What about the family home, then – where Aggie and DeeDee were brought up?' I suggest desperately.

'They've already looked there. Try not to worry so much, dear. Of course she isn't looking for DeeDee. She probably just decided to go for a walk. You know how addled she's been lately. They may be trying to phone me this very minute to say they've found her. I'll ring as soon as I hear anything.' The line goes dead.

I stare at the phone in bewilderment. I must look very dazed and strange, standing by the roadside, because someone approaches me and asks me if I'm lost. She's not Irish; I can tell from her expression, the down-at-heel look of her clothes, that she isn't a tourist, but she knows what it feels like to stand like this, wondering where on earth to go. 'Thank you.' I smile at her. 'Thank you, but… no, I'm not lost. I'm just… worried about something. A relative.'

She pats my arm gently. I can see she doesn't really understand what I've said. Then she walks on.

Diarmuid. I must phone Diarmuid. He'll be home now; around this time on Sunday afternoons, he cleans the mice's cages. He likes to keep to a routine with them; he says it makes them more secure and comfortable. Diarmuid will calm me down. He'll state the options, explore the possibilities, get out one of his maps and study the small side roads. He's good at this kind of thing. He's very organised and reassuring.

His phone is out of range again. I can't believe it. He's never there any more… Tears of anger spring to my eyes. He's never been there, not really.

I can't bear to think of Aggie lost and alone somewhere, saying crazy things to strangers. Maybe she's forgotten who she is; even if someone wanted to help her, they wouldn't know where to take her. Maybe she's injured, lying somewhere, cold and shivering and desperate.

I need to sit somewhere quietly and think about the places where she might want to go. I walk in a stupor towards the beach, across the road with the whizzing cars and then along a quieter, smaller road. I look for the small shady cement path that leads to the bridge across the railway tracks and the steps down to the waterside.

I used to walk here with Aggie. She showed me this place. It was only minutes from her beautiful, rambling old house. She loved walking by the ocean with Scamp racing along in front of her. The nursing home is near here, too. That's why she went there; people thought it would comfort her to be in a familiar area. My parents are just a quick drive down the dual carriageway, and my own seaside cottage isn't that far away either. It's like we all wanted to be near Aggie, near her warmth and her welcome, her shining, hopeful eyes.

I sit on the shingle and think. They've looked in all the obvious places, so wherever she is, it isn't anywhere obvious. I feel I *should* know where she is, but I don't. Maybe I should just join Mum and Marie. I'm about to get up and head for my parents' home when, as a last resort, I decide to talk to Aggie's angels. I know they aren't there, but I have to talk to somebody, and maybe speaking to them in my mind will help me to calm down.

The sun is shining fitfully as the clouds scud across the sky. How do you talk to angels? I used to know how, when we lived in California. Astrid used to ask them all sorts of things – what size breasts she'd end up with, whether the turquoise powder eyeshadow suited her better than the purple cream stuff, whether Rory Bennett from the high school football team would ever kiss her. I just used to ask them if Mum and Dad would ever love each other again, and they didn't seem to have any particular opinion on the matter.

'Look, angel... or angels... or whatever you are,' I whisper. 'I'm sorry for bothering you, especially since I don't even believe in you, but...' I'm wondering what to say next when my mobile rings. I grab it from my bag. Maybe they've found her –

'What's up?' It's Nathaniel's voice.

'Oh... oh, it's you.' Why couldn't it have been Mum saying they'd found Aggie?

'Your message – you said to drop off the notebook, but you didn't say where.'

I stare at the gulls gliding over the waves. 'I thought I had.

I thought I said you could leave it at Greta's.'

'Well, you didn't.'

'I'm sorry. I… I must have got distracted.'

'What's wrong, Sally? You sound strange.'

'Nothing,' I say. 'I'm just… busy. Leave the notebook at Greta's, like I meant to say. I'll collect it tomorrow.'

'Where are you?'

'I have to go now.'

'You're by the sea. I can hear the waves. Are you thinking about DeeDee again? Is that why you're sad?'

'I can't talk now, Nathaniel.' Oh, God, I'm crying. Tears are pouring down my cheeks. 'I really can't talk.'

'Why? Why can't you talk? Why are you crying?'

'It's nothing. Please…'

'I'm not going to get off the phone until you tell me.'

It doesn't seem to occur to him that I could just switch the phone off. It doesn't occur to me, either. 'Aggie's gone missing. She's… she's my great-aunt. She's eighty-nine.'

'The one who thinks her room is full of angels.'

'Yes.'

'Stay there. I'll drive over and collect you, and we'll look for her together.'

'There's no need.'

'There's every need.'

'No, really… a whole bunch of people are looking for her.'

'But you're the one who knows her best,' Nathaniel says. How does he know that? How does he know all these things I didn't tell him? 'Where are you?'

'Look, Nathaniel –'

'Where are you?' he repeats firmly.

I tell him. I tell him because I don't know how not to. He's so insistent, and I need someone like him, someone who cares and wants to be here with me, someone who isn't out of range or too busy. Erika will have her answering machine on because she's attending to Lionel's ankles, and I can't phone Fiona or Zak for obvious reasons. As I sit and wait for Nathaniel, I wonder how this has happened. How can I know so many people and end up turning to a man who is almost a stranger?

Minutes later, I hear the crunching sound of his footsteps. He seems so tall and bright, standing with the sun streaming on his face, that I get the old shyness – the wish to hide and be found, all in the same moment. 'How did you find me so quickly?' I look into his bright-blue, honest eyes.

'You gave me very specific instructions.' He smiles. 'Over the iron footbridge, along the road by the row of old grand houses, the grassy spot and the rocks and the bench… and here.' He sits down beside me, his lanky, jean-clad legs stretching out on the shingle. 'I know this place too. I'm staying just down the road with Greta.'

'Oh.' I don't know what else to say to him. I don't know what we're doing here together. But I don't have that cold feeling inside me any more, that feeling that I'm lost too and no one will ever find me. Nathaniel is so *here*, so present. I rest in the warmth of him.

'Where do you think we should look for her?' he says softly.

'I don't know. They're looking everywhere already, all the obvious places. There's a whole bunch of them. They should have found her by now. I just don't understand it.'

He picks up a pebble and throws it towards the waves. 'And what about places that aren't obvious?'

'I've been thinking about that, but I don't know where they are. Aggie's an obvious kind of person.'

'What do you mean?'

'She's straightforward. She's not complicated like…' I hesitate. 'Like me.'

'But now she's old,' Nathaniel says gently. 'So she might be a bit more complicated than she was.'

'What do you mean?'

'Well, her mind sort of strays sometimes, doesn't it?' He is being very tactful.

'Yes, it does,' I sigh. 'She's very different from the Aggie we used to know.'

147

'So where is she?'

I have a pebble in my hand. I don't even remember picking it up. I grip it so hard that it hurts my palm.

'I don't know.' It is a whisper. I feel so helpless, as though I'm somehow letting Aggie down, failing her at the worst possible moment, by not knowing where she is.

'If you were Aggie now, what would you be feeling?'

I stare at Howth Lighthouse in the distance; at the shimmering sea where there is no land behind it and the water seems to go on forever. 'I can't do this.'

'Yes, you can.'

'How do you know?'

He doesn't answer.

I feel like getting up and walking away. This is pointless. We should be in his battered old car, scouring the streets, instead of sitting here talking rubbish. We should be ringing places, checking if Aggie has ended up somewhere and they don't know what to do with her. The old Sally would tell Nathaniel to feck off... but this Sally, the one sitting beside him, can't do that. I feel the glimmer of something. Another kind of knowing.

'I'd be waiting...' The words seem to be wrenched out of me. 'If I were Aggie, I'd be looking for my old life. I wouldn't understand why it wasn't there any more.' Tears are streaming down my face. Nathaniel hands me a tissue.

'And then, every so often, I'd realise it was gone and I had to stop looking for it. And I'd think about DeeDee and get tired, terribly tired. It would all be a jumble.'

'And...' He touches my hand, just for a moment. My skin drinks in his warmth. His strength.

'And suddenly I'd know I'd made a mistake, that I shouldn't have done this. That I was lost and frightened and alone and old, even though I didn't feel it. I... she doesn't feel old, you see.' I look into his eyes again. The light in them is soft and tender. 'I'd want Joseph, my husband... Aggie's husband... with all my heart.'

Nathaniel stares out at the ocean.

'And I'd go to a place where he could find me. A place where we used to meet.' My breath is quickening. 'A special place. *Our* place.' I get up. 'The place where I went when I was sad, and where he always found me.' I walk quickly towards a tiny road you wouldn't even notice. It's overgrown; it doesn't even look like a road. But it is, and at the end of it is an old oak tree and a little mound of grass covered with wildflowers. It is a forgotten place. A special place. And it's only minutes away from the home. Aggie could have got there, if she wanted to with all her heart. And who wouldn't, in her circumstances? Who wouldn't want to turn back time and restore the present to something with love in it – real love, not just pity and kindness? I am almost running. Nathaniel is walking quickly beside me.

The path is still there. Aggie showed it to me after Joseph died; she said it was our secret. I had completely forgotten about it until this moment. I push my way through the brambles; I stumble over the long grass and beer cans. It isn't a secret any more. There are sweet wrappers and plastic bags blowing in the breeze. She must be there. She has to be there.

She isn't. The old oak tree is still there, brave and battered, its sturdy branches reaching for the sky. So is the grass mound, covered in daisies and discarded condoms. I stare at it. 'She isn't here,' I say, over and over. 'I was sure she would be here, but she isn't. She isn't here.'

Nathaniel taps my arm and points. 'Yes, she is, Sally. She's over there.'

And she is. Aggie is lying in a heap by the charred remnants of a bonfire. I race over to her. She is breathing.

'Aggie!' I shake her gently. 'Aggie, are you all right?'

Her eyes open. 'Joseph…Joseph, is that you?'

'It's Sally,' I say. 'I'm sorry, Aggie – it's not Joseph. It's me. Sally. You know me, don't you?'

She rubs her eyes sleepily. 'Of course, dear. Of course I know you.'

Nathaniel helps her to sit up. She looks at him but doesn't comment. 'I'm sorry,' she says. 'I'm so sorry.'

149

'Why are you sorry, Aggie?'

She looks at me. 'Because I'm a stupid old woman. I can't believe how stupid I am.'

'Are you hurt?' Nathaniel asks gently.

'I fell over. That walking frame is no use. I've been so stupid.'

'Stop saying that, Aggie. You're not stupid. You're not stupid at all.' I am brushing the wispy grey hair from her face, rubbing the bits of charcoal from her cheeks. Her legs are covered in scratches. I hug her to me. 'Oh, Aggie, I'm so glad we found you. I was so worried.'

'Can you move, Aggie?' Nathaniel asks. 'Are you in pain?'

'No. I just fell over. I often fall over. It's like being a kid again.' She manages a little smile. 'Old age is a bugger. A real bugger.' Nathaniel smiles too.

'You're not old, Aggie,' I say, cradling her in my arms. 'You're not old where it matters. You're not old in your heart.'

'I thought I could go back.' There is a faraway look in her eyes. 'I thought I could go back to how it was. But I can't, can I? I know that now, but I mightn't tomorrow. That's how I am these days, Sally. I'm sorry.' Small, tired tears trickle down her face.

'We understand.' Nathaniel says it for me. 'We understand, Aggie. We're just pleased we found you.'

I see her studying him. 'He's called Nathaniel,' I tell her. 'He's a… a friend. Diarmuid would be here, only he has exams. He's been very worried about you too.'

'Diarmuid,' Aggie says. 'Dear Diarmuid…' She looks at Nathaniel more closely, her eyes bright and curious, and then at me. 'I suppose we have to go now.'

'Yes,' Nathaniel agrees. 'It's getting late, and it looks like it might rain.'

'And I must phone Mum,' I say. 'Right now.'

'You bring me back to… to that place. I don't want them all here,' Aggie says pleadingly. 'I'd just like a little time with you and…'

'Nathaniel.'

150

'Yes. I don't want a fuss. Tell them to visit me later. Tell them I want a little nap first.'

I follow her instructions. Mum and Marie sound extremely mutinous at this message.

'It's what she wants,' I whisper.

'What about what *we* want?' Marie demands. 'We've all been crazy with worry.'

'And, if you really love her, you'll respect her wishes,' I say. 'It's hard for her too.'

'How are you going to get her home?'

'A… a friend is going to drive her.'

'Where's Diarmuid?'

'I couldn't contact him. He has exams.'

'On a Sunday?'

'I couldn't get him on the phone. He must be studying.'

Nathaniel whispers in my ear, 'Tell them she won't be back at the home for an hour or so. She wants to go to the pub for a sherry first.'

I repeat this message.

'Sherry!' Marie splutters.

Mum grabs the phone. 'Don't be ridiculous, Sally. Take her back to that home right now.'

'She doesn't want to go.'

'She's a very frail old woman. You can't go gallivanting off to pubs with her.'

'That's what she wants,' I say firmly. 'And tonight we're going to do what Aggie wants, not just what makes everyone else feel more comfortable about her. I understand your concerns, but please don't let's argue about this.'

'Sally!' my mother protests.

'See you soon, Mum.' I turn off the phone.

Aggie sits on a low wall by the roadside while Nathaniel goes off to get his car. When it arrives, I have a sudden surge of panic. How is Aggie going to get into it? She can't scoot across the driver's seat like I did.

Nathaniel sees me frowning. 'I had the door mended.' He smiles. 'Though the rest of it is as banjaxed as before.'

'What a lovely car!' Aggie exclaims. 'It's just like the car Joseph and I had when we first married. Very old and full of character.'

'Exactly,' Nathaniel says. 'She's full of character. Not everyone sees that. I'm afraid there's a dog called Fred in the back seat,' he informs me, as we virtually lift Aggie towards the vehicle. 'He gets lonely when he's left on his own.'

'Scamp!' Aggie cries when she sees Fred, who is a messy mongrel of no fixed pedigree. He is barking excitedly.

'It's not Scamp,' I say softly. 'It's Fred. Nathaniel's dog Fred.'

Aggie stares at Fred. 'Yes. Yes, of course, dear. I'm sorry. I forgot again.'

As soon as we get into Nathaniel's shabby old car, Fred starts trying to climb over the back seat onto Aggie's lap. 'He's really taken a shine to you, Aggie,' Nathaniel smiles.

'And I like him. Bring him with you, will you?' She searches Nathaniel's face hopefully. 'Bring him when you visit.'

'Of course.' I don't know how it happened, but Nathaniel has become part of all this.

We go to a quiet old pub that Nathaniel knows, a slightly shabby, cheerful place with big, comfy, faded chairs. I tidy Aggie up in the ladies'. I wash her scratches gently with warm water and rub the charcoal smudges from her face. I also comb her hair and put some of my coral lipstick on her lips.

By the time we get back to Nathaniel, he has ordered our drinks. Fred lies at Aggie's feet and licks her hand every so often. His tail is wagging happily. There is even a doggy grin on his face.

'We should ask them for some water for Fred,' Aggie says. 'He's probably thirsty. Scamp used to get very thirsty after a walk.'

We ask the waiter to bring over a saucer of water, and, as Fred drinks it noisily, Aggie starts talking about Scamp and their walks along the strand. She talks about her home – her real home, even though someone else owns it now. She talks about the garden and the geraniums and the cakes. She says that DeeDee knows that special place too, the one she went to. And then her eyes grow dreamy, and she says she misses the old music – the music she and Joseph used to dance to on the lawn, with the French windows open so that they could hear the melodies.

I haven't talked with her about these things for months. None of us do; we thought they would make her sad. Or maybe it was because they would make us sad; maybe we were the ones who couldn't bear it. Poor Aggie – she so needs to talk about these memories, and Nathaniel somehow knows it. He is prising them from her so gently.

'Crisps,' Aggie says suddenly. 'I'd like some crisps. Cheese and onion.'

I get up and go to the bar. 'Four packets of cheese and onion crisps,' I say, because I suspect Fred would like a packet too. While I wait, I look over at Aggie and Nathaniel chatting easily. Fred is sitting up; he seems to know food is on its way.

I want to hug this moment to me, this time in which we are all together eating crisps. I have turned my mobile off; when I check it, I see I have missed five calls, but I don't care. Sometimes you have to give yourself permission to know what's important. And this is. I know it in a new way. I know it in my heart.

Chapter Nineteen

I DON'T WANT TO leave the pub. I could stay here for hours talking with Nathaniel and Aggie. I've been talking to Fred, too; he's a very intelligent dog, even if he looks like a scraggy brown-and-white floor mop. We have ordered chips and sausages from the bar because Aggie's one sherry has made her a bit tipsy. Maybe this cheap-drunk thing is genetic. Even April has been known to cry after four glasses of vodka. We've got Aggie onto tea, but even so, a few minutes ago she started to sing 'Strangers in the Night' in a high, warbly voice. Then she looked at me and Nathaniel as though we were lovers. I think she has forgotten that I'm married.

Part of me is shit-scared that she's here when, by rights, she should be tucked up in bed at the home. All her scratches are superficial – I've cleaned them up and bought plasters to cover them – but she looks so old and frail... She doesn't want to leave yet, though. I keep telling her that maybe we should head back to the home, but she says she doesn't want to go. She's become a party girl. For months I've thought she was dying slowly – and maybe she is, but that seems beside the point at the moment. The point is that she's laughing. Her eyes are bright and playful. She could, I suppose, keel over right here after all her exertions, and the family would be furious, but frankly it doesn't seem such a bad way to go.

Sometimes it's lonely to follow your heart; that's what I'm learning as I gobble my second packet of crisps and pat Fred's sweet, scraggy head. It's lonely, but it feels right. It feels true. Without that gentle voice inside me, I would never have found Aggie. She would still be lying there. Maybe she's right about the angels. Maybe there is a vast world, not just out there, but inside us – mysteries and beauties and another kind of knowing; another kind of home.

'The mountains were huge.' Aggie is telling Nathaniel about her holiday in the Alps with Joseph. 'It was summer, but the biggest ones were still covered in snow. We went up one on a chairlift. The houses in the valley looked so small from the top... like ants lived in them.' She laughs; then she turns to me. 'What happened to that music box, Sally? The one I bought there. I'd love to hear it again. It played "Edelweiss", didn't it?'

'Yes. Yes, it did.' I bite my lip and scrunch the empty bag of crisps. 'I must look for it.' I can't bear to tell her that I suspect Mum may have delivered it to some charity jumble sale and then forgotten she gave it away. It's the kind of thing she used to keep when we lived in our rambling old home in California, where there was more space for all kinds of things.

'Ah, here are the chips and sausages!' Nathaniel announces. 'You must be famished, Aggie.' He sets the plate before her, and she stares at it. She's never really hungry these days. She eats because other people want her to.

'They've done the chips well.' Aggie picks one from the plate and munches it with what looks like pleasure. I can't believe I'm letting her do this. A year ago I would have dragged her back to her bed, whether she wanted to go or not. It would never have occurred to me to go to a pub with a battered, ancient aunt and a man I hardly know, not to mention a dog who looks as though he's been through a hedge backwards. I would have wanted everything to be tidier and more orderly. I would have wanted Diarmuid to come along and take charge and sweep us off to somewhere more sensible...

And in that place Aggie's eyes would have grown dull again. She would be lost to us, and I wouldn't have been sad, because I would have thought that was all that was left of her. I would have been wrong. What's shining from her now is her soul, her spirit; and, though she is old, that is timeless. And in this moment, this strange and maybe stupid moment, I simply can't believe that part of her will ever die.

Tears spring to my eyes, and Nathaniel senses it; he reaches out and squeezes my hand softly. Aggie is halfway through her chips and sausages, and she isn't even using a fork. I wish Mum were here to see this. She'd probably think she was dreaming. Even I can't believe this is the same Aggie who can sometimes hardly speak with tiredness, who can barely totter to the toilet on her walking frame and who spends most of her time lying blankly on her bed. Now she's like an excited child allowed to stay up way past her bedtime. Maybe she'll refuse to leave the pub until the fat lady sings.

Aggie is asking Nathaniel if he's lived in other countries. 'I wish I had,' she says. 'I only know one place, really: this part of Dublin. I haven't seen the world, apart from a few holidays.'

Nathaniel tells her about New York, the snow and the sirens, and the buzz of all those dreams humming electrically on sultry summer nights in Central Park. Then he tells her about Rio.

'Oh, you've been there!' Aggie exclaims excitedly. 'Did you meet my sister, DeeDee Aldridge?'

Nathaniel looks at me.

'She was probably wearing a wide-brimmed hat, a tangerine-coloured hat – she loves that colour. And in that sun, of course, she'd probably need a hat, wouldn't she?' Aggie is speaking very quickly, clasping and unclasping her hands. 'She has the kind of face you'd remember. Good bone structure, a very firm jawline. And her eyes look straight at you. They're blue. A big, bright, honest blue.'

I look at a beer mat. She could be describing Nathaniel's eyes. Mine aren't blue... and I doubt if they look that honest or straight. Why did Nathaniel say DeeDee's eyes in the photo reminded him of mine? What else did he see in that grainy black-and-white image?

'And good eyebrows. She has great eyebrows, never needs to use a pencil.'

'I don't remember being *formally* introduced to her,' Nathaniel says carefully. 'But who knows, I could have passed her in the street... or sat in the same bar listening to the same music, watching the same dancing. Rio has its very own folk music, called *chorinho*.' As he says these exotic words the

156

evening suddenly seems sultry and mysterious, almost sensual. 'The beaches are huge. The place is so vibrant and alive. There's so much colour, so much excess and... and sheer *life*.'

'Yes. DeeDee would like that,' Aggie says dreamily. 'She said she wanted to go there because it was a melting pot of different races. It was all sorts of things at the same time.'

'Oh, yes, there's been lots of mingling.' Nathaniel's smile implies that the mingling probably happened with considerable exuberance and enthusiasm. 'One survey says there are up to a hundred and thirty-four shades of brown and beige in Brazil. They even have names for them, like paint charts.'

'What do you mean?' I ask.

'The only names I remember are *alverenta,* which means "shadow in the water", and *café com leite* – that's coffee with milk. And *acastanhada* – that's cashew.'

'What very imaginative skin,' Aggie says. I can see she's disappointed that Nathaniel doesn't know DeeDee personally, but she is also comforted that he might have met her without knowing it.

'It's very far away, isn't it?' she adds, as if this has just occurred to her. 'The angels say DeeDee isn't that far away, but that's probably in angel miles. They don't have to take planes and that sort of thing.' She looks blankly at a wall. 'I promised Joseph I'd try to find her – and then I didn't.'

This is a new development. 'Why did Joseph want you to find her?' I enquire gently.

'Because he felt guilty.' The words slip off her tongue, and then she looks startled, worried that she has revealed more than she meant to. She doesn't talk about Joseph very much, since he died; I think she prefers to keep her grief to herself. Sometimes, when he's mentioned, a strange look comes over her face.

'Why did he feel guilty?' I persist. 'I need to know. I really need to know why it's so important to you that we find her.'

Aggie closes her eyes, and I can see that her body is exhausted even though her spirit wants to party. She is not going to answer my question. The old barriers have returned, and I must respect them. If I try to drag the truth out of her, she'll just start to cry. I feel a familiar irritation, a desire to shake her, demand that she answer my perfectly reasonable questions; but I must try to be patient. This day has been a superhuman effort for the part of her that is old, and it's extraordinary that she got so far on her adventure – and it has been an adventure, for all of us.

'We'll have to drive her home soon,' Nathaniel whispers in my ear.

She is slumped in her chair now, visibly drooping. It's an effort for her to keep her head upright. At least she's wearing shoes and not slippers, but she has a pink nightdress on underneath her coat.

I decide to turn my mobile phone back on. If Mum rings, at least I can reassure her that we have not bundled Aggie onto a plane for Rio de Janeiro. That's what I'd really like to do, if DeeDee were alive and Aggie was up to it: I'd like us all to go to South America and maybe never come back. 'She just ran off to South America with Great-Aunt Aggie, a young man she met at a reception and a mongrel,' Marie would have to tell people at her family gathering. How amazed they would be. How horrified and intrigued.

Maybe, if you're going to be a rebel, you should do it with style, like DeeDee. Letting mice out of cages, leaving husbands and taking a stand about spermicidal cream is fairly small stuff, when you could disappear and join the circus – or abscond to a tropical beach. Maybe Nathaniel and I could set up a community for runaways from nursing homes. I smile at the image of our vagabond charges frolicking with their walking frames on some exotic, palm-fringed beach.

'What are you smiling at?' Nathaniel nudges me.

'At wonderful, impossible things.'

'Lots of people have done wonderful, impossible things because no one told them that they couldn't. I read that somewhere. I wish I'd made it up myself.'

He's right, of course. Why are we all so quick to agree on what is possible? We let other people tell us who we are, and we listen to their stories until we feel we have to get married because the hotel has been booked and cousins are flying in from Canada and the entire family has bought expensive outfits. We promise to love someone forever because we love the idea, and because not doing it would be too bloody inconvenient.

I look at my watch. God, we must go. The family will be going apeshit.

Aggie is telling Nathaniel that he is very like a young man she once knew, who used to collect wildflowers for her in the Dublin mountains. They went to dances together on his bike, with her sitting on the crossbar. One summer evening they ran into the sea in all their clothes.

'We should have taken them off, of course,' she says. 'But it was warm. They dried quickly in the breeze.'

I stare at her. I'm seeing a new, wild side to her this evening. 'What happened to him?' I hope I don't look too surprised.

'He went to Australia. He wanted me to come too, but it seemed so far away.' She twists a paper napkin between her fingers. 'Sometimes I wish I had gone. Then DeeDee would still be with us.'

'What do you mean?' I say, too quickly.

The closed look comes over her face again. 'Nothing, dear. I'm just being a silly old woman.'

'Tell me… please, Aggie. I want to understand.'

'These sausages are overdone. I don't want any more of them.' She leans over and puts the plate on the floor. Fred gulps the sausages down in a nanosecond. 'But I'd like another cup of tea before we leave.'

I'm still thinking about what Aggie let slip about DeeDee when Nathaniel returns with the tea. Now that DeeDee is dead, maybe I shouldn't try to press Aggie for more details; but there is a part of me that likes being a detective. It's why I went into journalism. I used to love interviewing well-known people and trying to get a glimpse of what made them tick. I loved trying to get behind their masks to their truth. But then I bought the cottage and found there was a bigger market for my articles about interior decoration, and I had to pay my mortgage somehow.

My mobile rings. Oh, dear… it's bound to be a very angry relative, even though I did text Mum to say Aggie was tucking into sausages and chips and would be home shortly. I take a deep breath and gulp down the bit of red wine that's left in my glass.

It's April. 'I'm sorry, April, I can't talk now,' I say. 'Can I call you later?'

'It'll only take a moment,' April says quickly. 'Look, could you get Mum's birthday present for me? I'll send on the cheque when you tell me how much it costs. Spend about seventy bucks.' She is sounding more and more American. I imagine her sitting, blonde and tanned, by her apartment's communal pool, her skin buffed and toned and almost gleaming. She never gets freckles like I do.

'What do you want me to get her?' I ask resignedly. April only remembers family birthdays at the last minute. I seem to have become her official present-buyer, which is probably why I never get presents from her myself.

'Whatever you think she'd like.'

'But I don't know what she'd like. She's a complicated person when it comes to presents. She gets rid of anything she doesn't have an immediate use for.' I find myself remembering the house in California, with its trinkets and its coloured mugs and ten brands of tea; the seashells from the beach, the pieces of driftwood, the strangely shaped stones.

'Something that smells good.'

'She's very fussy about perfume.'

'Oh, just get her anything. Anything *nice*. And make sure to get it professionally wrapped. Presentation is so important.' April pauses. 'So how are you, anyway? Have you started dating again?'

I rise from the table. Nathaniel is putting sugar into Aggie's tea; he adds milk, then stirs it for her. It's almost like a ceremony. Aggie looks sleepy but contented as she watches. I want to hug Nathaniel and thank him for being here and being just as he is. I wouldn't change a thing about him, in this moment – not even his car, or his fringe, which is too long and partly covers his honest blue eyes. He feels me watching and looks up at me.

'I'll be back in a minute.' I point to the phone. I don't want Aggie to overhear conversations about dating. She may remember I am married to Diarmuid at any minute, and she is very fond of Diarmuid. Most people are. Even I am, sometimes.

I go out into the pub's garden. 'Look, April,' I say, when I've reached a rather grubby bench, 'of course I'm not dating again. And I can't talk now. I'm with Aggie.'

'Oh, how is Aggie?' April says, with surprising affection. 'Give her a kiss for me. I had a lovely chat with her just the other day.'

'You *phone* her?'

'Oh, yes. I phone her about once a month. We talk about men and gardening and cakes.'

I don't know what to say to this. It is just another reminder that April is a complete mystery to me – and maybe Aggie is, too, since she didn't even mention these conversations.

'Is she there now? Can I have a word with her?' April asks.

'No. I'm sitting in a garden. She's… she's indoors with a… a friend.' As far as I know, April isn't interested in gardening or cakes… but maybe she talks about men because she's got a boyfriend. She never tells us if she's in love or not. 'Why do you talk to her about men?' I try to make it sound casual.

'Aggie says she doesn't want me to get married young. She says she thinks the family were a bit too keen for you to marry Diarmuid.'

I stare at a spindly geranium.

'She worries about you. She says you talk a lot about Diarmuid, but you don't sound happy. She says it sounds as if you're *trying* to sound happy, just to please her.'

Oh, bugger. Aggie has always been able to see through me. 'Of course, I haven't told her that you've left him. You can tell

161

her that yourself.'

I take a deep breath. 'Look, I haven't left Diarmuid – not really. We might get back together any day now.'

'If you really loved him, you'd be with him,' April says flatly. 'You wouldn't be able to stay away.'

'I'm with Aggie in a pub,' I say quickly. Suddenly I want April to know. 'She tried to run away from the home, but I found her. We're with someone called Nathaniel; he's a man I met at a reception. Mum and Dad and Marie said Aggie should go straight back to the home, but we didn't listen to them. There's a dog here, too, called Fred.'

I'm waiting for April to be impressed. This is the kind of thing she'd do. I want her to know that sometimes I take a stand, that I can be brave, like her. Deep down, I have always yearned for April to like me.

There is a long pause; then April says, 'You'd better take her back soon. She's a frail old woman, Sally. And she's a bit crazy. I mean, she must be, to have done that.'

'What?'

'Fecked off from the nursing home. Where on earth did she think she'd end up?'

I clutch the bench's wooden armrest. I shouldn't have told her. I should have known she wouldn't get it. It's a sideways situation, and she is looking at it straight on.

'Aggie's given me some cake recipes,' April continues; briskly moving onto another subject is as close as she comes to being tactful. 'I tried the one for marble cake the other day. It was lovely. I had it with a friend on the beach.'

I know by the way she says 'friend' that the person is more than a mere acquaintance, but I suddenly don't care who he is or what he means to her. I want to go back to Aggie and Nathaniel and Fred. I look in at them, through the pub door. Aggie is drinking her tea, so slowly that we might still be here at midnight.

'Aggie said the marble cake was DeeDee's favourite,' April says. 'That's not why I baked it, of course.'

I decide to tell her she was wrong about DeeDee being

alive. April is so good at sounding right that I want to remind her that being convinced isn't the same thing as being accurate. 'By the way, April,' I say, 'DeeDee is dead. Marie told me so just the other day. She died in Rio de Janeiro fifteen years ago.'

Aggie has reached for her handbag and is looking around, wondering where I've gone. I get up from the bench. I shouldn't have spoken to April for so long. I suppose I had some forlorn hope that we might actually end up having some sort of conversation.

'Of course DeeDee's not dead!' April is almost spluttering with indignation. 'I heard Marie talking to her on the phone before I left for California – and that was only three years ago.'

I glare at an empty beer glass. What on earth is April on about now?

'She virtually screeched, "DeeDee!" She was in the sitting room and she didn't know I was in the kitchen; she thought I was out in the garden, having a cup of tea with Uncle Bob.'

'You're wrong,' I say firmly. 'It must have been someone else.'

'No, it was DeeDee. Marie said the name over and over. Then she said, "Where are you? Where are you, DeeDee?" She was sobbing.'

'That's nonsense,' I declare, mainly because I don't know what else to say.

'It's true. Girl Guide's honour.'

My breath catches. My chest feels tight with disbelief. April was once an unruly Girl Guide, and when she says, 'Girl Guide's honour', she is telling the truth. It actually means something to her. 'So… so Marie *lied* to me?'

'Yes, I suppose she did,' April says airily. 'I don't know why you're so surprised, Sally. She was desperate to stop you pestering her about DeeDee; it must have seemed like a convenient way to stop you asking all those awkward questions. Why do you care about DeeDee so much, anyway? I think you only find her fascinating because she isn't here.

You'd get bored with her after a few hours if she was actually in your sitting room.'

I'm too shocked to feel the sting in April's comments. DeeDee is *alive*. Part of me is happy, delighted that I might actually meet her, but part of me is dismayed. 'Marie *lied* to me.' I am almost in tears. 'That's an awful thing to lie about.'

'Our family lies about lots of things, haven't you noticed?' There is a crisp anger in April's voice – almost as if she's been lying about something too. 'Please don't make a big deal of it, Sally. It's completely understandable, in the circumstances. Don't even mention it to Marie; it would upset her. Just forget it. DeeDee's gone. If she wanted to see us, she would contact us.'

'But she *has!* If what you're saying is true, she contacted Marie!'

'Only to ask if Joseph was dead. She'd run into some distant acquaintance of an acquaintance, who'd heard he had "gone to a better place", so she wanted to know if Joseph had died or moved to Barbados. She put the phone down almost as soon as Marie told her he was dead.'

'Did she say where she was?'

'No, and she made Marie promise not to tell anyone she'd called. Marie only told me because I'd overheard anyway. I had to promise not to tell anyone, too.'

I don't know what to say.

'Marie thought DeeDee would at least send Aggie a condolence card, but she didn't. She sounds like a heartless bitch, frankly.'

Nathaniel is standing beside me, studying me quizzically. 'I wish you'd told me all this before,' I say brusquely. 'I have to go now.'

'What about a haddock?' April says.

'*Haddock?*' The line has got kind of gurgly.

'Not haddock, hammock.' April bursts out laughing. 'I think Mum might like a hammock for her birthday.'

'Look, April,' I say through gritted teeth. 'You send her something yourself, and I'll tell her it will arrive late. I have to go now.' I turn off the phone.

'You look angry,' Nathaniel says, as we walk back into the pub.

'I am. I'm furious – and happy, at the same time.'

'Why?'

'Because DeeDee isn't dead.'

'That's good news, isn't it?' I feel the heat of his breath on my cheek.

'Yes. But I can't believe Marie lied to me.' I sigh. 'And, anyway, I don't know what to feel about DeeDee any more. I mean, I might as well not know she's alive; I'll never find her.'

'How can you be so sure of that? You found Aggie.'

Butterflies have started to dance in my stomach. I'm filled with an impossible, wonderful yearning. Perhaps I could. Perhaps I could find her, after all. I ache to know her story and her mysteries. She is the crucial missing piece in the family jigsaw. If she's a heartless bitch, like April says, I want to know what made her that way. I can feel the shape of her absence, the huge gap she has left behind. We need DeeDee. We need her big heart and her contradictions. We need to forgive her, even though I don't know what we'd be forgiving.

Aggie is dozing on her chair. 'Why doesn't she tell me more about DeeDee?' I whisper.

'Maybe she thinks you mightn't look for her if you knew the truth,' Nathaniel whispers back. 'It's just a feeling I get. She hasn't said anything about it.'

Aggie stirs as we approach her. We have to virtually lift her into the car. Fred is scampering around excitedly; he loves car journeys. When Aggie is sitting sleepily in the front seat, he installs himself on her lap.

Nathaniel's car jerks forwards and grunts and groans and, at one point, seems to be muttering expletives in French. Nathaniel pats the dashboard affectionately. Soon we are chugging noisily along the road.

'Oh, well... back to the real world,' I sigh.

'What do you mean?'

165

'Everything that's just happened doesn't feel quite real. It's been like a… a sort of holiday.'

His glance is deep, penetrating. 'What if it's more real than this other real world you're talking about?'

'Would you like a mint, dear?' Aggie turns round and offers me a very crumpled bag of sweets. I take one and stare silently out the window.

Chapter Twenty

THERE IS A ROW of gleaming cars outside the nursing home. I recognise my parents' car, and Marie's – and, oh God, there's Diarmuid's. I freeze.

Nathaniel looks at me. 'What's up?'

'Don't go into the driveway for a moment. Stop here. I don't want them to see us.'

'Who?'

'My parents and my aunt… and my husband. They're here. They're all here.'

'Oh, bugger.'

Aggie is almost asleep in the front seat. She stirs and looks at us. 'Where are we?'

'We're back at the home, Aggie,' I say gently.

'Oh, good, I'm parched. We must all have tea on the lawn.'

'We're not at The Gables,' I say softly. 'It's the nursing home.'

'Oh, feck.'

Nathaniel smiles and pats Aggie's arm.

I stare warily at the cars. They must all be in the large sitting room twiddling their thumbs and waiting for us, getting their questions ready – and there will be questions, loads of them. They'll be relieved that I found Aggie, of course, but they'll also be angry that I disobeyed them. And when they see Nathaniel, they'll put two and two together and get fifty. They'll think I have become a woman with fancy men.

'Let's just get it over with,' Nathaniel says. 'You found her. Surely they should be grateful.'

The pebbles crunch in the driveway. A nurse bolts out the door as soon as we park, and three more arrive to help lift Aggie out of the car. They glare at me and Nathaniel reprovingly. Aggie is almost asleep now; there is a contented little smile on her face. Nathaniel reaches for her walking frame, and I collect her handbag and the bag of mints that has fallen from her pocket.

Marie, Mum, Dad and Diarmuid are staring at us from the hallway. 'Oh, Aggie,' they chorus, showering her with kisses. 'Oh, Aggie, are you all right?' She waves at them vaguely as the nurses bustle her down the corridor towards her bedroom. 'We'll be with you in a minute, Aggie dear,' they call after her. 'When they've got you nice and settled.'

Then they turn to stare at me and Nathaniel, as if we were the ones who made a run for it. Diarmuid's eyes are looking particularly steely and, frankly, not that surprised.

Dad takes a few steps towards us and cautiously extends his hand towards Nathaniel. 'Hello,' he says, trying to place some order on things. 'I don't believe we've met.'

'This is Nathaniel,' I say. 'He's... he's just a friend.'

Why on earth did I say that? The words have a guilty ring to them. And Fred has started to sniff Marie's crotch. She pushes him away roughly and says, 'Where did you find her?' She sounds as though she suspects that, far from rescuing Aggie, I may have snuck her out of the nursing home just for a lark.

'In a special place she showed me once. It's beside the beach, in a sort of clearing down an overgrown path. It's...' I stop. They look befuddled enough already.

'Well done, Sally.' Diarmuid kisses my cheek and gives Nathaniel a cold glance. He is remaining admirably calm, in the circumstances.

'Yes, thank God,' Mum says. 'None of us would have looked there. Aggie could have been lost... forever.' At this point she bursts into tears and Dad takes her hand.

'I tried to phone you, Diarmuid,' I say gently. 'But your phone was out of range, so...'

'So you phoned Nathaniel.' There is no edge to his voice; it is simply a statement of fact. Everyone looks at me. *Poor Diarmuid.* You can see it on their faces.

I don't want to say Nathaniel rang me; it sounds too incriminating. 'I... I needed someone with a car in case we needed to search the roads.'

'If you can call that thing a car,' Marie mutters to my mother. 'It looks like it belongs on a scrap-heap.'

I glare at her. 'Nathaniel lives down the road from here, and his girlfriend is a… an acquaintance of mine.' Why didn't I just lie, like April would have, and say Eloise was one of my closest friends? 'Her name is Eloise and she makes cabinets.'

'How nice,' Marie says, with crisp politeness. 'Did she join you?'

'No… she's…'

'At a trade fair in Paris,' Nathaniel completes the sentence for me.

'Diarmuid's phone wasn't out of range when we rang,' Marie says, rather pointedly. 'He raced over as soon as he heard.'

I study Diarmuid. I can't tell what he is feeling; his eyes have that distant look in them again. Where has he been all afternoon? He looks at me without warmth or reproach. When did he learn to hide himself so well from me? Has he always been like this and I just didn't see it?

Marie darts off down the corridor to check on Aggie. She returns almost immediately. 'She's half asleep,' she says. 'The nurses say she seems all right… in the circumstances.' She gives me an accusing look and I stare at her stonily, thinking of how she lied about DeeDee. I feel like screaming at all of them, *DeeDee's alive – and I don't care what you say, I want to find her!*

'We'll have to do something about the lock on the front door,' Dad says. 'Apparently Aggie managed to slip it off the hook when no one was looking.'

They start talking about locks and doors. They make it sound as though the solution to Aggie's situation is to make sure she doesn't escape again. Diarmuid even looks at the lock, comments on its sturdiness and makes some suggestions about replacements.

'I'd better go,' Nathaniel says, when they have been talking about locks for a full ten minutes.

'Yes,' Dad agrees swiftly. 'Thank you for… giving our

daughter a lift.'

Suddenly I yearn with all my heart to leave with him. I can't stand this. They love Aggie; why can't they show it? Why don't they want to hear about what happened? It was an adventure – a strange, sad adventure, but an adventure nonetheless. I wish I could tell them how she laughed in the pub, how she told us that she once ran into the ocean with all her clothes on. I wish I could tell them that, for one whole hour this evening, she was happy.

'Goodbye.' I glance up at Nathaniel. 'Thanks.'

'You're welcome.' I rest in the depth of his gaze for the briefest of moments. Then he departs swiftly, with Fred gambolling at his heels.

'Well done, Sally,' Dad says when Nathaniel has gone. 'Well done for finding Aggie.'

'Yes,' Marie agrees. 'It was clever of you to remember that special place. Where is it, exactly?'

I don't want her to know where it is. I want it to be Aggie's special place, our secret and Nathaniel's. 'Oh, it's just down the road from here,' I say vaguely. 'It's wasteland now, covered in used condoms.' Marie wrinkles her nose in disgust.

We all troop in to say goodbye to Aggie. I lean over to kiss her cheek, and when I reach for her hand I feel her give mine a gentle, conspiratorial squeeze. She's awake, but she doesn't want their questions.

'I love you, wild Great-Aunt Aggie,' I whisper very softly in her ear.

Outside in the car park, Dad jangles his keys. 'Well, I suppose you two will be off for a drink somewhere.' He looks at Diarmuid and me hopefully.

'Or a meal,' Marie adds quickly. 'That Indian place down the road is fabulous. You'd love it.' She is darting excited glances at us. Her voice is quivering with emotion. 'I had the chicken biriyani. It was almost enough for two, and –'

'Come on, Marie,' Mum interrupts. 'We'd better go.'

They drive off speedily, clearly not wanting to interrupt this tender moment – though why it should be tender I'm not entirely sure. After all, I did arrive here with another man; a man who has a girlfriend called Eloise, but another man nonetheless. Maybe they think this will awaken Diarmuid's proprietorial side, make him want to fight for me, or maybe they think he'll want to comfort me after a worrying afternoon.

'Do you want a lift to the bus stop?' he asks.

'Sorry?' I peer at him like someone trying to read in poor light. 'I'd drive you home, only I've promised to meet someone. In fact, I'm already late.'

Who? I want to ask. *Who have you promised to meet?* But I don't.

'We're going to revise together. The exams are tomorrow.'

'Oh, yes – of course.' I wonder if this person is a man or a woman. I wonder if this person is Becky and he's lying about the revision, lying about her being in Galway with a new boyfriend.

'I'm sorry. We must meet up soon to… discuss things.' He hugs me, kisses me on the nose like I'm a kid sister. 'Do you want that lift to the bus stop?' He's talking so casually, as though nothing has happened. 'Or I'll ring you a taxi if you want. Is there a particular company you use? Do you have the number? I'll pay, of course.'

'No.' I manage to smile at him. 'The bus stop is just down the road. I'd like the walk.'

'Are you sure?'

'Yes.'

He gets into his car.

'Good luck with the exams.'

'Thanks.' He smiles at me and waves as he drives off.

At least it's sunny. I try not to think about anything as I walk towards the bus stop. I look at the flowers in the gardens and feel the fresh breeze on my face.

Diarmuid no longer loves me. Why do I find that so surprising? I have never believed he loves me – not deep down; I've always believed he loved Becky more, just as my parents love April best. Maybe he's with Becky right now.

Why do I think about food so much more than I used to?

171

Sometimes I spend ten minutes wandering around the kitchen late at night, just looking for something tasty to stuff into my mouth. I go into a newsagent's and buy a bar of chocolate. I have walked way past my bus stop; I want to walk for miles, but I don't know where I want to go. *I can get used to this*, I tell myself. I can get used to Diarmuid not loving me. What have I done to show him I love him?

On my way out of the newsagent's, I notice the darling place has a special offer on my favourite brand of cheese-and-onion crisps. I'm about to grab four packets when I feel someone watching me.

'Hi, Sally!'

'Hello, Nathaniel!' I turn away from the crisps and force my mouth into a big fake smile. 'What are you doing here?'

'Renting a DVD. What are you doing here?'

'Oh…' I hope my voice doesn't sound too wobbly. 'I was just… you know… buying some necessities.' I show him the bar of chocolate.

'Would you like to eat that chocolate while watching a DVD?'

'What kind of DVD?'

'A funny DVD. Something really stupid.'

I think of Eloise. 'I should really be getting home.'

'Fred wants you to stay. He says you've had a difficult, though exciting, day and could do with a bit of company.'

I look at Fred. He is looking up at me expectantly.

'That's very kind of him, but… but I'm tired.'

'That's what Fred said, too. He said he thought you'd be tired and could do with a large plate of takeaway fish and chips.'

'Look, Nathaniel…' I gaze straight into his swimming-pool eyes. 'It's very kind of you – and Fred, of course – but…'

'Eloise really is in Paris.'

I wasn't even going to mention Eloise. I was going to say I needed to wash my hair.

'You look as if you want to cry.'

'I don't!' I protest. 'I look happy. See, I'm smiling.' I

stretch my lips as far as I can.

'They might even have spring rolls at the takeaway place. We could ask, anyway.' Nathaniel grabs a DVD from the shelf and goes to the counter. 'I don't share the house with Greta, by the way. I know she kind of frightens you. I've borrowed her ground-floor flat. It has its own entrance.'

'Nathaniel, I'd really –'

'Maybe you could give me advice on doing up the bathroom.'

'Look, I only pretend to care about that stuff.' I sigh. 'I don't care about it at all. I'm sorry.'

We leave the store together, and somehow I am getting into Nathaniel's car, while still discussing why I really should be going home. Fred is panting excitedly in the back seat and Nathaniel is trying to find the nearest takeaway.

'Diarmuid doesn't love me any more,' I say, as Nathaniel tries to remember the right turning. 'I think he's seeing someone else, actually. That's why I should go home. I think I should grieve a bit… in a bath.'

'Oh, dear.' Nathaniel grimaces sympathetically. 'Are you sure?'

'Yes. I find baths very comforting, especially when I add lavender oil.'

He glances at me, his eyes twinkling. 'I wasn't querying the bath, Sally. I was asking about Diarmuid. How do you know he's seeing someone else?'

'Well, I don't actually have any evidence,' I say slowly. 'But he doesn't seem to want to see me. He has a whole other life that he won't tell me about, and he says he's at home when he isn't. He lies, and he's become very good at it.'

We sit in silence for a while. Then I add, 'In fact, he's with someone else right now, and I don't even know who.'

Nathaniel squeezes my shoulder. 'It's weird, isn't it – all this love stuff? I think we should all be born with a clear instruction manual about who to meet and who to avoid… and who to marry. We're supposed to keep wanting to find love, even if we've been love-mugged and left gasping and can

173

scarcely summon up the enthusiasm to do our laundry.'

'And keep wanting to eat things,' I add. 'Even when we're not hungry. And we suddenly start wanting to find lost great-aunts just for the distraction of it, so we can escape from our own lives into somebody else's for a while.'

He glances at me dubiously. 'I think there's more to it than that.'

'But why should I suddenly care about DeeDee *now*?' I say. I've barely thought about her for years. I should spend more time trying to get to know the relatives who are actually here, instead of wondering about someone who didn't bother to hang around.'

'It is very intriguing, though.' His look is soft, searching. 'Even I'm getting pretty curious about what she got up to – and Aggie seems desperate to see her again.'

'Yes. That's the dreadful thing. It's like she wants to settle something, whatever it is, before she dies.'

We turn onto another road – another road without a takeaway. 'Should we get some wine?' Nathaniel asks.

'No,' I say quickly. 'I don't want any.'

'I think I've got a bottle at home, actually, if you feel like some later. You'll have to excuse my flat. It's a bit... dishevelled.'

'I don't mind that. You should see my cottage.'

'I'd love to see your cottage.'

I stare straight ahead and try to compose myself. 'Actually, Nathaniel...'

'Yes?'

'Actually, I might just stay for the food. I don't know if I really want to watch a DVD.'

Nathaniel doesn't seem to hear me. Where on earth is this takeaway? He clearly doesn't have a great sense of direction. But, just when I think we may spend the whole night hunting for fish and chips, he finds it. It appears clean and nondescript, and it doesn't do spring rolls.

'We'll just have to go to that Chinese place I told you about – you know, the one with scowly Henry.'

'Tonight?' I peer at him cautiously.

'No, of course not.' He grins. 'It's nearly in Howth. I mean another time.'

Another time. Maybe there won't be another time for us, but I don't say it. He's so casual about Eloise, but I can't be. Sometimes I think he's just as mixed up about love as I am. But, even so, I can't imagine him sitting alone somewhere, getting through a whole packet of Hobnobs in one sitting.

Chapter Twenty-One

WE PARK OUTSIDE A large red-brick building with a luxuriant garden. 'Aren't you going to lock the car?' I ask, as Nathaniel heads towards an ornate wrought-iron gate.

'It doesn't lock properly, and who would want to steal it anyway?' He grins at me resignedly. 'Greta says that, since I'm probably going to have to have it towed away one of these days, I should just put a card in the window that says "Classic Car, Free to Kind New Owner". I like the "classic" part. Greta knows how to talk things up.'

'It's a nice car.' I'm surprised to find myself defending it. 'I like it.'

'Well, if I go back to New York, you can have her. I think she likes you already.'

New York. Nathaniel may be going back to New York. I don't know why I'm so surprised.

The entrance to Nathaniel's ground-floor flat is at the side of the house, shaded by an old oak tree. By the door is a blue ceramic pot containing a sturdy red geranium. I wait as he searches frantically for his keys. For a moment it looks like we might have to ask Greta to let us in. I really don't want to meet Greta. She's bound to tell me about some amazing new tiling; she may even stuff the press release into my hand.

Nathaniel seems nervous, almost bashful. I suddenly feel protective of him. The vinegar from the chips is dripping stealthily onto my jumper. I'll smell of vinegar all evening, when by rights I should be at home in a bath.

'Oh, good, here they are,' he says, delving in a forgotten pocket of his denim jacket. 'Sorry about that.' The door creaks. It is white, with a small frosted-glass window at the top.

As I walk into the dimly lit hallway, I steel myself for the mess he talked about – papers spilling onto the floor, files and books cascading over armchairs. But we walk into a large room with a window that stretches expansively from the floor to the ceiling. It has orange velvet curtains; the armchairs are a restful dark blue, and the striped rug in front of the huge marble fireplace is a combination of all the colours in the room. It's a lovely room, a spacious, cheerful sanctuary. It bears all the hallmarks of Greta's good taste, but it also bears the precious hallmarks of Nathaniel: a jumbled heap of CDs by the stereo, important-looking books open and waiting by a wicker chair. A few mugs are dotted around, waiting to be retrieved and washed, and there is a crumpled navy sweatshirt on the comfy-looking sofa. There is an incense holder on the mantelpiece, and rocks and shells and a tiny replica of the Statue of Liberty. And, of course, there are boxes, boxes of things from the life he has left behind; some of the contents are already making a bid for freedom.

You can't go back to New York, I'm thinking as Nathaniel watches me. *You belong here ... with Fred. He'd miss you.* But what I say is, 'It's lovely. It's a really lovely room.'

'Eloise got me to tidy it up a bit.' He goes over to the small kitchen tucked away in a corner. I see a row of big, brightly patterned mugs and a half-eaten packet of chocolate biscuits.

Suddenly I feel angry with Eloise. I don't want anyone taking Nathaniel in hand. He's fine just as he is. He's scurrying around the kitchen, peering at cutlery to see if it's been washed.

'So you miss New York, do you?'

'Sort of. I like its restlessness – though I don't want that stuff quite as much as I used to.'

I curl up on his blue sofa. I feel like I'm back in the big wooden house in California and Dad is telling me bedtime stories, like he used to before his heart got broken. Stories about anything – the conversations between instruments in an orchestra; what two shoes might say to each other after a long walk.

'I'm not quite so antsy and unsettled as I used to be,' Nathaniel says. 'I like the buzz, but there are days when I just want to retreat with a good dog and a book. I've even been known to watch TV programmes for the under-fives.' He is opening and closing kitchen cabinets noisily. 'Feck it... I really thought I had napkins here somewhere.'

'I'm not a napkin kind of woman. I can eat perfectly happily without them.'

'I've got vinegar all over me.'

'So have I.'

'I'll have to shove it in the microwave for a minute.' I assume he is referring to the fish and chips. 'I don't really like microwaves. There's something unnatural about them, don't you think?'

'Absolutely,' I agree. 'They're like aeroplanes, and sugar-free biscuits.' I am fiddling with my wedding ring. It's always been a bit loose.

'I was surprised to find you in that newsagent's. I thought you'd be with...'

'Diarmuid.'

'Yes.'

'So did I.' The ring slips off my finger and I stare at it. 'He's got exams tomorrow. He says he's revising with someone, but I can't help wondering if he's with Becky.'

'Who's Becky?'

'His great lost love.' I sigh. 'When she was in New Zealand I didn't really worry about her, especially since she'd got engaged... but then she decided not to marry the guy after all, and now she's back here. Diarmuid says she's got a boyfriend and is living in Galway.'

'Maybe he's telling the truth.' Nathaniel presses buttons on the microwave and then backs away from it dubiously.

'Maybe I should find out,' I say. 'Maybe I should get a taxi and race round there and find out if they're *in flagrante delicto*... but he's probably just studying with some nice male friend and talking to the mice.'

'The *mice?*'

I put the ring on the arm of the sofa. Why am I wearing it when my marriage has become a farce? 'He's very close to some mice,' I say. 'They're part of a biology experiment he's involved in. He has long conversations with them.'

Nathaniel waits for me to go on. When I don't, he returns his attention to dinner. 'We should have vegetables with this stuff,' he says. 'I keep reading articles that tell me we should all be chomping on fifty carrots a day.'

'Not quite that many, surely.' I'm getting used to his exaggerations.

'And fruit. I buy loads of fruit, but I keep feeling that it should be sweeter. In Rio the oranges are sweet, but these poor ones are probably picked early and put in fridges and sprayed. They may even be painted.' He gives me one of his mischievous grins. His fringe is flopping over his eyes.

'You should get your fringe cut.' I don't normally make personal remarks like that, but this one just pops out of me.

'I know. Would you do it for me?'

'Not bloody likely,' I splutter. 'The last time I cut someone's fringe, they ended up with virtually no fringe at all.'

'Why?'

'I kept snipping at it to make it straighter.'

He studies me. 'It was your own fringe, wasn't it?'

I let out a yelp of surprise. 'How did you know that?'

'Because I've done the same thing myself. I think it's easier to cut a fringe if it's someone else's. You can see it properly.'

'Look, Nathaniel,' I say firmly, 'I am not going to cut your fringe. Get Eloise to do it.'

'I don't want her to. I want you to cut my fringe.' He is looking very determined about it.

I change the subject fast. 'Is that your guitar?'

'Now you're trying to change the subject.'

'Can you actually play it?'

'Sort of. Do you want to eat this at the table?'

I look at the table. It is covered in magazines and files and papers. 'No.'

'I don't have any trays.'

'That doesn't matter. We'll just put the plates on our laps.'

I decide not to ask Nathaniel more about the guitar. Maybe he just knows four or five chords that don't sound right. He may not even know how to tune it. I've spent hours with Erika while she tries to tune her guitar. She gets this dazed expression and hums tunelessly. It would drive my father crazy. He plays the cello so beautifully; a deep, soft look comes over his face.

'I'm sorry.' Nathaniel hands me my plate and sits beside me on the sofa.

'What are you sorry about? This looks lovely. You're a great takeaway cook.' I bite into a chip gratefully.

'I'm sorry about what you said about Diarmuid not loving you any more. Even though he still might, of course.' His look is soft, sympathetic. 'Some people just aren't very good at showing people that they love them.'

'And some people aren't very good at believing they're loved,' I say slowly. 'I think I'm like that. I think I want a love diploma.' I laugh hollowly. '"Diarmuid has passed his exams in loving Sally Adams." I would want it to be framed, too.'

'And signed.'

'Oh, yes. And then, of course, he'd have to have one from me – but I don't think they'd award it. I'm a marriage mitcher.' I start to laugh again, a high, stupid kind of laugh. I sound as if I'm drunk. I try to regain my poise. 'I... I may have been exaggerating a little about Diarmuid not loving me. Maybe he isn't with Becky. Maybe he really is just revising.'

'Yes,' Nathaniel says, stuffing five chips into his mouth.

'He's a good man,' I continue. Why do I spend so much time defending Diarmuid? 'This whole partial-marriage thing has been desperately hard on him. I really couldn't blame him if he's decided to stray. He's not a great talker, that's the truth of it. And it's amazing how helpful talking can be.' I chomp sadly on my cod, which is covered in crisp batter. 'When someone doesn't talk, you start to fill the silences for them. You start to think, "Have I upset him? Did I say the wrong thing at breakfast? Am… am I a bad lover?"'

'I'd say that's most unlikely.' Nathaniel shoots me a wry, bright glance.

'Maybe I'm just not meant to be married.' It's something I've been thinking for some time. 'Maybe I'm just meant to live alone and go to evening classes and comfort my friends and make lots of tea. I could do with a cat, too – a nice purry cat who runs up to me as soon as I get home.'

Nathaniel reaches for the bottle of ketchup, which is on the floor between his feet. 'I often think that, too – that maybe I'm meant to end up alone. It mightn't be all that bad. I have lots of other interests.'

The way he says it makes me laugh. 'You make love sound like salsa dancing or something.'

'Oh, you know what I mean.' He throws a chip to Fred, who catches it in mid-air. 'Do you think DeeDee found love?'

I sigh. 'Who knows? She sounds like a very complicated person. I alternate between disliking her and finding her fascinating.'

'I must remember to give you that notebook.'

'Yes. I could read the recipes out to Aggie. I bet she'd like that.

I might even try to make some of the cakes; we could have little tea parties in her room.' I pause. 'But I really wish I could find that music box. It would mean so much to her. I think my mother must have given it away and forgotten. She seems to have lost any trace of sentimentality.'

Nathaniel pats Fred with his foot. He has taken off his shoes; he's wearing thick navy socks, which have a small hole in one of the big toes. 'Have you ever asked your mother about DeeDee?'

'No. Not recently. I used to when I was little, when I first heard about her…' I am suddenly remembering why I stopped asking Mum about DeeDee. The last time I asked her, she actually cried. I was about eight at the time, but surely I should have remembered her tears. How could I have forgotten?

'I don't understand it,' I say softly. 'It's like DeeDee's

changed the family somehow. But how could she? She isn't even here.'

Nathaniel looks at me carefully. 'Sometimes things need to be healed that go back through generations. People don't realise how families can form habits, secrets, lies, because of someone like DeeDee.'

'What do you mean?'

'It affects how people love each other. That's what I think, anyway. Once you've closed your heart to one person, you can do it to others; you can even do it to yourself.' He fiddles with his watch strap. 'But maybe I'm wrong... It's just my opinion.'

I find myself staring at him. He's right. I sense it.

But I don't want him to be right. Suddenly I want to be like the rest of them; I want to forget about DeeDee, too. I want to find out more about Nathaniel, who's here, sitting beside me. I yearn to reach out and touch the smooth olive skin of his hands.

I have never felt so mixed up about anyone. Sometimes I long to kiss him, and sometimes I think it would have been easier if we'd never met. Maybe he feels the same way about me. He looks at me so intensely sometimes, but he just treats me like a friend... Maybe he doesn't know what he wants either.

I decide to try to lighten up.

'So what exactly do you do, now that you're not a social worker?' I ask, dipping a chip in the pool of tomato sauce on my plate. The minute I've said it, I regret it. It sounds like the sort of 'explain yourself' thing Marie would say. 'I'm sorry. I don't mean to sound... you know...'

'I help Greta out in the office most mornings. I'm sort of her temporary PA.' Fred jumps onto the sofa between us and puts his head on Nathaniel's lap. 'The rest of the time, I try to get on with my psychology course.'

'You're studying psychology?'

'Yes. I'm a perennial student; last year I was doing philosophy.'

'Oh.'

'And I also play the guitar in a restaurant.'

I gawp at him. I have never met someone who can actually play the guitar properly.

'Mostly flamenco music. I'm not that good, but I think the owner likes me.'

'I bet you are good,' I say. 'I don't think anyone would let you play the guitar in restaurants if you sounded like crap.'

'Thank you. We really need some wine, don't we?'

'No. Some water would be fine.'

'I have a bottle someplace.' He gets up, and Fred leaps off the sofa, follows him into the kitchen and starts pushing his food bowl towards him. 'OK, Fred, OK!' Nathaniel says. 'I came back here and fed him before I went out for the DVD. I really should be more firm with him.'

Fred cocks his head and fixes Nathaniel with a liquid, chocolate-brown stare.

'Oh, all right, then.' Nathaniel extracts a tin of dog food from a cupboard, and Fred dances around excitedly. 'I envy him his enthusiasm,' Nathaniel says, as Fred attempts to jump onto the kitchen sideboard. 'It's just as well I don't have children. They'd be delinquents. I'd be far too lenient.'

I think of Diarmuid and our arguments about diaphragms. 'Did you and... Ziggy...' I wonder if I've remembered his ex-wife's name correctly. 'Did you and Ziggy plan to have children?'

'We weren't sure. Ziggy worried about overpopulation and the world's resources, and she said she didn't have any real need to spread her genes. We thought we might adopt a street child from India.'

'That sounds... admirable.'

'Yes, but I don't think she could have dealt with the paperwork of adopting a child. She would just have wanted to grab one and bring him or her home. She hates form-filling and bureaucracy; she finds it offensive to be asked all those questions.'

'Is she a... a social worker too?'

'Oh, no.' Nathaniel laughs. 'She's an actress and a dog-walker. She was the person who showed me that maybe I didn't have to be one particular thing.'

'What do you mean?'

'Well, my family is full of doctors and solicitors and accountants and high-class civil servants. They're very disappointed in me, even though they try not to show it. Social worker sounded sort of OK to them, but now that I'm nothing in particular, they are mightily pissed off. They're very civilised about it, though.' He smiles at me ruefully.

'Does it frighten you?'

'What?'

'Being a… a disappointment?'

'Well, I have a little cluster of cousins who are disappointments too. That helps. They're off hill-trekking in Nepal and that sort of thing.'

'That sounds wonderful!'

'Yes, to us. But they don't own houses or cars, or want to do anything very impressive with their degrees, and none of them seem to have any plans to get married. I'm very grateful to them.'

'I wish I had cousins like that.' I sigh. 'There was a time when I thought one of them was a lesbian, but it turned out she just liked short hair and dungarees. She's a diplomat now. She'll probably have her own embassy any day.'

Nathaniel grins. 'Here's the wine. That should cheer you up.'

'How did you learn to be like this?' I stretch out on his sofa, cosily clutching a soft yellow cushion.

'What do you mean?'

'When did you learn not to let things get on top of you?'

'Do I seem like that? I feel like I go around looking like all sorts of things are on top of me.' Nathaniel hunts for the bottle-opener. 'In fact, there are days when I think I look like a skip. Eloise agrees with me about that. She says my shirts are shameful.'

I don't like the sound of the way Eloise seems to be

184

treating him. 'Your shirts seem fine to me.'

'That's because you've never had a good look at them. There are buttons missing and the cuffs are frayed, and some of the collars are almost falling off.'

'You're exaggerating again.'

'Yes, but only slightly. When I left my apartment in New York, I just grabbed the first clothes I saw. All the good stuff was in the laundry basket, and now I can't afford new clothes.'

'Why did you leave in such a hurry?' Fred is snoozing on my lap. Every so often his nose twitches excitedly, as if he's dreaming of chasing rabbits.

'I thought if I didn't leave in a hurry I mightn't leave at all. I thought… you know, that I might find myself thinking it was all OK. That I could get used to it.'

'What?'

'Ziggy falling in love with that guy.'

'The transvestite?'

'Yes. He's called Richard. He looks great in fishnet tights.'

'You've actually seen him wearing them?'

'I came home early one night, and there they were, cuddled up on the sofa. He was wearing a short black dress with purple sequins, and the fishnet tights. He has good legs, though he's a bit hefty around the calves.'

'I'm sorry.'

'I don't mind him having good legs. He would have to, to go around dressed like that. Ziggy enjoys dressing him up.'

'No, I mean I'm sorry that Ziggy didn't love you properly. Not in the way you needed.'

Nathaniel pulls the cork out with a pop. 'She believes in open relationships. She thought she could date Richard and still have me, and maybe fit in an affair or two when she got bored. She likes variety.' He reaches for two large glasses.

'Why did you marry her?'

Deep-red wine gurgles into the glasses. 'I loved her. At least, I thought I did.' There is a silence. 'I'd still be with her if she could be faithful to me, but it's just not in her nature. I'd have to share her, and I can't do that.'

185

I wonder if he talks to Eloise about Ziggy. He always speaks of Eloise so matter-of-factly. He enjoys her ruggedness, the way she just grabs what she wants; it's almost as if he enjoys being taken in hand by her, finds it amusing. I wonder if one day he'll resent it. I wonder if he loves her, or if she's just helping him to forget Ziggy.

'Ziggy was so shiny and bubbly and enthusiastic, in that American way,' he says, 'and so friendly to almost everyone – though some of that was fake. Nice fake, though. I'd never met anyone like her before.' He hands me a glass. It's so full it might spill. 'Don't worry; the carpet is very accommodating about spillages. It enjoys a good Chardonnay. It disappears into the fabric without a trace.'

I take the glass carefully and sip it. 'You must miss her.'

'Not as much as I thought I would. I miss the Ziggy I thought I'd married. It was fantastic at first; Ziggy is great at beginnings.' He sits on the sofa beside me and stretches out his long, denim-clad legs. 'She loves the discovery, the excitement. But the next part bores her – the bit where you're deciding whether you need more shelving, or whether you should try that new supermarket with the special offers. Buying food bored her. She wanted to eat out and meet people. We always seemed to have dinner with at least ten friends.'

'It must have got sort of tiring.'

'Yes, it did. It began to feel like we didn't have a home; our flat was more like a base camp. We never seemed to have private conversations. She crammed our lives with other people. After a while, I realised she was scared of letting someone really know her. She didn't want that intimacy.'

'And you did?'

'Yes. Yes, of course I did. That's the point, isn't it? For me, anyway.'

I feel a tingle in my chest. There is a kind of brightness between us, almost like a caress.

Nathaniel leans forward, and our foreheads almost touch. 'I wish we'd talked at the party.'

'Yes,' I whisper. Suddenly I want to remove this space

186

between us. I want to travel the miles from my soft blue cushion to his, take his hand and hold it to my cheek. I want to kiss his fingers softly…

Then I remember Eloise and Diarmuid. It's almost as if they are in the room with us, gazing at us reproachfully. I draw back and stare into my glass.

Nathaniel pats Fred, running a hand along his back in gentle sweeps. 'I wasn't as romantic about marriage as Ziggy was. I knew we'd have to work at it, but she didn't want that. She thought love just happened. So her solution was to find Richard and distract herself. We'd both got so lonely. That's what we couldn't deal with, really…' His eyes are cloudy and sad, bewildered. 'The dreadful, secret loneliness of being with someone but feeling alone. Not knowing how to reach them.' He might as well be talking about me and Diarmuid.

He empties his glass and gets up to refill it. 'Do you want some more?'

'No, thanks.' I've been sipping my wine very slowly. I really don't want to be a cheap drunk tonight. I want to have my wits about me.

'Would you like a chocolate biscuit?' He waves the half-eaten packet at me.

'No. It's OK.' That's the first time I've refused a biscuit in months.

Nathaniel stuffs one into his mouth and returns to the sofa, bringing the biscuits with him. 'So you're going to let me get drunk and morose on my own, are you?'

'You're not morose.'

'I get very depressed about it sometimes. I feel so guilty.'

'You didn't fall in love with a transvestite,' I say. 'What do you have to feel guilty about?'

'I've always felt that most people give up on marriages too easily.' He pops another biscuit into his mouth. 'I feel like I should have bought the right book or gone to the right counsellor. I feel like I should have been able to change her, somehow – make her see that dating other people while you're married is… well, *unreasonable*, I suppose.'

187

'It's like not being married at all,' I agree.

'And then she started on about adopting a child again. She got it into her head that we should do it within the year.' Fred is trying to get at the packet of biscuits, pawing at Nathaniel's knee. 'I felt sorry for this kid we might have – dragged over from India to be brought up by a couple who could hardly meet each other's eyes any more.'

He looks into mine, and then he stands up suddenly. 'Anyway, I'm sorry. I've been going on and on about myself, when you have your own problems.' He tucks his hands into the back pockets of his jeans. 'Would you like a cup of coffee… or tea? Or would you just like me to drive you home?'

'What about the DVD?' I can't believe he has suddenly disengaged from me like that. I felt so close to him, and now he's all business. I feel like I've been slapped.

'Do you really want to watch a DVD?'

'No.'

'Thought so.' He reaches for his denim jacket.

I stand up. I don't understand what's going on. Even Fred is staring at Nathaniel with a puzzled expression.

'Nathaniel.' I tug at his sleeve as he turns towards the door. 'What's happened? Did I say something wrong?'

His shoulders soften. He reaches out and takes my hand. 'Of course you didn't. You've been… lovely.'

'Is it because I asked you about Ziggy? I'm sorry. I shouldn't have.' I am looking down at the floor.

'Oh, Sally.' It is a deep, ragged sigh. 'Do you really want to know the truth?'

'Yes.'

'That glass of wine made me want to kiss you.'

I stare up at him. I feel like I might melt with longing and disbelief.

'It was only the wine, of course. If I'd gone for Earl Grey, I might have started to spout my opinions on quantum physics.' He moves closer. 'But, because of the wine, I wanted to kidnap you and prise you away from Diarmuid. I'm very annoyed with Diarmuid – talking to *mice,* when he

188

could have been cuddling you.'

'And I'm very annoyed with Ziggy,' I say quickly. 'Going off with a man in fishnet tights, when she could have been...'

He must read my thoughts. 'Indeed.'

'Why didn't the wine make you kiss me?' I have to know.

'I decided it would be unfair. You're vulnerable at the moment, and so am I. We'd be like two lost kids clinging to each other. Our friendship is important to me; I don't want to risk it.'

Friendship. Is that all it is?

His eyes darken. 'And then, of course, there are Eloise and Diarmuid to consider.'

'Yes,' I agree. 'There are all sorts of things to consider.'

'So it's probably best if you go now and have that lavender-scented bath.'

'Yes, of course it is,' I say. 'It's the only sensible thing to do.'

Chapter Twenty-Two

'AND WHAT HAPPENED THEN?' Erika is almost falling off her chair with excitement. 'Did Nathaniel kiss you?'

'No. He hugged me, and then he drove me home and I had a lavender-scented bath. It was only when I was drying myself that I realised I didn't have my wedding ring with me. I'd left it on his sofa.' It's been a few weeks since Nathaniel almost kissed me, but I didn't feel ready to tell Erika and Fiona until today. I knew they'd pester me for details.

'Oh, sweet Jesus!' Fiona exclaims. 'Did you phone him?'

'Of course. And he looked and looked for it, but he couldn't find it. Maybe it went down a crack in the floorboards.' I sigh. This has become yet another farcical detail of my marriage. But, since Diarmuid hasn't worn his wedding ring for weeks, I find myself being surprisingly philosophical.

'You could get another one,' Fiona says. 'I know a jeweller who'd be able to make an almost exact replica. Diarmuid would never know.'

'Thank you, Fiona.' I haven't the heart to tell her that the ring may not be needed anyway, even though she must have her suspicions.

Fiona seems somewhat distracted. 'Sally, could you help me with the tea?' she says. I follow her into her gleaming kitchen, leaving Erika to fuss over Milly in the sitting room. As soon as we reach her kitchen table, Fiona slumps onto a chair and sobs inconsolably.

I'm the only friend who knows her secret, so I am the only person she cries with. 'Zak is going to leave me,' she whispers piteously. 'He's going to leave me and Milly when he finds out the truth.'

'Of course he won't.' I decide to be very firm and authoritative, even though I have no idea whether Zak would leave or stay. 'He's not that sort of person. He'd be angry and *think* about leaving, but he wouldn't. It's not as if you've

190

been unfaithful.'

'But I have, in a way, haven't I? He's so convinced Milly is his baby.'

'And she is, in every way that matters,' I say. 'Anyway, he'll probably never find out that she isn't.'

Fiona's eyes widen plaintively. 'But he wants her to have a blood test.'

This is worrying news, but I manage not to change my expression. 'Why?'

'It's just something his family does, apparently. They keep charts with key medical details, including blood types. They're very organised about healthcare.'

'Well, tell him she's a bit young. And then he'll probably forget about it. Anyway, it's not as if he wants them to do a DNA test.'

'I think he will!' she cries. 'He'll want them to do all sorts of tests. He believes in doing everything thoroughly. I had to go to four gynaecologists before he found one he liked.'

I put on the kettle. Erika may come in at any moment and wonder where the tea is.

'It's his sperm, you see.' Fiona's eyes are puffy and red. 'He's worried that his slow sperm may have affected her development somehow – that it mightn't have had enough oomph in it, or something.'

'He's just being a bit neurotic.' I rub her back. 'I'm sure you'll be able to make him see sense.'

'I think he's suspicious, too. Sometimes he looks at Milly as if he suspects something. I bet that's why he really wants her to have a blood test.'

I'm not surprised. The truth is, Milly's eyes are beginning to look a bit Asian. Even her hair is coal-black.

I sit down beside her. 'Have you ever thought of just telling him?' I tear off a piece from the paper-towel roll and hand it to her. 'He knows you love him. You could tell him you thought he'd be a great father and desperately wanted to have a family with him.'

Fiona blows her nose noisily. 'He'd leave me.'

'You keep saying that, but maybe he wouldn't.'

'He hates lies – you know that. He hates any kind of deception.'

'Well... maybe you could say you'd gone for a fertility test or something, and the receptionist didn't speak English properly.' Fiona looks at me as if I'm a Tibetan yak. 'You could say there was a misunderstanding and... and they snuck the sperm into you without you knowing.'

'Oh, for God's sake, Sally.' Fiona makes another honking sound as she blows her nose again. 'That's ridiculous.'

I hear the sound of Erika's clattery sandals on the imported marble tiles. Fiona does too. She sniffs and dabs her eyes and is Fabulous Fiona again. You'd think she didn't have a care in the world, if it weren't for the slight redness of her eyelids.

'Sorry for the delay, honey,' she calls out as Erika comes in. 'We were just wondering if you'd want Lapsang Souchong, jasmine, Earl Grey or green tea.'

'I think she likes the cat!' Erika beams. 'She actually smiled and gurgled.'

The main reason why we are here is to give Milly the cat Erika made – a beautiful pink kitten, with a floral T-shirt that says 'Born to Boogie' in orange and turquoise letters.

'It's a beautiful cat,' Fiona says. 'It's... it's an *heirloom.*'

Erika sits down at the chrome and glass table and absorbs these words delightedly.

'What kind of tea would you like, Erika?' I ask.

'Whatever you're having. Milly's so beautiful, Fiona. I just love her eyes; they're so –'

'And a biscuit,' I interrupt sharply. 'What about a biscuit, Erika?'

'I'm completely off biscuits,' Erika says smugly.

'So am I,' I say. 'I haven't eaten a biscuit in... in twenty-eight hours.'

'But who's counting?' Fiona laughs her bright, happy laugh. I really don't know how she keeps up the pretence. She's already been in touch with people at work to discuss conferences and manuals and some new database that virtually cooks dinner. And she's knackered, of course, because of feeding Milly in the wee small hours and attending to her screeches, which may happen at any time. I'm amazed that she's sleeping so quietly in the next room while we talk. As far as I can tell, the nanny is mostly a backup who helps with the household chores.

'Sally must really like Nathaniel, because when she got home she found an uneaten bar of chocolate in her pocket. She had forgotten all about it.' Erika looks at Fiona excitedly.

'And how's Diarmuid?' Fiona enquires. She can never entirely forget that I'm married, which of course is quite true and something I should be more aware of myself.

'I don't really know. I phoned him about his exams, and he seemed pleased enough with how they went. Then he said he had to go because he was busy. He wants to meet up tonight about something – probably to discuss a divorce.' I get a familiar fluttery feeling in my stomach.

'Oh, come on, Sally, he might just want to see you,' Fiona tells me. 'It's important to keep the lines of communication open.'

'But he hasn't wanted to see me for weeks. I thought he'd call round after the exams, but he hasn't. I think he's found someone else, actually; he might even be back with Becky. I can't blame him, really.'

'He might just have been busy,' Fiona says soothingly. 'Are you sure you don't want a biscuit? These are really delicious. They're home-cooked, from the deli.'

'I don't even want to *look* at them,' I reply firmly. 'Keep them in that jar or I'll leave the house.'

'Nathaniel sounds lovely.' Erika has opened the biscuit jar and is sniffing it. 'I wish I could meet him.'

'He might be going back to New York.'

'Oh, *no!* He mustn't!' she cries, dipping her hand into the container and extracting a thick shortbread cookie stuffed with hunks of chocolate.

'He sounds like a nice…' Fiona pauses. 'A nice friend. And he's really cheered you up.'

'He's more than a *friend,*' Erika protests. 'He wanted to *kiss* Sally.'

'But he didn't, did he?' Fiona says loftily. 'He didn't kiss her because she's married to Diarmuid and he's dating Eloise. He knows there is such a thing as *loyalty*.'

'But… but Diarmuid wasn't loyal to Sally,' Erika protests. 'He was unfaithful with the mice. He left Sally alone for hours and hours every evening.'

'Oh, for God's sake, Erika!' Fiona splutters. 'You can't have an affair with a mouse.'

'You can have an *emotional* affair with a mouse,' Erika says heatedly. 'If a husband is getting more intimate with his mice than his wife, I think it's a perfectly good reason to leave a marriage. Especially if he also loves a woman called Becky.'

'Diarmuid never said that.' I feel a need to defend him. 'He never said he was in love with Becky.'

'But *you* said he was.' Erika glares at me.

'Look, there are hundreds of reasons to leave a marriage,' Fiona says with great authority. 'But there are more reasons to stay.'

'Such as?' Erika demands. She is clearly thinking of Alex.

'You *make* a marriage,' Fiona declares. 'That first passionate bit is only the start of it.'

'But Diarmuid and Sally didn't even have that,' Erika interrupts. 'They were more like friends… you said it yourself. There was none of that glowy stuff. They didn't even hold hands when they went for a walk.'

It's sort of fascinating to be discussed as if I am not present, but I'm not sure I like it. 'Diarmuid is shy about that kind of thing,' I interject. 'He's not very physically demonstrative in public.'

'Look, it's all right for you, Fiona. You've found yourself your perfect partner,' Erika mumbles rebelliously.

'Zak is not a perfect partner. There are loads of things about him that annoy me.'

'Why do you stay with him, then?' Erika demands.

'Because I like being married to him. I actually like

working things out together. It's like a journey you take with someone.'

'But… but what if the other person is off doing yoga three nights a week and then going for herbal tea afterwards with the teacher?' Erika demands.

Fiona raises her eyes to heaven. 'Look, I'm not going to discuss Alex with you, Erika. Whatever he and Whatsher-name–'

'Ingrid.'

'Whatever he and Ingrid are getting up to is their own business.'

'So…' I begin hesitantly. 'So you think anyone could marry anyone else and be happy, if they worked at it?'

'Of course not. Some people just aren't suited – but they should try to discover that *before* they get married, not afterwards.' She looks at me a little reproachfully. 'People go on about finding the right partner, but it's also about *being* the right partner. Being prepared to grow together.'

She is, of course, right. Sometimes I get tired of Fiona being right. Erika is shifting restively in her chair.

'Some people keep moving on to the next partner, thinking everything will be different.' She's getting into her stride. 'But they don't realise that, for things to be different, they need to be different too.'

Erika grabs another biscuit and stares moodily out the kitchen window. We remain silent for a while. Fiona's pronouncements have been rather sobering.

'Alex's wife has got suspicious now. He says we shouldn't see each other for a while.' Erika turns sharply towards Fiona. 'I bet you're glad, aren't you? Every decent man is married. I've been left behind on the sideboard.'

I assume Erika means 'shelf'. Fiona and I manage not to smile. 'That's nonsense,' Fiona says. 'I bet you've got all sorts of men lusting after you secretly.'

'Yes,' I say. 'You're so pretty, and… and you make such beautiful cats.'

Any compliment about her cats comforts Erika. Her eyes

brighten slightly. 'Milly really does seem to like this one.'

'Of course she does,' Fiona says.

'Yes, it's an *heirloom,*' I add. 'Fiona said it herself.'

'Maybe I should make some singleton cats,' Erika says dreamily. 'Singleton cats with attitude.' She picks up one of Fiona's gorgeous hand-painted mugs and stares at the intricate motifs.

Fiona fills the teapot and glances over at me. 'Did you get that notebook back from Nathaniel?'

'Yes, I was going to bring it round to Aggie tonight. I want her advice about some of the recipes. The chocolate cake sounds very nice – though I'd only make it if I was having at least five people to tea; I wouldn't want to be alone in the house with it.' Fiona laughs. 'But I'll have to visit Aggie tomorrow instead, because Diarmuid suddenly wants to see me.' I look at my watch. 'In fact, I'll have to leave soon. He's calling round to me.'

'Sally and I are going horse-riding any day now,' Erika suddenly announces. 'We're going to be women who run with the horses... or who let the horses run while we're on them.'

'Just trotting,' I say firmly.

'That's great,' Fiona says. 'I must go riding myself, but not just yet. I'm still a bit – you know...' Erika and I nod. Fiona has already told us in detail about the gruelling process of labour. 'But we'll have to go hill-walking one of these days.'

I think of Fiona's seemingly interminable hikes through the hills, and Erika probably does too, because she swiftly moves on to another topic.

'Lionel's got me helping bloody refugees. Can you believe that? He's actually bullied me into teaching a bunch of them how to speak English.' She sighs dramatically and crunches her cookie.

'Bloody refugees'? I can't believe Erika just said that. Her love for Alex has made her terribly heartless.

'Lionel doesn't sound like someone who'd bully you,' I say. 'Unless his loosened ankles have radically altered his personality.'

'He said he'd help me market the cats if I helped with the refugees,' Erika mutters.

'Why don't you bring him round here one day?' Fiona says eagerly.

'Oh, you wouldn't want to meet him,' Erika says dismissively. 'He's terribly boring and bashful. He has hardly any personality.'

Fiona and I exchange meaningful glances. Lionel sounds much nicer than Alex.

Erika cocks her head sideways. 'Was that Milly?'

I didn't hear anything, but Fiona scurries away to check. Erika and I put the tea things onto a tray and carry it out to the magnificent bog-oak coffee table. Milly is gurgling happily, and Fiona is staring at her, besotted, as though she can't believe she exists. I wish I could stay here all evening. I wish I could curl up on one of Fiona's big cushions and watch some soppy black-and-white film on the telly.

I also wish Nathaniel had kissed me, but he didn't. And soon I have to face my husband in my sitting room, even though I suspect I already know what he wants to tell me.

Chapter Twenty-Three

'I'M SORRY I CAN'T visit you tonight, Aggie.' I pause and gaze out the window at the sea. I need to give some excuse, but I can't say Diarmuid is coming round, since she thinks I still live with him. 'I've… I've got a meeting.'

'Oh, don't worry, dear.' Aggie sounds bright-eyed and bushy-tailed. 'I've already had a visitor today – a lovely old woman who wanted to see what the place was like. Her relatives think she shouldn't live on her own for too much longer.' Aggie frequently calls people her age 'old', but she also calls people like me 'young', which is rather comforting. 'She was a bit brash – dyed blonde hair in a big bun and layers of make-up, and expensive-looking knitwear that flapped around as she talked – but we had a great chat. I told her to stay in her own house for as long as possible and stop listening to people telling her how old people should behave.' There is a new, authoritative tone in Aggie's voice, as if she sees herself as something of a rebel now. 'Her name is Fabrice. She's a real character, and very posh – she mentioned something about being a countess. Her family comes from Germany.'

'Goodness,' I say. 'She sounds interesting.'

'Yes. She just came into my room because the door was open. She'd fibbed to the staff about visiting a relative. She said she knew they wouldn't tell her the real facts about the place; she needed to hear the truth, from a resident. So I told her about the overdone roast beef and the bossiness, and how they've changed the lock on the front door because of me.' Aggie starts chuckling – a deep, satisfied, almost roguish chuckle. 'She was very impressed by my silly bid for freedom. I told her all about how you and Diarmuid found me.'

I'm not surprised by this statement. Aggie has started to believe Nathaniel is Diarmuid; she has also told me that marriage clearly suits him, because he's so much more 'open' and 'light-hearted' now.

'It turns out Fabrice knew DeeDee when they were in their twenties.'

'But I thought she was German.' The journalist side of me likes to sort out these inconsistencies, but the minute I've said it I wish I hadn't. It's not fair to expect Aggie to have a firm grasp on the details. Only the other day she told me Marie was thinking of being a country singer in Nashville.

'Yes, she is, but her family came over here shortly after the First World War.' Aggie's voice sounds dreamy. 'Fabrice was only a young girl. Her mother was afraid the family jewellery would get pilfered on the ship, so she kept the best pieces in her bra. It was stuffed with gold and pearls and diamonds... DeeDee would have loved that story.'

'How did she meet DeeDee?'

'They met in the shop where DeeDee was working. It was just off Grafton Street and sold hats.' I hear a sucking noise; Aggie is on the mints again. 'It was quite famous; so, because Fabrice is so posh, I asked her if she had ever been in the place. And she had! She said DeeDee helped her to choose a lovely hat; Fabrice said it was the nicest one she ever owned.'

Aggie is so excited that I haven't the heart to tell her my 'meeting' may start at any minute. Diarmuid is usually pretty punctual.

'They sometimes met for lunch after that. Sometimes they just had cream cakes and coffee; they both found sandwiches boring.' I find myself smiling.

'Fabrice is an unusual name for a German, but she says part of her family is French. Some of her relatives have big castles in the Loire Valley.' Aggie gives a contented sigh; then her voice grows solemn. 'I asked her if she knew where DeeDee is now, but she doesn't. They lost touch when DeeDee left Dublin.'

'Oh, well – it's lovely that you had such a nice chat,' I say.

'Yes,' Aggie agrees. 'Fabrice has lived in this area for years, but even so, it's quite a coincidence that she knew DeeDee.'

I agree, though in Dublin there are loads of such unexpected connections. In fact, meeting someone who isn't already acquainted with a number of your friends can be quite a relief.

'I think the angels were involved,' Aggie adds. 'Fabrice did too. She saw them flying about the place.'

'Oh.' I don't know what to say. 'How nice.'

'She said she senses that what the angels want me to know, most of all, is that DeeDee still loves me.' Aggie's voice wobbles. 'She said that DeeDee often talked about her sister Aggie. She even told Fabrice she would always love me, no matter what. It was shortly before she disappeared.'

'Well, how *lovely,*' I exclaim. I do not, of course, add that I'm pretty sure Fabrice saw that she was desperate for reassurance and simply said whatever she wanted to hear. 'Are you going to see her again?'

'Oh, yes, she says she'll come visit me as often as she can, but it might not be for a few days. She says she has to visit London for a while; she's got some business to do there. And she's involved in the peace movement; she goes on marches to stop various wars. She's very sprightly. Her relatives think she shouldn't gallivant around so much.'

After Aggie and I have said our goodbyes, I sit on the orange sofa. The biscuits are on the plate and the kettle is full; the mugs are on a tray, and so is the jug of milk and the bowl of sugar. *So this is how you find out you are about to get divorced,* I think. *Over tea and almond biscuits on a bright summer evening.* I reach for my wedding ring – I've got used to twisting it round and round my finger – but of course it's not there. It's got lost.

I remember Fiona's pronouncements. When my marriage got lost, I really didn't hunt hard enough for it. I was half-hearted about it from the start, but that was because I didn't know what I really wanted. But I knew what I didn't want. I didn't want the nights alone while Diarmuid was with the mice, I didn't want a baby nine months later, I didn't want all the silences. And I became so obsessed with what I didn't want that I stopped seeing the good things I had. No wonder Diarmuid didn't want to talk to me; I kept complaining. We should have talked about the good things between us and helped them to grow. If I'd given him some compliments, I bet we could have negotiated instead of just arguing.

I throw a cushion at the floor. Feck it, why am I only realising all this now?

And then I know. It's because of Nathaniel. Because I was closed, too, just like Diarmuid; but Nathaniel has somehow opened me up, made me see the bigger picture.

I try to cheer myself up. There are plenty of advantages to being single again, of course. I can spend more time in the country. I could develop a rugged, outdoorsy side, like Fiona. That would sound good at Marie's family gathering. 'I cycled round Ireland last week. No, I didn't mind the rain; I had waterproof clothing. Yes, I know I've lost weight. I haven't eaten a biscuit for a month…' I need to relax. I'm all antsy and itchy and worried. I wish Erika were here to loosen me up with one of her massages.

I close my eyes and think of a beach with white sand and a hammock slung between two palm trees. I imagine a dusky-skinned waiter asking me if I'd like a piña colada. Palm trees and piña coladas, the soft swish of waves on white sand… that's what I want. I want to get brown and swim with dolphins… Then the waiter turns into Nathaniel, bending down to kiss me. He's touching my naked skin. He's dipping his finger into the piña colada and dripping it onto my breasts. He's…

The phone rings when he's expertly prising off my bikini bottoms. For a crazy moment I think it might be Eloise, telling me not to have imaginary sex with her boyfriend.

It's Erika, and she sounds very agitated. 'Oh, Sally, I've been such a fool!'

She says this a lot, and my job is to say that she hasn't been, and that whatever she's done is perfectly understandable in the circumstances. 'What happened?'

'I told him to get undressed.'

'Who?'

'The guy who came round here just now for a massage. I'd booked him in, and I was all prepared and excited. He was my first real client.' She sounds like she might cry. 'I didn't mention him when we were at Fiona's because I know you don't approve of me massaging strange men in my flat.'

I don't comment.

'Of course I didn't tell him to get undressed immediately. I brought him up to my bedroom, only you wouldn't know it's my bedroom because the bed is covered in cushions and I've got a screen in front of it...'

'And?' I'm getting rather worried.

'Then I showed him where the bathroom was, in case he needed... you know...'

'Naturally.'

'And then he started asking me whether there was a washing machine, which seemed a bit odd.'

'Indeed.'

'He also wanted to know if the area was noisy and if there was central heating. I thought he was just getting bashful, like Lionel, so I told him we could discuss that later. I said that once he'd got his clothes off and I started to work on him, he'd feel much more relaxed.'

'What happened?'

'He ran down the stairs like greased lightning, shouting that he wasn't the kind of man who visited prostitutes. He wasn't the massage client at all. He was a guy who rang me weeks ago about sharing the flat. I put up a notice in the newsagent's, in case Alex suddenly wants me to run off with him in a camper van.'

'Oh, dear.' I hope Erika can't hear my smile.

'He'd taken the address and said he'd call round sometime. I thought he'd forgotten. I shouted after him that it had been a misunderstanding, but I don't think he believed me.'

'Poor Erika,' I say. 'But I can see how it happened. It was... it was quite understandable in the circumstances.'

'Oh, bugger, the doorbell's going. It's probably the other guy. Bye.' The phone clatters down, and I wonder if I should march around and supervise Erika's massage; but then I'd miss Diarmuid, if he even bothers to show up.

The phone rings again almost immediately. It must

be Diarmuid. He just couldn't face me. He wants to say whatever it is from a safe distance.

But it isn't Diarmuid; it's Greta, and she's sounding very determined.

'Sally!' she gushes. 'I need a favour from you.'

Oh, shit. She wants me to say those awful table-mats that look like matted dog hair are must-buys.

'Sorry it's so last-minute, dear, but the tickets are booked, all you need is your passport.'

Passport?

'The flight is tomorrow at 10.30 a.m. – a very civilised hour. Of course, you'll need to be there about two hours beforehand.'

'Greta,' I say, wondering if she wants me to pop over to Birmingham to discuss rattan storage units. 'Where do you want me to go?'

'New York, dear, didn't I say that?'

I clutch the phone tightly. *'New York?'*

'Yes. Can you go? It's only for a few days.'

'Mmm….' I don't want to sound too available. I wait for three whole seconds before saying, 'Yes… yes, I think so. I could probably rearrange some meetings.'

'Oh, I'm so relieved. It's just a few interviews. I'm taking out a large ad feature in *Irish-American*, about top young Irish designers based in the Big Apple. I can get quotes from some of them on the phone, but I really want you to meet these three – they're *fabulous*. We need a sense of the buzz around them. And hammer home the fact that they're Irish, of course; the magazine's readers are very loyal to the Old Country. I'll send you an e-mail right now with all the details. You can collect the tickets at the airport.'

'That sounds great,' I say, trying to sound enthusiastic but not overexcited. And I am enthusiastic. *New York!* Suddenly, instead of being just a woman who has mislaid her marriage, I am a jet-setting cosmopolitan international journalist.

Greta hangs up just as the doorbell rings. I put down the receiver and walk slowly towards the door. I know Diarmuid will be looking solemn – solemn and sad, and a bit guilty about being late.

But he isn't. He's smiling broadly and carrying a big parcel. He looks both shy and excited, and a little nervous.

'You'll understand why I'm late when you see this,' he says, marching over to the coffee table and putting the parcel down.

'What is it?'

'Open it and find out.'

It's not my birthday; it's not the anniversary of my engagement or my wedding. I stare at the parcel dubiously.

Inside it is a music box shaped like a Swiss chalet. All the details are perfect. 'When you wind it up,' Diarmuid says, 'it plays "Edelweiss".'

Chapter Twenty-Four

'I'M SO GLAD YOU like it.' Diarmuid smiles at me. We are lying snuggled together in my double bed. The music box is on my bedside table. He knew I'd lost the one I loved, so he made me another one. It's gorgeous. Aggie will love it too. I burst into tears of happiness when I saw it. When you open it up, there's a small figurine of a woman in a pink dress – she was an ornament for a wedding cake, but he got his sister to give her a new outfit. She is smiling with all the joy of a new bride. Diarmuid hunted around for ages for 'Edelweiss'; eventually he tracked it down on the Internet. He made the box in the workshop in his parents' house, during study breaks (I was right about him studying at his parents' to get away from Barry's CDs). That's why his phone was out of range so often: his parents live in a valley north of Dublin, and Diarmuid has to climb a nearby hill if he wants his mobile to work.

Of course, I didn't need to sleep with him just because he'd made this lovely gift. In fact, it would have been more sensible not to, because we have so much to talk about. But he'd also brought a bottle of wine with him, and he insisted that we drink it with the almond biscuits… It was the cheap-drunk thing all over again.

By this stage of the evening I thought we'd be discussing our divorce. I'm still somewhat dazed by the sudden resumption of our affections. Diarmuid really is an amazingly forgiving man. After all I've put him through, the last thing I thought he'd be doing was making something so special for me. I've been so wrong about him; I've jumped to all sorts of unfair conclusions.

He must have spent ages making the box. No wonder he didn't have time to meet me. I thought he didn't care, but he does; he must.

'Would you like some tea?' I ask. I seem to have sobered up quite quickly. I'm hungry now; in fact, I feel a deep yearning for some takeaway fish and chips.

'No, let's just stay here a bit longer.' He nuzzles my shoulder. Diarmuid is a good nuzzler. He's great in bed all round, in fact. I particularly like it when he massages my toes. And the fireworks really get going when he kisses that special spot behind my ear. He went straight for it as soon as the bottle of wine was opened. Our lovemaking was very passionate. I just wish there weren't quite so many biscuit crumbs in the bed; all the bouncing around must have dislodged them from inside the pillowcase or something.

It feels strange, lying here and not talking. But maybe Diarmuid is right; maybe all this talking stuff is overrated. He is a wonderful lover, and he has made me this beautiful present. He still wants me. Surely that says all I need to know about his feelings?

I am the Sally who married him again, and I'm going back to him. I can't think of any good reason not to. We'll make the marriage Fiona talked about. We've got past the stupid part where you want everything to be romantic and schmaltzy. This is the cake, and it's nice. It's tasty. We can go to Marie's family gathering together, so I won't even have to cycle round Ireland to distract them from my divorce. Maybe we should start a family immediately, before I change my mind again. And if I get pregnant soon, that will stop Aggie talking about DeeDee; she'll completely forget about her in the excitement. I'm almost sad I used my diaphragm. I stare up at the ceiling and think of little Milly's gurgles. Yes, a baby would get rid of this ridiculous restlessness that lunges at me out of the blue.

It's in the family genes, I'm sure of it. DeeDee definitely has the same tendency, and so has my mother – after all, she almost went AWOL out in California. It definitely affects April, too. She couldn't wait to leave Ireland. She whooshed off as soon as she'd got her American passport – because she was born there, she didn't have to plead for a Green Card. And then, of course, there was Aggie's recent bid for freedom. Even at Marie's family gatherings, my cousins talk ardently about weekend yachting and hiking and windsurfing, as though they can't stand to spend protracted periods in their own houses.

I lean on Diarmuid's sturdy chest and listen to his heart. This feels so snug, so cosy. That's what I missed most when he was so taken up with the mice – that snug feeling we have when we nestle like this.

'I'm giving the mice back to the laboratory,' he says, as if he's read my thoughts. 'The research is over. They can just grow fat and old now and eat what they like. I think they'll be used for breeding… they might enjoy that.' He gives me a naughty smile. 'I'm sorry I got so obsessed with them. It's just that I didn't know what to say to you. You seemed so disappointed.'

I peer at him. 'Disappointed?'

'Yes. I could see it on your face. You were disappointed in me. I thought I bored you. All your friends are so much more… sophisticated, I suppose. I'm pretty basic.' He smiles at me ruefully. 'I have no hidden depths. I'm sorry.'

'Of course you have hidden depths,' I protest. 'You're a lovely man. And you're kind, too.'

He deepens his head on the pillow. It is ten o'clock at night and still light outside. We can hear the sound of the ocean through the open window, the soft swish of the wind through the leaves of the mimosa tree in the garden.

'I really did try to phone, that day Aggie went missing,' I say. 'I longed for you. I knew you'd be able to comfort me.'

'I'm sorry.' He runs the back of his hand lightly over my cheek.

'It's all right. You're here now,' I say. 'I'd even begun to think you were back with Becky.'

'She's in Galway with her boyfriend.'

'Yes.' I smile at him. 'I believe that now, but I didn't before. And, even if you were with her, I thought I had no right to be angry.'

'Why?'

'Because I was a bolting bride – that's what my Uncle Bob calls me. I really did think you might never forgive me. Especially

207

when you saw me with Nathaniel... even though he really is just a friend.' I kiss his forehead. 'You're a much better person than I am.'

Diarmuid seems to stiffen slightly.

'What is it?' I glance at him worriedly.

'Nothing.'

'Are you sure?'

'Yes.' He suddenly sits up and gets out of bed. Then he starts hunting on the floor for his boxer shorts.

'Are you going?' I stare at him disbelievingly.

'Yes.'

'*Why?*'

He pulls on his jeans and navy sweatshirt, finds his socks and ties the laces of his runners. Any minute he is going to march out of the room.

I leap up and race to the bedroom door to block his exit. I stand there like someone in a film, panting, almost hissing. 'I can't do this, Diarmuid. I can't be with you if you clam up every time we need to talk about something.'

Diarmuid suddenly slumps onto the bed and puts his face in his hands.

'What on earth is it?' I sit down beside him.

'Oh, Sally...' He looks at me bleakly. 'I haven't forgiven you. I've been furious. I've... I've felt so humiliated.' He runs his hands agitatedly through his thick black hair. 'I keep thinking of the wedding – those grand declarations in front of everyone, the presents, the photographs. I don't know what to do with the photographs, whether to keep them in an album or throw them away.'

'Oh, Diarmuid.' I lean forward. Our noses are almost touching. 'You're so faithful and kind and sweet. I really wish you'd married someone nicer.'

'Stop *saying* that!' He is suddenly shouting. 'It's not true. I'm not those things.'

'You are! Look how you behaved this evening, coming round with the beautiful music box, bringing the wine... and seducing me so expertly.' I trace a finger tenderly along his arm.

He pulls away sharply. 'I did it because I felt guilty.'

'Why?' I gaze at him. 'Because you weren't there when I phoned, when Aggie went missing?'

He shakes his head numbly. His eyes look dull and miserable. 'No. Because I got so insanely jealous when I saw you with…'

'Nathaniel?'

'Yes. I know you said you were just friends… but you looked so close. So right together, somehow. I couldn't stand it.'

'But you looked so calm – almost as if you didn't care.'

'I can hide my feelings; surely you know that. I can do it well… too well, probably.'

'OK, so you felt jealous,' I say soothingly. 'That's understandable. But he really does have a girlfriend who makes cabinets. I wasn't lying.'

'I know that now.' Diarmuid looks down at the cheap, multicoloured Indian rug beside my bed. 'I saw them together a couple of days later. They were in the newsagent's together, returning a DVD. She was holding his hand.'

'Sounds like Eloise, all right.' I manage to say it without any trace of emotion.

'I should have stayed with you that evening. You'd had a difficult day, and you were worried about Aggie… But I didn't. It all seemed to get to me suddenly. I'm like that sometimes; I let things build up.' He glances at me apologetically. 'I couldn't face revising that evening, so I decided to take Charlene up on her offer of dinner. She's the colleague I've been –'

'Teaching to drive.' I complete the sentence for him. 'Which is very kind of you. I'm sure she's very grateful. No wonder she wanted to cook you dinner.'

'Barry was having another barbecue,' Diarmuid continues. He is speaking so softly I have to lean forward to hear him. 'I didn't want to go home… to what was supposed to be our home.' He pauses and takes a deep breath. 'I wanted to be away from everything… everything that reminded me of you.' His words sound hollow, as though he's heaving them up reluctantly.

'Was the meal nice?' I ask, too brightly. I don't like the way he's talking. I almost wish he'd shut up. I miss his silence now. It was far more restful.

'She'd had an argument with her boyfriend. It's a very on-off situation. He's sort of volatile.' Diarmuid sighs. 'We drank far too much wine. We were both lonely. We hardly knew what we were doing.'

I sit completely still.

'Oh, Sally, it's such a mess. I can't believe it.'

'Just tell me, Diarmuid,' I say. 'Just tell me.'

'I slept with her.'

I stare at the Indian rug. I feel numb and cold and strange, as if I'm watching us talking. As if this isn't happening to me at all.

'I meant to go home, but I'd drunk too much to drive. She lives in Glencree, in County Wicklow; there's no way I could have faced the dual carriageway.'

'Do you love her?' I say, before Diarmuid starts to expound on the importance of sobriety when one is in charge of a vehicle.

'We were drunk, Sally!'

'Do you love her?'

He places his elbows on his thighs and hunches over. He appears to be intently studying the floorboards. 'I think she loves me. I didn't know that before. My mind was full of you, but I should have seen it.' He turns towards me suddenly. 'She wants me, Sally. She wants me to live with her.'

I can't meet his eyes. I feel fooled and angry. We have just made love. He should have told me beforehand; then we wouldn't have done it. I feel the way Diarmuid must have felt when I bolted out of the house and left him on his own with the photographs and the presents and all the new bouncy furniture. I want to be angry with him, but I don't know if I have the right to be. I always knew he might find someone else if I left him. I knew it might come to this.

Even so, I wonder if I should pick up the music box and hit

210

him over the head with it. I could also demand that he leave the house immediately. Or I could throw a jug of water at him. It wouldn't stain the carpet or the rug. It would just need to be mopped up with a paper towel.

'You're not even angry, are you?' Diarmuid says. 'Not really. Not the way you should be.'

'I am angry, but after the way I've treated you, I suppose I'm just not that surprised.'

'Are you in love with Nathaniel?' He searches my face.

'He's in love with Eloise.'

'That's not what I asked.'

'I know. You should have told me about Charlene earlier.'

'I almost didn't tell you about her at all, but I couldn't stand you putting yourself down like that and making me sound so... so bloody virtuous.'

'Were you planning to seduce me this evening?'

'No, honestly... I just meant to give you the music box. But you seemed so pleased and so fond of me again, and...' He looks at me a bit bashfully. 'The old chemistry came back for a while, didn't it?' I cannot dispute this.

He clenches his jaw. 'Maybe, if I'm honest, I also told you about Charlene because I wanted to see how you'd react.'

'Oh, Diarmuid.' I sigh. 'Maybe we've said enough about it all for the moment.'

After a moment he murmurs, 'Come back to me, Sally. Come back to me and let's try to forget this happened.'

I look numbly at a patchwork cushion. I can't believe what he's suggesting.

'What about Charlene?' I whisper.

'I can't live with her.'

'Why not?'

'Because we're too different. She comes from an entirely different culture.'

'County Wicklow?' I peer at him like I might peer at a strange creature in a zoo, a creature whose habits and predilections are still something of a mystery.

'She's from South Africa. And I don't feel ready, anyway.'

211

'Ready for what?'

'Ready to live with someone else. What about us, Sally? What about our marriage?'

'That's something you should have asked yourself before you slept with another woman.' I look away from him. He looks so lonely – lonely and lost and sad – and all I can feel is very, very tired.

Chapter Twenty-Five

'DIARMUID SLEPT WITH CHARLENE.'

'He slept with a *bean?*'

'Oh, for God's sake, Erika, why would Diarmuid sleep with a bean?'

'That's what it sounded like.' Erika is sounding extremely groggy. I must have woken her up.

'He slept with *Charlene.*'

'Good.' Her voice is thick with sleep. 'That's great.'

'What do you mean, that's great?'

'Now you can run off with Nathaniel and no one will mind.' She yawns. 'What time is it?' Erika tends to go to bed at ten-thirty unless there is a good reason not to.

'Midnight. I'm sorry for phoning you so late. Diarmuid only left ten minutes ago.'

'How did you find out?'

'He told me.'

'*Great!* So now he can't deny it. You can run into Nathaniel's arms and no one, not even Diarmuid's bitch of a mother, will be able to scold you.'

'I don't plan to tell everyone,' I reply, somewhat primly. 'And, anyway, Nathaniel doesn't want me to run into his arms. He has a girlfriend.'

Erika bursts into tears.

'What is it, Erika?'

'It's nothing,' she howls into the phone.

'I knew he had a girlfriend,' I say softly. 'Please don't get so upset about it.'

'It's awful,' she wails. 'Every wonderful man has someone else. I can't stand it.'

There is a long pause. Then she says, 'Alex doesn't want to see me any more. He rang this evening, just after my massage client left. I've been in bed since. I drank a whole bottle of wine.'

'Oh, Erika.'

'I bet it was the camping that did it,' she sniffles miserably. 'When they survived camping together, they probably realised they could stay married.' I still don't know why Erika thinks camping is so terrible, but this isn't the time to point out that some people actually enjoy it. 'He said he'd prefer to be with me but he couldn't bear leaving the children.'

'What about her and her yoga teacher?'

'He's gay. I should have known it by the prim way he carried his yoga mat.'

'Oh, dear. I'm so sorry.'

'That's it now,' Erika declares. 'I'm single forever. I'm on the sideboard.'

I try to cheer her up, but after half an hour I realise I should at least make some attempt to pack for New York.

'I'm sorry, Erika, I have to go. I've got to pack.'

'Why?'

'I have to go to New York. It's a last-minute assignment.'

'When?'

'Tomorrow morning.'

'Tomorrow morning?'

'Yes.'

Erika takes a deep breath; then she says firmly, 'I'm coming with you.'

I don't know how this happened. It is seven o'clock on a sunny July morning, and I am in Fiona's car, on the way to the airport. Erika is in the car too. We are all going to New York because we need to shop for shoes.

Of course, I'm also going to New York to interview three people about furniture and accessories, but that seems a mere extra. And Fiona is also going to New York because her husband may leave her at any moment. She is absolutely convinced of this: once he gets the results of the blood tests, she says, he'll be off like an Olympic sprinter. He's taken some days off to help out with Milly, and Fiona is leaving him with her in the hope that they may 'bond' more closely. This won't prevent him from divorcing her, she claims, but it would be nice if they could remain friends.

Erika is going to New York because she needs a new pair of flip-flops – they're the only shoes she can afford at the moment, especially since she borrowed the airfare from Fiona. She rang Fiona as soon as she spoke to me, late last night, to ask if she could borrow the money, and Fiona said she wanted to go to New York too. She's booked us all into some fancy hotel her company has some arrangement with. She and Erika are on a slightly later flight.

'New York, New York…' We're trying to sing the song, only we don't know the words, so Erika starts to shout, 'West Cork, West Cork!' She's a little overexcited. 'We'll just forget about men entirely,' she suddenly declares. She knows about Milly now; Fiona told her last night. She was naturally gobsmacked, but she seems to have adjusted to the news. 'We'll go horse-riding and start a drag boy band and sing songs about cats.'

Erika's slight hysteria is partly caused by the fact that she's terrified of flying and feels we might arrive in New York. She has about fifty kinds of calming herbal tablets with her.

'It's nice to be in this mess all together,' Fiona says. 'We might as well enjoy our failures. Life has passed us by, hasn't it? It hasn't been what we thought it would be at all.'

'Yes!' Erika and I agree cheerfully. We don't point out to Fiona that her life has been spectacularly successful. It is not a day for details. For example, they think my marriage is over – and so do I, only I can't seem to tell Diarmuid. It's almost as if I've got used to being a partial wife. Maybe it's the only way I can stick being married. Married to anyone at all.

I feel a thrill of excitement as I admire the suspension bridges and the soaring buildings, from the cab taking me to our hotel. I feel the caress of hot, muggy, agitated New York air. I look up at the huge sky. New York. I am in New York. Even the air seems bouncy and alert, electric. So many people, so many colours – people skateboarding, walking to work in smart suits and trainers, dog-walking, eating bagels. Big

215

brownstone buildings, old and grand. Scary-looking strangers. Smiles. A huge, exultant mixture.

I reach into my bag for my purse – I want to get the fare ready – but my fingers close over a notebook. I've somehow brought the recipe notebook with me. I must be careful not to lose it. The paper is dimpled; the roof of Nathaniel's car leaks slightly, and when he found the notebook on the floor it had got a bit damp after some rain. I put it back in my bag carefully, find my purse and keep it ready in my hand.

I sit back in my seat. The strong New York sun is streaming through the window, and everything seems bright and shiny; the windows on the buildings we pass are gleaming like fluorescent bulbs. I put on my sunglasses and wonder if it was a bad idea to ring April from Dublin airport. I told her I was coming to New York, and she said I should fly on to California and visit her, but I said I couldn't. I said I was too busy. It's the kind of thing she probably would have said herself; but I don't talk to her like that.

I'm the one who's usually more polite and sensitive. She even sounded slightly hurt. I'll never understand April – but I wish she'd come home occasionally. My parents miss her terribly, but they don't say it. I've always known they love her more than me. That's why I needed Aggie so much when I was younger: with her, I never felt second best.

My parents didn't love April more at first. When she was born, they were both understandably reluctant about her. My father could hardly bear to look at her; and my mother cooed and clucked over her dutifully, but her heart wasn't really in it. She was tired and sad and scared. Sometimes, when April cried, Mum held her and cried too. It wasn't the most ideal introduction to the world, and one could almost sense April's outrage. Even then, she was a fighter. Her demands grew louder; she screeched and hollered and punched the air with her tiny hands.

My father normally ignored this. He glanced at her and walked away, waiting for someone else to attend to her. But then, one day, Mum was out getting something from the store and I was left to look after April, and she wouldn't shut up. Her face was puce and her whole body was taut with anger. I lifted her up and cradled her, but she wriggled around so much she almost fell out of my arms. My father came over and told me to put her back in her cot; Mum would be home any minute. When he spoke, April fixed him with her big brown baby eyes.

Something happened in that moment – something that made him take her from me and hold her, rather warily. His arms were stiff and angular; there was no tenderness in them. But April leaned her plump little cheek against his chest anyway, with a deep sigh. All of her body suddenly relaxed, and his did too. Dad moved slowly to a chair and sat down, resting his chin on her head. They just sat there, silently. And when Mum came back they were both fast asleep.

My reverie is interrupted as the cab driver leans out the window and shouts an expletive at another motorist. He's gruff and burly, and the hunched look of his back does not encourage conversation. I look out the window again and drink in the skyscrapers, the gleaming Hudson River, the green tops of the trees in Central Park in the distance. But I am still thinking of April. She has always been a puzzle to me. I want to love her, but I don't know how. I don't know how to reach her.

I let my mind return to that day when Dad surrendered to his love for her. My mother was so relieved that the baby who could have parted them had somehow become their strongest link. April needed love, and she wasn't going to go without it. Where another child might have grown quiet and listless and resigned, she had grown more determined. You couldn't help admiring her spirit, her cunning baby instinct that love could, in certain circumstances, be demanded. And, once my father found he could love April, something softened in him. He no longer looked at Mum with that hard glint in his eyes. And so they stayed together, even though I could see Mum often dreamed of leaving. They stayed together because of April, not because of me.

It makes no sense, of course. If you were to look at it straight on, you could see that clearly Dad should have remained dubious about this baby, who probably wasn't even his. But the heart doesn't work in that way. It has its own reasons. And when April began to look more and more like him, it seemed like a kind of miracle. It was almost as though she had chosen him as her father when she could have chosen someone else.

I don't know why being in New York is suddenly reminding me of all this. New York is so different from California, it could almost be another country. As the cab growls its way towards central Manhattan, I suddenly have a terrible yearning to be back in the golden hills outside San Francisco. I want to see April again, but I also want to find the part of me I lost.

Because I see, now, that when my parents turned their love to April I decided something. I decided that, when it came to love and I had a rival, I would always end up second best. I would not be the first choice, but the backup. That's why it made perfect sense to marry Diarmuid, even though I thought he preferred Becky, and it's why I can accept Nathaniel's love for Eloise so calmly: because it's what I know. It's what I'm used to.

I gaze up at the skyscrapers. I used to think I wanted love like the house we had in California – love that was big and rambling and somehow cosy too; love with lots of rooms and sunshine, and weird sentimental stuff laid out on the mantelpiece. But the house lacked storage space and the wooden floorboards creaked, and the big lawn often got too brown and wild and scraggly. That's why we left California eventually: Mum began to long for a semi-detached home in the Dublin suburbs. She wanted to go home to a house that was orderly and tidy, and this is what she now has. And maybe she's right; maybe that kind of home is better. It makes life simpler. You don't have to decide what colour mug you want, because they're all the same, and Mum and Dad must save hours each month not having to mow the lawn. As you get older, you begin to long for convenience. Maybe love is like that too: when you get to a certain age, you need it to be tidier. That's why I should be glad Nathaniel has Eloise. He is too boisterous and messy for me. Life with him would never be settled.

The cab reaches the hotel. It's a tall white building with potted palms on each side of the large glass door. I pay the driver, and the hotel's uniformed doorman puts my small suitcase onto a trolley. I follow him into the foyer. It's cool and airy, and there is a large glass chandelier hanging from the high, sky-blue ceiling. The reception desk has a white marble top, and the auburn-haired woman behind it is immaculately manicured and smiling at me somewhat fixedly.

'I'm Sally Adams,' I say. 'My friend Fiona O'Driscoll made the booking, so it could be under her name. She'll be arriving in an hour or so.'

'Fine. I'll just check for you.' The woman smiles. She's wearing very shiny red lipstick, and I'm so tired that I can't help staring at it. It has obviously been applied with great care; you can see that she used a lip-liner to emphasise every curve.

As she's reaching for the keys to my room, I feel someone nudging my elbow. I turn around sharply and find myself facing April.

Chapter Twenty-Six

'YOU KNOW HOW YOU keep telling me I should be more open?' April says. 'Well, I've decided that maybe you're right. It's time you knew.'

'Knew what?' We're sitting in the hotel's swanky lounge, and I'm drinking a cup of tea. I am light-headed with jet lag. I feel as though I'm dreaming – but April does look very real, sitting there in her trim navy trouser suit. I can even smell her. She always wears very expensive perfume. She looks very blonde and tanned and grown-up.

'I've bought Mum's birthday present.'

'Oh.' I sit back in my seat. I don't know why she should think this is a secret, but the workings of April's mind have always been a mystery to me. 'That's nice.'

'Will you take it back with you? I don't know if it'll arrive in time if I post it.' She opens her handbag and hands me a small box. 'It's a diamond brooch. I think she'll like it.'

'Goodness, yes. I'm sure she will.' I stare at the box. It is exquisitely wrapped in gold paper and has curly pink ribbons cascading from its top.

'It was expensive.'

'Yes, I'm sure it was. She'll be thrilled with it.'

'It's a kind of guilt-gift, really. I know I've upset her.'

I think of Diarmuid's music box. 'Why would you say that?'

'Let's have some champagne.'

'OK...' I look at her warily as she bounces to her feet and marches towards a waiter. I'm feeling drunk already, but seeing April again surely calls for some kind of celebration. I still can't quite work out why she flew over from California on the spur of the moment. Perhaps the brooch really is very expensive and she wanted it delivered personally.

'This is such a lovely surprise, April,' I say as she returns. 'You must have dashed to the airport as soon as I phoned.'

'I have some business to do here anyway.' Her voice is

220

crisp and toneless.

The champagne arrives, and the waiter opens it expertly with a quiet pop. I put down my cup of tea and reach for my glass. April empties hers in one determined gulp.

'You look great,' I say.

'You've put on weight... but it kind of suits you.' She gives me a calculating glance. 'I'm sorry about Diarmuid. I didn't quite know what to say to you about him. And, anyway, I think marriage is outdated, don't you?' She fills her glass again. 'What we have these days is serial monogamy. Most people just aren't meant to stick with one person forever.'

I want to disagree with her. I want to say that sticking with one person forever must be wonderful, if you know how to do it. It's a skill – I know that now. It's not just icing and cake; it's also weird casseroles and leftover quiche and low-fat biscuits.

'I've got used to being a partial wife.' I smile at her. 'In a strange way, it sort of suits me. The sudden reconciliations can be quite exciting... and sexy. And you get nice presents.'

'Do you think you'll stay a partial wife?'

'You know something?' I stretch my legs out languorously. The champagne is already going to my head. 'If Diarmuid agreed to it, I just might. Some people do that, you know. They get married and live in different houses.'

'It wouldn't suit you,' April says. 'You're too much of a romantic for that kind of thing. You'd begin to yearn for long, rambling midnight conversations about the meaning of life and love and laundry.'

'*Laundry?*' I tilt my head sideways. It feels very heavy suddenly.

'You want to understand *everything*, Sally. Haven't you noticed that? I bet you could already write a thesis on why you got engaged to Diarmuid and why you married him and why you left him. I bet you already have about a thousand theories.'

'Not quite that many.' I hiccup. This champagne is particularly fizzy.

'But I don't think we can understand everything. Some things are just mysteries.'

'Yes.' I look at her. April doesn't normally talk about this sort of thing.

'I think you should start dating again.'

'You've told me that a number of times already, April, but I just don't feel like it. If I can't be a partial wife, I want to be a contented and eccentric spinster. I'll keep busy trying to help my friends; they seem to get themselves into all sorts of weird situations.' I think of Fiona and Milly, and Erika, and Diarmuid... Oh, God, am I already thinking of Diarmuid as a *friend?*

'I'm sorry I didn't come to your wedding,' April says abruptly.

I don't know what to say to that. It perplexed us all, frankly, but naturally we didn't talk about it. My parents remained tight-lipped and disappointed, and I was too busy worrying about crucial things like how many layers should be on the cake and whether it could, just possibly, contain chocolate. (I left the chocolate out, eventually; the bakery said it might affect the texture.) Marie was the only member of the family who kept phoning April for an explanation.

'It's all right, April,' I say from my champagne haze. 'We understood. You... you had that conference.'

'No, I didn't. I just couldn't face them.'

'Who?'

'Mum and Dad.' April's face is wan and tense, and her lower lip is trembling.

I lean forward and touch her arm. 'But they love you, April. They love you so much.'

'Oh, Sally... Haven't you ever guessed? Haven't you ever even suspected?'

'What?' I am feeling extremely jumpy.

'That's what I came here to tell you. I couldn't keep it a secret any longer. It's been so lonely.'

'What?' By now I'm almost hopping around in my seat.

'Al is my father. Mum and Dad have known for years.'

I am completely dumbfounded. I gawp at April as though I

222

have just swallowed the hotel's very large and fancy chandelier.

'They had the test done when I was one. That's why we went back to Dublin. Dad said he couldn't stand having Al hanging around wanting to visit me – and Mum, of course. He decided we should all go back to Ireland and pretend I was his child.'

'How... how did you find out?' I am almost whispering, though what surprises me most is that I am not more surprised. Because when I look at April now, really look at her, I see she doesn't look like my father at all. I must have convinced myself of the similarities because I wanted to, and my parents must have encouraged the deception; but, deep down, I must always have had my suspicions.

'I found out when I was twelve. I overheard Mum and Dad talking about it one day. They thought I was off with friends, but I'd come back to ask them for money – a whole gang of us had decided to get our ears pierced. They were in the sitting room, talking about when they should tell me, and I walked in on them and said, "Well, now you don't have to." Mum burst into tears. She made me promise to keep it a secret.'

I feel numb. The whole landscape of my past has been altered. It seems to me that April shouldn't have just announced this. There should have been more of a build-up. There should have been some hints.

But, of course, there probably were hints – loads of them, if I had chosen to see them. I think of the hushed conversations that ended when I walked into the room; the way Mum kept repeating how alike April and Dad were. I even remember, suddenly, the day April shouted, 'You're not my proper father!' at Dad when he said she couldn't get a tattoo. I put it down to teenage petulance. I just thought we were a normal, slightly dysfunctional family.

'Mum kept saying she was sorry and it had no effect on how much they loved me.' April twists the leather strap of her bag round her fingers. 'But I knew it did. I knew that was why they'd always loved you more.'

I gawp at her. This declaration is almost as surprising as the last one. 'But they've always loved you more, April,' I correct her. 'They really have.'

'That's nonsense, Sally! They didn't care when I went off on my mountain bike for hours. They didn't even ask what I was getting up to.'

'That's because you were that kind of child. You seemed to *need* to whiz around the place.'

'They wouldn't have let you do that.' She looks at me accusingly. 'They gave you piano lessons. They drove you there and brought you home, and Mum always gave you a mug of tea and biscuits after the class. She never gave me tea and biscuits like that.'

'It's only because she knew I hated my piano lessons!' I get the vague sense that we're going off on a tangent, but suddenly this seems terribly important. 'You should have seen the way Dad held you when you were a baby.'

'That's because he thought I was his.'

'No, he didn't, April. He really didn't. I can see that, looking back on the time just after you were born. At first he didn't want to have much to do with you, actually…' I wish I didn't have to say that, but it's true. 'Then one day you were crying and Mum was out, and I couldn't comfort you. You were screeching.' I take her hand. 'Dad was about to walk away when he looked at you – and something happened. He fell in love with your big, bright spirit and the way you wouldn't be ignored. He fell in love because you pulled it out of him, and that's so special. It's never gone away. Mum and Dad stayed together because of you, I'm sure of it. You taught them how to love again – in a different way, maybe, but they found they could stay together.'

April is sniffing and dabbing her eyes. 'You just made that up, didn't you?'

'No, really. It's true.' I feel terribly tired. I wish I could go to Central Park and sit under a tree and collect my thoughts. Instead, I say the first thing that comes into my head.

'Maybe they love us both equally, but in different ways.' It's only when I've said it that I realise it's probably true.

224

'They decided you were the wild one, and I was quiet and studious and dutiful. I suppose it was more convenient. You know how Mum likes things to be tidy and orderly. They somehow didn't see that we were both mixtures of all sorts of other things, too.'

April sniffs dubiously.

I decide just to say it. 'I love you, April.'

'And I love you,' she says. 'Even though I wish you'd stop wearing that awful lipstick.'

I have to laugh. I laugh because sometimes I love April's rugged unsentimentality, and sometimes I hate it.

April remains serious. 'I came to California because I needed to get to know Al – I call him Al; I don't call him Dad. I didn't really plan to stay, but I like it there. I know Mum and Dad are disappointed that I've got close to Al.'

'Have you ever talked to them about it?'

'No.'

'I think you should.'

April just says, 'You should visit me. I'd love you to visit me.' She looks at her watch. 'I'll have to go soon. I've got to meet someone and then I'm getting a flight back to San Francisco.'

Just as she announces this, Erika and Fiona arrive. 'So here you are!' Erika exclaims. 'We'd thought you'd be in your room...'

'Or in the Jacuzzi,' Fiona adds. 'We even checked.'

They look at April.

'This is my sister, April.'

Fiona smiles. 'Oh, yes, of course. How lovely to see you again, April. You look fabulous.'

April does in fact look extremely glamorous and cosmopolitan, and Erika stares at her with undisguised awe. 'We only met once,' she says shyly. 'You probably don't remember, but I made a cat for you when you left for California – or, at least, I made it for Sally to give to you. I came round to your house with it and –'

'Wow! I love that cat!' April interrupts. 'It's on my mantelpiece. Loads of people admire it.'

Erika almost purrs with joy, and I look at April gratefully. She seems to be telling the truth. Though her eyes are a bit puffy, she is regaining her usual poise and briskness. In fact, I suspect she's happy that we've been interrupted. I don't think she could have dealt with that emotional intensity for much longer.

'So what have you two been talking about?' Fiona says as she sits down. 'Catching up on all the gossip?'

April and I glance at each other. 'Yes,' I say. 'We've had a great chat. She just decided to fly here to see me – isn't that great?'

'Wonderful.' Fiona beams.

'So are you over here on business too?' April enquires. There is something lighter about her. Though her eyes are sad, I can see she's relieved she has finally shared her secret with me. The tension has gone from her face; she looks less guarded.

'No. Fiona and I are here to shop for shoes,' Erika says solemnly. You can see she's savouring this declaration.

April begins to give her advice on shops, and Fiona listens eagerly, since she is the one who can actually afford to buy herself top-class Italian footwear. The thing is, she is also wondering if she should go back to the airport and fly straight home. She's fretting terribly about Milly, even though she left a supply of expressed breast milk in the freezer – she has been methodically storing it since Milly's birth and sometimes feeds her using a bottle. Her breasts are aching; in fact, her whole body is yearning to hold Milly, immediately if not sooner.

'I hope Milly's all right,' she says, for the hundredth time.

'Look, you left five pages of notes about her for the nanny,' Erika points out. 'And Zak is there, and your mother. The poor child is probably longing for some time to herself. And, anyway, we'll be flying home tomorrow. You'll be seeing her in a few *hours*.'

Fiona calms down slightly.

'So what kind of shoes are you looking for?' April turns to Erika.

'Flip-flops. They're the only kind I can afford.' She bursts into embarrassed giggles.

'I know a place where you could get fabulous flip-flops. They decorate them with all sorts of stuff – flowers, mermaids, cats…'

'Have you any advice on where to buy really good socks?' I ask April, when Erika has drawn a small map of where to find the flip-flop shop and is peering at it cautiously. She doesn't really understand maps; she prefers to keep asking people for directions.

'Socks?' Erika and Fiona stare at me.

'Yes. Since I can't afford new shoes, I want new socks.'

April bursts out laughing.

'You know something, Sally?' Fiona says grandly. 'I think we should discuss this important matter over some more champagne.'

Chapter Twenty-Seven

ERIKA HAS A FABULOUS new pair of flip-flops and I have a magnificent new pair of socks. They are hand-knitted cashmere and have an intricate design in a variety of pleasing colours. They're the kind of socks rich women from Connecticut wear on skiing holidays to Aspen, and because I own them I feel richer and blonder and more tanned. April bought them for me. She dashed through her 'business meeting' in fifteen minutes and joined us.

It has been a wonderful afternoon – even though, by rights, it should be late evening. Somehow the fact that time has got jumbled up is helping me to adjust to the news that April is my half-sister. If time can rearrange itself like that, other things can too. It's almost as if I believe April was my full sister until I met her in the hotel, and then the details suddenly altered, so I just had to adjust to this parallel version.

It takes me time to absorb huge information like this. I only truly realised I was married a month after the wedding. This will probably happen in stages, too, until one day I'll say, '*Oh my God, Al is April's father!*' in the middle of an interview about wallpaper. In the meantime I'm in semi-denial and trying to comfort Erika, who is crying because she'll always be on the sideboard. We are all in another swanky room in the hotel, having coffee and cakes.

'I loved him so much,' Erika is telling April. 'I can't imagine life without him.'

The waiter arrives with the cakes. They look gorgeous, like ornate and luxurious hats with strange, delicious things poking out of them. The chocolate ones are virtually sculptures. Erika briefly forgets her almost unbearable grief and decides she wants the meringue, which is stuffed with fresh cream and raspberries and tiny chocolate truffles.

'I just can't believe it,' she says. 'I really did think he'd leave her... Oh, this cake is delicious. Do you think they make them or buy them in?' Her mouth is stuffed with it and she has a bit of cream on her nose.

'I don't know if I'll ever be happy again after Zak leaves me,' Fiona says. 'It's so unfair that she can't be his child. He'll probably leave after the christening. He'll put on a good show, and then he'll go.' She chooses the chocolate cake, rather than the virtuous pastry full of tropical fruit, and stares at it.

'At least you got a really nice pair of shoes, Fiona,' Erika says. 'That shop was so huge and gleamy – and did you see that assistant's nails? She must spend hours looking after them. That's why I could never live in New York.'

'Because of the nails?' April looks at her.

'Yes, and the hair and the teeth. They're all so magnificently *groomed*. I wouldn't be ready until five o'clock, and then the day would be almost over.'

'A lot of them get the grooming done professionally,' April says. Her own sleek blonde hair has all the hallmarks of a salon blow-dry.

'Yes, but I can't afford to go to a hairdresser every three days,' Erika replies. 'If my cats sold better, I might be able to, but the sales are very sporadic.' She bites into her cake again and looks at me. 'Remember the time you tried to cut your own fringe, Sally? And you ended up with almost no fringe at all.'

'Yes,' I say, and tears suddenly spring to my eyes, because I am thinking of Nathaniel. I should have cut his fringe, and then I should have insisted that he kiss me. I should have demanded his love, like April demanded it from Dad.

No one comments on my tears. It's that sort of day. 'My hair is very unruly,' Erika continues. 'I've never learned how to blow-dry it properly. Lionel says it's lovely, but that's only because he has no sense of style.'

'Who's Lionel?' April asks.

'Oh, some stupid guy from the office,' Erika says dismissively. 'And now he wants me to help a load of refugees speak English. I mean, my English isn't that good; how am I supposed to teach a bunch of foreigners about grammar? A lot of it's instinctive. I don't even know some of the terms.' She scoops some cream from the plate with her finger and pops it into her mouth. 'So I've decided I'll bring my guitar along and sing to them, and then we'll talk about the lyrics.'

Fiona and I exchange concerned glances. Erika can hardly sing, and she is awful on the guitar. What's more, the only song she can remember is 'The House of the Rising Sun', which is a sad song and could have a depressing effect on people who may be feeling miserable already.

'I suppose I might as well busy myself with good deeds, since I'll never meet anyone else like Alex.' Erika sighs dolefully. 'Does anyone want that éclair?'

We shake our heads, and she grabs it. I've chosen a chocolate cake with layers of mousse; it's creamy and light and delicious, and it doesn't even taste fattening.

'The sad thing about men…' Erika pauses to munch on her éclair. '…is that they're so *unsatisfactory*. Most of them just don't understand us, and the ones that do are married or gay or monks.'

'That's not fair,' Fiona protests. 'Some men are lovely. I bet a lot of them feel the same way about us.'

'Look, let me enjoy being unfair for a moment, will you?' Erika says sharply. 'I keep trying to be fair, and you know something? Sometimes it's a right pain in the arse.'

I laugh, and the others do too. Erika looks so fierce and ruffled, like a kitten.

'Anybody want more coffee?' I ask. I am droopy with jet lag. Fiona shoves her cup towards me.

'I wish I could put on my flip-flops now,' Erika says. 'It feels wrong, being in New York without wearing my new shoes.'

'And I want to put on my socks,' I add. 'My New York socks.'

'Let's all go down to the spa,' Fiona says. 'You can put them on there.'

'But you're supposed to take your clothes *off* in the spa,' Erika says.

'Yes, and then you put them on again.'

'We should go to Central Park afterwards,' Erika says. 'It's such a lovely afternoon, even though it's a bit muggy. My flip-flops should feel lovely and fresh.'

'But it will probably get a bit cooler later, and then my socks will be nice and cosy,' I say.

'You should all come and visit me in California,' April suddenly announces. 'There's enough room in my condo.'

'Condom?' Erika frowns at her.

'Condo. Condominium. It's got a swimming pool. You could all fly out there tomorrow.'

We stare at her. Just for a moment, I can sense we are all feeling that this is a good idea. Once we've shopped for shoes and socks in New York, we need to move on, and California is ideal. We could hang out in San Francisco for a while, and then maybe travel south and drop in on L.A. We would naturally travel in an open-topped car and play loud music about love and cars and moving on down the highway. We'd stop in motels and have wild sex with hunky, bronzed men who drove beat-up Chevys. Then Paris would beckon... or Rio. I look at Erika and Fiona. Their eyes are soft and dreamy.

'I have to get back to darling Milly.' Fiona is the first to break the trance. 'I can't believe I just left her like that.'

Erika looks at me excitedly. 'But *we* don't have much to go back to, do we? We could stay in the condom for a while.'

'Condo,' April corrects her.

'We could stay there for a while and then get a camper van, Sally. We could get a camper van and roar into the desert.'

'I don't know, Erika.' I look at her warily. Maybe those calming herbal remedies have a bit more in them than she thought. 'It all sounds very... interesting... but I don't think a camper van would really suit me.'

'But they have loads of different types,' she protests.

'And we'd need more money.'

'We could be buskers. I'd buy a new guitar. And I could make more cats. And... and you could write articles about it.'

'I think we should go home and discuss this when we've had more time to... you know... think about it.'

Erika purses her lips stubbornly.

'Look, Erika, Sally is married,' Fiona adds carefully. 'Even though she sometimes seems to forget it, she has acquired a husband.'

'That she doesn't seem to know what to do with!' Erika splutters. 'Especially since he slept with Charlene.'

'What?' April exclaims.

'Diarmuid slept with someone else,' Erika says casually. 'But Sally doesn't really mind, because she's in love with Nathaniel.'

'Who's Nathaniel?' April leans closer.

'He's a gorgeous guy who's in love with Eloise. It's like Pass the Parcel.'

'I see.' April looks at me thoughtfully.

'I'm not in love with Nathaniel!' I protest. 'I might be if I felt he was available, but I know he isn't, so I've… I've reined in my feelings for him.'

'You rein in horses and ponies,' Erika says. 'And even then they sometimes don't stop.'

'It's an expression, Erika. You can rein in other things too… such as wild wishes to roar into the desert in a camper van. Sometimes it's necessary.'

'I'm going to have to go soon,' April says.

'Oh, no – you can't!' Erika exclaims dramatically. 'You're the only sensible person here.'

'So you're not going to come to California with me?' April smiles at us.

'I'd love to… another time.' I get up and hug her. 'It's been wonderful seeing you again. We really must keep in touch now. I'm sorry I haven't phoned more often.'

'Don't tell anyone what I told you, will you?' She looks at me cautiously.

'No, of course not. But I'm glad I know. Thanks so much for telling me.' I throw my arms around her again and we hold each other. There must be a number of Aprils. I'm so glad I finally got to see this side of her.

'Oh, feck – I forgot to get Mum a birthday card!' she

232

suddenly exclaims. 'Would you buy it for me? Nothing too sentimental. Nothing with teddy bears on it. I'm not that sort of person.'

'OK.' I smile. This is a more familiar April. I'm not sure I could have got used to her being huggy and sweet indefinitely.

As she reaches for her bag, I say, 'Actually, April, there's something else I meant to ask you.'

'What?' She looks at me solemnly.

'What exactly don't you like about my lipstick?'

Chapter Twenty-Eight

THERE'S A BLACK WOMAN on the small stage, swishing a pink feather boa as she sings some jazz song. She sounds husky, experienced, weary in a way that isn't plain tired. She thought life was going to be different, that's what she's singing: it's been OK, but she thought she was going to get more out of it. She's not complaining, but she'd just like us to know that. And she still has the diamond ring he gave her, the one she almost threw away.

There's a saxophone solo at the end. It's good. The whole thing amounts to something – I can't say what, exactly, but it's not cheap and not too simple. It's an old song. We need the old songs. They remind us that what we humans want and need, deep down, really doesn't alter.

Erika and Fiona and I should be eating dinner, but after we left Central Park we walked down some scary side-streets and got a bit lost and met a guy called Samuel. He told us the way back to the hotel, but he also told us about this place. It's called the Furry Avocado and we were virtually standing outside it. Samuel said it was funky and we'd like it here. He also said he'd be singing himself in a while, and we got intrigued. So now we're sitting here in this dusky little room. It's smoky and shabby and wonderfully weird.

Erika and Fiona and I have decided that we are the kind of women who get down and boogie. Erika isn't talking about Alex, and Fiona isn't calling Zak every twenty minutes to check on Milly's welfare. I have even managed to stop continuously thinking about April and what she told me, but I seem to have transferred my anxiety to the diamond brooch; I look in my bag every five minutes to check that it's still in there safely. I'm somehow comforted by the fact that I am wearing lipstick that is a deeper shade of pink and isn't 'awful'. April said the other stuff was verging on white and didn't suit my complexion.

Before he went off to tune his guitar, Samuel told us he works in a health-food store. That's what I'm gradually figuring out about this place: all the performers haven't quite made it. It doesn't seem to worry them. They're good, but they haven't got that other thing – that thing that would make them famous and rich and on television and in big concert halls. But I sense they don't mind too much, because they're still singing. They're still doing what they love on their own terms. And I like their terms. I like that we are in this dark, almost poky little room together. I like that a guy called Rik is singing about his banged-up old car that took him across the Midwest. He isn't comparing himself to others and fretting that he doesn't have a CD in the top forty. I bet he's happy – and I really wish he were a first cousin. He's just the sort of guy who would bring a real buzz to Marie's uptight family gatherings.

Samuel comes on next. He's short and chubby and smiling, and his hair looks as though he asked a friend to cut it when they were both drunk; it sticks out in strange places. Samuel picks up his guitar, and Erika starts clapping as though he's Bob Dylan. And then he starts singing, in a strong, raspy voice, about this woman he knew and how he'll never forget her; how being with her felt like home, the home he'd never had. And then she dumped him for a truck driver and he became a vegetarian, though his cat, Chuck, still eats meat. Erika is utterly enraptured.

They've lit some candles, old white candles stuck into beer bottles. A fellow starts playing the didgeridoo, big earthy vibrations. Erika and Fiona are getting through their beers pretty fast, but I am sipping mine; I have three interviews to do tomorrow, and I don't want to have a hangover.

'I'm ravished,' Erika suddenly announces; then she blushes. 'Sorry, I mean I'm famished.'

'I'm ravished too.' I smile. The only food they seem to serve here is nachos with melted cheese.

'And me,' says Fiona. 'Let's go and get some food.'

I suddenly realise I really want to leave this place, even

though I love it. I love it, but it scares me, too, because it's reminding me of Nathaniel. It seems like just the kind of club he and Ziggy would have come to with their friends. I can almost see them laughing and joking and dreaming at one of the small round wooden tables. Maybe he and Eloise will be sitting here together in a few months, and I can't bear the thought of it. As I reach for my handbag and negotiate my way through the crowd towards the exit, I begin to wonder what Diarmuid would make of this place. A few months ago I would have known that he would hate it, but now I don't know this – and the fact that I don't know this seems far closer to the truth.

'I wish I'd brought my guitar with me,' Erika says as we try to find our way back to the hotel. 'They seem to be allowing all sorts of people up to the microphone.'

Fiona and I don't comment. We pass a hotdog stand and are suddenly even more ravished than before. 'Easy on the mustard,' Erika says to the guy, who looks rather gruff and businesslike. She sounds like she does this every day.

We eat our hotdogs and savour the hot, sultry evening. Every so often a jogger pounds past us – a New York jogger, determined and driven. Some of them are listening to Walkmans, hearing the latest news about the yen or lost in jazz, Bach, the Red Hot Chili Peppers; they could be listening to anything at all.

When we get back to the hotel, we go straight to our rooms. It's wonderful to be staying in such comfortable surroundings. Fiona has got such an enormous 'business' discount that I can even afford to repay her the money, out of the pretty basic expense allowance Greta has given me. Fiona has told Erika she can pay her back with massages. She says she'll need loads of massages after Zak leaves her.

Even though I'm tired, I decide to watch a bit of television. American TV guides are as big as the *Reader's Digest*. You could spend a whole evening channel-hopping. A mahogany-coloured guy with a black moustache is waving his arms around and shouting about low-cost diamonds. He suddenly breaks into Spanish. I watch the news for a bit, but it jumps around from big stories to small ones so much I get confused. They get all excited about a new bridge, and then there's something about various wars and famines and terrorists and muggers. The newsreaders seem to be coated with super-thin transparent plastic; even their smiles remain unchanged for far longer than is normal. They get all joky about a lost dog that got on a train to Newark, New Jersey. That makes them laugh. Wally – that's the dog's name – gets five whole minutes. He's some kind of terrier. When he got to Newark, he walked into a hairdresser's and lay under the reception desk until someone called his owner. The number was on his collar.

I am so groggy I almost expect the next news item to be about April and this new father of hers. I get a panicky feeling just remembering what she told me, but then it mixes with the general strangeness of the night. I still don't believe it, really. Every so often it lunges at me, but it seems unreal. In another way, though, it feels like something I've always known but couldn't admit to myself. Like the fact that I didn't love Diarmuid when I married him. I lied in that church. I thought he loved me, and his love would be enough for us both.

I search desperately for the Public Broadcasting Service channel, the one that does *Armchair Theatre* and imports all the best drama from the BBC. I feel sure I'll end up watching *Upstairs Downstairs*, but what comes on is a wildlife documentary about baboons with big red bottoms. I turn off the television. The sound of the city is a background hum. Every so often there are big, scary whoopy noises.

I go to the window. It's almost dark, but the streetlights cast an orange glow on the trees sprouting at the edge of the sidewalk – New York trees; trees that could tell you about rap music and prostitutes and drugs and women in brown fur coats carrying white poodles that wear red nail varnish. Taxis are drawing up at the front door of the hotel, disgorging businessmen with briefcases and svelte young women talking into mobile phones.

An elderly couple are walking arm in arm. They look as though they've just gone out to dinner. They must be in their seventies, but they don't look old; there's a spring in their step. Even their wrinkles seem enthusiastic. She's wearing a cerise dress with a long indigo scarf slung around her shoulders, and he's wearing a brown suit and a white shirt; he's taken off his tie, you can see it peeping out of a pocket of the jacket he's carrying. They've been to a musical *and* a meal. That must be it. Their hearts are still full of big swathes of longing – *pleasant* longing, longing that has some point to it. Dad says that certain chords reach the heart in the same way.

Suddenly April's secret seems to fill the room. I have to talk to someone about it. Erika and Fiona are probably snoring by now. Who should I phone? I want to talk to Nathaniel, but I mustn't. He's probably with Eloise, anyway. Diarmuid – I'll phone Diarmuid. He's usually pleased to hear from me, and he's very discreet. And sharing this secret with him will keep the lines of communication open.

He picks up the phone right away. Good, he's actually at home. He so often isn't these days. 'Hello, Diarmuid.'

'Oh.' He sounds hesitant. 'Oh, hello, Sally.'

'I'm in New York!'

'Oh.' Now he sounds perplexed. 'What are you doing there?'

'It was all very last-minute. I've got to interview some people tomorrow, then I'm flying home.'

'I'll collect you from the airport if you like.'

'Really? Are you sure?'

'Yes, of course.'

I tell him when the plane is supposed to arrive. 'This means a lot to me, Diarmuid,' I say. I'm about to add that I'm feeling a bit odd, because of what April told me, when I realise he doesn't sound like himself. In fact, he sounds very distracted.

'Diarmuid... have I phoned you at an inconvenient time?'

'Well, I...' I can almost hear him scratching his stubble. Diarmuid's facial hair grows at an alarming rate. 'Well, actually, I'm just–.'

'Diarmuid, do you want me to open the wine?' A voice. A woman's voice.

'Yes... fine,' he says. I can almost hear him blushing.

'Who's that?' I demand.

'Just a friend.'

'Where's the bottle-opener?' The voice is closer now. This friend clearly doesn't want her presence to remain a secret.

'In that drawer.'

Silence. He must have put his hand over the receiver. 'It's Charlene, isn't it?'

He doesn't answer.

'Just tell me. It's her, isn't it?'

'Yes,' he says, after a moment. 'It's just dinner, that's all. We needed to talk about some things.'

You should be talking about things with me, Diarmuid! I want to scream. *How come you've got so talkative suddenly? You never wanted to 'talk about things' when we were married.* But I don't say it, because he knows my feelings about all this already. I have shouted and screamed and hollered and let his mice loose.

Maybe he just feels more comfortable talking with Charlene. And I'm tired. I just want to curl under my duvet and dream of nothing.

'Sally?'

'Yes?'

'I'll meet you in the arrivals hall.'

'OK.'

'Good night.'

'Good night, Diarmuid.'

I don't even get undressed. I just fall onto my bed. I dream that DeeDee is holding me, drying my tears and telling me she understands. Suddenly I wake up with a start and find myself reaching for my handbag. I can't remember what I'm looking for, but my fingers close over the notebook. I draw it out and open it in a kind of daze.

There are some handwritten pages at the back that I didn't notice before. The sides of them are frayed, as if they were stuck together with glue. I remember how the notebook got damp on the floor of Nathaniel's car: the dampness must have

239

softened the glue and released the pages. These notes aren't about recipes. I can tell at a glance that they are intimate. Secret.

'*Nobody believes that Joseph forced himself on me.* They think I'm making it up – Aggie most of all. She says she won't talk to me again until I admit that I've been lying. They all think I'm jealous. They think I love him and want to marry him myself. And now I'm pregnant, and I don't know who to turn to. They don't love me. If they loved me they'd believe me about Joseph. "Oh, that's just DeeDee – you know what she's like." That's what they think. But they don't know what I'm like. None of them really know me. I'll have to go away and have the baby adopted. And then I'll become an actress. I never want to see any of them again.'

Chapter Twenty-Nine

I HAVE SPENT THE day interviewing Top Young Irish Designers about fancy furniture and accessories. I met the first hip, happening person in a loft in SoHo and discussed his fabulous wallpaper. Then I moved on to a cramped studio in Greenwich Village and discussed the very latest developments in lamps. After that I bustled off to a small shop off Fifth Avenue and met a woman who can make coffee tables in any shape that appeals to you – breasts, cats, fruit, butterflies, parsnips, you just name it. She had a metal stud in her nose and a dog called Frankie.

After hearing about symmetry and textures and organic curves and angles for two and a half hours, I staggered out into the late-afternoon sunshine and bolted into this coffee shop, where I am having a large cappuccino. I've kept my sunglasses on. I've decided I'm that sort of woman now: I wear sunglasses in shady corners of cafés.

I feel like I have suddenly been thrown into the Truth Club. Within hours, I have learned that April is my half-sister and that DeeDee got pregnant by Joseph and that Diarmuid is talking to Charlene – not just teaching her to drive and having sex with her, but actually cooking her dinner and having long conversations. I'm almost scared to phone my parents in case they suddenly announce that I am, in fact, adopted.

I wish Erika and Fiona hadn't flown home this morning. We all got up early and sat in the jacuzzi for half an hour, and I told them about DeeDee. It made them both cry – which is not, I suppose, that surprising, since they've been close to tears ever since the jet landed. It made me cry too. We must be the only people on the planet who come to New York for a good sob.

Poor DeeDee. She was treated like an outcast. The thing is, now that I've discovered why she left, I don't think it's advisable to try to find her. She might march into Aggie's bedroom and shout, 'You old bitch!' and rant and holler. I doubt very much that she could forgive what happened – surely Aggie must know that. But I'm fairly convinced that Aggie has now blanked many of the sadder details from her memory. How could she have dismissed her sister's version of events so easily? She talks about loving her now, but did she love her then? Did any of them understand her?

I sigh and fiddle with the sugar sachets. I'm so disappointed in Aggie. I find it hard to accept that she was so callous. I liked Joseph, too, but now he seems like a brute – and DeeDee's parents sound extraordinarily insensitive. I'll never be able to think of them in the same way again. In fact, the truth about what happened to DeeDee is so horrible that I'm beginning to suspect it is, perhaps, best forgotten. What's the point of bringing it up now? In the circumstances, it's almost more comforting to think that she just disappeared.

I never want to see any of them again. That's what she wrote.

I must respect that. It was silly of me to ring International Directory Enquiries in the middle of last night to ask if they had a number for a DeeDee Aldridge in Rio. They didn't, of course. She will have changed her name. She wouldn't have wanted to keep any reminder of the family that spurned her. She's probably married. I hope life brought her lots of hats and marble cake – and, most of all, I hope it has brought her love.

I check my bag to make sure the diamond brooch is still in there. I wish April hadn't made me promise not to tell Mum I know who her father is – her biological father. Dad is her father too; of course he is. When he hears April is on the phone, his eyes light up. I admire him even more than I used to. He must have a big, forgiving heart.

I'm about to close my bag when I see the notebook. I take it out and reach for the small, faded photo of DeeDee. That's all we have of her now. I wonder what she would have made of our big, friendly house in the golden hills outside San Francisco. Maybe April was conceived there. Dad was often away giving concerts, and I came back from school late in the afternoons. I used to feel it was a truthful house; it had huge windows, and in a weird, childish way I thought that meant we were open, too – transparent. But, of course, we weren't. That's where Mum learned how to lie and I learned about love. I felt its presence, the contours, the textures; the shy, wispy shapes of its absence. It seemed to disappear and return like the tide, and I knew I would never understand it. I wanted love to be 'one dear perpetual place', like Yeats wrote in a poem. Only it wasn't.

'Sorry I'm late, there was a big queue in the supermarket… No, it can't have been my car. I was with Veronica. She's just bought a hammock… Don't worry about those strange calls. Our number is almost the same as that Indonesian takeaway's…' So many lies. And Mum was really good at it, too.

Like Diarmuid. 'I was studying at home all evening… Charlene and I are just friends… My mother really likes you, Sally.'

Like me. 'I love you, Diarmuid. Yes, I want to marry you.'

How do people learn how to lie so expertly? Sometimes they don't even know they're lying, because they are lying to themselves too. I'm good at that. That's my speciality.

I stare at DeeDee's eyes. They look truthful. I'd say she would have liked our California home, but only for a visit. She seems more of a city girl. I can't see her growing flowers, but I can see her getting them in big, extravagant bunches from a florist. I'd say she often didn't even know who they were from, and that made her smile. She has that look about her – the look of a wounded child and a thief, a spy and a black-and-white film star, all mixed together. She has a sturdy glamour. Men would have liked to have her beside them, arms linked, in the street. It's not easy to be that kind of woman, to be wanted for things other than yourself. But DeeDee wouldn't have known that, because she was restless; she felt her answer was somewhere else, somewhere exotic, so she wouldn't have noticed the little aches and sorrows. The little nudges. The habits and ordinary yearnings of her heart.

The evening sun is streaming through the window. I stare out the window at the people striding by on the sidewalk. They want to get to the next place – the next meeting, the next meal, the next love affair, the next shop. Sometimes I wish I had been born in a quieter century, but maybe there never was a quieter century. Maybe people have always been like this. Maybe even cavemen went haring out each morning with their clubs.

The waiter asks if I want another cappuccino – waiters are so attentive here. I say yes, and I add that I want a chocolate brownie. This is not a day to go without chocolate, or crisps. I must buy a stack of them to eat on the plane.

I glance at the headline of a newspaper someone has left on a nearby table: 'Fake Fur – How to Make Your Dog Feel like a Millionaire!' I catch my reflection in the window. I appear to be sipping cappuccino calmly. I even look quite smart: I'm wearing a flatteringly tailored navy jacket and a thick turquoise shirt, and there's a chunky pop-art brooch shaped like a terrier on my lapel. My sunglasses make me look mysterious.

I don't have to go home – that's what I find myself thinking. I could fly out to April in California. What's there to go back to, really? I don't even feel the same way about Aggie, after what she did. And, anyway, she has Fabrice now. Fabrice is going to visit as often as she can. Aggie talks about her as if she's known her all her life. She says the angels brought them together.

I frown and bite into my brownie. I used to believe in angels. Our house in California was crammed full of them. There came a point when I really thought some of them should move into the attic; there were at least twenty of them in my bedroom, and it wasn't all that big. At night, when Mum and Dad were arguing, I knew the angels were watching over me. If I stared hard enough, I saw a sort of golden glow above the curtain rail. Sometimes I thought I heard their wings banging off the ceiling, and I said, 'Ouch!' in sympathy. One of the great things about the angels was that you could pour them a great big glass of Coke and they could drink it all and leave the glass completely full. They were really low-maintenance.

And then, one night, I stared really hard at the golden glow over the curtain rail and realised it wasn't there. That's when I knew I'd just made the angels up because my friend Astrid kept going on about them and because I was scared Mum would leave us. It was only the moonlight dancing through the gaps between the curtains. I don't know why I hadn't noticed that before; probably because I just didn't want to. That's the thing about the truth. Sometimes the lie is infinitely preferable.

I must ring Diarmuid, I decide suddenly. I must tell him we can't go on pretending any longer. Our marriage is no longer even semi-detached; it appears to be over.

I pick up my mobile phone and am about to dial when it rings.

'Hi, there!' I'd recognise that voice anywhere. It's Nathaniel. 'Greta told me she sent you off to New York. How are things in the Big Apple?'

I make circles in the air with my foot. 'Oh, you know – very calm and quiet. It's a great place to get away from it all. And I bought a really nice pair of socks.'

He laughs. He has a great laugh. 'I'm almost tempted to ask you to get my shirts back, but I don't think you'd want to.'

'You're right about that.'

'You sound weird.'

'No, I don't.'

'Yes, you do. What's happened?'

I don't know how he does this. 'I don't know what you're talking about,' I protest. 'I'm having a cappuccino and a brownie in a lovely café. I'm sitting on a sofa –'

'Couch, Sally – you're in New York.'

'OK, I'm sitting on a couch, and the sun is shining. I'm wearing sunglasses – I mean shades.'

'Wow… a woman of mystery.'

'I'm also learning how to make a dog feel like a millionaire.'

'What?'

'It's the headline on a newspaper.'

'That figures.'

'Look, Nathaniel, I'd better go,' I say firmly. 'I've got to

245

buy some crisps and catch a plane.'

'Get some for me too.'

I hesitate and look wistfully out the window. I don't think Nathaniel even guesses how much he means to me. He's so chatty and sociable; he's probably like this with everyone.

'I need to see you, Sally.'

I clutch the phone more tightly. Maybe he feels more for me than I thought.

'Why?' I ask quietly.

'I need to talk to you about something.'

'What?'

'I need to talk to you about DeeDee.' His voice sounds urgent, excited. Like he knows a secret he wants to share.

Chapter Thirty

IT'S 3 P.M. AND I am curled under my duvet. I got back from New York a week ago, and I'm allowing myself a siesta because of the general weirdness of my life. I'm thinking about the conversation I had with Nathaniel just before I left the Big Apple.

'I've met someone who used to know DeeDee!' he said excitedly. 'Her name is Fabrice. She was with Aggie when I visited today.'

'Actually...' I frowned. I didn't want to disappoint him, but I felt I might as well tell the truth; there seemed to be a lot of it about lately. 'Actually, I've heard about Fabrice already. Aggie told me.'

'Oh, dear, I wanted to tell you first,' he sighed. 'This great-aunt of yours has me kind of intrigued, Sally. I love mysteries.' It's funny, but I found myself thinking that he was leaving something out – that he had more information about DeeDee than he was sharing with me. But I knew I must be imagining things. I've got so used to people having secrets that I'm even suspicious of Nathaniel, the most honest, guileless man I've ever met.

'Call round soon,' he said before he hung up. I suppose I should, because I need to hunt for my wedding ring. I should also attend a time-management course, because I don't seem to be able to find time to think about my marriage, let alone coax Diarmuid into talking about what the feck is going on between him and Charlene. Instead I've been sweating over my articles about Top Young Irish Designers. I have also written an ebullient column about how to make your home look like a Provençal cottage. I tossed in references to lavender and candles and whitewashed walls, thick glass vases full of sunflowers, espadrilles and wide-brimmed straw hats. I am basically being paid to be an opinionated bossy-boots. The headline on last week's column said, 'Ultimate Vases:

Sally Adams Falls in Love with the Latest Floral Chic'. My life is all style and no substance.

At least I've given Mum the diamond brooch. She burst into tears when she saw it, and I didn't ask why. I just said it was 'lovely' and avoided any significant emotional interchange. I had quite enough of that in New York. I think she was crying with joy – I hope she was, anyway. My own birthday present to her was rather meagre by comparison – a collection of creams and bath oils and soaps – but she seemed pleased enough with it. The card I bought on April's behalf had tulips on it, and mine had a rural landscape. There wasn't a teddy bear in sight. Once I'd made my delivery and shared a glass of wine with Mum in the sitting room, I trotted off to see Aggie, but Fabrice was with her and I didn't stay that long.

Fabrice is an odd woman. If I was to be charitable I might call her a 'character', but I'm tired of calling people 'characters' to excuse all sorts of silliness. She appears to be in her late seventies and was once probably quite pretty, but now she is, frankly, mutton dressed as lamb. She was wearing so much make-up that I have no idea what she might look like first thing in the morning. Her dyed blonde hair was piled on top of her head, and she was strewn with silver jewellery and semi-precious stones – she was even wearing extraordinary glasses with small fake diamonds around the rim. She had a long indigo scarf tossed around her shoulders, and her pink blouse was low-cut and revealed rather too much cleavage. She told us that she had been a nightclub singer in Belgium and a model in Paris, and that she'd never married but had been in love 'many times' and in most of the major time zones. Aggie was entranced by it all. She was gulping up each word as if it were caviar.

'And what about you, Sally?' Fabrice suddenly fixed me with an intense stare, and that was when I began to get suspicious of her. Because her eyes are unlike the rest of her showy appearance. They are serious, almost solemn, the eyes of a woman who knows what she wants and has thought long and hard about it. And they made me wonder why she wants to visit

Aggie so often. There are people who prey on the elderly and try to extract money from them, and I began to wonder if this was what Fabrice was up to. But Aggie looked so happy that I decided not to interfere. Maybe Fabrice is just lonely, like Aggie. Maybe she just needs someone to listen to her stories, which I suspect are mostly dreams of what might have been. It would be easy enough to become like her.

When I left, Aggie called out, 'Bye, Sally, dear,' rather vaguely. I'm probably jealous, that's the truth of it. And I'm also angry with Aggie for behaving so badly towards DeeDee, I've scoured DeeDee's notebook for more revelations, but the rest of it is just recipes and doodles.

Though I adore my duvet, it seems to me I should perhaps emerge from it and face the strange, and sometimes downright daft, outside world. I really should go round to Nathaniel's and look for my wedding ring – its loss seems far too symbolic – but there are so many other things I should also be doing that I can't decide which to attend to first. This is clearly some sort of reaction to all the truth that has tumbled upon me so suddenly. I always regarded the truth as important, but right now I find myself thinking that ignorance, in certain cases, does indeed contain some bliss.

I also find myself thinking that Diarmuid is *my* partial husband, so if Charlene has suddenly decided to make a grab for him there should at least have been some sort of discussion. I was the one who was supposed to be having doubts about my marriage, but now Diarmuid has raced ahead of me. He even has an alternative partner lined up for himself, if he wants her. That's just like Diarmuid, of course. He doesn't drift. He has plans and goals and a surfboard stomach. He isn't a confused and dawdling biscuit-eater.

I manage to push myself out of the house, and blink in the sudden sunlight. Part of me is still in New York. I almost expect to see skyscrapers and yellow cabs and bagel-sellers. It's one of those days when summer appears for a while and then turns into autumn; there are billowy white clouds and patches of blue, and a breeze that is bordering on chilly. I cross the road and walk down the steps to the beach. The leaves on the sturdy Dublin palm trees are being tossed about in the breeze, and a crisp packet is dancing in the air.

I want to be totally in the present moment. I want to just walk and smell the sea air, hear the gulls, feel the crunch of sand under my feet. I manage to do this for thirty seconds, and then I start thinking about the conversation I had with Diarmuid when he collected me from the airport. It was the perfect opportunity to talk about our marriage and what we wanted to do with it, but instead we ended up discussing horse-riding. It reminded me of a dinner party I once attended, at which the guests discussed fish-farming for an entire hour.

I said Erika wanted us to go horse-riding and Diarmuid said it was a good idea. Then he said that he used to go horse-riding when he was a teenager, and I said he'd never told me that, and he said he was telling me now. The conversation got very prickly for a bit, because his dinner with Charlene was hovering around in my thoughts and I felt furious with him for sleeping with her and giving her driving lessons – and, most of all, for *talking* to her. I suddenly felt sure he had said all the things to her that he hadn't said to me. What's more, I felt he had actually *saved up* this conversation for just such an occasion. At one point I thought I couldn't stay in the car with him a moment longer. I almost leapt out at a traffic light when I saw a taxi rank, but then I realised my purse was full of dollars. So I just closed my eyes, and Diarmuid started to talk about this horse he'd got very fond of and how he loved the smell of her sweat on his hands after grooming. He said there was nothing like a good gallop across an open field. I said, rather frostily, that I didn't want to gallop across an open field; I wanted to be on a smallish horse that was happy to walk and didn't run off with me. I wanted a horse I could *trust*.

We sat in silence for a while after that, and I thought of Fiona, who gets on big gleaming thoroughbreds and gallops off across fields. She even has her own jodhpurs and riding boots and a hard hat. Erika and I went to some posh equestrian place with her once, and we were, as usual, left completely in awe of her streamlined, gutsy beauty. We ended up having scones and tea in the little café by the stables.

As Diarmuid drove on sombrely, I found myself thinking that knowing someone like Fiona really rubs one's nose in it. That's why this situation with Milly doesn't seem right, somehow. It just isn't the sort of thing that happens to Fiona. I suppose I could almost feel relieved to discover she isn't perfect after all, but instead I'm heartbroken for her. I love her. I want her to be happy. I want her to be the Fiona who made us all feel a bit inferior.

'How was New York?' Diarmuid asked, when we were nearly at my cottage.

'It was fine. It was very nice.' I told him a bit about the interviews and the swanky hotel.

'Good. I'm glad you enjoyed it.' He leaned forward and kissed me on the cheek. 'You must be tired. I'll call around soon.' He helped me carry my bags into the living room and asked me if I needed a lift to the shops to get some milk. I felt a brief return of affection. It was so typical of Diarmuid to remember a detail like that. I probably married him for just that sort of question.

I said I would get the milk tomorrow, so he gave me a quick hug and drove off. I suddenly felt terribly lonely – but I also found I was almost relieved that we had managed to avoid all the crucial emotional topics. Life and love are sometimes so strange that I really don't know what I think about them.

As I watch a young girl run along beside the waves with her dog, my mobile phone rings. It's Fiona, and she's in tears. 'Should I tell him, Sally? I really want to tell him,' she asks, through sobs and sniffs. Then she blows her nose. It sounds like an off-key trumpet. For such a pretty, streamlined person Fiona is a very noisy nose-blower.

'Not yet,' I say with as much authority as I can muster. What Fiona needs at the moment is someone who has an opinion – any opinion, as long as it sounds calm and considered. She keeps ringing me in tears and asking if she should tell Zak he isn't Milly's father, and I always tell her to wait for a while, mainly because I don't think she could deal with Zak storming out of the house and leaving her on her own with Milly and the nanny. Of course, he mightn't do this; but he has such lofty opinions about telling the truth that I think she should wait a bit, at least until Milly settles down and stops bawling at all hours of the night.

Then Fiona says she wonders if she should postpone the christening, because Zak will probably have the results of Milly's blood tests by then. I tell her that Milly will have to get christened sooner or later, and even if Zak knows he isn't her father, he may feel obliged to put on a good show for the relatives. I say this might in fact be very useful, because it would delay his departure – even though he probably won't leave anyway – and give them more time to discuss the situation.

'He's getting suspicious. I've heard him whispering on the phone to his relatives.'

Frankly I'm not surprised. Every time I look at Milly, I can't help wondering if her father is Chinese or Japanese or perhaps even Tibetan. The fertility clinic really should have a look into their filing system.

'Maybe I should have brought Milly to New York with me and just stayed there,' Fiona says.

I try to calm her down. I say that Zak may understand; he's a very understanding man. And he loves Milly. He is also besotted with Fiona.

'Maybe you don't know him quite as well as you think,' I add. In normal circumstances this might not be comforting, but in this case it seems to offer a mild reassurance. 'There could be a part of him that can come to terms with this. Look how my father loves April.'

'Zak's not like that,' Fiona says, and I know she's wrong to be so sure about what he is and isn't. At least that's something the last few months have taught me. Then her voice suddenly brightens, and I know Zak must have appeared. 'Yes, I just loved that film too. We must go to the cinema soon, Sally. Lovely to talk with you. Bye.' She hangs up.

I trudge along the seashore and wonder what I can do to help her. I decide that just being supportive is the most sensible approach. It's best not to interfere in other people's marriages, especially if they have managed to stay under the same roof. A gust of wind turns the waves into white horses. I gaze at them and wish there was a dog I could borrow. I love the way dogs dart into the waves and fetch sticks and scamper along the sand. They are a wonderful reminder not to take things too seriously.

Thinking of dogs reminds me of Fred, and Fred reminds me of Nathaniel. I am walking in the direction of his flat. I should pop in and see if he's there and hunt for my wedding ring. I start to walk more quickly; there's an ice-cream van parked by a Martello tower, and I need to get away from it. People are munching cones with chocolate stuck into them. I fix my eyes on the horizon. I simply must lose some weight before Marie's party.

I am relieved to see Nathaniel's bashed-up old Citroën in front of Greta's house, but then I get a sudden urge to just go home. What am I to do with these feelings he calls out of me?

I stare at the large red-brick building with its luxuriant garden. Then I gingerly approach the wrought-iron gate and try to open it. As is often the case with gates like that, it involves a certain amount of tussling.

As soon as I'm in Nathaniel's spacious sitting room, he starts squinting suspiciously out the window. 'I think that ice-cream van is stalking me. Look, it's just pulled up outside the gate. It turns up outside this house every afternoon, playing some tinny Viennese waltz.'

'I want to hunt for my wedding ring.'

'Yes, but let's buy some 99 cones first.' He smiles at me. 'The guy won't go away until I relent.'

He starts to hunt for some change on a bookshelf. I glance out the window. 'He's pulling away.'

'Bugger!' Nathaniel says. 'He usually waits.'

'So you *want* an ice-cream cone.'

'Of course. He's been pushing the stuff at me for weeks.

I'm addicted.'

Fred is snoring on a large cushion by the window. Every so often he growls. He is probably dreaming of chasing rabbits. 'So you've been visiting Aggie,' I say.

'Yes. I promised I would. I get the impression she thinks I'm Diarmuid, but I don't mind. John, Cedric, Gervaise – she can call me anything she wants, as long as it isn't Maisie. I'd like to retain my gender.'

Nathaniel heads for the kitchen and starts making tea, washing mugs, sniffing milk and staring cautiously at the sugar bowl.

'Ants,' he mutters. 'Bloody ants. They treat this place like a hotel.'

'I have them too,' I sigh. 'I suppose I could resort to heavy chemicals to get rid of them, but it seems rather drastic.'

'I agree.' Nathaniel opens a window and flings a handful of ants and sugar into the shrubbery. 'I suppose we'll just have to freeze them out with our disapproval.'

There is a silence. An easy silence. Then he says, 'Have you been trying to phone me?'

'No.'

'Just as well. Fred buried my mobile phone somewhere in the garden. Sometimes I think I should have him shot at dawn.' Nathaniel hands me a turquoise mug. He didn't ask me how much milk or sugar I take; he remembered. 'I've been asking people to ring me and skulking around the garden trying to find it... Greta thought I was listening to the geraniums, until I explained what I was up to.' He sits down beside me and takes a large gulp of tea from his mug.

'Who cut your fringe?'

'Eloise.' He languidly stretches out his legs. 'I think she made quite a good job of it.'

'An excellent job.'

Fred suddenly jumps up from his cushion. 'Walk time.' Nathaniel looks at me wryly. 'He'll start howling if he has to wait too long. He's awfully bossy.'

Fred is now dancing around our feet with excitement. 'Let

us at least finish our tea,' Nathaniel tells him sternly. Fred runs off into the hall and jumps up and down until he manages to dislodge his lead from a coat hook.

'It's ridiculous,' Nathaniel says. 'I am being bossed about by a mongrel. I'm going to have to let him take me for a walk. You can stay here if you want.'

I drain the last drops of tea from my mug. 'Well, I had planned to look for my wedding ring…'

'I'll look for you.'

I smile gratefully. 'Really?' He nods. 'OK, I'll come with you. I'll walk home along the beach. I'm trying to get more exercise.'

It's nice walking along the strand with Nathaniel. I find myself thinking that, if I were on a bus and saw us, I might think we were a couple, a real couple with their crazy dog.

'I'm so glad you called round,' Nathaniel says. 'I really enjoy our talks.'

'So do I.'

'I find it easier to talk to women. Most of my friends seem to be women these days.'

I pick up a shell. How many women friends does he have? Am I just one of a big bunch?

'I know it's a cliché, but women do tend to be more in touch with their emotions. Julia hates it when I say that; she says I shouldn't generalise.'

'Julia?'

'Haven't I mentioned her? She's a computer whiz; I keep ringing her for advice. She prefers sensitive men, but Eloise keeps telling me that women don't want their men to be wimpy. I sometimes suspect she'd like me to take up body-building.'

As he laughs affectionately, I wish he had found himself a gentler girlfriend. Eloise is clearly a pretty tough cookie. She's beautiful and sexy and bright, but I don't think I'd want to talk to her about my feelings.

Fred keeps bringing us sticks and demanding that we throw them for him. Even though Nathaniel throws them onto the sand, Fred scampers after them through the water.

'Look at that.' Nathaniel sighs. 'He insists on getting drenched every time we come here.'

I look at Nathaniel quickly, and then I look away, towards the curve of Killiney Bay and Bray Head in the distance. 'He'll miss you if you go back to New York.' I almost add, 'So will Eloise,' but I don't. Maybe she'll join Nathaniel there. She'll have a whole new market for her cabinets.

'Yes.' Nathaniel frowns. 'Greta said she'd take him on, but she'd probably want to turn him into a party dog. Everyone in her life gets roped into helping out at her PR receptions. She'd probably train him to hand out press releases.'

I bite my lip. 'When would you go back – if you go back?'

'I don't know – I haven't decided. Maybe in a couple of months.'

A couple of months. He says it so casually.

We aren't taking notice, and we've wandered far too close to the water. A wave crashes over our shoes, drenching our socks and jeans. We both gasp with surprise.

'Oh, feck!' Nathaniel laughs. I giggle too. The water is freezing. We must get some dry clothes on. I stare into the distance. My cottage is only ten minutes away; we must have been walking faster than we thought.

'Come to my place and we can dry out. I'll make you tea.' I've said it before I can even think about it.

'OK.' Nathaniel's eyes meet mine.

We walk purposefully, silently, along the beach.

'I really should take off these jeans,' Nathaniel says, when we're in my untidy sitting room. 'Do you have a radiator I could put them on?' He is already taking off his socks and shoes.

The afternoon seems to have acquired its own momentum. 'Yes,' I say. 'I'll get you my dressing-gown.'

Soon we are sipping tea. I have changed clothes, and Nathaniel is in my blue gown, which is covered with tiny pink roses. Steam is rising from his jeans, which are on a plug-in Dimplex radiator. I don't know quite how this has happened.

We could have just gone back to his flat, even though my cottage was closer. The cushions on the sofa seem to be sagging towards the middle, sort of shoving us together. My hand touches his knee when I offer him a biscuit. My skin drinks in the feel of him, the smell, the warmth.

Then I start laughing. It's a belly laugh; it bursts out of me. I laugh so hard that I have to put down the plate.

'What is it?'

'You look so funny in that gown.'

Our eyes meet again. 'Oh, Sally…' Nathaniel says. But then the doorbell rings. It's probably one of my small neighbours, wanting me to retrieve a ball from my back garden. I am still giggling as I go to the front door.

It's Diarmuid, and he's holding a bunch of flowers. My stomach lurches. He mustn't see Nathaniel; he'll put two and two together and get fifty.

'Hi, Diarmuid! It's good to see you!' I want my voice to sound welcoming, but it's a high-pitched squeak. 'I – I was just about to go to the shop for some milk. Could you give me a lift?' The shop is only a minute away by car, but it will give Nathaniel time to pull on his jeans and leave. 'Then we can come back here and have a nice chat.'

I try to move out the door, but Diarmuid is standing in front of me and he doesn't budge. 'But what about your visitor, Sally – your *other* visitor?' His voice is cold and angry. I gulp. How does he know I have a visitor?

He pushes past me and marches into the sitting-room. He glares at Nathaniel. Then he flings the bunch of roses on the floor, turns on his heel and walks out.

Chapter Thirty-One

'I'VE MOVED IN WITH Charlene.' It is eight in the morning, and the bedside phone has woken me up.

'Hello,' I say vaguely, rubbing my eyes. 'Is that you, Diarmuid? I'm sorry. I didn't hear what you just said.'

'I've moved in with Charlene.'

That's what I thought he said, but it can't be. Diarmuid wouldn't just say something like that so bluntly.

'She and I had a long talk about the whole situation, and I've decided that my marriage to you is a sham. I have to get on with my own life.'

This is a Diarmuid I have never encountered before. 'Oh.' I don't know what to say. I pull my duvet up under my chin and lie there with the phone stuck to my ear.

'When I saw you with Nathaniel, I knew our marriage was over.'

'But – but didn't you hear the messages I left on your phone? I explained the whole situation. He was only in my dressing-gown because –'

'I don't believe you.'

'Well, it's the truth.' I feel like crying. 'He's just a friend, Diarmuid. That's all he is, really.'

Diarmuid decides not to be sidetracked. 'We'll have to sell the house as soon as possible. Do you want me to contact the estate agents?'

'You've moved in with Charlene?' I feel the need to confirm this fact.

'Yes.'

'You're living with another woman, even though you're still married to me.'

'Yes, yes,' Diarmuid says, somewhat impatiently. 'How many more times are you going to say it?'

'As many times as I need to,' I say with a note of steel in my voice. 'You can surely see why it may take me a little while to get used to the idea, Diarmuid.'

'Well, I had to get used to you running off without a word of explanation.'

'I did explain.' My voice has risen in anger. 'Only you didn't listen. But you listen to her, don't you? You listen to Charlene.'

'This isn't a competition, Sally,' Diarmuid says wearily. 'I listen to Charlene because she listens to me.'

'I listened to you too!' I am now sitting bolt upright in bed. 'I listened to you going on and on about the bloody mice and your carpentry classes and how once we had a baby I'd feel more settled. I even listened to you talking about *football*. As far as I recall, you went on about new bathroom shelving for an entire *week*.'

'But I never said what you wanted to hear, did I?' Diarmuid says sadly. 'That's why I stopped talking. You just didn't want to hear what I was saying.'

'You – you could have asked me what I wanted to talk about,' I splutter indignantly. 'When we were engaged, we used to talk about all sorts of things.'

'It was mainly about the wedding, as far as I remember.' Diarmuid sighs. 'You were determined to impress your relatives.' This is indeed true.

'Do... do you love her?' I bite my lip and wait for his answer.

'She loves me.'

'That's not what I asked you.'

'She loves me, and now I suppose I love her. We kind of fit together, somehow. We seem to want the same things.'

I stare at a picture of a lavender field in the south of France. It's on the wall opposite my bed. There are sunflowers, too, and a little path leading down to the blue ocean. I wish I were there. I don't know if I can stand Diarmuid's callousness.

'I know it doesn't sound very romantic,' Diarmuid says, 'but I'm not like you, Sally. I don't need some grand romance – in fact, I don't think I'd know what to do with it if I found one.'

259

I blink away the tears. I don't want him to know I'm crying silently. It might even please him.

'I thought you were that sort of person too,' he says. 'Before we married, you kept saying that you wanted someone uncomplicated. You said you wanted someone steady, someone you could trust.'

This is true too. I did want someone uncomplicated and steady, because I didn't want my marriage to be like Mum and Dad's. Their eyes had met across a crowded room, and when I was little they were besotted with each other; sometimes I even felt excluded by their high-octane intimacy. But when Mum met Al, she seemed to forget all that. Their grand romance suddenly seemed terribly flimsy, like a house full of ornaments and pictures but without a proper foundation. That's why I couldn't bring myself to talk to Nathaniel when I first saw him at that party. I didn't want those intense feelings, that flamboyance. I didn't want to want anyone that much.

'I… I thought you were worried about Charlene being from South Africa,' I say. 'You said you were too different.'

'We'll work out the cultural differences as we come to them. I did think my family might have problems accepting her –'

'Especially your mother.' I almost hiss the words into the receiver. 'She's a right bitch, Diarmuid. I don't know why you keep making excuses for her. You always take her side, but you should have stood up for me.'

'Yes, you're right about that.'

I almost drop the receiver.

'I mean, I'm not saying she's a bitch. But she didn't really make you feel welcome. I'm sorry.'

Why on earth couldn't he have said this before?

'She was reluctant about our marriage because she wanted me to marry Becky, even though Becky didn't want to marry me. She keeps forgetting that.'

I look out the window. It's a cloudy late-July day, and it must be windy too; I can hear my neighbours' wind chimes tinkling in their tiny patio garden. 'Did you ask Becky to marry you?' I have to know.

There is a long pause. 'Yes, when I was in my early twenties. I phoned her in New Zealand. It was kind of silly. We hadn't seen each other since we were teenagers.'

'But you loved her?'

'Yes.' Diarmuid's voice sounds funny, sort of empty and doggedly resigned. 'But she never loved me the same way. The truth is, I don't think I'll ever be able to love someone so totally again, Sally.' He sounds as if he wants to cry. 'I think I put that part of me away forever.'

I wish he'd told me this. He kept saying he'd forgotten about Becky, that he loved me now, not her. He lied. But, deep down, I knew anyway.

Now I understand that distant look in Diarmuid's eyes. Now I understand why I never really felt I could reach him. He didn't want me to. That part of him was closed off and carefully forgotten. And I know, suddenly, that many people do this; it isn't just Diarmuid. My parents did it with their love. They made it into something else, businesslike, determined; the ornaments are gone, and all that's left is the structure. I did it too, that day I saw Mum kissing Al. I didn't trust love any more. I knew it was something flimsy and prone to alteration. It didn't seem a safe thing to want. And I stopped believing in the angels – I simply couldn't summon up the faith. And when I stopped believing in them, I stopped seeing the shiny, gentle shapes floating near the ceiling. Maybe love is like that too. If you don't believe in it, maybe you just don't notice it. All you sense is the contours of its absence.

'I'm sorry for ringing so early.' Diarmuid's voice sounds softer. 'I've only just looked at my watch; I thought it was later. You probably haven't even had a cup of tea. Why don't you go and make one and I'll ring you back?'

I find myself grimacing. Why can't Diarmuid be bad or good? Why can't he be one thing, instead of this strange mixture? I want to hate him, but now he's remembered how much I need tea first thing in the morning. It's like when he asked me if I needed to buy milk. He remembers this kind of thing. On our very first date he gave me his jacket because it was raining.

I hang up and go downstairs. I feel like I have suddenly landed in another country, a foreign, odd place with a stark, strange landscape. Even the kettle and the teapot and the mugs look different. They've lost their cosiness; they're just things in my kitchen. The ants are still trying to get into the jar of honey. I leave them to it. *South Africa*, I think. Why does Diarmuid make it sound like another planet? It would be funny, if his new love didn't come from there.

As I pour the boiling water over the teabag, I catch a thin reflection of myself in the glass pane in the back door. I recognise the expression. It is my mother's, the one she wore on the long, lost days after she left Al. Suddenly I love my mother, in a way I have never loved her before. She came back to us, even though she could have left. It must have taken such courage. It must have taken a bigger kind of love. She must have set so many of her dreams aside for us. She saved her marriage – but I can't save mine. It's gone. I wish with all my heart that I could step back in time and alter the part of my past that I have chosen to belong to. I wish I had noticed my mother's courage and faith, instead of her brief infidelity. I would have become another kind of person. And I would have spoken to Nathaniel at that party.

The phone rings just as I am stirring in the half-spoon of sugar. Diarmuid even knows how long it takes me to make a cup of tea. He knows the side of the bed I prefer, my favourite Chinese takeaways and crisps and chocolate; he knows I keep forgetting to return DVDs on time. He used to do it for me. There are so many things we know about each other, small crucial details. I used to be able to recognise the sound of his car hundreds of yards away. What are we to do with all this knowledge? Where are we to put it now?

'Have you got your cuppa?'

'Yes, thanks.'

'I should replace that plug on the kettle for you. It's getting a bit loose, isn't it?'

Don't do this, Diarmuid, I think. *Don't keep pretending*

you're still in my life. You're not, not really. You've wandered
hundreds of miles away. I didn't know you could move that
fast. I didn't even know you wanted to.

'I know how to change plugs, Diarmuid,' I say firmly, to
myself as much as to him. I am about to add, once again, that
Nathaniel is just a friend and that Diarmuid seems to have
given up on our marriage because of a misunderstanding, but
he speaks first.

'Anyway.' His voice is calmer now. 'I suppose I should
explain why I've changed my mind about Charlene.'

I don't say anything, so he continues. 'I've decided it
doesn't matter where Charlene comes from. The important
thing is that I feel comfortable with her. My family will just
have to get used to it. Charlene says there's a kind of love you
sometimes want, but the important kind of love is the kind you
need.'

I almost tell him to shut up about bloody Charlene, but her
words seem wise. They seem like words I need to hear.

'I did love you.' He sounds sad now, bereft and bewildered.

'But you don't any more?'

There is a lengthy pause; then he says, 'Surely this can't be
too much of a surprise to you, Sally. You've found someone else
too. We've both moved on. You don't even wear your
wedding ring any more.'

So he noticed. I decide this is not the right time to mention
that I suspect Nathaniel's dog may have eaten it.

'If you'd talked to me, Diarmuid, you would have
discovered that I haven't moved on and I haven't found
someone else. Nathaniel is just a *friend.*'

'As you said in your telephone messages.' Diarmuid sighs
wearily.

'Look, Diarmuid…' I take a deep breath. 'You think I've
been having an affair with Nathaniel, but I haven't. He was
only here because we went for a walk by the sea and a wave
drenched us. He came to my cottage to dry off a bit.
That's why he was wearing my dressing-gown.'

'And I'm supposed to believe that?'

'Yes. If you'd stayed for a moment, you would have seen his jeans on the heater.'

There is a significant pause; then Diarmuid says, 'Look, I don't know if his jeans were drying or not –'

'They were, honestly they were.'

'But that doesn't change the fact that you love him. I knew it from the first moment I saw you two together. You love him, Sally. You love him in a way you've never loved me.'

I feel like he's punched me. Am I really that transparent? Can other people see things that I can hardly admit to myself? 'He's a *friend*.' I decide to be defensive. 'That's all he is, Diarmuid. That's all he wants to be.'

'I think you should confirm that with him,' Diarmuid says. 'I've seen the way he looks at you. I saw the way you were both snuggled up on that sofa.'

'*What?*'

'I looked through the window before I rang the doorbell.'

'You were *spying* on me?'

'Yes, and who would blame me in the circumstances?'

'What are the circumstances, Diarmuid?' I feel a sob rising in my stomach. 'I really don't know any more. I thought we were both taking time out to think things over.'

'You're the one who wanted to do that.'

'Yes, but then you said you wanted to do it too.'

'I don't know what I said.' Diarmuid sighs. 'You got me so muddled about the whole thing, I could have said anything.'

I suddenly feel desperately tired. Why on earth couldn't Diarmuid have called at a civilised hour? I can't even bear talking to him any more; it seems utterly pointless.

'I don't want to talk to you any more right now.' I just say it.

'Oh.' He sounds surprised. 'I thought you wanted me to talk more to you.'

'Not about this kind of thing!' I scream. 'Not about how you don't love me any more. I've never felt you loved me.'

'Did you love me?'

I don't answer. That's the thing about wanting to be loved:

you don't spend enough time thinking about giving love back. And just wanting to be loved isn't real love. I start to cry. How can I have been so ignorant about being a wife?

Diarmuid hears me crying. 'I'm sorry. I've been far too blunt. I thought it would make it easier.'

'What do you mean?' I sniff.

'I... I didn't want to think about all the things I like about you. I thought it might make me change my mind about Charlene.' His voice lowers. 'Do you want me to change my mind about her?'

'No.' It's a whisper, but I mean it. I say it before I even think about it. The word just scoots out of my mouth.

'I didn't want it to end like this.'

'Neither did I.' I clench my hanky in my hand. 'I'm sorry, Diarmuid. We just kind of lost each other somehow. I don't think either of us meant to – to be so careless.' I start to sob.

'No.' Dear God, Diarmuid is crying too. 'I'm so sorry about the mice, Sally. I kind of got obsessed with them. At first I was just fascinated with the research, but then each one of them seemed like a little friend, somehow. They always seemed so glad to see me.'

'And I didn't?'

'You seemed disappointed, Sally. I couldn't stand seeing you so disappointed with me.'

'I disappointed you too.'

Diarmuid doesn't answer.

'At least we've *talked*,' I say. 'This is the most open conversation we've ever had.'

'Do you want me to ring the estate agents?'

'OK.'

'Bye, Sally. I'll phone again soon.'

'Bye, Diarmuid.'

The line goes dead.

I go back to bed and cry until my pillow is soaking. I just cry, letting the tears leave me – big, fat tears that stream down my face. Some of them find their way into my ears. I can't name the feelings behind them. There are too many. I just know I need to cry.

Half an hour later I dry my face. I get up and pad down to the kitchen in my thick pink socks. I make myself a very large mug of tea and stare numbly out the window at the potted plants in my back garden – the geraniums and sweet peas, the large terracotta pot full of lavender. There is a water lily flowering in a blue glazed bowl.

The phone rings. I almost let the answering machine take it. But it could be Diarmuid. Maybe he's changed his mind… It's Nathaniel.

'Hi, Sal. I've found your wedding ring.' He sounds very bright and perky. 'It was wedged into a chocolate chip cookie in a particularly complicated part of the sofa's upholstery. I also found three euros and a packet of mints.'

'Oh.' My voice must sound like it's travelling through cement. I try to raise it a few octaves. 'Oh! That's *great*. Thank you.'

'What's up? You sound kind of down about something.'

'Really?' I try to sound surprised. 'Maybe it's because I haven't had my second cup of tea yet.' I don't like this any more. I don't like it that Nathaniel knows all these things. It makes me want to tell him everything, but I can't – not after how appalled he was when Diarmuid found him on the sofa in my dressing-gown. He even wanted to phone Diarmuid, to reassure him that nothing had happened between us. He even collected Diarmuid's roses and insisted I put them in a vase. Any secret hopes I had had about Nathaniel vanished in that moment. He looked so scared and guilty, so upset that Diarmuid had jumped to the wrong conclusion.

So had I, for a while. Nathaniel is naturally affectionate, and he exaggerates. I used to like his exaggerations, but now I don't; they're very misleading. I am just one of his little coterie of female confidantes.

'I have to go, Nathaniel,' I say quickly. 'I must make myself some breakfast.'

'How's Diarmuid?'

'He's… he's fine. We've just had a long talk on the phone.'

'Oh.' He sounds surprised. 'That's good. You said you wanted him to be more open.'

'Well, he was,' I say. I try to make my voice sound chirpy. I don't want Nathaniel to know what Diarmuid and I said to each other. I might start bawling and he might want to come round, and I couldn't bear that. I don't want him to feel so close and yet so far away.

'What do you want me to do with the ring?'

'Could... could you just post it?' I get a horrible hollow feeling in my stomach. 'I don't think I'll be able to collect it. I'm very busy at the moment.'

'Fine.' He sounds a little puzzled. 'I'll send it recorded delivery.'

'Yes. Yes, that would be good.'

There is an uncomfortable pause.

'How's Eloise?' It seems appropriate to mention her. Nathaniel should mention her more often. He should use the 'we' word: *We went to the cinema, we went to the park...* It would remind his female friends of his true affections.

'Busy too. She's got an order from a posh hotel in Connemara. We went to Scowly Henry's restaurant to celebrate. She's determined to make him smile.'

We. 'Oh. That's great.' I try not to feel too jealous.

'Yes, she's really getting known now.' It seems to be a morning in which men extol the merits of other women to me.

I'm just about to say I have to go, again, when Nathaniel adds, 'You should get to know Fabrice.'

'Oh, really?' I say dubiously. 'And why is that?'

'You'd like her. And she likes you. She told me on the phone.'

'You *phone* her?'

'Yes. When I met her with Aggie, she gave me her phone number. She said we should meet for tea and cake.'

'And did you?'

'Yes. It was great fun. She's a breath of fresh air. She's led the most amazing life.'

God, I think. *Now Fabrice is part of Nathaniel's little*

267

coterie of female friends too. She probably fancies him. She probably likes her men young and nubile. Maybe I should warn him about her. He's so trusting.

'You'd like her, Sal. You two have a lot in common.'

I clench the phone in outrage. I think of Fabrice – her tall stories, her layered make-up, her rattling, showy costume jewellery; her solemn, calculating, calm eyes. How dare he compare me to her? He mustn't know me at all.

'I think she could be a good friend,' Nathaniel continues. 'Aggie has her mobile number. You should give her a call.'

I am so flabbergasted that I just stare out the window. What does Fabrice do to people? Both Nathaniel and Aggie can't stop talking about her.

'She'll be going away soon, on business; she might be away for a while. You should phone her soon.'

'Look, Nathaniel,' I say firmly, 'I have no wish to get to know Fabrice. I don't even like her.'

'But you don't know her,' Nathaniel persists. His voice sounds odd; once again, I get the vague suspicion that there's something he's not telling me.

'I have to go now, Nathaniel.'

'OK. By the way, I found my mobile phone. Fred had buried it near the hydrangeas.'

'Good. I mean, I'm glad you found it.'

'What is it, Sally? You sound really weird. Do you want me to call round?'

Yes. Yes, I do, I think. *I want you to call round and hold me. I want to rest my head on your chest and hear your heart. I want to make you tea. I want you to tell me your stories. I want to know you, Nathaniel. I want to love you. I want to stare into your clear blue eyes and remember my dreams and hopes and who I once wanted to be. I seem to have forgotten.*

Only I can't say this. It isn't what he wants to hear. He wouldn't know how to answer; he would be embarrassed. It would frighten him off. 'No – no, I really don't want you to call round, Nathaniel. Maybe… you know… we shouldn't see each other for a while.'

'Yes,' Nathaniel says slowly. 'Yes, of course. I'm sorry. I shouldn't have suggested it.'

I know he thinks I'm saying this because of Diarmuid, and I let him. I can't just be friends with Nathaniel any more. It would be easier if he just left my life; then maybe I could forget him.

'Bye, Sally.'

'Bye, Nathaniel.'

After I've hung up, I stare at the phone. I don't even know what I'm feeling. Erika's cats are all looking at me from the shelf beside the fireplace. Some are smiling and some are solemn and some are inscrutable and mysterious. I can't cry; I've cried enough this morning. Instead I make myself some toast and another cup of tea, put them on a tray and go back upstairs to my duvet. It is a duvet day. I just want to hide away under it and maybe watch something comforting on the telly.

I am halfway through my second slice of toast when the doorbell rings. I decide to ignore it, but the person won't be ignored. Whoever it is thumps the door and shouts, 'Salleee!'

It's Erika. I plod gingerly downstairs and open the door. She is looking very bright-eyed and bushy-tailed, and she's wearing cord trousers and thick leather boots.

'You'd better hurry up and get ready,' she says. 'We're supposed to be at the stables soon.'

I stare at her. Then I gulp. Oh, *feck*! Today is the day we're supposed to be going riding. The last thing I feel like doing is getting on a huge animal who may run off into the hills with me.

'Fiona's giving us a lift,' Erika says. I look out onto the road. Fiona waves. She's borrowed Zak's jeep for the occasion, and Milly is sitting in her baby seat in the back.

'I tried to ring you, but you were on the phone for ages,' Erika says.

I wonder if I should just say I can't go riding today. If I tell her about Diarmuid's phone call, she'll surely understand.

'Go upstairs and change. Fiona brought her jodhpurs in

case you needed them.'

'There is no way I could fit into Fiona's jodhpurs,' I say grimly.

'I've been so looking forward to this!'

I look at Erika warily. She is almost bursting with excitement. She needs this, and she needs me to be with her. I sigh and smile. And then I trudge upstairs to dress.

Chapter Thirty-Two

THE CREATURE IS HUGE and brown and snorting. She's called Blossom, and I don't like the look of her. Saffron, the boot-faced woman who has herded us and the horses into the paddock, tells me that Blossom is very gentle, which is clearly a lie worthy of the most devious politician. Saffron has one of those frightfully solemn faces that make everything seem very serious. Whoever named Saffron clearly thought she was going to be someone else entirely. Saffrons should have long flowing scarves and smell of patchouli. This one looks as if she's taking a quick break from the army.

She informs me that Blossom sometimes puffs out her stomach when you try to fasten her girth. 'When you get on her, you'll have to check the girth again and make sure it's tight enough.'

'Saffron, do I have to do that with Bluebell?' Erika pipes up.

'No,' Saffron says, unsmiling. 'It's only Blossom you have to watch out for.'

I glower at Blossom, while also reluctantly admiring her subterfuge. If I had to spend the day hauling strangers around the Wicklow hills, I'm sure I would resort to all sorts of ruses. In fact, I might dump the strangers in a large hedge at the earliest opportunity. Blossom is stamping her feet, and I can't say I blame her. She probably wanted to lead an entirely different kind of life. Today might be the day when she finally makes a break for it. She will probably gallop desperately towards the distant hills, with me on her back. I glance enviously at Erika's mount, Bluebell, a short, stubby creature who is probably half Shetland pony. Why couldn't I have been given Bluebell? I feel like I'm back at school. Saffron is talking to us as if we are teenagers.

My marriage is over. The thought lunges at me, and I suddenly feel like I'm on another planet. *How can everyone be acting so ordinarily? How can the sun be shining? How can Diarmuid be in love with Charlene? How am I going to tell my relatives at Marie's party? And why, oh, why did I have to meet Nathaniel?*

'Put on your hard hat, Sally,' Saffron says. 'Everyone has to wear a hat before we go on the ride.'

I feel like shouting, *Fuck off, you bitch, my husband's just left me,* but then Erika and Fiona would know too, and I can't bear to talk to anyone about it at the moment. I can hardly admit it to myself. They said I seemed very quiet in the car, and I said it was because Diarmuid had been talking about maybe moving in with Charlene. Erika and Fiona were suitably outraged and wonderfully biased; Erika showed no evidence of her annoying even-handedness. Then they said that riding would 'take me out of myself' and help me to forget my worries. This, of course, is utter nonsense. It is just a brand new worry to add to the steaming heap that's there already.

I plonk the hat on my head and glower at Saffron. *What will I do with my wedding ring? I think. Should I give it to Diarmuid or hand it over to Oxfam?*

There are five riders in my group, and I am the only one who hasn't got on her horse. Saffron offers me a leg up, which I clearly need, since Blossom is the equine equivalent of Mount Everest.

'Feel the fear and do it anyway,' Erika whispers.

'Oh, shut up,' I bark at her. Saffron is marching towards me, and I fear she may lift me up and plonk me on Blossom whether I like it or not. All the riders are looking very smug. Some of them must have spent hundreds of euros getting the right gear. Only Blossom seems to be looking at me with a slight trace of sympathy. We are both in the same boat: neither of us wants to do this. She'd prefer to be munching grass in a field and I'd prefer to be at home watching daytime television and trying not to think about my life.

Saffron appears to be hanging on to my left leg. She obviously expects me to cling onto the saddle and sort of claw my way upwards, while hanging onto Blossom's mane. I notice a large stone nearby – a stone that has clearly been used many times before by people in my situation.

'I'm going to use that,' I say to Saffron, in the gruff military voice she employs herself. Then I get on the stone and attempt to throw myself across Blossom's enormous back. She stands very still while I make a total arse of myself. Eventually I manage to haul myself aloft, even though the saddle is slipping. And then Blossom puffs out her stomach, so that the saddle stabilises and I am not left clinging to it under her stomach. I am actually on her back. I feel like punching the air like a footballer.

'Thanks, Blossom,' I whisper. Her ears twitch back and forth. She's listening.

'All right, now that we've got *that* finished with, we can start the ride,' Saffron says joylessly. 'Tighten Blossom's girth.' She frowns at me. 'Bluebell, you go behind me, and…' She starts to reel off various names, which all seem to be connected with flowers. Blossom has to be at the back because she occasionally kicks. I am on a rebel horse. A horse with attitude. How on earth did I allow myself to be talked into this?

Fiona darts forward as we are all about to set off. She has a new digital camera. She's probably been recording the entire saga, and we haven't even left the paddock yet. I smile. That's the stupid thing about photographs: you feel you have to smile. My marriage was like the smiling Olympics.

Nathaniel has such a wonderful smile. It lights up his whole face.

'Oh my God!' Erika suddenly screeches.

We all look at her. 'What is it?' I enquire. Blossom is dancing up and down as if she may make her bid for freedom at any minute; she's champing at her bit and backing towards Bluebell as if she's about to give her a quick belt on the shin.

'It's Alex and his wife,' Erika moans. 'They're over there. Look. In the advanced ride.'

'What is it?' Saffron demands. 'Are your stirrups too short?' She glides towards us on her gleaming thoroughbred to

273

inspect Erika's legs.

'I… I have to make a phone call,' Erika whimpers.

'You'll have to make it later. We're going now.' Saffron glares at her.

Erika ignores her. She takes out her mobile phone and dials, while Bluebell starts to snatch mouthfuls of grass from the side of the path.

'Pull her up!' Saffron roars. 'She's not supposed to eat until we get back.'

'Oh, shut up, you bossy woman!' Erika roars back. Then she starts to whisper urgently into the phone. I wonder if Saffron is going to send Erika back to the stables and tell her to write a hundred lines, but she seems too surprised to get angry; she merely waits until Erika stuffs her phone back into her pocket.

'Who did you ring?' I ask, but Bluebell is trotting forwards to take her place behind Saffron's mount, who is called Primrose. Poor Erika. I wish I could get closer to her and offer her some comfort.

In normal circumstances, my day would have been full of Diarmuid. I would have thought for hours about what I could have done differently, in between watching the telly and drinking tea and soaking desolately in the bath. I would also have got angry about Charlene and felt desperately betrayed and rejected. Then I would have got miserable about Nathaniel not wanting me like I want him, and eaten a whole packet of chocolate biscuits.

By this stage I would probably have phoned Erika and she would have joined me. We would both have been wailing about being on the sideboard and wondering why we were such eejits.

But I can't think any of these things, because my thoughts have contracted into one major concern: staying on Blossom while she slithers down the bank of a river and splashes across. Then she has to climb up the other side. She trips, alarmingly, a number of times, and I cling to her mane. What on earth can Saffron be thinking of? Doesn't she know we're *beginners*?

We reach a leafy path and have to duck to avoid the branches. Two kids on frisky ponies are riding up and down policing us, making sure that we are all in the correct order and behaving ourselves. They must be Saffron's staff sergeants.

Saffron now wants us all to climb a steep hill; then, apparently, there will be some trotting. I sigh stoically and try to keep the sense of panic from rising too rapidly. But then Blossom does something unexpected. She turns to the left while the others walk on. We're on a small path bordered with wildflowers and blackberries. Blossom walks on, steadily and contentedly. I try to get her to turn round, but she politely ignores me.

I am beyond caring. I'm tired and pissed off and very far from the ground. I am perched precariously on top of a huge animal who has absolutely no respect for me and who may take off at any moment. And so, since I am now virtually a prisoner on Blossom's back, I decide just to try to enjoy myself. I'm tired of waiting for the circumstances that will make me happy. The right job, the right house, the right man, the right marriage... they were all supposed to be the answer. But they weren't. I was – I am – still the same Sally. Having big articles in newspapers didn't increase my sense of worth; being married didn't make me feel more loved. Maybe the only way to be contented is to accept where I am and make the most of it. I should drink in this moment, especially since I may soon find myself deposited unceremoniously in a ditch. I smile. How did I become so serious about things? So worried and earnest?

It's good to be away from Saffron. It's good just to be with Blossom. I pat her shiny brown neck. She is innocent of the intentions I gave her; I don't know how I know this, but suddenly I'm no longer frightened. I listen to the birds. I watch a small squirrel darting around, collecting nuts. That's the thing about nature: it only knows how to be who it is. It doesn't know how to pretend. It doesn't know how to lie. Suddenly I am the little girl who wanted a mountain bike so she could pedal into the wilds, who wanted to learn the names of every bird and every tiny animal. DeeDee was right when she said parts of us are like the Serengeti and parts are like the back yard.

Poor DeeDee. Did she consider coming home, when Marie confirmed that Joseph was dead? Maybe she wanted to be sure she wouldn't have to see him. Why else would she have phoned? But then she probably decided she couldn't face the rest of us – especially Aggie...

Blossom knows where I – we – need to go. She takes us to a calm lake, where there are blackberries and tall, lush grass for her to eat. I get off her and let her munch. I lie back on the earth and stare up through the trees, at the clear, high, singing blue sky.

'So you sometimes want to get away, too,' I say to Blossom. 'Get off the old path and try something different.' I know Saffron will probably be going apeshit, but I find that I don't care. The world will always have people like Saffron in it. You just have to learn not to take them too seriously.

I want to do things like this more often, I think. *Have more adventures. I want to travel more. And why shouldn't I? I'm a single woman now. I've never really felt single before; I've felt married to my job, my family, my friends, even my house. I want to be more like Nathaniel. I love his carefree ways, his humour. And I want not to care so much what people think of me. It makes you feel small and trapped and scared.*

'My husband has left me,' I whisper to the wind, which carries the words away into the distance. 'I've made a mistake. I have made a lot of mistakes.' The lake stares back at me, calm and gentle, undismayed and unsurprised.

Eventually I feel I should make some attempt to get back to the others. I'm worried about Erika. We'll have to whisk her away from Alex's vicinity as soon as possible. I find a tree stump and manage to clamber onto Blossom's back. As I wriggle around arduously, I remember the way Fiona puts one foot in a stirrup and swings herself upwards so that she lands neatly on the saddle; but I am tired of comparing myself to Fiona. Why should I? We're different people. Why can't I just accept myself as I am, instead of wanting someone else to do it for me?

Blossom heads back down the path without protest. Suddenly I hear the sound of trotting, so Blossom and I hide behind a large bush. I peep out at the riders. It's the beginners. Erika is hanging grimly onto Bluebell's mane and bouncing up and down on her saddle. When the last rider has passed, Blossom and I creep out from behind the bush and fall in at the back. No one even comments on our absence, apart from one of the small staff sergeants, who says, 'Did you like the lake?'

'Sorry?'

'It's Blossom's favourite place. If she likes people, she takes them there.'

'And you didn't stop us?'

'No. Saffron said Blossom would look after you. Blossom's very good with people who are frightened and don't really want to go riding at all.'

Saffron is roaring instructions about some gate and telling Erika to shorten her reins. How hard it is to tell who people really are! I feel a warmth in my heart, a surge in my spirit. It's been a lovely morning, lovely in a way I didn't expect at all. It hasn't just been helpful; it has been necessary. It happened just when I needed it to.

The horses are walking faster, towards the stables and food. As we reach the paddock, I see Erika glancing around nervously. The advanced ride will be returning soon. She'll probably want to flee before Alex and his wife get back here. Fiona is taking more pictures, and Milly is looking at us all with great interest.

There is a man resting his elbows on the wooden fencing. He is tall and dark and lithe, with soft brown eyes and a lovely, open face. He's watching Erika, watching her every movement. He looks shy but determined.

'Who's that?' I nudge Erika as she loosens the girth on Bluebell's saddle.

But suddenly I know, even before she says it. It's the person she phoned. It's Lionel, and he's *gorgeous*.

Chapter Thirty-Three

I STUMBLE INTO THE day from a thick sleep, with no wish to go anywhere. I want to spend the day in my cosy wee cottage. It's lashing rain outside. I have to write my column, and this one's going to be different. It's going to say things I actually believe, for a change. I'm tired of feeling like a fake. I'm tired of telling people to paint walls and buy woven rattan baskets. There's quite enough of that advice around already. I want to write something different, but I don't quite know what it is yet. I need a cup of tea first.

I propel myself from my bed. I can barely stagger. Erika's wildflower liqueur has set off a foggy, dull ache in my head, and the muscles in my legs and thighs and bum are complaining mightily. I wince with every step. Who would have thought sitting on a horse for an hour could do this to you? I inch my way downstairs towards the kitchen and the kettle. I feel as though I'm ninety.

As I gingerly sip my tea, I decide to phone Erika to see if she has recovered from seeing Alex and his wife. When we sat on her saggy sofa last night, I spilt the beans and spent most of the time talking about Diarmuid and Charlene and Nathaniel. It didn't help that the sofa's cushions were sliding gradually onto the floor. It's a cheap sofa with a rickety wooden base, and it seems to have aspirations to become a carpet. By the time we were virtually on Erika's multicoloured ethnic rug, I was announcing that I was a failure and clearly knew nothing at all about intimate relationships, so I would obviously be alone forever. The brief serenity I had found when riding Blossom had disappeared entirely. How could I believe I knew anyone again? I hadn't had the slightest suspicion that Diarmuid was about to ditch me so dramatically. Yes, I agreed, I hadn't been entirely sure about my marriage, but I'd thought it would at least drag on a little longer. Erika pointed out that 'dragging on' didn't sound that satisfactory, but I proclaimed that it could, at any moment, have got better. Diarmuid had given the mice back to the college. He was a great lover. He remembered things like milk and black bean sauce. He washed up, for God's sake, and he knew how to put up shelving. I started to cry when I mentioned the shelving. Charlene would have his shelving, and I was on the shelf.

'The sideboard,' Erika said. 'It's not the shelf, it's the sideboard.' I didn't correct her.

At around that time she got up and fetched chocolate biscuits, which she actually put on a plate. As she handed the plate to me, I said that that was what I'd done with Diarmuid: I had virtually handed him to Charlene on a plate, like a biscuit. Then we spent the next hour discussing what type of biscuit Diarmuid would be, if he were a biscuit – and, after four glasses of Erika's wildflower liqueur, I wouldn't have sworn he wasn't. We decided that he wouldn't contain much sugar but would be alarmingly deceptive – the kind of biscuit that seems wholesome and bland until you get to the bits of raw chilli pepper and have to race to the sink and rinse out your mouth. Alex, on the other hand, would seem to be sweet and delicious, but he wouldn't really be a biscuit at all; he would be full of salt and pepper and sour mayonnaise. I don't know where the sour mayonnaise came from. By that stage we were basically talking gibberish.

Erika wanted me to describe what kind of biscuit Nathaniel would be, but I couldn't. I said he was Eloise's biscuit and I had no right even to taste him. I started to cry again, and Erika decided to cheer me up by playing the guitar. I got a taxi shortly afterwards. I wonder what sort of state she is in this morning. It's nine-thirty; she should be at her desk.

'International Mouldings.' Her voice has acquired the sing-song tone of public announcements at airports.

'I thought it was International Holdings.'

'That's what I said.'

'No, you said International Mouldings.'

'Oh, feck.'

'It's OK, most people wouldn't notice.'

'I don't know what's wrong with the stapler. There's another one in the stationery cupboard.' I'm getting used to this now. Erika sounds groggy and a great deal less patient than usual.

'How are you, Sally? Are you feeling any better?'

'I don't know. I rang to find out about you,' I say. 'I'm sorry. I hardly let you say a word last night.'

'Right and proper, too,' she says. 'I'm furious with Mouse Boy for being so horrible to you. You needed to let it all out.'

'Please don't call him Mouse Boy.'

'But it suits him.'

'No, it doesn't.'

'You should be more angry with him.'

'I am angry with him,' I say. 'But I've been angry with him for months; it's a normal feeling for me now. I want to talk about you. How are you?'

'I wish I didn't have to waste my time at this stupid job,' Erika sighs. 'It's outrageous. Life is far too short for this sort of rubbish.'

I know exactly how she feels.

'We should be swimming with dolphins, Sally. We should be sitting under olive trees in the sunshine, eating figs.'

I agree with her entirely.

'Let's get a camper van and just run away.'

I'm not so sure about that one.

'How's Lionel?' I ask casually.

'Same as ever.' Erika sighs. 'He made a pig's arse out of pretending to be my boyfriend, didn't he? I wanted Alex to think I'd found someone who adores me. I wanted to... to regain some dignity. I even hoped he might be jealous.'

'I... I thought his hand lingered on your elbow with genuine feeling,' I say.

'But you missed the rest of it when you went to the café.' Erika sighs reproachfully. When Lionel was supposed to be pretending to be Erika's boyfriend, I darted into the small café beside the stables to get some sugar sachets for Blossom.

'What happened?' I ask. She didn't feel capable of talking about it last night. It was all too raw and disappointing and ridiculous, and she wanted me to talk about my raw and disappointing and ridiculous marriage instead.

'I wanted him to kiss me,' Erika says. 'Yes, I know it says it's out of paper, but it isn't. Just turn it off and turn it on again.' This is clearly the highly advanced photocopier, which sometimes gets a bit confused. 'I said, "Lionel, when Alex and his wife appear, you must kiss me on the lips with great feeling." I told him to pretend he was in a play.'

'Yes, I saw you discussing something rather earnestly. What happened?' I'm beginning to wish I hadn't run into the café at the crucial moment, but Blossom was looking at me so hopefully. I suspected she shared my sweet tooth. I really loved her for a while. That's the kind of woman I am now: I fall in love with a horse at the slightest encouragement. My next significant other may quite possibly be a gerbil.

'It was awful,' Erika moans. 'Alex and… and that woman turned up, and I kept waiting for Lionel to do something, but he just stood there looking like a mortified marmoset.'

I'm not sure what marmosets look like, but I'm pretty sure Lionel does not resemble one. In fact, he cut quite a dashing figure as he waited for Erika outside the paddock. His long legs looked most attractive in his fashionably faded jeans, and he was wearing a light-brown woollen jumper that was clearly expensive and might have been made in Italy. He looked rather Italian, actually, with his olive skin and brown eyes. His dark hair was short and stylishly unkempt, and his face had a soulful look about it. He was handsome enough to appear in a coffee advertisement. I don't know why Erika doesn't seem to notice his charms.

'So – so I had to sort of grab hold of him,' Erika continues. 'Only he started to back away from me, so I grabbed his jumper and plonked my lips on his. And then he opened his mouth and our teeth bashed together, and I yelped and stumbled and landed on my bum in a pile of horse shit.'

'Oh, no.'

'It was dry horse shit,' Erika says bravely. 'I could brush it off fairly easily.'

'I was wondering what that pong was in the car. I thought it was Milly.'

'I must have looked desperate – and Alex must have seen the whole thing.'

'Lionel opened his mouth when you were kissing?' This seems like an important detail.

'Yes, and then when he'd helped me up he ran off. For a man with tight ankles he can move pretty fast. He mumbled something about needing to go to the toilet and just disappeared. It was ridiculous.'

'But he *did* go to the toilet,' I remind her. 'It's a pity he didn't add that he was going to have a short walk and then sit in the saddle room and have a cigarette, but at least we found him.'

'After twenty minutes of shouting, "Lionel!" as though he was a German shepherd,' Erika snaps. 'We should have just left him. What on earth can Alex have thought?'

Alex threw us an extremely quizzical glance before driving off with his wife in their flashy jeep. I bet they don't really need a jeep. Why do so many city types want to look like they live up some long dirt track?

'Lionel's just a boy, basically,' Erika continues. 'He's five years younger than me and very immature for his age. I've been trying to train him into adulthood, but I think I'm going to have to drop him, even though he's sold seven of my cats so far. At least it will let me off the refugee thing.' Her voice lowers to a whisper. 'He's coming over. I have to go.' Her voice returns to its normal level. 'No, Lionel, I don't want your bloody organic stem ginger biscuits.' The line goes dead.

What a pity, I think. Lionel seemed very sweet, if extremely bashful, and he looked at Erika with such longing. He just needs a little coaching – and there will be plenty of women willing to coach Lionel. I sincerely hope he doesn't bump into Fabrice.

Fabrice. The word lands in my brain with a thump. Aggie's

still going on about Fabrice and her travels and her views on world peace.

I creep, bow-legged, upstairs. It is clearly time to have a long soak in the bath, because I'm walking like some gunslinger in a Western. As I sink into the warm water, I think about my conversation with my parents last night. I decided to phone them from Erika's, after my first glass of wildflower liqueur; I needed company and Dutch courage. They were aghast and disappointed to hear that my marriage is over, but they weren't as surprised as I expected. I am no longer their 'good' daughter. In fact, the main thing I am to them at the moment is a puzzle. I am a puzzle to myself, too. I thought I could train myself to live a conventional life, marry a conventional man, have a conventional – if stylish – house and make conventional chicken casseroles. I should have known from the casseroles that I wasn't up to it; I don't know what I did to them, but they tasted like oregano-flavoured mud pies.

'Take it easy, now,' Mum said softly. 'Be kind to yourself. Do you want to come over for lunch? I'll make your favourite chicken casserole.' I almost cried at the word 'casserole', but I managed to smile bravely. I said I would love to come over for lunch, but not just yet; I would phone very soon. Then I got off the phone quickly, before she suggested I take up tennis. Mum has been wanting me to take up tennis for the last fifteen years. She loves tennis herself. There is a whole tennis world out there, apparently, and she thinks it would make me happier. I have never told her that, any time I've attempted to play tennis, it has taken me ages to actually hit the ball, and when I do, I send it over walls and hedges and wire fencing. On one occasion it ended up in the middle of a dual carriageway.

I suspect that she and Dad were relieved that it was Diarmuid who finally called an end to our marriage. This way I can seem like the wronged party, and it will sound so much better when they have to explain it all at Marie's gathering.

'Poor Sally, do you think she'll ever find someone?' The overheard conversations between my parents and Marie return to me while I soak in my lavender-scented bath.

283

'I wonder if I'll ever have grandchildren. Neither April nor Sally seems to have any intention of getting married.'

'She keeps meeting these awful men who leave her.'

'She leaves some of them, too.'

'Yes, but with good reason. None of them really seem to want to make a commitment to her.'

'What do you think she's doing wrong? Should we talk to her about it?'

'When she meets the right person it will be different.'

'But she isn't getting any younger.'

Of course, I shouldn't have listened outside the kitchen door; I should have just marched in and made myself a cup of tea like I wanted to. Why did I care what they said? Why did I believe it?

People make up stories about other people, and those become their truth. And if you don't watch out you may start believing their version of you. You forget how to be anchored in your own life; you become the product of other people's fears and hopes and weaknesses. But we are more than our stories. We are more than our past and our mistakes. I knew that when I was riding Blossom, and when I found Aggie. DeeDee knew it, too. She refused to believe in the limits that were being set for her. I hope she became an actress even though they thought she wasn't that type of person. If only she had returned to challenge the family's view of her. She let Joseph off far too easily. She should have returned with his baby and forced them all to face the truth.

Suddenly I long with all my heart for Nathaniel. I wish I could tell him what has happened. We fit, somehow. I don't have to struggle to make him understand me. He doesn't make me feel alone. That's the worst kind of loneliness: feeling alone when you're with people who are supposed to know and love you.

'My beautiful stranger…' I say the words out loud, just to hear them. He really would make the most wonderful biscuit.

I get out of the bath and dress quickly. I need, urgently, to eat something. I go downstairs and make some toast and another cup of tea. Then I go to the sitting room and turn on the computer, and start to write.

'The nicest house I ever lived in had faded carpets,' I write. 'The curtains were old and the lining was worn, and the floorboards were a bit loose in places and squeaked. The lawn needed mowing and the bathroom tiles needed re-grouting. There was a sign above the toilet that said, "Flush sharply," the shelves were stuffed with shells and stones we'd found on beaches, and there was no particular colour scheme. But that house had love and hope and faith in it, and forgiveness. It was a shelter and a sanctuary. We were larger in it. There was a heartbeat in its silences. I never felt alone there.

'When we lived in that house, we weren't trying to impress anyone. It was a home. It didn't have to look like the magazines; we knew what we needed, and we didn't compare the house to other places. I've begun to remember something I'd forgotten: you can have a house, or you can have a home. And a home will sometimes be a bit inconvenient. There will be things you can't throw away, and it will sometimes be a bit messy – like life, and like love. But, because you aren't seeing it through other people's eyes, you will know what fits there and what is cherished. And you won't fuss around trying to make everything perfect, because that's an endless, pointless task.

'So buy the sofa you want, even if it's bright red and clashes with the wallpaper. Change things at your own rhythm or leave them as they are. Most of all, don't worry about what other people think. What's the point? Everyone has their own tastes and preferences. And maybe you'll be alone in that house, or maybe you'll share it; but, whatever your circumstances, you will know more about the largeness of life and love and how to belong somewhere. How to listen to your heart.'

Chapter Thirty-Four

FIONA IS BEAMING. HER smile hardly fits on her face. 'It's a kind of miracle, isn't it?' she says, cradling the mug of tea I have made her. We are sitting in my kitchen in the company of numerous ants.

I am smiling too – smiling with relief and happiness, and trying to hide any slight trace of suspicion. I'm finding it hard to believe what she's telling me. The main thing that makes it plausible is that it happened to Fiona. These sorts of things happen to Fiona quite a lot.

It looks like Zak's sperm may not have been quite so slow after all. In fact, according to Fiona, it seems highly likely that Milly is Zak's daughter. He himself is in no doubt about it. Milly is, apparently, the spitting image of his great-grandmother Mabel – who, it turns out, was one-quarter Chinese.

Zak hardly knew anything about Mabel and her exotic provenance until the day before yesterday. He was up in the attic, hunting for the antique lace tablecloth that Fiona wanted to use at the christening party. He plonked a photograph album on a wonky table; it promptly slid off, hit his shin, landed on the floor with a wallop and burst open at a two-page spread entitled 'Bella's Christening'. Fiona is quite convinced that the angels guided Zak to the album. I think this angel thing is catching. Ever since I told Fiona and Erika about Aggie's angels, they've been keeping a beady lookout for their own.

Zak knew that his grandmother had been called Bella; and, since he was soon to be deeply involved in a christening himself, he glanced at the photos with mild interest. His eyes fixed on the woman who was holding Bella. Someone had written 'Mabel and baby Bella' underneath the photo in tidy blue ink. Zak had seen photos of his grandmother, but Mabel was only a thin and distant name, more of a story than a fact. Though the image was brownish and faded, he could make out Mabel's features quite clearly. He gazed at her almond-shaped eyes; her pert, charming nose; her high, exotic cheekbones. She was virtually an adult replica of Milly. You could see that she was more European than Eastern, but there was a distinct suggestion of improbable exoticism.

Zak took out his mobile phone and called his mother, who said that Mabel was a strange woman. She had met Zak's great-grandfather when he was working on a building site in London. He had brought her home to County Westmeath, and no one had really known what to make of her. She was basically English and had a Cockney accent. There was some talk of her having a Chinese grandfather, but even Mabel was vague about the details; the main thing she knew about him was that he had wanted to go to America but had somehow got off the boat in Liverpool. For a long time, many people thought that Mabel herself had ended up in the wrong country – but then the differences slowly softened, and she was just Mabel, who had somehow landed in the middle of them all like an exotic bird. She was quiet and shy, and even her genes seemed to share her reticence: her children all looked like their father, and her grandchildren didn't seem to resemble anyone in particular. 'It's almost like she went back to where she came from and didn't leave a trace,' Zak's mother said.

'Yes, she did,' Zak said. 'Milly looks like her.'

His mother debated this point. She said that, at three days old, Milly had been the spitting image of her Aunt Sasha – 'Though your father says she looks more like me,' she added. 'She has my eyebrows.' Zak began to realise that, at the christening, Milly would be likened to half of his relatives. They would see what they wanted to see, and he would not correct them. He smiled to himself and put the phone back in his pocket. He himself knew that Milly had his hands and his chin and his ears, but he had been very disappointed that she didn't look more like Fiona. And he had sensed that, in some way, Fiona was worried about Milly's appearance. Now he could explain it to her.

'I really want to find out more about Mabel,' Fiona says as

she stoically munches one of my rice cakes (my house is now a biscuit-free zone). 'It's like you and DeeDee. Families are so strange, aren't they? There are so many hidden, secret things. It's fascinating.'

'Yes, indeed,' I agree, deciding not to tell her that I've put DeeDee in the 'too difficult' file for the moment.

'Apparently, some family characteristic can skip generations,' she continues enthusiastically, 'until you get a son or a daughter like Milly. Zak says there are families who don't know they have a black relative until a lovely dusky little baby suddenly appears. I know it sounds funny, but I almost feel like Mabel's genes suddenly decided to reassert themselves through Milly. And, once they decided to do it, they really got down to business. I mean, how else can you explain it? I was told over and over, by people who are supposed to know these things, that Zak would never be a father – a biological father. I felt so guilty about hiding the truth from him, but now I'm glad I did.'

'Why?'

'Many people have done amazing things because no one told them that they couldn't. The only person who said Zak could be a father was that acupuncturist. He gave him herbs he had to boil up and drink. They tasted really awful, but I think they must have helped.' Fiona's eyes shine with joy. 'He found that album at just the right time. It sort of jumped out at him. It wouldn't let him ignore it.'

I try to eat a rice cake myself. I desperately want to lose weight for Marie's party. Ditched, divorced and fat would just be too demoralising.

'I was going to tell him about the fertility clinic that very night,' she says. 'I just couldn't keep it to myself any longer. I'd even phoned my mother to say I might need to come and stay for a while.'

'Oh, poor Fiona.' I touch her arm sympathetically.

'If Zak ever finds out what I did, he'll be furious.' She frowns. 'I don't think he'd leave now, but it just wouldn't be the same between us.'

'Don't think about that,' I say gently. 'I'm so pleased for

you.'

'I so wish you could meet someone you love as much as I love Zak.' Her eyes are sorrowful. 'I'm so sorry about Diarmuid. And I've been no support to you. I've just been going on and on about myself.'

'Well, I think we all kind of knew it wasn't a marriage made in heaven,' I mumble. 'I'm beginning to think you marry the same way you live. I haven't listened to my heart enough, Fiona. I haven't believed it. It… it seemed to want some things that frightened me. Things that seemed like too much of a risk.'

'Like your beautiful stranger at that party,' she says softly. 'Like Nathaniel.'

'Yes.' The word is a whisper. 'I don't know who I'm becoming, Fiona, but I'm different. I can't lie to myself like I used to. I miss that, in a way. It seemed easier, even though it wasn't.'

'So you lied to yourself when you married Diarmuid?'

'Yes, I did, but I didn't know it. I didn't listen to that little voice that kept whispering, "This isn't right. You don't love him. Don't be so frightened of being alone." I was so scared, Fiona – so terrified that I mightn't find anyone who wanted me. I didn't want people saying, "Poor Sally, she never married…"'

'Well, at least they won't say that now.' Fiona smiles.

'Yes, but they'll say all kinds of other things instead. They're going to judge and comment, and some of them will blame me. And these feelings I have aren't going to stop until I decide other things are more important.'

'Like what?'

'Like honesty and compassion and courage. Like love – real love.'

She reaches out and hugs me. She is so warm and sweet and kind – and she works so hard at being Fiona. She puts her beliefs into practice. She is brave and true, and she doesn't expect everything to be easy.

'So how are preparations going for the christening?' I ask, as she rises to leave.

'They're a mess,' she sighs. 'Zak found the album, but he didn't find the antique tablecloth; I must have thrown it out by mistake. And the house is a tip – there's stuff all over the place. We're just too tired to put things away, and we never seem to get around to cleaning. Milly has thrown up on almost all my good clothes. I go around smelling of stale milk. I've forgotten who I've invited, and I keep phoning people to check if I've told them. I've never been this disorganised.' She smiles happily. 'Sometimes we have muesli for dinner.'

'Sounds a bit like my life,' I laugh. 'At least you don't have ants.'

As Fiona drives away, the phone rings. I wonder if it's Diarmuid phoning to discuss the house sale. He has made an inventory of all the furniture, and he wants to know what to sell with the house and what we should keep. I don't know if I want any of that furniture. It seems alien to me now, like remnants from another life. And I wouldn't be able to fit any more furniture into this cottage anyway. Maybe I'll say I just want the nice bright mugs I bought. They wouldn't take up too much space.

'Sally.' It's April. 'Sally, is that you?' Her voice sounds strange, breathless and excited.

'Yes, it's me. What is it?' She's normally so calm on the phone – businesslike, almost brusque.

'I've been thinking.'

'About what?'

'About Marie's party. I've been thinking that maybe I should come over after all.'

'Oh, that's – that's great.'

'You'll be there, won't you?'

'I don't think I have any choice, April. Marie would probably send out a search party if I was ten minutes late.'

'I don't think I can keep this a secret any longer. It's ridiculous. It's high time they all knew.' Her voice quivers. 'I've been living a lie. Mum and Dad said they'd tell people when I was twenty-one, but they didn't. My therapist says it's really affected me.'

'Your *therapist*?'

'Yes, I started going to him after we met in New York. I've been bottling up all sorts of things for *years*. I really needed to let it all out.'

I don't know what to say.

'I'm going to tell them, Sally,' April declares, in a tone that makes me realise she has been drinking. 'I'm going to tell them, at Marie's party, that Al is my father.'

'Don't be ridiculous, April!' I exclaim. 'You can't do that. Mum and Dad and Marie would be devastated.'

'You're the one who keeps saying people should be more open.'

'Yes, but not quite so dramatically. I mean, you have to consider people's *feelings*.'

'They haven't considered mine.'

'Wait,' I say urgently. 'Come over another time. Talk to Mum and Dad about it first.'

'No, I've talked to them about it countless times.' She takes a deep breath. 'I told them I'd tell people if they didn't.'

'Oh, April, please…' It's like she's a teenager again, the April who went to cider parties and stole clothes and stumbled home at three in the morning.

'I want to come over, Sally. I want to tell them,' she says firmly. 'I thought you, of all people, would understand. I just want them all to know the truth.'

Chapter Thirty-Five

THE WEEK HAS GONE by in a busy blur. Since I don't know what to do about April's phone call, I've been trying not to think about it. But I have thought about it. There is no way that April can announce who her real father is at Marie's family gathering. I have been saying this over and over again to myself. But my phone calls to her don't seem to be having any effect and she isn't answering my e-mails. Now she isn't even answering the phone.

I have been imagining Mum's distraught expression as April makes her announcement. I can almost sense the hush, feel the disbelief, hear the uproar as Dad grabs Mum's bag and coat and sweeps her out of the room into the car. His face will be stony and expressionless. His jaw will be clenched with outrage. And Marie will try to blink back the tears as she rushes around with plates of soggy lemon meringue pie, while everyone stares at April as though she has suddenly turned into a duck-billed platypus. She'll regret what she said almost immediately – and, because she will be angry with herself, she will become angry with me and say I should have stopped her. But how can I stop her without actually going to California and somehow finding a way to make her see sense?

I get up from my desk and go to the kitchen to make a cup of tea. As I wait for the kettle to boil, I long with all my heart to phone Nathaniel. He'd understand; he'd say something wise and comforting. But I can't hide my feelings for him any more. That's why I haven't phoned to tell him about Diarmuid. I'm free, but he isn't. He has Eloise, with her film-star-bright, ruthless beauty.

Someone like Nathaniel would never love me anyway. He's way out of my league.

I reach for the box of Earl Grey tea bags. I wish I didn't keep getting these little nudges, these little whispers saying that Nathaniel cares for me more than I think. My head knows it's nonsense, but my heart won't give up on him.

What was he going to say to me, that evening when Diarmuid found us together? He started to say, 'Oh, Sally…' as if he was about to make some kind of declaration. Sometimes I feel the heaviness of his gaze when he watches me. There's an intensity in his eyes, a heat in his touch… or maybe it's just my imagination. If he really cared for me, he would have done something about it by now. He's that sort of person.

I pour some milk into my orange mug and add a spoonful of ant-free honey. Then I find myself staring at the phone. Should I just pick it up and ring him anyway? Some of April's defiant new candour seems to have found its way to me. I said I wanted to follow my heart more – and my heart is far more courageous than the rest of me. I will ring him right now and get it over with.

As I'm thinking this, the doorbell rings – not just one ring, but four. Whoever it is doesn't want to be kept waiting.

It's Greta. She marches in a bit haphazardly and nearly stumbles over a heap of files by the large wooden table I use as a desk. Then she says, 'Oops,' and smiles, and slumps onto my orange sofa. It is two o'clock in the afternoon and I suspect she's had a rather liquid lunch.

Great, I think. *This is just what I need.* I look at her warily. 'Would you like a cup of tea, Greta?'

'He's driving me crazy,' she declares, waving her arms for emphasis. Alcohol tends to make her a bit dramatic. 'He's howling at all hours of the night and he's made huge scratches on the front door. He won't even eat properly; he just grabs a couple of mouthfuls and goes back to his cushion.'

'Who?' I say. 'Who's howling?'

'Fred, of course. He's howling for Nathaniel.'

'But… but why?' I get a terrible stricken feeling in my heart. 'Isn't Nathaniel there to look after him?'

'No, he's gone off with some fancy woman – Fabrice, I think she's called. His writing was a bit scrawly, but I could read the name quite clearly.'

I just gawp at her. *Fabrice?* Surely I'm dreaming.

293

'I was away at a conference, and when I got back I found this scribbled message about flying out of the country with this Fabrice woman for a few days. He didn't even say where they were going.'

I fidget agitatedly with a cushion tassel. Fabrice and Nathaniel have flown off somewhere together? It's not true. It can't be.

'It's been a week now, and he hasn't even phoned. They really must be very taken up with each other.'

I lean forwards anxiously. 'Are… are you sure you read the name correctly?'

'Oh, yes, absolutely. It definitely said Fabrice.'

I gulp.

'I think I heard him planning the trip, actually,' Greta continues. 'It was a very odd conversation. I don't normally eavesdrop, but I went into his flat one day, the sitting-room door was half open, and I heard him talking on the phone. He sounded very strange.'

'Strange in what way?'

'Well…' Greta stretches out her long and rather muscular legs. 'I heard him saying, "Yes, I'd love to go with you, but you'll have to buy the plane tickets. I'm a bit short of cash at the moment." Then he added, "I wish I could tell people, but I suppose we'll just have to keep it a secret for the moment." Then he saw me, and his face went blank and he said, "Pepperoni and mushroom, yes, with extra cheese." He wanted me to think he was ordering a pizza. I should have asked him what he was up to.'

I feel like I have suddenly landed in Outer Mongolia. Is Nathaniel having an affair with *Fabrice*, of all people? No wonder he couldn't stop talking about her.

'Do you know anything about the woman?' Greta enquires.

I don't know what to say. If Greta finds out her cousin may be the toy boy of an elderly blonde, she'll have a hissy fit – and I really could do without that just now, since I feel like wailing myself. I don't know why I'm so surprised. Nathaniel is far from conventional; he believes other people's opinions are none of his business. But surely he has some taste. I can admire him for not caring about Fabrice's age, but why would he fancy a woman who cakes her face with make-up and piles her hair, which is probably the texture of straw, on top of her head like a small mountain? Hasn't he noticed her coarse laugh and the fact that she jangles with cheap jewellery? And what about Eloise?

Greta is staring at me, so I force myself to make some sort of comment. 'I met Fabrice once,' I mumble. 'She's… she's a bit older than Nathaniel. And a bit flamboyant. She's probably just a friend.' Now that I've said it, I suspect that it's the truth: he just enjoys her company. But then why did he say he wished their relationship didn't have to be a secret? Come to think of it, every time he has mentioned her, I have sensed there is something he's not telling me. Dear God, I hope she hasn't lured him into some dodgy escapade.

'Poor Nathaniel,' Greta sighs. 'Women keep falling in love with him. I think it makes his life rather complicated.'

'In what way?' I gaze at her disconcertedly. It's like she's talking about someone else. Not my Nathaniel. Not my secretly lonely and charmingly bewildered friend.

'Well, Eloise and Ziggy have been calling every evening asking where he is,' she says wearily. 'When they can't get him on the phone, they call me.'

'Ziggy?' I frown. 'I thought they weren't that close any more.'

'Oh, no, she's still in love with him – though it's pointless, of course, since she loves Richard too.'

'The guy who wears fishnet tights?'

'Yes. They've moved in together, so I suppose she's accepted that the marriage is over, but she still wants to talk to Nathaniel. She's a very strange woman. I don't think she knows about Eloise.' Greta looks at me sadly. 'I've told him over and over again, you can hurt people by being too soft-hearted.'

'What do you mean?' I'm sitting on the edge of my seat. The cushion tassel has come off in my hand and I'm weaving the threads through my fingers.

'He hates people to feel rejected. Surely you've noticed?' I just look at her.

'Even when Ziggy tried to start a *ménage à trois* with Richard, I don't think Nathaniel really told her how much it upset him. He put up with so much in that marriage – but that's Nathaniel for you. He's amazingly tolerant.'

'And Eloise?' I prompt bleakly.

'Oh, *Eloise*,' Greta says meaningfully. 'She's beautiful, of course, and her cabinets are *excellent*, and she was sweet to him at first; but now she seems to think she can boss him into loving her. She's forever trying to change him, smarten him up. Eloise is so used to men adoring her that she thinks, if she says, "Jump," Nathaniel should say, "How high?" But he just listens and takes no notice of her. It's really beginning to irritate him, actually. That's probably why he's gone off with this other woman. He's told Eloise he just wants to be friends with her, because he can't change himself to suit her, but she won't accept it.' Greta studies her nails, which are long and shiny and painted dark red. 'And then, of course, there's Sarah.'

'*Sarah?*'

'Yes, she's a psychologist friend from New York. She keeps wanting to come and stay. I think she's in love with him too. She says he's the only man she can really talk to. Women just seem to love Nathaniel.'

Oh, stop rubbing it in! I want to scream. Greta seems to have absolutely no suspicions about my feelings for her cousin. She isn't to know, of course, that I find these revelations dismaying because they have turned my quiet adoration into something almost comically predictable. I knew Nathaniel was popular, but I didn't realise he was a minor love celebrity. For a weird moment I imagine me and a bunch of other Nathaniel devotees chasing him down Grafton Street waving our knickers.

'I think he should take a break from the whole thing, frankly.'

'What do you mean?' I don't know why I ask – or why on earth she is telling me all this. The Greta I thought I knew only shares personal details with a tiny circle of trusted confidantes. And then I suddenly know why she is telling me these things. She *does* know my feelings for Nathaniel. She must have seen me gazing at him longingly at that reception; and last time I visited his flat – which is, after all, in her house – I saw her curtains twitching. He may even have told her that he was worried that I was becoming a little too fond of him. And now she's trying to warn me off him because she knows I have already made a total arse of myself with my marriage. She arrived just in time. Oh, God, I was just about to phone him!

'He just seems to go from one woman to another,' Greta says. 'There's always one waiting in the wings, as far as I can tell. If only he could meet the right person – someone who could help him get over Ziggy. He feels so betrayed by her... He needs someone who can be loyal to him and love him for who he is.' She gazes at me earnestly.

There is a long silence. I stare at my rubber plant. It's grown very big lately; in fact, it's too big for this room, but I'm fond of it. It's so enthusiastic, somehow. I really should re-pot it.

'Sometimes he comes into the kitchen and steals my dinner,' Greta suddenly adds. 'Then he runs off with it and eats it in the sitting room.'

I think this is rather thoughtless of Nathaniel, but the details just wash over me distantly. I'm too numb to take them in.

'Of course I try to forgive him, considering the circumstances. But I don't know why he needs to go out so late at night and wander round the garden.'

I just nod. Very little about Nathaniel could surprise me now.

'And I really wish he hadn't developed this awful habit of burying my jewellery in the middle of the hydrangeas. I have to lock it away now.'

The words land with an improbable thud. Nathaniel may be

daft enough to fly off with Fabrice, but he is not daft enough to bury Greta's jewellery. She must have switched the conversation to Fred.

Confirming this, Greta adds, 'And his paws get so muddy. I'm going to have to get the carpets cleaned.' She peers at me. 'Are you all right, Sally? You look a little...'

'I'm – I'm just a little tired,' I mumble quickly. Then I sit up straighter and say, 'Actually, Diarmuid has moved in with another woman. Our marriage is over.' I know what I've done – telling Greta is a bit like taking out an ad in *The Irish Times* – but people have to know sometime.

'Oh, I see.' She studies me solemnly, but she doesn't seem the least bit surprised. 'To be honest, I never felt you were that suited.'

Greta has only met Diarmuid once. Was it that obvious? How on earth wasn't it obvious to me?

'Marriage is a strange old business,' Greta continues. 'I think some people just aren't cut out for it. That's why Nigel and I have stayed single. He stays with me at the weekends, but by Monday I can't wait for him to leave so I can clean the house and put things where they're meant to be. He moves things around.'

In normal circumstances I would be itching to hear more about Nigel, who is Greta's mysterious boyfriend. He has been sighted waiting for her in his car outside receptions; he appears to be about her age and is portly and distinguished-looking, though his clothes are crumpled. On this occasion, however, I have absolutely no wish to hear about Nigel. I just want Greta to leave. I want to be on my own so I can rearrange my views on Nathaniel.

When Erika asked me what kind of biscuit Nathaniel would be, I didn't answer. I said it was because I had no right to think of him as a biscuit because I wouldn't ever be allowed to taste him; but, deep down, I know it was because I was thinking of him more as a house – the kind of house we had in California, with its quirks and its crannies, its idiosyncratic beauty. I thought I knew him in the way love reveals a person to you – a one-off way, not mass-market. I was wrong. Nathaniel's golden intimacy is lightly given, and even more lightly prized.

'What on earth are you doing with your column these days?' Greta suddenly enquires. Her eyes are glinting. Maybe she's a bit miffed that I haven't asked for more fascinating revelations about Nigel. 'The last one seemed to advise people to live in squalor,' she adds with an indignant sniff. This is the Greta I am used to.

'Of course it didn't,' I snap. 'You obviously didn't read it properly.'

'I was talking to your editor, and he was very disappointed with it too.'

I feel a twist of fear in my stomach.

'He said the advertisers were appalled. You're supposed to drum up business for them, Sally, not tell people that their houses are just fine as they are. This business thrives on discontent and aspiration. What's happened to you? You used to know that.'

'Maybe I just want to be a bit more truthful, Greta.' I glare at her. She can be extraordinarily insensitive sometimes – but, since the world she inhabits is tough and somewhat ruthless and liberally laced with cynicism, this is probably an advantage. 'Maybe I've decided the most important things in life are not *things*.' I think of the beautiful dark curve of Nathaniel's eyelashes. I suppose all his women feel the same way about them.

'I'm not saying *things* are the only things that matter!' Greta splutters indignantly. 'But they make people happy. Many people lead very boring lives. The thought of a new sitting-room suite is genuinely uplifting.'

'We buy all this stuff, and then we have to pay for it.' I'm thinking of the small fortune I spent on my marital home. 'We get into debt, and that leaves us with fewer choices. We can even feel trapped in jobs we loathe, because of – of some daft notion that we have to replace our fitted kitchens every few years!'

Greta looks at me as though I've just said no one should

299

wash because after a few weeks one doesn't really notice the smell. I suddenly realise we could have a frightful argument. Greta must sense this too, because she says gently, 'You're just a bit upset at the moment because of Diarmuid. I know you don't really mean these things. It's not like you at all.'

I decide not to protest.

'Anyway,' she says softly, 'will you do this article for me? There's no rush; it's not needed for two weeks. They want two and a half thousand words.'

'What article?'

'Oh, didn't I mention it?' She sounds genuinely surprised. She's sobered up somewhat, but she still looks a bit droopy. 'The ad feature about hotel accessories. It's for a new client.'

Two and a half thousand words on hotel fucking accessories. I feel like screaming. But I need the money. I need to pay off my mortgage and take some interest in my overdraft limit. It would also be nice to eat occasionally. Diarmuid and I spent a fortune doing up our home, and now I don't even want the furniture. Any profit we make on the sale will mainly go towards paying for all the cabinets and the tables and the chairs and the armchairs and the… I can't even list them any more. I don't know how I got so carried away. I must have thought that, if the house was just right, our marriage would be right too. And then, of course, there are the lawyers who will charge big bucks to separate us. This cottage also needs some refurbishment. On top of the other defects, it turns out that the ants are getting in through a mysterious hole in the kitchen wall.

'That… that sounds great, Greta.' I manage a smile. 'Who do you want me to contact?'

'It's all down here.' Greta puts a neatly typed memo on my coffee table. Then she sighs, and her rather severe face suddenly looks lost. 'Maybe I should cook some mince for him. He probably needs some coaxing.'

It takes me a moment to realise she has returned to the subject of Fred. Poor Fred; I feel just like him.

Greta sweeps off soon after that – she doesn't leave a room, she sweeps out of it, and the air behind her shakes for a moment like the wake of a substantial ship. I envy her firm sense of her place in this world, the way she's so sure of who she is and what she wants. She doesn't feel trapped and owned by situations. She moulds and manipulates. If she had been married to Diarmuid, she probably would have ordered him to bring the mice back to the college. She would have insisted on romantic meals and meaningful conversations. And, strangely enough, Diarmuid probably would have obeyed her and been relieved to get some direction, some training. Because he didn't know how to be a husband, any more than I knew how to be a wife.

And now he wants me to have these long conversations about the house. He wants me to make lists. He wants everything tied up and organised. Most of all, he wants it all to be *fair*. And he doesn't seem to know that I can't bear it. Our conversations seem so empty and practical, almost as if we never knew each other at all.

I sit on my orange sofa and stare out at the sea through the bay window. *I could just walk out of this house*, I find myself thinking. *I could just pack a suitcase and go somewhere else for a while – Galway, perhaps, or West Cork. I could rent a cottage in the wilds for a week...*

This is not the way to write two and a half thousand words about hotel accessories. Of course I can't just go off for a week. I have receptions to attend and columns to write and Aggie to visit. I also have to meet Diarmuid and visit what was supposed to be our home, so we can discuss the whole furniture thing in more gruesome detail. And, of course, I have to somehow convince April not to come to Marie's family gathering.

I sigh and head stoically towards my computer. How could I ever have thought I could change? This is how I am, and this is how things are. I will always have dreams of leaving, but I'll stuff them back in their box and try to ignore them. 'Have to' is the only way I know how to live.

Chapter Thirty-Six

NEARLY TWO WEEKS LATER, I am deeply engrossed in the world of hotel accessories. I have devoted myself to trouser-presses and chrome cafetières. I know I should be phoning April, since it is now August and Marie's party is in September, I know I should be discussing the house sale with Diarmuid, I know I should make an appointment with a therapist immediately if not sooner, but these things will all have to wait.

Yesterday I picked up Diarmuid's music box. I was going to store it away, somewhere where I couldn't see it, but instead I threw it at the floor and the lid flew open and the music started and the little dancer fell off and scooted under the sofa. I haven't bothered to find her. I will probably Hoover her up next time I actually get around to cleaning my cottage.

Every so often I think of the wedding presents. What am I going to do with the table-mats and the Waterford crystal and the recipe books and that plug-in thing that cooks casseroles? I should clearly have other priorities, but at the moment I have so many priorities I don't know how to prioritise them. If I had been sensible, I would have told Greta I was taking a short holiday because of 'personal circumstances', but instead I have allowed myself to wander into the terrible desert of soap dispensers and shower mats. I have become obsessed with them.

It's beginning to remind me of the weeks before my wedding. I knew I should be thinking about my doubts about Diarmuid, but I was more worried about my veil. I am using hotel accessories as a displacement activity. There are so many things I don't want to think about that hotel accessories are a sort of incredibly boring refuge. I thought I had completely lost myself to them – which is why I am extremely surprised to find myself heading towards Dublin airport.

I actually came to this part of Dublin to discuss wall-mounted coffee units with a man called Gervaise, who had so much to say on the subject that he didn't think a phone call would be sufficient; he wanted me to see the showroom. The bus I caught had 'Dublin Airport' on the front, but I asked the driver to let me know when we reached Old Wish Road. It's such a lovely, poignant, percussive name – and I must have been thinking about its poetry when we actually passed the place. The driver must have forgotten my request. When I realise we are nearly at the airport, I know I should get off the bus and call a taxi, because I'm already a little late and Gervaise will be fretting. But I find I want to stay on the bus. I want to go to the airport. I want to have a creamy cappuccino and ponder the latest developments in the cordless kettle. I decide that I'll ring Gervaise from the airport, explain that I'll be a bit late and apologise profusely.

I gaze out the bus window. It's raining again. I find myself dreaming of California, of the young girl I was there. I want her freedom and innocence; I want to see the round brown hills that she loved, the hummingbirds and the palm trees, the high and huge blue sky. No one asked me if I wanted to leave. We just packed up and left. April went back, and I always said I was going to go back too; but I never did, not even for a holiday. It was one of those things that had to wait – perhaps forever.

I begin to wonder what I should do about April. One option is simply to kidnap her when she arrives for Marie's party. I could ask Fiona to drive me to the airport, and then once we'd got April into Fiona's car we could drive to Fiona's huge home, say we were just going to have a quick cuppa in the dining room that Fiona hardly ever uses, and then lock April in there. I think about this for a full five minutes, but then I decide that perhaps kidnapping April isn't such a good idea. What I really need is to talk to her, face to face. I'm her big sister; she does sometimes listen to me. But if she's actually travelled to Ireland she'll be harder to dissuade. The best thing would be to talk to her in California. The thought makes me feel so jumpy that I stare out the window again, at the dreary, rainy day. I wonder if Nathaniel is somewhere sunny. I wonder what he and Fabrice are getting up to.

To distract myself from these miserable thoughts, I reach into my handbag for the half-bar of chocolate that's been there since three o'clock yesterday. I am amazed to find my passport. It must have been there for *weeks*. I took it into town with me ages ago – it was almost out of date, and I planned to apply for a new one, but I got sidetracked and forgot. I glance at the expiry date. There are still a few months to go. I can still use it.

I get out of the bus at the airport and head into the building. People are bustling past me with trolleys and cases and that sense of compact purpose that foreign travel gives some people. I am in the departures area. Am I really just here for a cappuccino? A faint thrill runs through me. Have I in fact travelled here for another purpose entirely?

What is there to keep me in Dublin? I think. Aggie has Fabrice; she seems to have forgotten all about me and DeeDee. Fiona has Zak and Milly, and Erika has Lionel, even if she doesn't want him. Mum and Dad have each other and tennis and music. April and I seem to be the only ones who are alone now. Nathaniel has Ziggy and Fabrice and Sarah and Eloise, and even Diarmuid has Charlene.

A shudder runs through me; then it stills into a faint tremble, like the flapping of a tiny bird. I can't allow April to make her grand declaration at Marie's gathering. I can't allow her to break Mum's heart – it has been broken enough already.

Almost without thinking, I go to the standby counter. 'I want to go to San Francisco,' I tell the woman. 'As soon as possible. I don't have any luggage.'

She tells me a seat may be available on a flight that leaves in three hours. She will announce my name as soon as she has news. Yes, the price will be greatly reduced, but I won't be able to choose my seat; I'll just have to take what's available. I say that's fine and ask if I'd be able to hear her announcement in the café. She says yes. My smile trembles and I head numbly towards all the people going God knows where.

When I was going to New York, I had luggage; I had

knickers and T-shirts and tights and bras. I was even wondering whether to buy perfume in duty-free. That's how I am at airports. I check in punctually and make sure I know which boarding gate to head for; I look in my bag over and over again, to make sure I have my tickets and my passport and the address of the place where I'm planning to stay. I sit on those strange, endless-looking seats and make lists to discover if I've forgotten something crucial. Only today I don't feel like that. I'm not just preparing to be somewhere foreign; I am in a foreign place already.

I didn't know one could feel like this, I think as I sip my cappuccino in the nondescript, functional café. I didn't know how things can just fall away. Nothing lasts. All the things we cling to – houses, jobs, marriage – are just little specks of shifting sand. We build our lives around them, and then in moments like this we see the impermanence. All we truly have is this moment.

Who am I to be, now that I'm not Diarmuid's wife? I'm 35, that's still quite young. I want to be somewhere new. I want to be somewhere that won't keep reminding me of who I planned to be. I want a place that won't ask for explanations, a place where I can start a new story about myself – a story that won't be continually contradicted.

I think of April. I wonder if she'll understand all this. Probably. It's one of the main reasons people go to California, the land of the reinvented self.

But I'm only going to California for a visit, I tell myself. I'll probably be back here in a week. April needs me now; she's opened up to me in a way she never did before. I must help her to see sense. And I must make her know I love her.

There seem to be endless announcements about not leaving luggage unattended. Since I don't have any luggage, I wish they'd just shut up. Maybe I should go to one of the shops and buy something – a face-cloth, perhaps, or a toothbrush – but instead I stay in my seat and watch people bustling past me with their preoccupied airport expressions. I should be looking more like them. I delve into my bag and take out my lipstick, the lipstick April helped me choose in New York.

My mobile is switched off in case Diarmuid calls again to discuss furniture. I don't know why it upsets me so much; it almost seems enough reason in itself to leave the country. Is that why I'm leaving – because I want to avoid conversations about furniture?

Mum and Dad will understand when I tell them I've gone to talk to April, I think. When they hear that she wants to spill the beans at Marie's party, they'll probably be very grateful that I'm trying to make her see sense. I get out my mobile phone and ring April's home number. There is no answer. Because of the time difference, she's probably asleep. I leave a message to say I may be arriving in California this very evening and will phone her when I have my flight details. Flight details… Am I actually planning to get on a jumbo jet without even my toothbrush?

I ring Gervaise and tell him that, much as I would love to talk with him face to face about wall-mounted coffee units, I may need to phone him about it from America. He is clearly waiting for an explanation, so I say I've just found out I have to fly to San Francisco because of a family matter. My voice gets trembly, and I know if I don't stop talking soon he'll know I'm crying, so I say, 'Bye,' briskly and hang up. At least I have my laptop with me; I wanted to type up the interview with Gervaise on my way home and get it over with. And this evening I planned to have Swedish meatballs for dinner. I even took them out of the freezer to defrost.

I should stay. I can't just leave; I have responsibilities, *duties*. The ants must be attended to, and I have to go to Milly's christening. And there are so many people I'd miss. This whole idea of leaving is daft; I don't know how I can even have considered it. I want my mugs. I want my orange sofa. I want my view of the sea and the sky and the gulls and the windsurfers. I want my mother's chicken casserole. I want to watch Dad playing the cello, his eyes closed, a deep peace on his face.

But I don't rise from my seat. I can't believe it, but I just stay there, waiting for my name to be called. Did DeeDee feel like this? What was she looking for? What hopes were in her heart when she left? I don't think I would even consider doing this if it weren't for DeeDee.

Will I even come back here? I think as I look around me. Of course I'll want to – I'll have to – but maybe not for a while; maybe even years. And I will miss it so much. I try to memorise the scene – Dublin airport; my home town. When the plane lifts off, everything will seem so small and distant, so unlikely, as the houses turn into tiny boxes. We might even fly over my home, where there is a half-drunk orange mug of tea on the table. I feel a stab of almost unbearable grief. Aggie – will I ever see Aggie again? Even though she isn't that excited about seeing me any more. Fabrice has replaced me in her affections.

I blink hard to stop the tears. Erika and Fiona must come over and visit me as soon as possible. I'll miss them so much, but I think they'll understand. I'll pay Erika to get the cottage ready for a new tenant. I'm sure Fiona would store my belongings if I asked her to. And when I get to San Francisco I must look up Astrid. I'd love to know what became of her; I'd love to know if she still believes in angels. There are plenty of people I'd love to see again. I could write articles about America and anything except interior decoration. That's the great thing about freelancing: it's flexible. You can do it in different places.

I should phone people to say goodbye, but if I do they'll try to dissuade me. I must tell someone, though; I can't just leave here without telling anyone. The only person I've told is Gervaise. I feel a tug at my heart. I so wish I could ring Nathaniel, but it would be just another ardent message clogging up his answering machine.

I ring anyway, just to hear his voice. 'Fred and I are out,' the answering machine says. There is a loud woof; then Nathaniel adds, 'Please leave a message. If you don't, we'll never forgive you.'

Maybe that's the last time I'll hear Nathaniel's voice.

Then I hear my name called. 'Sally Adams,' the sing-song

voice says. I rise slowly from my seat and head towards the standby desk.

Chapter Thirty-Seven

'WHAT'S YOUR NAME?' THE woman at the standby desk peers at me. She is slim and tanned and has shiny blonde hair.

'Sally Adams,' I say. 'You just called me.'

'No, I didn't.'

'Yes, you did. I heard my name called just now.'

'Well, I didn't call you. Maybe it was the information desk.'

I am about to explain that nobody knows I am at the airport, apart from her, but then I feel a shudder of dread. Has Gervaise followed me here? I did tell him I was flying to America. Is he going to follow me to the boarding gate talking about wall-mounted coffee units?

'It's just over there.' She waves vaguely to the right. I suspect the information desk is at the other end of the building and she can't be bothered to give me directions. I get a daft urge to explain my whole situation to her. I want to look into her detached, slightly bored face and ask her if she's met other women like me. When a woman marches up to her and says she wants to go to San Francisco and doesn't have any luggage, doesn't she get ever so slightly *curious*?

My name is called again. 'Please go to the information desk,' the woman's voice says. Now that I hear it again, I realise that's what she said before. Perhaps April has heard my message and phoned Marie, and a family delegation has come to persuade me out of my idiocy. Maybe I *want* them to.

'You'll call me if you have news about a flight to San Francisco?' I say to the woman.

'Yes, of course. I've got your details here.' She gives me a brief smile. 'You might be able to leave on the three o'clock flight. I'm just waiting for confirmation of your seat.'

'Thanks.' I bite my lip and walk in the direction she indicated. I don't see the information desk, but... Dear God, it

309

can't be. Is that really *Nathaniel*?

'Sally!' He sees me at the same moment and bounds over. 'I knew I saw you a while back, but then you disappeared on me. That's why I had you called.'

'I've been sitting on the same seat for almost an hour,' I reply primly, though I feel like tipping slowly sideways and lying down on the floor.

'No, you haven't.' His blue eyes hold mine. 'I was going over to talk to you, and then suddenly you weren't there.'

That must have been the time I dashed into the loo, I think. But I don't say it. What on earth is he doing here?

'What are you doing here?' Nathaniel gets to the question first. He is standing too close. I can feel his breath on my cheek.

'I'm waiting.' I look up at him; then I look away.

'Waiting for what?' He leans towards me. Our foreheads are almost touching.

'For a flight to San Francisco.'

I can feel the words land on him. I can actually feel his surprise. 'San Francisco?'

'Yes, that's what I said,' I reply briskly.

'Why?' He is just standing there, amazed and bewildered.

'I want to visit my sister, April.'

He absorbs this information solemnly. 'When's your flight?' It's only now that I notice he has luggage with him, a compact leather holdall. He must have just arrived back from his trip with Fabrice. I look around anxiously. Thank goodness, she doesn't appear to be with him.

'I don't know. It might be at three. They're going to call me.' As I say it, it sounds more and more improbable.

'Where's your luggage?' His blue eyes have darkened. No one has ever looked at me like that before. No one has searched my face so hard for my secrets. I suppose all his women feel like that. '*He makes you feel like you're the only person in the room. He has such charisma...*' I can almost hear them saying it.

'It's none of your business where my luggage is.' I turn to

leave – I can't face explaining it to him – but he grabs my arm and holds it firmly.

'You just decided to go to San Francisco today, didn't you?' His eyes are boring into me.

I try to pull away from him, but he won't let me go.

'Maybe.'

'We need to talk. You need to talk, Sally,' he says firmly.

'Let go of my arm.'

He does. I consider dashing away like a sprinter; then I realise that's ridiculous. This whole situation is ridiculous. Maybe I should just go home and have a long bath.

'What's happened to you, Sally?' He brushes a stray strand of hair from my cheek. 'What's made you so desperate?'

'Nothing.' The word trips off my tongue like it used to when I was a teenager and I thought everyone, especially my parents, wouldn't understand.

'OK, so you're just fine, are you?' He is guiding me gently towards the café. 'You're just fine and dandy, but you thought you'd like a change of country.'

'And I need to see my sister April.'

'Why?' he asks gently, softly. I wish he didn't speak like that. I wish he didn't know how to lure these details out of me.

'Because... because she wants to announce that my father isn't her father, at this stupid family get-together we're having.'

I splurge it out in one breath and then slump onto a chair in the café. It isn't a very comfortable chair. Nothing about this airport seems comfortable or tender. It should be, with so many people saying goodbye to things, to the people they love.

'And is that true?'

I stare at him dumbly.

'About April. Is she really your half-sister?'

'Yes, of course it is.' I sigh. 'But she doesn't need to make a scene out of it. She could... she could break it to people more gently. Or let my parents find a way to say it themselves.' I feel terribly tired suddenly. I feel like I'm already

311

jet-lagged. This day seems to have lasted an entire week, and it's only 1.30.

'And that's the only reason you're going to California?'

'I don't know.' I drag the words out of myself. 'Maybe. It's complicated.'

'You need a cup of tea, don't you?' Nathaniel looks at me so sympathetically that I feel I might cry. Why did he have to turn up now? It makes leaving so much harder.

'Yes, a cup of tea would be nice,' I mumble.

'What kind?'

I just sit there for a moment. I have no idea what kind of tea I want – herbal or Earl Grey, English Breakfast or Darjeeling. It seems like a huge decision. 'Just tea… any kind of tea. You decide.'

'OK, but promise to stay there until I get back.' He glances at me anxiously.

I nod. I'm too exhausted to run off. How can I have thought I didn't have any luggage? I have so much emotional baggage I should get a trolley.

Nathaniel seems to return in a matter of moments. He has remembered how much milk I take, and when I sip the tea I discover he has put in just the right amount of sugar. Just sitting here with him makes things better. I decide not to mention Fabrice. I really don't think I'd like to hear the details.

'You've… you've just flown in from somewhere, haven't you?' I say slowly.

He nods.

'So why are you in the departures area? You should be in arrivals.'

He grins sheepishly. 'I got lost. I was trying to find the bank. I've been going up and down the escalators like a total bloody idiot. I thought I was going crazy, because I know where the bank is – or, at least, I usually do. It began to feel like looking for a Chinese takeaway – do you remember that evening?'

Of course I do. How could he have thought I would forget

it?

'I suppose I was looking for you, only I didn't know it.' He reaches out and touches my palm. He makes small circles in its centre. It is such an intimate and unexpected gesture, and so totally right. This is just the kind of thing I don't need right now. It might make me tell him I've fallen hopelessly in love with him. And he'd be understanding about it – because, let's face it, he must hear that kind of thing pretty often. He'd probably even be sympathetic.

I shift restlessly in my seat. 'I should go, Nathaniel. They may call me any minute.'

'I once did what you're planning to do,' he says calmly.

'Where did you go?'

'New Orleans. I wanted to go to Costa Rica, but I didn't have enough money. I just needed to get out of New York for a while, be somewhere different – I wanted to be someone different. I was having doubts about everything – Ziggy, my job, the ridiculously expensive new suit I'd bought that didn't fit me properly. I think it was the suit that did it, actually.' He laughs his bright, gleeful laugh. 'It seemed fine in the shop, but that was because I hadn't actually walked in the thing. I had to contort my entire body just to get across a room.'

I find myself smiling. He always manages to make me smile, eventually.

'People kept saying what a lovely suit it was, even though it made me feel like a hunchback. My life felt just like that suit: I had to contort myself to a ridiculous extent to fit into it, and nobody seemed to notice. It was the loneliest feeling. Should I get some biscuits?'

'No. I don't eat biscuits any more,' I say. 'I'm on a diet.'

'Of course it seems crazy now, flying off somewhere because of a bloody suit. I should have just chucked it and put it down to experience.'

'What happened in New Orleans?'

'It was fun, even though I found a cockroach under my bed in the dirt-cheap hotel. I went out. I wandered around and looked at things. I ate. It's a lovely city. It was different, but I

313

was still the same. That's when I knew I had to let some things go – some beliefs about myself.' He starts to fiddle with a spoon. 'And that's hard. It's what I'd been trying to avoid, I suppose. I'd been living with this idea that there was some better place I had to find. But what I realised was that finding it might be more an internal decision than a question of location – though, of course, some locations are better than others. I still have a hankering to go to Costa Rica.'

'What did you do with the suit?'

'I gave it to Ziggy. She got it altered. She wears it with a feather boa. Of course, I could have got it altered too, but it didn't occur to me at the time. I think I'd wandered into a rather primitive part of my brain. I really should have made more of an effort to use my neo-cortex.' He looks over at the food counter. 'Do you think they do baked beans on toast?'

'Probably. What's a neo-cortex?'

'It's the part of the brain that can see the bigger picture – along with other things, of course. It sees a whole range of alternatives. But you can't access it if you're too emotionally aroused, so things seem black and white.' He looks at someone carrying a loaded tray. 'Come to think of it, I wouldn't mind some scrambled eggs too.'

I remember the important-looking psychology books on the floor of his flat. 'So is this why we're talking, Nathaniel?' I say slowly. 'You wanted to calm me down?'

'Yes. Of course, I wanted to talk to you, too,' he admits cheerfully. 'To be honest, Sally, if you're going to California I think you should pack. I really missed not having a spare T-shirt or boxer shorts in New Orleans. I didn't even have an extra pair of socks.'

I suddenly feel defensive. 'This is an entirely different situation, Nathaniel. My sister needs me. I am calm. I'm very calm.' I lift my cup with trembling fingers. 'I've thought it all through very carefully.'

'I'll miss you.'

I stare at the table.

'And Diarmuid will miss you, won't he? What

314

about Diarmuid?'

'Look, it's only a visit!' I snap. 'It's not like I'm planning to
—'

'Disappear like DeeDee?'

'Don't finish my sentences,' I protest. 'That isn't what I
was going to say. I've forgotten about DeeDee; I know I'll
never find her.'

'What were you going to say, then?'

'I was going to say...' I clench my fingers into my palms
so hard that it hurts. 'I was going to say that none of this is
your business.'

'What's happened with Diarmuid?' Is he psychic? He
reaches for my hand and touches the tips of my fingers. 'I'm
sorry he found us together like that. It was all very... very
awkward.'

'As you made clear at the time;' I say tightly, recalling the
appalled look on his face.

'Is it over, then?'

'What?'

'Your marriage.'

Am I really that transparent?

'And now you're wondering how I know. It's because I
know that look on your face, Sally. I've seen it on my own.
You feel things leaving and you don't know what's going to
take their place, and everything seems very stark and strange,
almost unreal.'

I feel an ache in my heart. How can I not love someone
who knows these things about me? But what do I know about
him? He is basically a stranger. He flew off somewhere with
Fabrice, for God's sake! He has a whole hidden life that he
never even mentions.

I can't even look at him. 'Yes, you're right. Diarmuid has
found someone else... and it's not a mouse.' I smile feebly. It
isn't even funny. 'It turns out Diarmuid's very decisive. He
doesn't hang around and fret, like I do. He replaced me with
surprising speed and efficiency.'

'And you find that just a bit offensive?'

'I suppose I have no right to feel offended, really,' I say hesitantly. 'I mean, I'm the one who left him first.'

'Feelings aren't quite that clear-cut, though, are they? From what you've said, it sounds like you feel he left the marriage almost as soon as it started – only, of course, he was in the same house.' A faraway look enters Nathaniel's eyes. 'That's what I felt with Ziggy, anyway. She was there but she wasn't there, if you know what I mean.'

'At least she didn't have long conversations with mice.'

'She had long conversations with her lover instead,' he says. 'I think I would have preferred mice.'

I know I should say something sympathetic, but I can't – not now that Greta has told me about Ziggy's phone calls. Nathaniel is leaving that bit out, of course. There are probably loads of things he leaves out every time we talk.

'The thing about the mice,' I begin, realising how stupid and improbable it sounds, 'was that I couldn't really complain about them without sounding daft. A lover would almost have been easier, in a way.'

'I once had a client whose husband was obsessed with a stick insect.'

I want to burst out laughing, but then I see Nathaniel's expression and realise it's true.

'He used to take Candice – that was the insect's name – out to the garden every weekend and sit with her. He said she needed to get out and about a bit. Then he'd go upstairs and clean her cage, and go to the pet shop to make sure she had all the food she needed, and by that time it was too late for him and his wife to go out for the day. No one believed his wife until they actually saw him sitting on his deckchair, watching Candice and ignoring everyone else.'

'What did the wife do?'

'She boiled Candice up and fed her to him in a tuna sandwich.'

I gulp.

'No. That's what she would have liked to do.' He laughs. 'She left him and got very involved in Buddhism. She said she would never marry again.'

'I can understand that,' I say softly. 'I don't want to marry again either. It just doesn't suit me.'

I wonder if I should go to the standby desk. I've been listening for my name. Maybe the woman has forgotten me. Instead I say, 'If it's not mice or stick insects it's the Internet, or golf, or the pub. Haven't you noticed that, Nathaniel? People get married and then, after a few months or years of romance – if they manage to have them – they start to devise ways to be apart from each other.

Especially the men, I'm afraid.' I look at him reproachfully. 'Women keep saying, "Please talk to me," and men keep saying, "Not now, dear, I'm watching football."'

'Not all men,' Nathaniel corrects me. 'It was Ziggy who didn't want to talk to me.'

'Yes, yes, but you're not typical!'

'Thank you.' He grins at me. Am I actually blushing?

'Everyone's looking for love, Sally,' he says softly. 'Everyone and everything in this universe wants to be loved and to love. It's just that sometimes we get a bit battered about and forget that. Or we look in the wrong place and then decide it's not anywhere, that it's some sort of awful twisted joke.'

Then he adds, 'I got a call from her about a year ago. She's married again and living in New Mexico.'

'Who?'

'The stick-insect woman. And her ex-husband now talks to a dog – which is a step up the communication ladder, I suppose. He sometimes phones her and says he misses her, and she tells him to take the dog for a walk. It seems to be working.'

'What do you mean?'

'Well, people stop him and say, "What a lovely dog! What breed is it?" and he tells them it's some exotic kind of spaniel. He's even got quite pally with a woman he met in the park. Life can be so bloody difficult sometimes that some people just end up feeling more comfortable with animals than with people.' He smiles wryly. 'There's been some fascinating research about the number of women who feel, deep down, that their closest significant relationship is with their cat.'

I remember the sudden adoration I felt for Blossom when I went riding. She seemed to care about me unconditionally. And, of course, she didn't buck me off. I was immensely grateful to her. 'By the way, I read your column – the latest one. I really liked it.'

It takes me a moment to register what he has said. I'm still thinking of Blossom and her big, understanding eyes, the lovely smell of her shiny hair. 'I'm glad you liked it,' I say. 'But Greta thinks it's crap.'

'Good old Greta. She's delightfully mercenary.'

'Fred has been driving her crazy. He's been howling and scratching at the door and trying to bury her jewellery.'

'Oh, poor Fred.' Nathaniel's face grows solemn. Suddenly it feels like Nathaniel and I are in our own little world at this table, but we're not. He's being kind and thoughtful and sweet, and I wish he'd stop – because then I wouldn't want to kiss him. I even love his stupid car. It seems right that it isn't sleek and shiny like everyone else's. It seems like our car, somehow – the kind of car people like us should have.

'Greta told me about you and Fabrice flying off together.' I decide just to say it.

'Oh, did she?'

'Yes. Did you have a nice time?'

'Yes, thank you. Very nice.'

I wait for him to say more, but he looks tight-lipped and secretive. 'So you really want to fly somewhere today, do you?' he enquires suddenly.

'I don't know any more.' I sigh. 'Maybe you're right. Maybe it isn't such a good idea.'

'We should go somewhere closer.'

'What?'

'Now that I come to think of it, you really do need to get away, Sally. Let's just do it.'

'Do what?' I frown.

Nathaniel's eyes have brightened. He suddenly looks very enthusiastic. 'Let's go to London.'

318

'Now?'

'Yes!'

'I don't want to go to London.'

'You will when we get there.'

I hear my name called. Suddenly I don't want to go anywhere. I just want to go home.

'You have to come with me. It's really important. There's someone I want you to meet.'

I gawp at him. Why on earth is he saying this now? Why London, of all places?

'Come on, Sally. Let's go to that standby desk of yours,' Nathaniel says. Then he grabs my arm and pulls me from my seat.

Chapter Thirty-Eight

NATHANIEL AND I ARE walking down a swanky street in Chelsea. There is an autumnal chill to the late afternoon. I don't know what I'm doing here. I can't believe I let him talk me into this.

I went to the standby desk when my name was called, and the woman said that there wasn't a seat on the three o'clock flight to San Francisco after all. Then Nathaniel said, 'What about London?' and she checked her computer and said that two seats were available, but we'd have to rush to get on the flight. Nathaniel handed her a credit card, and she issued our tickets without so much as a murmur of surprise.

After that I found myself running after him towards the boarding gate, the way you run when you are gripped with a real sense of urgency about your intended destination. Somehow the running inspired this feeling in me. I really didn't want to miss the flight, even though I had no idea why I was getting on it. I was also getting extremely curious. Who on earth did Nathaniel want me to meet in London, and why? I began to suspect he'd just said it to make me go along with this crazy adventure. And, even though I was tired, I began to feel I needed an adventure. I needed this day to be different. After all, I'd spent a good part of it thinking I'd be in California in time for lunch. Going home to a bath would, in truth, have been a bit of an anticlimax.

So now I'm trying to keep up with Nathaniel and wondering how much the tickets cost. He does, after all, claim to be pretty short of money. I am also thinking that I'm hungry, and that I should phone April to tell her she doesn't have to get her spare bed ready. And I'm itching to ask Nathaniel more about Fabrice and what they got up to together. But for some reason I stay completely silent. I am probably in shock because I don't do this kind of thing. April gave me a reason to go to San Francisco; but I have no reason to be here on this spacious, austere street with its rich, white, colonnaded houses.

Suddenly I long for somewhere warmer – somewhere Latin and passionate, like Rio. London doesn't seem to be the right destination for a heedless, almost frantic journey. It looks far too sensible and self-contained in the crisp late-afternoon sunlight. There should be music and the scent of blossoms, bright dark eyes and tanned skin and languid street-side cafés. No wonder DeeDee was lured by Rio's embrace, its beckoning. A place like that would understand her need for it.

Since Nathaniel and I seem to have run out of conversation, I find myself glancing into windows and wishing it were later in the evening. Snooping is so much easier when it's almost dark and the lights are on in people's flats and houses. I like glimpsing the fancy lamps and paintings and furniture; a paprika-coloured wall or an antique chaise longue, a round table covered in silver-framed family photos. I enjoy watching lovers embracing as they return home from work, or some glamorous basement-flat bachelor preparing a stir-fry at a marble table.

'Where are we going?' I decide it's high time I asked again. Nathaniel has just ignored my question on previous occasions.

He glances down at me. One of the many annoying things about the opposite sex is that they are so often taller.

'Who is this person you want me to meet?' I persist. 'Or did you just make that up?'

'You'll find out soon enough.'

I stop in my tracks and glare at him rebelliously. 'This is ridiculous. You should tell me now.'

'We're almost there.'

'Where, for God's sake?'

Nathaniel takes out the A-to-Z guide to London that he's bought and squints at the dense thicket of information. It looks like he's lost. We'll probably be traipsing around these swanky streets until it's time to go back to the airport.

The potent lure of his company has dramatically faded.

He's not being his usual charming, witty self at all; in fact, he almost looks worried. I suspect he has realised that this was an idiotic idea and that he will soon have to introduce me to someone I have no particular wish to meet. I'm even beginning to wonder if this 'someone' exists.

'This is outrageous, Nathaniel,' I declare. I am extremely pissed off with him. 'Why are you being so mysterious? I haven't even had a proper lunch.' I realise there isn't really any connection between him being secretive and lunch, but I don't care. They only gave us a cup of tea on the flight, and there wasn't even a biscuit with it.

He just walks on, so I tug at his arm and say, 'I want to eat something. I want to go into that crêperie over there.' I point at a cheerful establishment with red and white tablecloths.

He turns away from me and gets out his mobile phone. He starts to talk, but I can't hear what he's saying. He did this at the airport too, before we got on the flight. Who on earth is he calling? Why won't he tell me? Maybe this 'friend' is yet another of his female admirers...

I start to fumble in my bag for my mobile. I know people in London too; I could phone one of them. We might even go out for a meal together. Nathaniel clearly isn't enjoying my company. I never thought he would be this moody. I don't want to traipse after him any more. He is really pissing me off.

'You go on, Nathaniel,' I say when his call is finished. 'Give me my ticket and we can meet up at the airport.'

He looks at me quizzically.

'No, really, you go on,' I insist. My bag is doing its trick of turning into a cavernous lagoon full of miscellaneous objects. I may need to get a torch to find my phone.

Nathaniel looks at his watch; then he takes my arm and yanks me towards a side-street.

'Let me go!' I protest. 'What on earth are you doing?'

'Goodbye, Sally.' He leans forward and gives me a light peck on the cheek. Then he shoves something into my hand and disappears.

I stare into the crowd. I can't believe it. He has, basically, dumped me. He hasn't even given me my plane ticket. I knew he was in a bad mood, but I never dreamed he'd be this horrible. I just stand there, trying to blink back the tears, until I notice I am holding a piece of paper and suddenly remember him shoving it into my hand before he disappeared.

It seems to have an address on it. I check the name of the street I'm on; it's the same as the one on the paper. I am to go to number 70. Why on earth couldn't he have just shown me the place himself? Why all this subterfuge? It's absolutely ridiculous.

I pass the newsagent's and the dingy laundrette and the mobile-phone shop, but I can't seem to find number 70. If this is Nathaniel's idea of a joke, he'll get some sharp kicks on the shins. What I need is a cup of tea and a large sofa and a quiet weep, but of course this isn't the kind of place that would offer such comfort.

I quicken my step, but then something makes me linger outside a shop that doesn't seem to fit in with all the rest. It's like an exotic bird in an aviary of pigeons. The walls and the door are a dramatic lapis-lazuli blue flecked with gold. In the window are a large orange hat, some very comfortable-looking red Chinese slippers, a stack of turquoise bowls, a large plate of scones and a big yellow teapot. It's number 70. Maybe Nathaniel was just giving me directions to the nearest café because he knew I was hungry.

I look up at the arty pink neon sign. 'Extravaganza,' it says. 'Specialities: Tea, Recycled Sofas and Hats. Proprietor: DeeDee Bertorelli.'

Chapter Thirty-Nine

I STAND OUTSIDE EXTRAVAGANZA for a full five minutes. I gaze into the window and then up at the sign. Any minute now I'll wake up and find myself on a seat at Dublin airport. This whole afternoon has been a dream. And in my dream it has started to rain.

I place my hand gingerly on the golden door-handle. It feels very real and solid. I turn it and the door swings open. The interior is low-lit; there are lamps and candles making a dusky glow.

I scan the room. Is DeeDee in here – and is she my lost great-aunt? The sign said DeeDee Bertorelli; but her name is, or was, DeeDee Aldridge. She said she wanted to be an actress. She said she wanted to live in Rio. How did she end up here, on this drab, damp London street? Or maybe she didn't. Maybe Nathaniel has got the whole thing arseways.

I stare at a tanned, plump woman who is engaged in an animated conversation with a ponytailed young man. They are sitting on a large yellow sofa, cradling steaming mugs; before them, on a dolphin-shaped turquoise table, is a big orange bowl full of what appear to be home-made chocolate chip cookies. They are the only customers in the shop – or is it a café? It seems to be both. If DeeDee were here, would I even recognise her? I try to remember the photo of her as a young woman. I recall her firm jawline and strong eyebrows, the straight look in her eyes. She was smiling even though she was sad. I knew she had longings she couldn't speak of, longings she felt no one would understand. But was it myself I was thinking of when I found these feelings in the grainy, faded image? Is that why I became so fascinated with her?

She isn't here, I tell myself. *Of course she isn't. Finding DeeDee wouldn't be this simple. I'd have to trawl through thousands of pages of South American parish registers and spend days on the Internet. She would have hidden her tracks very carefully. None of us even know where she settled, though Rio is the place that suits here. She should be in Rio, not here.*

Hello, DeeDee, how wonderful to meet you at long last... I prepare the words, even though I've convinced myself there will be no need to say them. If DeeDee were here, she would have somehow known who I was. She would have welcomed me with a warm embrace, and by now we would be seated and talking. I wouldn't be standing hesitantly by the door of this strange, almost surreal room, wondering if I should sit down.

Hi, DeeDee. I'm your great-niece Sally. Nathaniel gave me the address of your shop – you know Nathaniel, don't you?

The words in DeeDee's notebook return to me: 'Nobody believes that Joseph forced himself on me...' They have been etched in my memory ever since I first read them – and I have read them many times, each time hoping to find something new, something I hadn't noticed.

She isn't here, I think, as I walk past a large sculpture of a unicorn and almost fall over a fawn-coloured Labrador, who is dozing by the counter. *And, if she is, she won't want to see me. She may even throw me out. I'd be a reminder of everything she's wanted to forget. I should leave now. I should just go to the airport.*

'Would you like something?' a young girl behind the counter asks. She seems surprisingly conventional and is wearing a crisp white blouse and a navy cardigan.

I just look at her.

'A cup of tea, maybe?' She peers at me in the half-light. I must look very puzzled and lost, and extremely tired.

I think of the long journey and the lack of lunch. Tea... the word sounds like an old friend in all this strangeness. 'Yes, thank you. I'd like a cup of tea, please.' I no longer feel hungry.

She doesn't ask me what type of tea, or point to the rows of boxes behind her. She simply reaches for a teapot and says, 'I'll bring it over.'

I turn round like a sleepwalker and wonder which of the

three unoccupied sofas I should choose. My eyes are drawn to an amazing collection of exotic hats, scattered across a wall so white it could have been bleached by the sun on a Mediterranean island. A strategically placed lamp illuminates the collection.

I decide on the red sofa by the window and cross the room again, this time stepping carefully over the Labrador, who is now snoring gently. Where on earth is Nathaniel? I reach into my bag and turn on my mobile phone. Maybe he'll ring me. He has my plane ticket. Surely he's not just going to abandon me. Whatever I may feel about Nathaniel just now, I can't believe he would be that careless.

I check my phone to see if I have any messages, but nobody has tried to call – not even April. I really should phone April to tell her I haven't got that plane to San Francisco. I dial her number quickly and get her answering machine; I leave a brief message and don't mention that I have somehow ended up in London instead.

One of Bach's Brandenburg Concertos is playing softly in the background. I sit on the sofa and survey my surroundings. Even though the room is not particularly large, it contains many unusual objects. I notice a large cushion shaped like a toaster, and a painted wooden mermaid who seems to be overseeing a collection of antique teddy bears. What this room does, I suddenly realise, is it takes objects that might seem bizarre and strange elsewhere and it gives them a home – a place where they fit in.

The young girl arrives with the tea. 'Here you are,' she says, with a beaming smile. It seems to me suddenly that I am just one of the many unusual objects and people who have found their way here. Whoever owns this place knows about solace and sanctuary. It isn't a bad place to find oneself on a lost August evening.

The tightness in my chest relaxes and a thrill of excitement suddenly runs through me. What if Nathaniel is right? What if DeeDee is here? *Of course* I want to meet her. How can I have had any reservations? A woman who owns a place like this wouldn't be bitter and unforgiving. She wouldn't refuse to talk to me. And I need to talk to her. She has surely unearthed plenty of wisdom during her long and unusual life. She may even tell me how to endure my love for Nathaniel; the feelings he evokes in me are as odd as this room and its contents – which, of course, include me.

'Is… is DeeDee here?' I hopefully ask the girl, just as she's about to move away.

'Sorry, who?'

'DeeDee,' I repeat. 'I came here to see her.'

'I'm sorry, I don't know who you mean,' the girl says.

My heart sinks. So this whole crazy trip to London has been for nothing. What on earth can Nathaniel have been thinking? If DeeDee were here, I could understand why he might have absented himself. He might have seen it as an act of tact and kindness; he wouldn't have wanted to intrude on a reunion. But he has brought me here on a wild-goose chase, and for the flimsiest of reasons. There are thousands of DeeDees in the world. The name on the sign has probably been there for years and no one has thought to change it. No one thought that it would mean this much to anyone.

I am unprepared for the sharp, almost physical ache of desolation. In a flurry of misery, I grab my bag and get up. My love for Nathaniel has clearly been misplaced; I must reclaim it and forget him, forever. And I must forget DeeDee, too. I should have gone to San Francisco. Maybe I'll fly to San Francisco this very evening.

'She means me.' The plump, tanned woman is walking slowly across the room, and I notice she is limping. 'She means me,' she repeats, to the girl. 'I'm DeeDee.' She looks at me. 'I've been expecting you, dear, but I thought you might like a cup of tea before we talked.'

I sink back onto the sofa. I gaze at her and swallow hard. My mouth is dry and my heart is thumping. This isn't true. Of course it isn't. I've got so desperate I'm making it up, like Aggie with her angels.

But then I know it is happening. I know it from her smile. It is the same smile I saw in the photo, only it's happier; it's a

327

real smile, not just one plastered on for the camera. She has the same firm jawline, though it's thicker now with age. And the look in her eyes is unchanged. It is still straight and true and extraordinarily gentle.

I want to rise from my seat and embrace her; I want to find the right words to mark this momentous, extraordinary occasion. But I stay rooted to my seat. It is she who sits beside me and takes my hand.

This softly lit room, with its lamps and candles, made her seem much younger when I saw her from a distance. Now that she's closer, I can see that her face is considerably wrinkled and her wispy brown hair has streaks of grey at the parting. It is the plumpness, the general sense of roundness and tanned radiance, that convinced me that she was a middle-aged woman who had, perhaps, just returned from a sun-filled holiday. The impression was deepened by the thick silver bangle on her arm and the picture on her T-shirt, which sends a tropical sunset streaming across her ample breasts. She has the face of an old woman who doesn't know she's old.

'Would you like an omelette?' she asks. 'Nathaniel phoned me to say you were very hungry and hadn't had any lunch.'

'So you know him?' I lean forward, desperate for an explanation. 'You know Nathaniel?'

'Yes, I met him a while ago. He's a lovely young man.' She smiles at me. 'I think we also have lasagne.'

I realise we are still discussing my supper. 'Omelette,' I say. 'That omelette sounds just right.'

'With some cheese, maybe?' She squeezes my hand. Hers is warm and soft and very comforting.

'Yes.'

'Chips would be nice with it, too, wouldn't they?'

'Yes,' I agree quickly. I want to get on to more important matters.

She gets up and goes over to the girl behind the counter. They have a quick chat, and then DeeDee returns.

'Sorry Ita didn't know my name when you asked her,' she says as she lowers herself slowly onto the sofa. 'She only started here last week. I'm rarely here these days. Craig is the manager now.'

'So you know Nathaniel?' There are so many things I should be asking her about, but this is the one that seems most urgent and extraordinary.

'Yes, I met him a while ago,' she says vaguely.

'*How* did you meet him?'

'It was an amazing coincidence. We sort of bumped into each other and got talking. Would you like a biscuit?' I get the distinct impression that she doesn't want to explain this matter more fully; but she sees me waiting eagerly for more details. 'I know a friend of his. They came here together for coffee one day when Nathaniel was visiting London. And then, of course, he met you and heard you talking about your great-aunt DeeDee, so he phoned me one day to ask if I was this mysterious DeeDee – he said he knew it was a long shot, but it is rather an unusual name.'

'And you told him?' I am almost falling off the sofa with curiosity.

'I said I wasn't, but he still went on about you and how much you wanted to meet your lost great-aunt. So I phoned him the other day and told him who I was. It seemed time to finally admit the truth.'

I feel a glow in my heart. Nathaniel is completely redeemed in my affections. He has found DeeDee for me. He's just as special and sweet as I imagined. Of course I love him – I will always love him, even though he just sees me as a friend. That will have to be enough for me. I'm just glad he exists and that I met him. He has solved the family's biggest puzzle through a chance visit to a café. It seems more than a coincidence. It somehow seems that it was meant to be.

'Aggie so much wants to see you too.' The words come out of my mouth in a torrent of hopefulness. 'It would mean so much to her, DeeDee. I don't know how much longer she'll be with us. She's desperate to tell you that she loves you.'

DeeDee looks down at the table.

'I know about Joseph.'

DeeDee grows even more still and silent.

'I read your notebook.'

'What notebook?'

'The one with the recipes.'

She just looks at me.

'Someone must have found it,' I say quickly. 'It was in my parents' attic. You'd gummed together the pages that were… were more personal.' Suddenly I feel guilty. 'I would never have seen those pages if they hadn't got damp and opened on their own.'

She is still looking at me strangely.

'Don't you see, DeeDee? It's like I was meant to read them. So many strange things have been happening lately, it's almost like…' I take a deep breath. 'It's almost like we were meant to find you because of Aggie. You must visit her. Please say you will.'

'I don't know if that's really called for.' She says the words slowly, flatly, almost as if she's decided already. 'I want you to keep this a secret, Sally. I don't want you to tell anyone that you have met me.'

I stare at her, aghast.

'I just wanted to meet you because Nathaniel has told me so much about you.' She touches my arm gently. I maintain a mutinous silence, but I decide not to argue with her. Maybe when we know each other better I can persuade her to see Aggie. 'Do you like Extravaganza?' Her eyes search mine keenly.

'Yes, I do. I love it. It's… it's just great.'

'Oh, good. Some people say I should get rid of the sofas and the hats and the cushions, and put in more chairs and tables.'

'Oh, no!' I protest. 'The hats and the sofas and the cushions are… are essential.'

She laughs. 'No wonder Nathaniel says you and I are so alike.'

I wish I'd made a list of the questions I want to ask her. There are so many that I don't know where to start.

'What happened to your baby, DeeDee?' I say softly.

She gazes out the window at the rain and the cars and the people walking home from work. 'That's a long story, Sally.'

'I want to hear it.'

I'm afraid she may be about to tell me that's a secret too. But then she begins to speak.

Chapter Forty

'IT WAS AN AWFUL situation, of course,' DeeDee tells me calmly as I eat my omelette and chips. I'm amazed that I can eat, given the circumstances, but something about DeeDee is so loving and gentle that my hunger has returned. I even remembered to ask for tomato ketchup.

'I hadn't planned to have a baby for years, if ever,' she says. 'I was never the sort of woman who felt she had to have a child.'

I just listen. As DeeDee speaks, the light from the pink candle on the table seems to glow a deeper gold.

'I didn't really even know Joseph. He wasn't my type at all. He was rather solemn and lugubrious, to be honest with you.' DeeDee sighs. It sounds like an old sigh, one she has sighed many times already. 'He was the type of man who actually *liked* wearing pinstripe suits and braces. And he regularly talked about his large collection of cufflinks. He seemed to bask in the comfort of conformity. He and Aggie were engaged at this point, but I really never understood what Aggie saw in him. There was no spark to him. No *bounce*.' DeeDee's voice rises slightly in indignation. 'I wanted Aggie to find her prince, but she seemed perfectly contented with that smug, plump frog.'

The music in the room has changed to jazz. As the silver notes of a saxophone cavort through the air, DeeDee smiles at me with mild apology and rises to attend to a new customer who is clearly also a friend. This place is a kind of haven, I realise. People come here sure of their welcome. London can be a lonely place, but there is nothing lonely about this room. There is no rush about it; there is time for what needs to be attended to. There is a rhythm and a faith in its sounds and its silences. It has what no interior decorator can ever offer: it has love – a wise, embracing love that is there for whoever needs it.

DeeDee's sudden disappearance is almost useful: it gives

me time to recall my own impression of Joseph. I always thought of him simply as Aggie's husband. He didn't intrigue or even interest me; he was just there, and at Marie's family gatherings he was the only one who relished her soggy lemon meringue pie. He seemed a man of cherished routines and habits – routines and habits that he and Aggie shared. By the time I knew him, he had moved on to smart navy suits; even in retirement, he kept up his sartorial standards on trips to town. When pottering around the house he favoured a rather shabby blue cardigan and slacks, and sometimes he wore gumboots in the garden. He was usually very polite, even friendly, but he didn't give the impression of a man who wanted to be known by all and sundry. He saved his intimacies for Aggie, whom he appeared to love and who clearly loved him back. They did crosswords together and went to bridge parties and always had some plan or other to improve the garden. They planned their yearly holiday well in advance and in great detail, and sometimes they even tried to acquire a perfunctory knowledge of the local language via books borrowed from the library. There was a regularity to their relationship that was almost comforting. Joseph seemed like a man who could be relied upon to remain much as he was. This is the story we told ourselves about Joseph. We didn't question it, because we had no reason to. He fooled us all. Perhaps he even fooled himself.

As I am thinking these things, DeeDee returns with two steaming mugs of tea. She also brings a bowl of sugar and a small jug of milk, and an orange plate full of the chocolate chip cookies. 'Help yourself, dear,' she says. I reach for a cookie and crunch it gratefully. All thoughts of my diet have gone, though I don't feel any need to munch my way through the entire plate. That is another kind of hunger, one that is satisfied by simply being in this room with DeeDee.

As she sits down on the sofa she winces slightly. 'The creaks and groans of age, I'm afraid,' she says. 'Sometimes my joints make as much noise as a loose floorboard.' She laughs – an exuberant, almost youthful laugh. She wears her years wonderfully. She doesn't flaunt them and she doesn't deny them; she is simply herself. She is wearing cerise lipstick and a light brush of mascara, and in the low light her tan looks real and glowing.

I think of Fabrice – her low décolletage, her showy jewellery and the caked powder that covers her wrinkles like uneven cement. Fabrice's eyes are so covered in mascara and eyeshadow that I can't even imagine what she might look like without it. *If only she could meet DeeDee*, I find myself thinking. *Then maybe she would realise that age can be beautiful.*

'Of course, the family all thought Joseph was wonderful,' DeeDee continues. She is clearly used to picking up the threads of a conversation after interruption. She takes a cookie herself; small crumbs fall onto the floor, and the Labrador jumps up from his slumbers and watches her eagerly. 'They liked his neatness. I was never neat enough for them. I wasn't one thing or another. I suppose I've always been a bit like this room, really – full of ideas and plans that don't seem to quite fit together.' She looks around her as though trying to see the room through another's eyes. 'Only they do fit together. They do in my heart.'

I reach out and touch her hand. As her face softens, I realise this is what I have been wanting to do: just reach out and touch her hand like this, to let her know she can share her truth, and it will not be ridiculed or questioned.

'What happened, DeeDee?' I almost feel guilty asking. 'How did he... you know... how did you find yourself in that situation with him?' I find I can't bear to mention Joseph's name.

The air seems to stiffen. 'I was working in a hat shop off Grafton Street,' she says slowly. 'Joseph came into the shop one day. I was surprised to see him, but he said he wanted to buy a beautiful hat for his beautiful Aggie. I was delighted, of course. I thought maybe he had some dash about him, after all – a bit of romance. We laughed about how it would surprise her and how she mightn't even want to wear it – she had this set idea of herself as a person who didn't do certain things…' DeeDee's words trail off miserably.

'I told him a famous hat-maker had said that the courage to wear a grand hat came from wearing it. Once you put it on, you could do it. The hat gave you the conviction.' She sighs. 'I even joked that he would have to steal up behind Aggie and put it on her, so that this transformation could happen. What I wanted him to understand was that Aggie had a wildness in her – a wildness she wouldn't allow.

'Anyway, Joseph and I were having such a pleasant conversation about this hat he wanted to buy for Aggie that I agreed to go out for a drink with him. The shop was just about to close, and I thought it would be nice to get to know my future brother-in-law better, especially since he seemed so much nicer than I'd thought he was. So we went to a pub. I only meant to have one glass of wine, but it was the kind of evening that happens sometimes – you know, when you keep meaning to go home, but you end up getting tipsy and giggling and smoking French cigarettes. Joseph bought them for me.' She smiles wearily. 'I suppose I mainly stayed drinking with him because I was often bored in those days. At least this was something different.'

A couple wearing thick knitted jumpers under open wax raincoats come into the shop. They both have fair hair streaked with rain. They are hand in hand; they are close and obviously happy. DeeDee smiles at them, and they smile back.

'Hi, DeeDee,' the woman says. 'We came in for some of that scrumptious marble cake of yours.'

'Help yourself, dearie,' DeeDee smiles. 'I think there's a few slices left. There's been quite a run on it today.'

'You… you were saying that you were in the pub with Joseph…' I prompt, afraid that she may decide not to tell me the story after all. Surely she has tried very hard to put it behind her.

'Yes.' She turns towards me again. 'We talked about Aggie – how special she was, how loving, even though she sometimes hid it out of shyness. We talked about the wedding, and of

335

course we talked about hats. Joseph was laughing, and he seemed so carefree. Then suddenly I knew I should go. I'd stayed too long with him. I wanted to get the bus; I didn't want him to drive me.'

'Why?'

'Because when I looked into his eyes, really looked, I saw he wasn't being truthful. He didn't want to discuss hats or Aggie. He wanted to forget himself. He wanted to leave behind the Joseph everyone had come to know and expect. He was hearing whispers from another life he might lead, one that wasn't so bound by convention. It must have been devastating to him; he was usually so controlled and correct. I brought it out in him, you see. I was everything he disapproved of and suddenly wanted.'

The words seem to cool the air around us. I sit stock-still. I can almost feel Joseph's fear and longing, the heat in him, the confusion. 'What happened then?'

'We started to have a stupid argument about public transportation. We suddenly wanted to place a distance between us – the one that had always been there before. I said there should be more buses and Joseph said there were quite enough already. And I said he only said that because he had a car. He debated this hotly. All affection between us seemed to have evaporated. I got up and went out of the pub, but he followed me and insisted on driving me home. It was raining outside and I didn't have an umbrella. I got into his car.' She looks away towards some unseen point in the distance.

'And in the car he asked me why I had been flirting with him. I told him that I hadn't been flirting. I reminded him that it was he who had come to the shop; I hadn't sought him out. Then he asked why I had agreed to have a drink with him. I said it was to discuss Aggie's hat, and he laughed as though I was lying. It was like we were in Eden and I had handed him an apple.' She smiles ruefully. 'I suddenly realised he was the kind of man who saw women as saints or wives or whores, and I was pretty sure which category he had placed me in.'

She cradles her blue mug. 'He lived in his head, you see.

336

His mind was trained to categorise and judge and apportion blame. He couldn't live with ambiguity. All he felt was his own hunger, and his need to tame what he felt I was doing to him. It was the cruelty of weakness.

'Of course, I wasn't thinking these things at the time,' she continues, almost briskly. 'I just wanted to get home and away from him. He was drunk – I saw that suddenly. He started to drive me home, and I noticed we were taking a strange route, one that wandered off on small side roads into the mountains. I asked why, and Joseph said we were in no hurry, after all. He said he wanted me to see the lights of the city in the distance. I said I just wanted to get home, but he didn't listen. When he was changing gears, his hand brushed against my leg; I moved it away from him, and I saw his hand trembling as it moved back to the steering-wheel. I told him I was thirsty and asked him to stop at a pub so that I could get a drink of water – though, of course, I would have run away from him if he had.'

She looks towards the window. The rain is pouring down, belting against the window in small, deft droplets. I haven't moved for five minutes. I wish I could step back in time and yank her from the car. I wish I could have saved her.

'Of course, part of me just felt I was being foolish,' she continues matter-of-factly. 'Joseph wasn't that sort of man. But, even so, my mouth was so dry with panic that I could hardly speak. He handed me a thermos flask – he said it had cold tea in it, from a picnic he and Aggie had gone on that weekend. I gulped back most of the contents without thinking – it was about a third full. Then I coughed and spluttered and screamed at him. It was neat whiskey. He apologised and laughed. He said he'd forgotten it was in there; he'd mislaid his hip flask. I didn't believe him. I told him to stop the car; we were on a small side road in the middle of nowhere, but I said I would walk home, or go to the nearest house and call a taxi. I said I couldn't stand being with him any longer. I said he was a liar and not good enough for my sister. Then I lunged for the door-handle. He stopped the car. We started to struggle. I bit his arm and scratched his face and kicked him on the shins, but

337

it only seemed to make him more determined.'

DeeDee's face is flushed, and she is twisting her thick silver bracelet round and round her arm. 'I suddenly realised I was far too drunk to fight with him properly. He was very strong. I felt the weight of him on top of me; he was holding the door-handle. I realised I would have to stay in the car and try to humour him, tell him I hadn't meant what I said. But he didn't listen. He said, "I love you, DeeDee" – he actually said it; only of course I knew he didn't. It was just an excuse to press his lips on mine. To force his tongue into my mouth. To undo my blouse and pull up my skirt. To force himself on me and not listen to my cries.'

She looks away. 'It was over quickly. Afterwards he straightened his clothes and just sat there. Then he turned on the light in the car and told me to tidy myself up. He was cold, almost angry. He said I must realise that this hadn't really happened. It had been a mistake. It was the kind of situation any man might find himself in, with an attractive woman of my type.'

'Your type?'

'Yes. He didn't explain what he meant, but he didn't have to. I had seduced him, tricked him somehow. He said I mustn't tell anyone, and if I did they wouldn't believe me. The whole family knew I was fanciful, prone to exaggeration, and they also said I was jealous of Aggie's engagement to him – why else would I criticise him? He had heard what I'd said about him behind his back. Aggie had told him.'

The couple who came for marble cake are leaving. It seems like they arrived only seconds ago.

'And then... you found out you were pregnant?'

DeeDee nods. 'I couldn't believe it at first. I'd kept the whole thing to myself, like Joseph had told me to. I'd been a virgin, but I felt ashamed somehow; I had almost convinced myself that I was the "type" of woman he'd talked about, and that it was my fault.'

'But then you told your family, and they didn't believe you.'

'Yes. Joseph told Aggie that I'd tried to seduce him several times and that he had, of course, resisted. A few of his friends told her that I had tried to seduce them, too; he must have got them to lie for him. He portrayed me as a loose woman, someone who was quite prepared to steal her sister's fiancé out of petulance. The family took his side because he was, after all, Joseph, a man of impeccable character, whereas I… Well, they didn't know what to make of me, especially when I said I wanted to be an actress. I think they thought I was acting.' DeeDee actually laughs.

'But eventually my father did believe I was expecting a baby. I'd moved to a poky flat in Ballsbridge, and he visited one day and saw the bulge under my dress. He hit the roof. He said it was because of the kind of life I'd been living. He said he would give me money to go abroad and have the child and put it up for adoption. He would tell everyone I had been studying Italian in Tuscany – he wanted me to take Italian lessons, to make the whole thing more plausible.' DeeDee's eyes crinkle slightly at the absurdity.

'My mother visited the flat a few times, and cried quietly and said the situation was terribly difficult for them all. And Aggie was furious with me. She said I had tried to blame her darling Joseph for my own foolishness; she said I had clearly got drunk and couldn't remember who I'd slept with. Then she started to cry and said, "Why are you so jealous of me and Joseph? Why couldn't you just find a nice young man for yourself?"'

'Oh, DeeDee, I can't believe they were so horrible to you.' I feel like crying, though DeeDee seems quite cheerful.

'They didn't think they were being horrible,' she says. 'They felt they were trying to get me to mend my ways. My father even found a pleasant young engineer who had often admired me at parish fêtes – we had once had quite a long conversation about topiary; my father was prepared to give him a large cheque to encourage his affections. Once I'd had the baby, I was told, I must return to Ireland and marry John – that was his name – almost immediately. That's when I knew I had

339

to go. I couldn't stand all the lies, and the narrowness of their hopes for me. And, of course, I was outraged that they believed Joseph instead of me.'

'So what did you do?'

'One day I got up very early and packed my most essential belongings, and got the ferry. I scarcely thought about it. It just seemed like something I had to do. My father had given me the cheque so that I could go abroad, so I had enough money to last me for months. I didn't even say goodbye. I just wanted to forget about them all and start again.'

DeeDee looks away from me, and we sit silently for a few moments. Then I decide to change the topic of conversation. 'Did you get to Rio? I've heard you wanted to go there.' I decide not to mention that it was Aggie who told me.

'Only recently, dear – about ten years ago, with my late husband Alfredo. We spent two blissful weeks there.'

'So you married!' I exclaim happily.

'Yes. I'm DeeDee Bertorelli now. Alfredo was Italian.'

'I… I thought you might have changed your name for… other reasons.'

'Oh, no. I married Alfredo in my forties; before that, I was DeeDee Aldridge.'

Dear God, I think. *The family could have found her so easily if they'd just looked in the right phone directory. But they wouldn't have, because that wasn't the cryptic story they had told themselves about her. In their version, she had hidden all her tracks and travelled great distances. She had become a stranger – and all the time she was just across the Irish Sea.*

'It took me a long time to learn how to be happy. When I first arrived in London I was heart-broken and lost and…and very *annoyed*.' She smiles at me conspiratorially. 'The details of my past seemed so very unsatisfactory. I had wanted my life to be big and beautiful…but suddenly it seemed so small. I began to blame myself for not being more lovable.'

I gaze at a sculpture of a white horse with large, knowing eyes.

'I know it sounds odd but sometimes I believed that if I were more lovable these things wouldn't have happened. Maybe I was a fallen woman all along and Joseph had sensed it.'

'Oh DeeDee don't say that!' I protest.

'But then I looked around me and saw so many other women...so many other people who felt just as isolated as I did. And I saw that, in some ways, I had always been an actress. I hadn't let people know the sorrows I felt. I hadn't known where to place them in myself.'

I watch a candle on one of the tables flickering and dancing in its own soft light.

'When I was pregnant I lived in a shabby flat near here and I hated it. The lino in the kitchen was torn and there were ants in the sugar...'

I clutch my mug more tightly.

'Big buses roared by outside and it kept raining that winter. And the table in the sitting room used to make me cry.'

'The table?'

'Yes' she smiles. 'It was rickety and stained and small. It rocked back and forth whenever I tried to use it. It seemed to me that life should have given me a better table.'

She laughs. 'Those first months in London felt very dark. I couldn't stand the shadows in myself. I had always wanted the light. And then one day I went into a dingy cafe called La Dolce Vita and the man behind the counter smiled at me and gave me a slice of banoffi pie with my coffee. I hadn't asked for it and he didn't want me to pay for it. He must have seen my eyes were puffy from tears.' She nods a greeting to some new customers.

'It was the best pie I had ever tasted. And as I sat there I noticed that though the cafe was dingy and low lit, when the sun shone through the window it seemed brighter than usual. I liked the mixture of it. And suddenly I didn't mind that my life was such a mixture too because I knew that if I didn't learn from my pain I wouldn't learn what brought me joy. That was how beauty entered my heart Sally. On a damp November day.'

Her words feel so soft and translucent. Like water. 'What happened then?'

'I went into a paint shop and bought turquoise paint. I went home and painted the table. And then I decorated it with primroses...the kind of wild primroses I used to love as a girl. I got a small piece of wood and put it under the table leg that was shorter than all the others. It was no longer a shabby cast-off. It looked really pretty. A real feature.'

'A statement object' I smile, recalling one of Greta's favourite expressions.

'I started to buy small pieces of second-hand furniture and I decorated them too. I put up photos of them in La Dolce Vita announcing they were for sale. I didn't make much money from them, but some arty folk bought them and I made new friends. I needed that. They actually seemed excited about the huge improbable bump in my stomach. And suddenly the baby wasn't just Joseph's...he was mine too.'

The glow in her eyes caresses the space between us. 'That's how my life changed Sally. Not through some great love affair or adventure or being spotted by a Hollywood producer. I simply decided to paint a table.'

We both sit in a silence that is somehow unaffected by the clinking cups around us, the laughter and tapping rain on the window.

'I still have that table. Alfredo used to love it.'

'How did you meet him?'

'In a small record store. We were both looking for old American jazz records. I was determinedly single, but we got talking anyway. And suddenly I was sharing all sorts of intimate details. He knew how to lure them out of me.' She chuckles. 'He didn't look like the sort of man who loved jazz. He seemed a bit plump and ordinary actually, but he had a huge smile that was like sunshine. If I hadn't met him in that shop I probably wouldn't have even noticed him. But I liked that he wasn't quite what he seemed. He was special in a way I wouldn't have known how to see before.'

'Were… were you happy with Alfredo?'

'Yes, I loved him deeply. He was soft and kind and wonderful with Craig. He helped me start this place. Before that, I worked in a theatrical costumier's. I loved meeting theatrical folk – though I didn't become a professional actress. I did a lot of amateur shows, though. I especially loved the old musicals.'

I drink in this information; and then I suddenly realise she mentioned someone called Craig. 'Who's Craig?' I ask, almost casually.

'My son. Joseph's son.' DeeDee looks into my eyes. 'I kept him, you see. I didn't have him adopted. Actually, he's the one who insisted that I meet you. He said it was time for me to tell the truth again. And this time it might be believed.'

Chapter Forty-One

'SHE KEPT THE BABY. He's called Craig,' I tell Nathaniel. 'He was the one who persuaded her to see me.' I try to match Nathaniel's long, loping strides. We are rushing to catch a train to the airport. 'He said it was important that someone in the family knew the truth – though, of course, I knew it already because of the notebook.'

Nathaniel grabs my elbow. We are at a busy intersection, though I hardly notice the traffic. My head is full of DeeDee and her story, and the seeming miracle of our meeting. 'Craig manages Extravaganza now, but he's also involved in some kind of peace movement. They have workshops at the...' I wonder if I should call it a café or a shop. 'They have workshops at the café every Thursday evening. They bring people from different cultures together and get them to share recipes. It was DeeDee's idea; she says, whatever culture or belief system a person comes from, everyone enjoys a slap-up meal.'

'Very impressive,' Nathaniel says distractedly. 'Do you have any change on you?'

We are at the ticket counter of the train station. I delve into my bag. Thank goodness I went to that bank machine when Nathaniel and I were traipsing around Chelsea; since I hadn't had any lunch, I felt it was perfectly permissible to buy a largish bar of chocolate. I hand him an English fiver and some pound coins. He extracts some coins from his own wallet, leans towards the gruff-looking man behind the glass partition and buys our train tickets.

'Whew, we had just enough to cover the fares,' he says as we walk quickly away. 'Come on, Sally!' He grabs my hand. His feels warm and strong and very nice.

'Oh, thank God!' I exclaim, when we are actually sitting on the train. We are surrounded by people who are catching planes – they're virtually hugging their luggage – and others who have probably been working late and appear to be somewhat pissed off. And there is a small scattering of unsavoury-looking teenage boys holding beer cans and bragging loudly about their misdemeanours. The regular travellers on this route are glancing warily at their watches and then staring resignedly out the window; they clearly don't believe the train is actually going to leave at the appointed time. They have the look of stoical veterans.

At last the train judders and starts its journey, and I find myself thinking that, if this were New York, I would be far more excited and impressed by my circumstances. But this is London and it's familiar to me. I get a thrill when I see the great sights of the city, but I'm also acquainted with its irritations and routines. What makes it special to me now is that it's DeeDee's home. Big cities need people like DeeDee to give them warmth and humanity, to help create little villages, within the sprawl, where people can belong – places that feel like home.

'I didn't meet Craig,' I tell Nathaniel. 'He wasn't there. But I saw a photo of him. He looks rather handsome and dignified, in a casual kind of way. He's in his fifties. He used to teach Italian in a secondary school – his stepfather was Italian, you see. DeeDee married an Italian man called Alfredo in her forties. They were very happy together, but he passed away a few years ago. He left her a lovely villa in Tuscany.'

'Goodness, you managed to extract a great deal of information.' Nathaniel smiles.

'Once she started talking, it just spilt out of her.' I sigh contentedly. 'It's so nice to finally have a relative who really enjoys talking about things.'

'I thought April had suddenly got rather fond of that, too,' Nathaniel comments wryly.

Oh, God, I'd almost forgotten about April! I take out my mobile phone and check my messages. There is a call from Gervaise, saying he hopes I'll phone to discuss wall-mounted coffee units as soon as possible. There is also a call from Fiona, asking whether I think she should wear a hat to the christening.

Erika has phoned to reveal, in outraged tones, that Lionel won't accept her refusal to meet him for coffee; in fact, he is insisting on turning up at her flat with a Chinese takeaway that very evening. She wants me to call around and help her persuade him that his affection for her is entirely misplaced. And, of course, there is a call from Diarmuid about furniture – in this case, a pine cabinet that he thinks could fit into my kitchen if he made it slightly smaller, which he says he would be happy to do. Diarmuid has never felt that I have enough storage space in my kitchen, and he's right; but I really don't want him dashing around with his tool-belt, measuring things. I might just possibly spit at him.

I insist on buying Nathaniel champagne on the plane home. 'To dear friends who find lost great-aunts.' I clink his glass happily.

His blue eyes shine with pleasure. 'Well, one does what one can to help.' He tips the slender glass back and drinks it all in one gulp. 'Finding a lost great-aunt is thirsty work – though not quite as difficult as looking after a highly opinionated mongrel called Fred.' He sighs dramatically. 'Apparently he's just buried Greta's best gold bracelet.'

'Oh, no!' I reach out and touch his arm, in a very friendly though entirely platonic manner.

'Yes, she phoned me just before I arrived to drag you away from DeeDee and take you to the airport. She was having a real hissy fit.' He gives me a look of mock misery.

'Oh, you poor thing.' I decide not to touch his arm again, even though I would very much like to. 'I'll help you find the bracelet. We'll have to hire a metal detector. We'll... we'll scour the coastline if we need to.'

'It's probably just in the back garden.' He grins at me cheerfully. 'Though I rather like the idea of scouring the coastline with you, Sally. Shall we do it anyway? Who knows what we might find?' He is leaning close. I feel his breath on my cheek. The champagne is going straight to my head. I need peanuts or crisps or at least a biscuit. I try to catch the attention of one of the air hostesses.

'Here.' Nathaniel nudges me, and I find myself accepting a packet of cheese-flavoured corn chips. 'I bought these for just such an occasion.' He smiles at me wryly. 'It hasn't escaped my notice that, when you're hungry, you can get very... very insistent on finding nourishment.'

He is clearly referring to the crêperie incident. I consider explaining, once again, that I hadn't had lunch and had got tired of traipsing around London streets in what seemed an entirely aimless manner, but I decide not to mention this. Instead I open the packet and start crunching the contents gratefully. He isn't to know that I don't want to become too tipsy in case I declare that I love him or something equally stupid.

'Would you like some chips?' I enquire, suddenly remembering my manners.

'Oh, no, I'm not hungry. I had a very substantial pizza with a friend. It was almost the size of one of DeeDee's larger hats.'

I decide not to ask who the friend is. It is more than likely to be another female admirer. I just want to enjoy Nathaniel tonight as the plane hurtles through the sky. And I want to bask in my memories of DeeDee – how lovely she is, how gentle and wise. I've told Nathaniel most of the crucial details already. He listened with real fascination once we were on the train to the airport and he could relax a bit. I saw a more serious, almost solemn side to him.

'It's so sad that DeeDee doesn't want to see Aggie, though, isn't it?' I say, when every corn chip is eaten and I have peered into the packet for stragglers. 'She has such a big heart, I really thought she would find it in herself to visit a sister who...' I stare bleakly out at the clouds. 'Who may – you know.'

'...Shuffle off this mortal coil before too long.' Nathaniel finishes the sentence for me.

'Exactly.'

There is a long silence, in which I peer at the other passengers and remember that I am in a large piece of machinery that is currently soaring over the ocean even though

I don't know how it stays up. In the circumstances, it seems extraordinary that people are talking and laughing and reading newspapers and books.

'But she'll change her mind about seeing Aggie, won't she?' I find myself saying. It's more a statement than a question. 'I mean, she must. Everything's in place for a reconciliation. It would mean just as much to her as it would to Aggie, I'm sure it would. It would be… what's the psychological term for it?'

'Closure.' He says the word with a sigh.

'And we would have helped to make it happen,' I continue excitedly. 'We've done the hard part; we – you – have actually found her. Now we have to convince her to come over to Dublin. She just needs a little encouragement, that's all. Once the family hears what really happened –'

'You promised her you wouldn't tell anyone.' Nathaniel's look is cold and reproving, and I suddenly feel my euphoria fading. Up until this moment, I had almost managed to convince myself that DeeDee's obsession with secrecy would surely alter in a matter of days.

'Yes… yes, but how could I mean something like that?' I splutter. 'I planned to talk her out of this daft notion. Of course I wouldn't tell people until I've got her to change her mind.'

Nathaniel's blue eyes seem very steely suddenly.

'Her life has been clouded by lies,' I declare dramatically. 'Terrible lies. People need to know the truth.'

'I hope you'll forgive me for saying this,' Nathaniel begins carefully, 'but it seems to me you're beginning to sound a little bit like April.'

'What do you mean?' I glare at him.

'Well, she's convinced everyone has to know the truth, too, isn't she? And in her hands it's a blunt instrument. You have to be careful with the truth sometimes, Sally. There are many truths to most situations, because people can see the same situation in many different ways.'

'This is different,' I reply, bristling with indignation. 'We don't have to have a philosophical discussion about this. Aggie *wants* to see DeeDee. I wouldn't talk to her about what Joseph did – of course I wouldn't. I'd just tell the rest of the family, so that… you know… so that they'd welcome her like they should. I couldn't bear for her to be treated as an outcast.'

'But what do you think it would be like for DeeDee, sitting with Aggie, knowing that she still believes these awful things about her?' Nathaniel says. 'Aggie might even expect her to apologise.'

'I think she's forgotten most of the details.' I frown. 'She keeps saying that she just wants to tell DeeDee that she loves her.'

'It's a complicated situation, Sally,' Nathaniel says flatly. 'I know you'd like it to be like *The Waltons*, but it isn't.'

'I hardly ever watched *The Waltons*,' I protest, my lower lip quivering. 'I… I only want to be *helpful*.'

'Then you'll just have to respect whatever DeeDee decides to do,' he says firmly.

'But… but don't you find it a bit *surprising*?' I lean towards him and almost knock my glass off the small fold-out table. He grabs it just in time. 'I mean, she agreed to see me; why can't she agree to see Aggie and the rest of the family? She might as well go the whole hog while she's at it, don't you think?'

'What I think is incidental,' Nathaniel replies. 'It's what DeeDee thinks – what she feels, to be precise – that matters.'

Suddenly he reminds me of Erika's sporadic and very annoying even-handedness. He should agree with me about this. We should be discussing ways to make DeeDee change her mind.

'I know we could use emotional blackmail on her, but she's had quite enough of that already,' he says, as though he has somehow read my thoughts. 'There's absolutely no point in pushing her, Sally. She's trusted you to keep your meeting with her a secret.'

'Yes, but what if she regrets it – you know, later on?' I persist.

'DeeDee is the sort of woman who decides what she needs to do in her own good time.'

'Yes, but what if she decides too *late*?' My voice has risen in consternation. 'She can't dawdle about this, Nathaniel. Aggie needs to see her as soon as possible.'

'Let's not argue about this, Sally.' He picks up the in-flight magazine and starts perusing shopping tips for visitors to Copenhagen. I feel like grabbing it from him. It reminds me of Diarmuid and the mice and all the times he just didn't want to talk about things I needed to talk about.

But of course men are like this, I find myself thinking as I pick up my own copy of the in-flight magazine. I flick through articles about luxury weekend breaks in rural England, the joys of spaghetti and the amazing stonework on some cathedral in Belgium. *Talking to them is pointless; any semblance of closeness is basically just a mirage.* I pour myself another glass of champagne. *They back off as soon as they feel uncomfortable.*

'I think it was unfair of her to make me promise not to tell anyone,' I mumble mutinously, more to myself than to Nathaniel. 'If she knew she was going to say that, she shouldn't have seen me at all.'

'But you did promise not to tell anyone, and I've promised too,' Nathaniel says. 'And I don't know about you, but I take my promises very seriously.'

I can't stand this. If we were on land I would get up and march right out of the room. He's not just referring to DeeDee; he is also referring to my marriage. He's reminding me that I left a perfectly good husband, whom I promised to love forever, because of a bunch of mice. He, on the other hand, left his marriage because his wife had fallen in love with a man who wore dresses. In this competition, he is the clear winner.

I can't bear to sit with him a moment longer. I get up sharply and stumble towards the toilet. I sit on the lid for a full five minutes until someone starts to yank rather desperately at the door.

When I get back, Nathaniel stares at me bemusedly. 'What is it?'

'You know perfectly well.' I glower. 'Let's just not talk,

OK? It's easier that way.' I stick my nose into the magazine.

'Are you really that interested in snowboarding in Aspen?' he enquires, peering over my shoulder.

'Yes. I am absolutely fascinated by it,' I reply. 'Please don't interrupt me.'

'When I said that thing about promises, I really was just talking about DeeDee.' He nudges my arm gently. 'I'm sorry if it seemed like I might be referring to – you know... other situations.'

I glance at him cautiously. He's said just the right thing, yet again. I feel a sudden urge to ask him all the things I have wanted to ask him all day. I want to know what he got up to with Fabrice and why. I want to know more about Ziggy and Eloise and Sarah. I want to know why he shares his affections so easily with so many people. And I want to tell him that it isn't really fair, in some ways, because it would be so easy to form the wrong impression. It would be so easy to think that one is somehow special to him – more than just a friend.

I put the magazine away and start to rummage in my handbag.

'What are you looking for?'

'Some marble cake that DeeDee gave me. It's probably turned into crumbs by this stage. I should have eaten it on the train.'

'Have you tried your coat pocket?'

'It's up there.' I point wearily to the overhead rack.

He stands up, finds my coat and delves into a pocket. 'Is this it?' He shows me a small plastic bag.

'Yes. I think so.' I take it from him. 'Thank you.'

He grins. 'Is there anything else you'd like me to locate, now that I'm at it?'

I just stare up at him and think, *Yes, I'd like you to find the belief I used to have, that there was someone out there for me. Someone like you, actually, Nathaniel. Someone just like you.* Instead I say, 'I insist that you eat some of this cake. It really is delicious. I shared a slice of it with DeeDee.'

'Thank you.' Nathaniel sits down beside me, and I feel that

soft feeling I sometimes get when he's near. I want to be angry with him, so I won't feel this yearning. Surely he can see that this visit to DeeDee has, in some ways, changed nothing? The thrill of actually meeting her has waned, now that Nathaniel has reminded me starkly that I can't tell anybody about it apart from him. In fact, I suddenly realise that finding her like this is almost harder to live with than her dramatic disappearance.

I hand Nathaniel half the slice of cake and he pops it into his mouth. 'Delicious!' he declares. 'Do you have the recipe, in that notebook?'

'Yes,' I say. 'I could bake it for Aggie. It would be a... a sort of link to DeeDee, wouldn't it? A little – you know – secret acknowledgement.'

'I'm sorry,' he says softly.

'About what?'

'About sounding so haughty about DeeDee a while back. To tell the truth, I'm disappointed that she doesn't want to see Aggie, too.'

'Really?' I gaze at him with relief.

'It's just that I also feel that, if she's meant to see her, she will.' He searches my eyes. 'Does that make any sense to you? We must leave it up to her. She'd resent it if we tried to influence her. But I think meeting you may have helped to make her consider it, at least.'

'OK.' I fold the white paper napkin the cake was wrapped in. 'It's not simple, is it? Finding DeeDee. It's really just the start of something else. I don't know why I thought that finding her would be enough.' And what I want to add, only I don't, is that maybe it's a bit like love. It's not enough to find it; you have to know what to do with it, how to nurture and cherish it. I gaze with a sudden, terrible yearning at the deep curve of Nathaniel's eyelashes. Surely he must see it in me? Surely he must know what I feel for him?

His eyes stay on mine for a moment, and then he leans back. 'So how do you feel about going to California now?' he asks.

352

'I don't know,' I mumble. 'I mean, if April has made up her mind to come over to Marie's party and make her grand announcement, I don't really think I can stop her. Going out to California to talk to her about it might even make her dig in her heels. She's very stubborn.'

Nathaniel looks at me solemnly.

'And my views on America are rather mixed, these days, anyway,' I say. 'I don't really know what it stands for any more. It doesn't seem to be like… like it was. It's even sent me off on protest marches.'

'I think there are many Americas,' Nathaniel says dreamily. 'There are things about it I love and things I hate, but it's a special place for me. I love its buzz and enthusiasm. I love the innocence and honesty you can find there, when you get away from the crap… and there's plenty of that.' He yawns and rubs his eyes.

'I think mainly I just loved the house we lived in there. That's what I wanted to go back to,' I whisper. I would love to lean over and rest my head on his shoulder. We are both sleepy; it's been such a very long day.

'I wish I could have met Craig,' I say drowsily, 'but he was off getting some tiling put up in the villa in Tuscany, the one Alfredo left to DeeDee. It has an olive grove and orange trees. She showed me pictures of it. She spends part of the winter there.'

Nathaniel doesn't reply. I glance at him warmly and find myself thinking he seems more like DeeDee than Craig did in the photo. He is exactly the sort of son I imagine she would have. It is extraordinary how he found her so easily He is asleep, his head tilting towards mine. He moves closer and closer, until his cheek is resting on my shoulder. I don't move away.

Chapter Forty-Two

'THERE REALLY ARE THOUSANDS of hotel accessories on offer, ranging from the popular Corby trouser-press to the very latest in wall-mounted coffee units and even fine bone china! The right accessories can play a crucial part in a hotel's success, for they offer a panache and sense of comfort that discerning guests will note and savour.'

Phew! I press the Send button, and the feature is on its way to Greta with only minutes to spare. I hardly know what it says. I think the main theme was that hotel accessories are frightfully important.

I now have less than an hour to get to the church for Milly's christening. At least I've already showered and put on deodorant. I rush up to the bedroom and tumble into a thermal vest, a pair of tights and the Mediterranean-blue cotton dress I've bought for Marie's party. I am the sort of person who favours layers, even in summer. This dress is covered in small pink roses and looks suitably seasonal, but it's long-sleeved and loose enough that I can secrete a thin woollen jumper underneath it, should this be called for.

I check my answering machine and mobile, just in case Nathaniel phoned me while I was typing frantically. He hasn't. In fact, I haven't heard from him for days, not since we returned from London. He's probably off with Fabrice or hunting for Greta's gold bracelet in the garden. Whatever he's up to, he clearly hasn't had time to ask me how I am doing with my enormous and extremely cumbersome secret. I feel like I'm dragging it round with me. I keep wanting to tell someone. I mustn't drink too much at the christening party or it might burst out of me. How did my life become so complicated?

I find myself thinking of the long talk I had with Mum last night in her spotless kitchen. She kept saying that I mustn't allow Diarmuid to put me off marriage. She is very angry with Diarmuid. She seems to have forgotten that I left him first. I haven't gone into the mice situation with her, but I have admitted that, during the first months of my marriage, I felt somewhat neglected. I think she suspects that Diarmuid became romantically involved with Charlene shortly after the wedding. I have tried to tell her that I think this is enormously unlikely, but she won't listen. 'I never really trusted him,' she said, even though I know this is untrue and she thought he was very loyal and steady. 'He seemed shifty somehow. And he never really looked you in the eyes.'

I helped myself to a shortcake biscuit as she listed his shortcomings. It was fascinating to watch her editing her memories, tweaking the details into a story that suited her.

'Mum, do you remember the house we had in California?' I said during a brief pause. Of course, I knew she must remember.

'Yes.' Mum gave me a strange look. 'Why do you mention it?'

'It was lovely, wasn't it? So big and soft, somehow. Remember how there was a hammock in that old oak tree?'

She busied herself filling the kettle.

'And the sprinkler on the lawn... I used to love running into the jets of water in my swimsuit.'

I realised I shouldn't have mentioned the word 'lawn'. It's a loaded word in our family. My mother can't hear it without feeling she is being reproached.

'The garden was nice, but it was too big,' she said briskly. 'I was the one who had to look after it. I was the one who had to rake the leaves and water the flowers and cut the grass.'

But you enjoyed it, I wanted to say to her. *I know you did. I saw it on your face. You even went to the garden centre to buy complicated plants that came with long lists of instructions.* But I didn't say this, because she has forgotten. It is part of the world she left behind.

'I know about April's father.' I decided to just say it.

Mum remained with her back to me, staring out at the concrete.

'It doesn't matter.' I went over to her and put an arm gently around her shoulders. 'It was just something that... that happened. It happens to lots of people.'

'How did you find out?' she said in a whisper.

'April told me when I was in New York. When she gave me your birthday brooch.'

'Oh.' She didn't move away from me. I could feel the sadness in her, but I could also feel the relief. 'Well, I suppose you had to know sometime.' She turned to face me. Her eyes were glistening. 'We should have told people before, I suppose, but then we left it so long that it became... it became harder to explain, somehow. And anyway, who would understand it? We don't really come from that kind of family, do we? They all seem so very...'

'Well behaved?'

'Yes, exactly.' She smiled at me. 'But I don't want you to worry about Marie's party. I'll be there for you. If they get too nosy about Diarmuid, I'll interrupt and tell them about that wonderful solo concert your father gave the other day. Some of them are quite impressed that I married such a talented musician.'

I felt a stab of guilt that I hadn't made it to the concert myself, but it was a lunchtime concert in a faraway hall and I was very taken up with hotel accessories. I should have found the time to attend, I realised. My father enjoys being a member of an orchestra, but his occasional solo concerts are what really buoy his spirit. He rehearses for them for months.

After this there was a long silence, in which Mum tried to adjust to the news that I knew about April's parentage. She did this by tidying things – wiping the table and drying cutlery, which she then placed carefully in a drawer. When the phone rang, she answered it and had a conversation about the charity shop where she sometimes works; from the snatches of conversation I heard, it seemed that they were going to have a really big sort-out soon, because they had far too many men's jumpers on display and not enough 'quality women's wear'. It seemed to be just the sort of conversation my mother needed. She returned looking much more cheery.

'Well, I suppose you had to know sometime,' she repeated, mostly to herself, as she started making freshly ground coffee. 'Of course, your father loves her as much as if she were his own child. He always has.'

'I know,' I replied, not adding that he probably loves her even more than that. There has always been a fierce bond between them. She demanded his love, and he gave it. He would feel so betrayed if April announced, in front of the entire family, that Al was in fact her biological father.

'Mum,' I began slowly. 'You know April says she wants to come over for Marie's gathering?'

'Yes.' My mother beamed. 'It's wonderful. We haven't seen her for so long.'

'I... I think she wants to tell people about Al.' I forced the words out of me. 'She's angry that you haven't told people. She's been in therapy. She... she feels we've been living a lie.'

'Oh, don't be ridiculous!' Mum shrugged this off. 'She wouldn't do that. April's not like that. I've told her we'll tell people when... when the time feels right.'

'But you said you'd tell people when she was twenty-one, and you didn't,' I reminded her.

'Maybe people don't need to know,' Mum said. 'I think April realises that now. *She* knows; that's the important thing. And she's spent time with – with her father in California. It's not like we've prevented her from seeing him.'

'She told me she was going to make an announcement at Marie's party.'

'Of course she won't!' Mum declared. 'She would have told me. She just says things like that sometimes. She has a dramatic side.'

'Have you spoken to her?'

Mum looked at me somewhat guardedly. 'No. Not recently.' She poured the boiling water on my tea bag and poured herself a mug of coffee from the gleaming cafetière. 'Let's not talk about it any more. When she comes over, we'll take her out to a nice dinner.'

And that is how we left it. My mother refused to believe

that April had any plans to tell people about Al. But over dinner, she said, she and Dad and April would discuss how and when April's parentage might be revealed. They would also give her her birthday present – a large, hand-cut Waterford crystal bowl – in advance; that would surely placate her. I wish I felt more convinced about this, but I don't have time to think about it now. And I've just noticed that my hair looks like I've been through a hedge backwards.

The doorbell rings as I am tussling with my tresses. I put some styling gel on my hands and pat it onto the more rebellious parts. I've put on too much; now my hair just looks plain greasy.

'Sally, are you there?' I hear Erika calling. We agreed that she would call round so that we could share the taxi fare. I rush to the door.

'Don't say anything about my hair,' I say, as soon as I've let her in. 'I know it looks awful.'

'No, it doesn't; it looks just fine,' she smiles. 'Very sleek and shiny.'

'That's some jelly thing I've put on it,' I mutter. 'Bits of it will start dribbling down my neck during the service.'

'You look lovely,' Erika insists.

'And you look extremely…' She looks different. I can't quite find a word for it. 'You look extremely pretty and – and *satisfied*, Erika.'

She almost blushes.

'What's happened?' I ask curiously. 'Have you sold some more cats?'

She lowers her eyelashes bashfully, places a foot in front of her like a ballet dancer and makes little sweeping movements on the floor.

'Has Alex phoned you?'

She goes over to the bay window. 'The taxi should be here any minute, shouldn't it? I really don't want to be late.'

'Have you actually managed to teach the refugees some English?'

'I haven't given them any classes – not yet, anyway.' She

sits down, almost skittishly, on the sofa. 'I think it might be quite fun, really, once I've got used to it.'

I stare at Erika long and hard. She seems to have got over the disappointment of not being Milly's godmother. I have not, of course, told her that Fiona wanted me to be the godmother, only she was worried that it would make Erika feel rejected. We had a long discussion about it and agreed that it might be best if she asked a cousin called Louisa to be the godmother instead.

'Sorry I didn't phone you back,' I say, vaguely recalling Erika's indignant message about Lionel and his Chinese takeaway. 'Things have been pretty busy. In fact, I had to go to London a couple of days ago.' If only I could tell her what happened there!

'Oh, that's OK.' Erika tosses off my apology with rather too much nonchalance. 'Your hair really does look nice, Sally.'

'Did he turn up?'

'Who?' She looks at me innocently.

'Lionel. Did he arrive with the Chinese takeaway?'

Erika looks at me blankly, as though I have asked her to recall a distant and not particularly significant detail. 'Yes, he did, actually.' She gets up and goes over to the window again. 'Where on earth is that taxi?'

'Something happened between you and him, didn't it?' I say.

'Who?'

'Lionel, of course.'

'Yes, I had a meal with him.' She takes out her make-up bag and carefully freshens up her lipstick. 'It was a very nice meal – one of those meals for two you can buy; it must have cost him at least thirty euros. We had –' She is clearly about to list every morsel.

'Did he bring some wine?' I ask.

'No, he didn't, actually. He wanted to go out and get some, but I told him we didn't really need it.'

'What did you drink instead?'

Erika shifts uneasily in her seat.

'You gave him some of that wildflower liqueur, didn't you?' She looks sharply away from me.

'*That's* why you're looking so satisfied!' I exclaim delightedly. 'You slept with him. You slept with Lionel!'

There is a potent silence; then Erika sighs. 'Yes, I did sleep with him, actually. I suppose I might as well admit it.' She peers at me, worried. 'Do you think it was very foolish of me, Sally? I really didn't mean to.'

'Was it nice?'

'Yes,' she answers, without the slightest hesitation. 'It's just that it came as quite a surprise; I never really saw him in that way before, you know. To be honest, I was going to tell him that I hadn't the slightest interest in him and he should go after someone else.'

'What made you change your mind?'

'I think it was the ear-nibbling. He's a very good nibbler. He's actually been getting lessons.'

'In *ear-nibbling*?'

'*No!*' she laughs. 'In overcoming shyness. He must be a fast learner.'

'That's because he adores you, Erika,' I say softly. 'He is gorgeous and extremely desirable and far nicer than Alex. I hope you see that now.'

She still looks doubtful. 'We had a very nice evening, that's all. And we're going to a film at the weekend. I suppose he'll do for the time being.'

'What do you mean?'

'Well, I just can't take our relationship that seriously... though he really is an excellent lover.' A broad and extremely satisfied smile spreads across her lips. 'And he takes direction without a murmur of complaint.' I can almost sense her toes curling contentedly. Then the taxi arrives, and we both sprint to the door.

Five hours later, I lurch slightly tipsily into Aggie's bedroom. I have been neglecting her lately. I want to sit and hold her hand and talk to her; only I find that she is sleeping.

I sit by her bed anyway. The christening was magnificent.

360

Fiona eventually hired a small and highly professional team to attend to the more important details – 'It was either that or muesli for the main course,' she laughed. She was wearing a soft apricot and rose jersey dress that looked like it had just been flown in from Paris, and she, naturally, looked very beautiful. There seemed to be hundreds of people there, but it wasn't a frightening kind of gathering; nobody left it wondering if they'd said the right thing or worn the right clothes or brought the right presents. The christening, of course, was solemn and beautifully poignant, but the party that came after it was greatly aided by ebullient hits from the 80s and large quantities of excellent wine and food. Guests wandered happily between the large dining room, whose more ample furniture was stored elsewhere, and the huge sitting room with its vast windows and views of one of the area's grander leafy squares. Fiona's mother seemed particularly attracted to the kitchen; she watched in awe as plates of stuffed leaves and sushi and prawns wrapped in filo pastry were carried guestwards.

'What are these, exactly?' she asked Erika and me before she ate anything. Then she added, 'Didn't little Milly look wonderful? She really takes after our side of the family.'

And Milly did look lovely. She only cried, very briefly, when she was leaving the church. She seemed to enjoy the attention. At one point during the ceremony she appeared to be smiling and gurgling.

'Erika slept with Lionel,' I whispered in Fiona's ear, when the party was winding to a close. She looked knackered and extremely contented and she had a milk stain near the right shoulder of her new dress.

She looked at me with a mixture of joy and amazement. 'Wildflower liqueur,' I muttered. She beamed from ear to ear. No further explanation was required.

I am just about to kiss Aggie and go home when she stirs and looks up at me. 'Is that you, Sally?'

'Yes, Aggie.'

'How lovely to see you, dear. What have you been up to? I haven't seen you for a while.'

I ache to tell her about DeeDee. I still can't believe that I have to keep it a secret. It seems so unfair.

'Oh, I've been pretty busy with this and that,' I tell her cheerfully. 'In fact, I've just been to a christening. Fiona – you know, my friend?' She nods vaguely. 'Well, she's had a lovely little daughter called Milly, and –'

Aggie reaches out and clutches my hand. 'I'm sorry about Diarmuid, dear.'

I gulp. 'What do you mean?'

'That he ran off with that other woman. Your mother told me all about it.'

'Well, actually, I sort of –'

'Yes, yes, I know. You left him and went back to your cottage, but that's only because you sensed things weren't right between you.' She holds my hand more tightly.

'The details are a bit odd, to be honest with you,' I mumble. 'Mum seems to want to blame him, but it was my fault too.'

'Let her be biased, dear,' Aggie says softly. 'She enjoys standing up for you.'

'We didn't really love each other, you see,' I say. I don't know why I'm telling her this. It must be all the wine. She was always my confessor. 'He only became involved with that woman when he realised that. He asked me to come back many times.'

'Your heart wasn't in it, dear. I sensed that.'

'Did you?' I stare at her.

'Yes. Sometimes, when you talked about him, I felt you were talking about someone else.'

I blink hard. Age hasn't diminished her intuition. I think of Nathaniel. That's who I was talking about: the man who will always be just a dear friend.

'Anyway, we'll stand up for you at Marie's party,' Aggie announces gutsily. 'Don't worry. If anyone starts pestering you about Diarmuid, I'll tell them about the angels in my bedroom.'

I smile. I never realised my close relatives were going to be quite this supportive. It seems that some of them also find Marie's parties rather awkward. I really wish I'd known this earlier.

'Marie's gatherings have got very staid,' Aggie continues, almost as if I've prompted her. 'There's no real oomph to them any more. Joseph used to bring along jazz records when you were younger.'

I wish she hadn't mentioned his name. Jazz records... yes, I vaguely remember the strange, floaty music livening up my enjoyment of fizzy lemonade and crisps and sausage rolls.

'I've asked Fabrice to come along, to give the whole thing a bit more style and bounce. A bit more fun,' Aggie says firmly. 'She's such a dear friend, and I think she's rather lonely.'

I don't know what to say.

'She says she might even do some songs from the shows.'

'What shows?' I frown, somewhat irritably.

'Oh, you know – the big shows.'

'Can she sing?'

'I don't know.' Aggie chuckles happily. 'Anyway, she's been so kind to me, I feel I owe her a little treat. She has no real family of her own, you see.'

I bite my lip. Aggie never mentions DeeDee any more. It's as if she's decided to forget her because she knows she will never meet her again. Who am I to complain if she has turned to Fabrice for comfort and friendship? But I still resent it somehow. I don't like Fabrice, especially now that I know she's become so pally with Nathaniel too. There's something odd about her.

'Well, that's nice,' I say, lying politely. 'Maybe I should invite my friend Erika along and get her to play her guitar.'

I laugh ruefully, but Aggie says, 'Perhaps they could do the songs from the shows together.'

'No, I don't think I'll invite her, actually,' I reply quickly. 'She's not very good at remembering the words to songs, and she can't really play the guitar.'

Aggie chuckles. 'Did you bring any mints?'

'Yes.' I hand her the bag.

She unwraps one and pops it into her mouth. 'Well, at least Marie's party should be a bit livelier this year,' she smiles.

'Yes,' I find myself agreeing. 'In fact, it might be the least boring party Marie's ever given.'

Chapter Forty-Three

'I LOVE YOU.' 'I love you,' I repeat very carefully. I am in a large and somewhat shabby room near central Dublin, teaching English to Erika's refugees. Time seems to have flown since I returned from London: it's September already, and Marie's party is tomorrow. I suppose I should be glad I'm not at home fretting about it.

They are not, of course, *Erika's* refugees, if one is to be strictly accurate; but, in a way, we have all become refugees from Erika herself – or from her guitar-playing and singing, to be precise. She persuaded me to come to her first class, and as we listened to her wailing, I felt these poor people had been through quite enough already. She sang 'The House of the Rising Sun' over and over again, and then kept trying to get her students to discuss the lyrics. Since it is a rather sad song, this wasn't particularly uplifting. She also didn't remember all of the words and kept asking me to prompt her. No one laughed; they just watched us solemnly.

'I think it's a bit too advanced for them,' Erika hissed at me. 'What should we do?'

'What about just... just general conversation?' I suggested.

'But what is a general conversation?' Erika enquired. She can be rather pedantic at times.

'It's about anything, anything at all.'

Erika stood up before the group, visibly quivering with nerves. She has a fear of public speaking, but not of public singing – which is ironic, since she has quite a nice speaking voice. 'How much English do you actually know?'

No one answered. 'English,' I said, standing up myself. 'Speak? You?' I pointed at them.

There was a long silence, and then someone mentioned the name of a pop song. A rather dashing young man stood up and said, 'This is the BBC World Service' in a very gentrified Home Counties accent. He had obviously listened to this announcement many times. 'Please have exact fare ready,' someone else commented. 'Stand clear of the doors,' one woman remarked. 'Guinness is nice thing,' a young girl giggled. Soon they were all giggling. Some of them were almost falling off their seats with laughter.

'They're getting out of control,' Erika whispered nervously. 'Should I start playing the guitar again?'

'No,' I said firmly, because if she did there would be an exodus, and I had noticed that some of them were talking to each other – and they appeared to be speaking very broken English. The laughter was easing their self-consciousness. I decided to address the confident-looking young woman who was sitting nearest me.

'What is your name?'

'Katya.'

'It is nice to meet you, Katya.' I held out my hand and she shook it. Then I turned to the class and said, 'It is nice to meet you,' and they stared at me blankly.

'It is nice to meet you,' Katya replied suddenly. Then she turned to her classmates and waved her arms around like a conductor. 'It is nice to meet you,' she said encouragingly.

'It is nice to meet you,' they chorused in unison. We clearly had a leader in our midst.

'What would you like to talk about, Katya?' I asked her, thinking I would have to repeat the sentence several times and possibly draw a diagram.

'Love,' she replied, her big brown eyes shining. 'I very much need talk love. And forms.'

'Forms?' I enquired.

'Yes, forms you fill after.'

'Fill in,' Erika corrected her.

'Yes, many forms.'

'Do you have the forms with you?' I asked. This was clearly just the sort of practical help she required.

'No,' she sighed.

'Bring them next time,' Erika said.

'Yes,' I said, speaking very slowly, to the class. 'Make a list of the things you most need to talk about.' I thought of the bewildering array of bureaucracy they must have encountered. 'And give it to us at the end of the class, so that we can prepare next week's lesson.'

'Love,' a middle-aged woman said. 'She need talk love, too.'

And so the entire class learned of Katya's attraction to a man called Sergei – a man with big legs and arms and 'many shoulders'.

'Not many,' Erika corrected. 'People do not have many shoulders.'

'Broad shoulders?' I suggested.

'Big, like so.' Katya made an expansive gesture. 'And white teeth and many hairs.' The language of love was losing something in translation, but the class seemed eager for more details.

It turned out that Sergei was staying in the same B&B as Katya and her family. Sometimes he gave her his fried tomatoes at breakfast. This was clearly enough reason to desire him – or at least it had to be, because her grasp of English wasn't sufficient to go into greater detail.

This is how I have found myself trying to improve her vocabulary. 'I love you.' I say it many times.

'I love you,' a young man near the front says. 'Your arse, it is like a rhino's.'

'No! Don't say that,' Erika says firmly, while I try not to giggle. 'Whoever told you to say that was… was very naughty.'

There follows a long, and sometimes virtually incomprehensible, discussion about whether Katya loves Sergei or simply likes him, in which case she should say, 'I like you,' or perhaps just, 'Thank you very much for the tomatoes, Sergei, you are a very nice man.' I begin to get rather worried about Katya and Sergei. What if he just wants her as a friend? What if he already has many other admirers he hasn't told her about?

'Sex,' a matronly women comments. 'Men, that is thing they want.'

I begin to feel rather frustrated that most of the people in this room don't speak better English. We could have a most interesting philosophical discussion. I might even ask them what I should do about Nathaniel. Should I say, 'I love you,' and see how he reacts? He hasn't phoned me in weeks – not since we got back from London. Surely that tells me everything I need to know. I gaze sadly out the window. Maybe he's beginning to realise how much I care about him, and he doesn't want to mislead me. Maybe Greta has had a word with him and told him he needs to be more careful with his affections.

Erika is saying, 'Not all men just want sex. Some can be very kind and considerate and... and forgiving.' She is clearly talking about Lionel. He's growing on her. I knew he would.

The class ends shortly afterwards. As we spill out onto the street, I realise I have enjoyed myself. This was better than sitting at home worrying about April and DeeDee and whether I want Diarmuid's slimmed-down kitchen cabinet – not to mention Nathaniel. In the circumstances, it's probably best not to mention Nathaniel at all.

When I get back to the cottage I get a call from Mum. Apparently April has decided to get a later flight and won't be arriving in Ireland until tomorrow morning, the day of Marie's party. So they won't be able to take her out to dinner and give her the Waterford crystal bowl and discuss where and when they should tell people about Al. She's going to take a taxi straight from the airport to Marie's house.

'Oh, God,' I moan. 'Oh, well... I suppose the plane could be delayed.'

'Don't say that, dear!' Mum exclaims. 'Everyone is so looking forward to seeing her.'

Mum obviously still believes April will not make her grand announcement. But, judging from the conversation I had with April yesterday, she hasn't changed her mind about it at all.

'I even suggested to Mum that she just tell Marie to start with,' April said. 'That would have been enough for me – for the moment, anyway. But she wouldn't even do that. She just went on about some special birthday present she's bought me.' April sounded almost tearful. 'I don't think she plans to tell anyone – not ever.'

I didn't say so, but I suspected she might be right.

Since I can't seem to prevent April from attending Marie's party, I feel a real yearning to absent myself from it instead. This is not a new yearning, of course; I've been feeling it for most of the summer. But this time it isn't my own distress I'm concerned about. I can't stand to think of Mum and Dad, and even Marie, being so hurt. But I need to be there for them. I wish I had someone to bring with me, someone wise and kind, someone… Feck it, I must stop thinking about Nathaniel.

I get out my laptop. Even though it's late in the evening, I might as well get on with my column. This week it's about the glories of – wait for it – wicker chairs.

'These chairs have elegant curves and laid-back personalities,' I write. Chairs with personalities? Oh, well – that's how they describe them in the brochure. 'They come in softly coloured and textured seagrass, on a wooden frame, and have elegantly tapered legs.'

I stare hard at the letters on the keyboard. I want my column to be different, because I'm different. Or maybe I'm closer to the person I've always been without knowing it. Maybe I'm just remembering, at long last.

'But if you feel like something a bit different, why not check out some of the charity shops that sell second-hand furniture?' I find myself typing. Then I mention a large warehouse that helps fund hostels for the homeless. It is where Erika buys most of her furniture.

'There can be a real thrill in finding something second-hand and making it your own,' I type. 'I have a friend who has made a very pleasant coffee table out of an old wooden crate she found at a fruit market. And I know of a shop in London that offers recycled sofas – along with hats and cakes and its own very special brand of friendship.

'So play around a bit with different styles, if you want to. Have fun – and don't take it all too seriously. Paint golden angels on your bedroom wall if you feel like it. Keep things as light and as juicy as you can.'

Chapter Forty-Four

'I LEFT THE QUICHE too long in the oven.' Aunt Marie is sobbing 1 on the phone. 'It's all hard and leathery-looking. And the pastry's gone brown.'

'Calm down, Marie,' I say. 'I *prefer* quiche that's… that nice and firm.'

'But I want it to be perfect.' Marie's voice is like a little girl's.

'Well, the truth is, Marie, it probably won't be – and that's just fine. No family gathering is perfect.' I want to add that this one may be less perfect than usual, but I decide not to worry her. She gets into a terrible tizz about these parties. I really don't know why she bothers to have them, since they cause her so much anxiety.

'No one really appreciates them,' she says.

'What?'

'My parties. No one really enjoys them. It's a chore for everyone.' She sniffs miserably. 'This may be the last family gathering I ever organise.'

'Oh, Marie, don't say that!' I exclaim dutifully, wishing I could share my true feelings on the matter. 'It's a great chance for everyone to meet up and – you know…'

'Lie to each other?' Marie says tersely. 'That's what your cousin Annabel says.'

I almost drop the phone. I vaguely recall Annabel: a dewy, sweet creature who has done a number of postgraduate courses and was wearing an engagement ring last time I met her. She also seemed to be rising up the ranks of the diplomatic service and wasn't even slightly overweight.

'Yes, Annabel says she can't come to the party because it's too much of a strain,' Marie continues. 'She says she spends the whole afternoon trying to prevent Wayne – that's her father; he doesn't look like a Wayne, somehow – she says she can't enjoy the parties because she's too busy trying to prevent

Wayne from getting at the wine.'

'Why?' I grip the phone more tightly.

'Wayne is an alcoholic, only no one is supposed to know that, of course. They bring a special bottle of some herbal drink that's red and looks – well, you know.'

'As if he's drinking wine?'

'Yes.'

'I didn't know he had a drink problem,' I say in amazement. Annabel's father has always seemed one of my most well-behaved relatives.

'Well, he doesn't most of the time, these days,' Marie says sadly. 'It's just that at my parties he meets Cedric – you know, he married –'

'Yes, yes,' I say, not wanting Marie to go through the entire family tree. 'I remember Cedric; he's a lawyer or something, isn't he?' At least five of my relatives are successful lawyers.

'Yes, and he had an affair with Annabel's mother when Wayne was off sailing around Europe in that yacht race ten years ago. Wayne gets very edgy any time he's in Cedric's company. And Annabel's mother is forbidden to speak to him. That's why she spends so much time helping me in the kitchen. And I thought she was just being friendly.' Marie blows her nose and sighs.

Dear God, I think. *This is what really goes on at Marie's parties?*

'I didn't know about any of this until Annabel told me,' Marie whimpers. 'And there's other stuff, too. You know Louise's son, Sam? The one who's doing so well in construction engineering?'

'Yes,' I say eagerly.

'Well, the reason he never comes to my parties is that his family won't allow him to bring his lover, Pierre.'

'*Pierre?*' I press the phone to my ear.

'Yes. He's homosexual.'

'Well, a lot of people are,' I say soothingly, hoping she can't hear my relieved smile. I suddenly realise I always suspected all this, somehow. The image that my relatives present at Marie's parties has always been that little bit too perfect. But, instead of trusting my intuition, I chose to ignore it. I chose to believe that my flaws were the exception.

'It's like *Dynasty* or something,' Marie sniffs disapprovingly. 'I don't know how I'm going to face them.'

'It really isn't all that *unusual*, Marie,' I say. I feel like a huge weight has suddenly been taken off my shoulders. 'In fact, if anything, it was more unusual that none of them seemed to have any personal issues whatsoever.'

'I wish Annabel had just not told me,' Marie continues resentfully. 'I feel like calling the party off, but I can't, because of dear April.'

'Well, if you feel like that, maybe you should,' I say quickly, sensing a chance to prevent April's grand announcement. 'I'll help you ring everyone. I'm sure April would understand.'

'No, it's my duty,' Marie sighs, and I realise that she feels it is. 'Who on earth would have thought they had all these *secrets*? And how on earth have they managed to keep them for all these years?'

I think of my own secret. As Marie starts to go on about the quiche again, I begin to wonder if families can form certain habits. I begin to wonder if the fact of not talking about DeeDee, hardly acknowledging her existence, has helped my relatives to remain silent on other matters. After they had done it once, they found they could do it again. Maybe it became a familiar solution. After all, I remained entirely silent about my doubts about my marriage; I almost thought that, if I ignored them, they weren't there. But they were. They didn't go away. And now Mum thinks she can just somehow forget that Al is April's father.

'At least the lemon meringue pie is nice and moist,' Marie says, and I realise she actually thinks people *like* it soggy.

'Actually, Marie...'

'What?' she demands.

'Actually, maybe you might put it in the oven for just a bit longer.' I feel I have to tell her. 'I personally like it a bit firm – like that lovely quiche you've just made.'

Marie is considering whether or not to be offended, but then she suddenly shouts, 'Oh my God, I forgot to buy garlic bread!' and hangs up.

I look out the window. There is a swivel-hipped, Latin bravura to the way the sea falls and rises and suddenly embraces the shore.

The phone rings again. 'I got a good price for the sitting-room suite, and the hall table and the lamps.' It's Diarmuid. 'In fact, I've sold most of the contents of the house. And someone seems very interested in the bedroom wardrobe.'

'Oh.'

'Since you said you didn't want the furniture, I put an advertisement in the paper. It was almost brand-new, after all.'

'Thank you,' I say, realising this comes as a relief. I do rather need the money.

'When I come round to measure up the kitchen for the cabinet, I can give you a cheque. A lot of people have seen the house, too. The estate agent has the key.'

'I see.'

'When do you want me to come around with the cabinet?'

I take a deep breath. 'Actually, Diarmuid, I don't really want the cabinet either.'

'But – but you *need* it,' he protests. 'You don't have enough storage space in that kitchen.'

'This isn't about storage space, Diarmuid. It's… it's about whether I want you wandering around my home.'

There is a stiff, hurt silence.

'I'm not going to be that kind of ex-wife, I'm afraid,' I say softly. 'I mean… I won't want to meet you for coffee, or have you and Charlene round to dinner. I won't want to attend the christening of your first child.'

That silence again.

'I'm sorry, Diarmuid, but it would just seem very false. I know some people get all pally with their exes, but I don't want that. It's not that I hate you, or anything like that; it's just that there are… there are still too many things I don't understand.'

'About what?' he asks. His voice sounds tight, upset and bewildered.

'About us. About how we ended up together.'

'Maybe…' he begins slowly. 'Maybe it seemed like a kind of answer, only we hadn't been asking the right questions.'

I didn't expect him to say something like that. I didn't expect him even to have those thoughts.

'Look, give the cabinet away if you don't want it,' I say.

'But it's a really nice cabinet.'

'Yes, and that's why lots of people would be happy to have it.' He says nothing.

'I have to go, Diarmuid. I have to get ready for Marie's party.'

'Oh, it's today, is it?' He sounds sympathetic. 'Try not to worry about what they think of you, Sally. Just be yourself. Most of us find that only a few people ever really understand us anyway.'

Can this really be the same Diarmuid? I think as he hangs up. *The same Diarmuid who wouldn't skinny-dip in the hotel swimming pool at midnight on our honeymoon?* Being with Charlene seems to have changed him. At long last, he's had to take a stand about something he believes in.

I sit for a while after our conversation. I feel things leaving me – things that were ready to go. I can't quite name them yet, but that's OK. I want to get used to this new feeling I sometimes glimpse – this feeling that it's OK to be Sally Adams, just as I am, a great big mixture like DeeDee's shop. Of course, it would be great if I could share my life with someone like Nathaniel – he himself clearly wouldn't want to – but there are so many other people I cherish. I would have missed them if I'd taken that plane to California.

At twelve-thirty on the button, Mum presses the doorbell. I am in my new dress, with a thermal vest and a thin woollen jumper underneath; it isn't a very warm September day.

'Well, isn't this just grand,' Dad keeps saying as we head for

Marie's house. It's in a very large estate, and it's very tidy and somewhat devoid of character. Even from a distance I can sense the air of anticipation. Marie is peeking out from behind the net curtains; I can see her round, worried face.

Dad beeps the horn as we park in the driveway. The door opens and Marie, flushed and smiling, surveys us. Her smile is so broad it looks like it's going to fall off the edges of her face. She looks extremely nervous. She is wearing an apron and fidgeting with her hands. 'Welcome!' she cries. 'I'm so glad you're here on time.'

'Hello, Marie!' I call out.

She waves back as though we were still at the other end of the road. 'Aggie's here, and so is… that friend of hers.' She manages to keep smiling. Uncle Bob, Marie's husband, agreed to collect Aggie good and early so that she could put her feet up and have a little rest before the social exertions.

'The nurses said we shouldn't bring her back too late,' Marie whispers as we get out of the car. 'They weren't sure about her coming here, actually, but of course she insisted.' Marie's face softens, and I can see she feels grateful for Aggie's enthusiasm. 'This may be the last family gathering she attends.'

'Yes, yes, there's no need to be morbid, Marie,' Mum says brusquely. 'We all know that. I've brought along some sausage rolls.' She hands her sister a large plastic tub.

Uncle Bob joins us on the driveway. He is a tall, balding man with a serious face and kind eyes. 'I even mowed the lawn in honour of our visitors,' he proclaims innocently.

'Go inside and see to the drinks, dear,' Marie says quickly. 'And fill up the crisp bowl. And use the small sherry glass for Aggie; she says she doesn't want wine.'

'Keep an eye on Wayne,' Marie hisses at me as we go into her hallway. Her whole house is painted in very muted pastel colours, which match the furniture and the curtains and even the cushions. 'And make sure Fabrice doesn't eat all the crisps, or there won't be any left by the time the others arrive.' *So Fabrice is a crisp-eater too?* I think. For some reason this surprises me; I hadn't expected Fabrice to eat anything as un-dramatic as crisps.

Fabrice is swathed in a loose, fluttery dress, liberally dotted with sequins. It is a strident pink, and so are her large round earrings. Her white-blonde hair is now in frothy curls; part of it is in a chignon, and the rest almost forms a thin veil across her face. There is, however, a gap in the middle where her nose and parts of her mouth and eyes are clearly visible – and she is, as usual, caked in make-up. Clumps of mascara have gathered on her eyelashes.

'I wish April had allowed us to collect her from the airport,' Mum says to me fretfully, while Dad listens to Fabrice talking about snorkelling amidst the grandeur of some Australian coral reef. 'It doesn't seem right that she has to make her own way here, but she was adamant about it. Dad, of course, will pay the fare. Should I phone her to see if she's landed?'

'No. I will,' I say quickly. 'You sit with Aggie.' Aggie is installed in a very large armchair and swathed in a blue mohair rug. She is looking around her with great interest and sipping her sherry.

I go into the back garden and take out my mobile. 'April, it's Sally. Have you arrived in Dublin?'

'Yes,' she says rather breathlessly. 'I'm watching luggage on one of those carousels. Ah, good – here's my case.' There is a pause and the sounds of mild tussling.

'Please say you've changed your mind about –'

'I'm not going to talk about it now, Sally. I have to get a taxi.'

'I'll persuade Mum and Dad to tell people another time. Aggie's here; she's so old, and she's enjoying the party, April. Think of her too.'

'There'll always be reasons not to tell people,' April says briskly. 'I have to go now. See you soon.'

I walk back into the room in a daze. I can't believe I am allowing April to come to this party in her current state – but how am I to stop her? I hoped she would change her mind once she actually got on the plane, but she hasn't.

'Wayne,' Marie hisses at me as soon as I get indoors.

'You'll have to get someone else to watch Wayne,' I hiss back. 'I have to talk to Mum.'

'About what?' Marie demands, seeing my worried expression.

'April. She's… she's a bit upset about something.'

'Was her flight all right?'

'Yes, I think so. It's just that she seems a bit emotional.'

'Of course she is!' Marie exclaims. 'She hasn't been home for ages. It's only natural. She must have missed us all so much.'

'No, it's a bit more complicated than that,' I say, only Marie is now telling me how thrilled everyone is that April is attending the party. 'Your parents have talked about nothing else for weeks,' she adds. 'Have you seen the Waterford crystal bowl they've bought her? It's exquisite.'

I pull myself away from her and head towards Mum. 'She's become such a dear friend, you see,' Aggie is saying to Mum. I assume she is referring to Fabrice. 'And I think she gets lonely. She likes to pretend she's still a young thing, but…' They both look over at Fabrice, and Aggie smiles.

'Excuse me, Aggie,' I say, 'I need to speak to Mum for a moment.' I feel Fabrice glancing at me keenly. I look away and steer Mum towards the garden.

'What is it, dear?' Mum says.

'April,' I whisper. 'She really does plan to make some kind of announcement.'

'She's just teasing, dear. You know what she can be like.'

'But it's like she's a different April,' I say. 'She has this obsession with the truth now – she keeps saying people must know the truth. Maybe it comes from living in California.'

This seems to be the first remark about April that actually reaches my mother. For all its modernity, California is still the Wild West. It is a vast, mixed place with an extraordinary number of opinions. It can change people – often people who wanted to be changed anyway – and my mother knows this better than anyone.

'Ring her again,' Mum says suddenly, as though this is the first time I have mentioned April's announcement to her. She must see the look of very genuine consternation on my face. 'Tell her Dad will collect her from the airport.'

I take out my phone while Mum darts across the room and tugs at Dad's sleeve. 'April,' I say, when she answers, 'Dad will collect you at the airport. He really wants to. Please let him.'

'I'm sorry, I'm already in a taxi,' she replies. 'Gee, I'm glad I brought my sweater. It's not exactly warm today, is it?'

Mum is at my shoulder. 'Tell her he'll collect her in Dublin,' she says, rather desperately. But April has turned off her phone, sensing, I suppose, that we were launching an attempt to ambush her.

'Does Dad know about this?' I ask.

Mum nods and sighs. 'Oh, dear... I should have listened to you before.'

The room is getting crowded. The guests are all very well dressed, and some are bordering on beautiful. Any minute now they are going to start asking me about my marriage.

'I've read your columns,' a cousin called Seamus tells me. 'I agree with you entirely about the importance of kitchen storage.'

'Have you been doing any courses lately?' a relative called Suki enquires. She is tall and blonde and could easily be a model.

'Not really.'

'I've been studying art history – it's so fascinating, Sally – and...'

I look as though I'm listening to her for the next ten minutes. She seems a nice enough person, and genuinely enthused by her subject matter. Then Mum nudges me sharply in the ribs.

'How wonderful, Suki,' I say. 'I'd better go and... you know... mingle.'

'What is it, Mum?' I whisper, when we're out of Suki's

earshot.

'I've asked your father to head the taxi off at the entrance to the estate,' Mum says agitatedly. 'He'll wave it down.'

'What?'

'He'll get it to stop. And then he'll ask April to get into the car, and drive her to a nice lunch at that hotel in Killiney she likes so much.' Mum is almost quivering with subterfuge. 'If she says she wants to make her – her announcement, he won't argue with her; he'll pretend that he's going to drive her to Marie's party later. Then he'll get her drunk.'

'Oh.' I notice my father leaving the room hurriedly and dashing towards the front door. I'm rather shocked at this daring plan.

'Orla, our daughter, has just met a lovely young man at her salsa class,' a distant relation by marriage tells me. 'Have you ever tried salsa, Sally? Apparently it's great fun.'

She's talking to me as if I'm single, I think. *She's talking to me as if I was never married at all. But she must know I married Diarmuid. Everyone in this room does. Marie rounded them all up and got them to come to the wedding. They have given me wedding presents. They have showered me with confetti.*

'Dear Marie – she puts on a great spread, doesn't she?' Cedric says. I try not to stare at him as I recall what Marie said about him and Annabel's mother. 'How are you, Sally? Are you still involved in windsurfing?' The man must have a great memory. My crazy windsurfing days were years ago. I only managed to stand up on the surfboard for about five minutes.

'I've always rather liked the look of windsurfing,' Cedric continues. 'It must be wonderfully refreshing.'

'Yes, I suppose it is,' I agree. He hasn't mentioned Diarmuid, either. In fact, I don't think anyone is going to. I thought they'd be pestering me with questions, but they seem to have edited the subject out of their conversations. I'm grateful, but I shouldn't be that surprised: they have done that with so many other subjects already.

I feel Fabrice watching me again, as she straightens the

mohair rug so that it covers Aggie's knees. Maybe she's jealous of my friendship with Nathaniel. I would love to march up to her and ask her about him, but of course I don't.

I take a large gulp of red wine. I'm glad that Dad has decided to intercept April – and I'm so relieved that he and Mum finally believed me. Of course, now people are asking where April is, and where my father has gone; Mum is making vague comments about her being collected from somewhere at the last minute. 'It will be so lovely to see her again,' someone says. 'She must be lovely and brown. I've always wanted to visit San Francisco.'

I wonder how Mum will explain April's non-appearance, I think, cramming crisps into my mouth. Marie is serving some sort of main course later. Whatever one may say about her parties, there is no shortage of food.

'Sally, could you help me to bring in the plates?' Marie says. Then she looks around and cries, 'April. Oh, darling April!'

I nearly drop my glass. What on earth is April doing here? She should be with Dad. Did she get out of the taxi and sprint past him? Where is he?

'April, darling!' Mum rushes towards her, arms outstretched. She is managing to hide any reservations very convincingly.

'Hi, April!' I hug her too. It is, after all, expected in the circumstances. April is looking very tanned and slim, though her expensive trouser suit is a little crumpled after all those hours on the plane. Other members of the family move forward to greet her and kiss her cheeks, and Uncle Bob hands her a large glass of wine.

'You must be tired after your journey, dear,' Mum says. 'But you've arrived at just the right time. Marie is serving lunch.'

'Why on earth was Dad waiting at the entrance to the estate?' April leans over to whisper in my ear. 'He wouldn't let us get by. It was ridiculous.'

'How… how did you get past him?' I whisper back.

'There's another entrance, a smaller one. A kind of dirt track.' April's eyes are glinting. 'He was trying to stop me coming here, wasn't he? I can't believe it!'

She grabs a spoon and taps her wine glass imperiously. 'Excuse me!'

It takes a while for people to quieten. I try to grab April's hand and lead her from the room, but she pushes me away. Mum is cowering in a corner, Dad has just arrived back and looks haggard with worry, and Aggie is watching the whole thing very closely.

'I'm sorry to interrupt,' April says, when the room is almost silent, 'but there's something I'd like to share with you.'

I can't just let her blurt it out. I grab a wine glass myself and tap it furiously. Maybe I can give Mum and Dad a chance to bustle April away.

I almost run into the middle of the room. 'Yes, and I have something I'd like to share with you, too!' I say, almost shouting. 'My marriage to Diarmuid is over.'

No one looks in the least surprised.

'I left him because... because he was getting too fond of some mice.'

I see a number of raised eyebrows.

'I let them loose in the tool shed, only he lured them back with cheddar cheese.'

There is a sprinkling of murmur.

'Shut up, Sally!' April roars suddenly. 'Everybody knows about your ridiculous marriage, but they don't know that –'

'An honoured visitor is now going to sing us some songs from the shows,' a tremulous voice interrupts. It's Aggie.

People glance at her kindly, but their gaze returns to April. Her face is flushed and there is an urgent, slightly crazy look about her.

'Of course, not everyone likes songs from the shows,' Aggie continues; she is now standing, with Fabrice's help. 'But I thought a little music before lunch might... might help the party atmosphere.' She looks pointedly at April. 'And, anyway,

382

I thought that even those who don't like musicals might enjoy them this time. Because this time they are being sung by...' Aggie's voice breaks. 'By my dear sister DeeDee.'

Every jaw in the room drops in amazement.

There is uproar. People are pushing their way towards Fabrice – DeeDee – staring at her, wanting to clasp her hands. April is forgotten in the melee; I see Dad taking her hand and leading her carefully from the room.

I just stand motionless for at least a minute. It can't be true. How has that creature Fabrice managed to persuade dear Aggie that she is her long-lost sister? Is this what she's been up to during all those visits? Fabrice bears absolutely no resemblance to the lovely woman I met in London. It's outrageous. It's dastardly. It's... I stare at her more closely.

Dear God, it's true.

DeeDee has taken off her wig, and I can see her face properly. The heavy make-up has been applied very expertly, but I can discern her features underneath it. DeeDee has come back to us – and she has arrived just in time.

'Did you always plan to attend this party?' I say, when things have calmed down a little and she has removed most of her camouflage. Even the lurid pink dress has been briskly pushed into a shopping bag; she is now wearing a rose-pink cashmere jumper and neat brown trousers.

'No.' She smiles at me. 'I was very doubtful about it, actually.'

'I'm so glad you came.' I say. 'In fact, if you hadn't–'

'April might have told everyone about her father.'

'You knew that!' I gasp.

'Yes. Nathaniel told me and I told Aggie. But Aggie knew about Al already; your father mentioned it to her shortly after you all returned from California.'

Poor April. I suddenly long to hold her, comfort her. But Dad has probably taken her off to that lunch.

'So... so did Aggie always suspect you were DeeDee?' I say slowly.

'No, not at first,' DeeDee says. 'She saw me as a rather

dotty but entertaining new friend.' I smile. 'When I first visited her, it was mainly out of curiosity. And I wanted to see if I could pull it off; Aggie never believed I could be an actress. I didn't really feel that kindly towards her, you know. Only then we got chatting and laughing, and Aggie kept saying how interesting I was, and I began to enjoy entertaining her with tall stories. And she talked about me – DeeDee, not Fabrice – and she seemed to genuinely miss me… I had only planned to visit her once, but for a while I even stayed in a guest-house in Dublin so I could see more of her.

'And after a while I sometimes forgot to be Fabrice. We fell into our old ways, the types of conversations we had before.' She looks down at her hands. 'Anyway, after a while I think I wanted her to know. I dropped some hints. And then, after your visit, I came over to see her again and decided to broach the subject of Joseph. I said… I said I'd heard from someone that DeeDee had lied to her about Joseph. I needed to see if she was still bitter about it. I knew she would never accept the truth, but I hoped that time had lessened her resentment.'

'What happened?' I'm almost falling off my chair with curiosity.

'She burst into tears, and I started to apologise. I said I shouldn't have mentioned something so obviously hurtful; I was, after all, just someone she had got to know quite recently.'

'What did Aggie say?'

'She said she longed with all her heart to see DeeDee again, so she could beg her to forgive her. She said she knew DeeDee hadn't lied – it was her own husband who had deceived her.'

'Oh, DeeDee, you must have been so relieved!'

'Yes. I told her who I was then, of course. I took off the wig and told her about the layers of make-up, and we just sat there hugging each other for at least ten minutes. "I always knew there was something special about Fabrice," Aggie kept saying. "Something *familiar*."'

'How did she know you had told the truth about Joseph?'

'Shortly before he died, he told her he had raped me.' DeeDee's voice is almost a whisper. 'He couldn't live with the guilt of it any longer. At first Aggie thought she shouldn't look for me because I wouldn't want anything to do with her. She was sure I would never forgive her.'

'What made her change her mind?'

'Her heart,' DeeDee says softly. 'She listened to her heart. She... she says the angels helped her.'

'She thought they were floating sheep at first.' I smile.

'Yes, she told me.' DeeDee chuckles. 'I don't know if I believe in these angels of hers, but I still feel grateful to them.'

Suddenly I feel grateful to them too. It seems to me that we accept many extraordinary things as normal – birth, life, death, the sun and the moon and the stars, love. So why shouldn't we leave room in our hearts for the possibility that there are tender, wise beings out there who want to help and guide us, if we ask for their assistance?

'Did I really stand up and tell everyone I left Diarmuid because of some mice?' I say.

'Yes, you did, dear.' DeeDee smiles and brushes a stray strand of hair from my face. 'I'm sure you oversimplified matters, but it was very valiant of you.'

'But it was no match for your bit of theatre. You put on an amazing show as Fabrice. You're an excellent actress, DeeDee Aldridge.' I kiss her cheek very tenderly.

Then Marie marches up behind me and grabs my hand and drags me into the conservatory. 'I can't believe you didn't tell me this!' she splutters in outrage.

'What?' I reply, wondering if she has somehow discovered that I visited DeeDee in London.

'About April, of course!' Marie snaps. 'That your father isn't her real father. Your mother came up to me and just announced it in the kitchen. I'm sure Cedric overheard her.'

'Oh.' I try, but I just can't hide my smile.

Chapter Forty-Five

IT IS NEARLY SPRING, and the first snowdrops are nudging their way through the earth in my small garden. During the winter we almost lost Aggie a number of times, but she's still with us and as curious about my love life as ever.

I don't tell her I have no love life to speak of, though Erika, Fiona and I often rent passionate DVDs and develop major crushes on the leading actors. We watch these DVDs in my cottage so that Lionel and Zak are spared the sight of their beloveds drooling over some hot young Hollywood heart-throb. Love hasn't dented Erika's and Fiona's admiration for a nice bum or a pair of well-toned biceps. I, of course, am free to ogle any hunk I want to. Being single really does have many advantages, including a complete absence of mice.

Nathaniel has gone to London instead of to New York. He has some social-work job there and occasionally sends me cheerful postcards. I haven't asked him, but I suspect he may have finally chosen someone from his horde of female admirers; he hasn't actually said as much, but on the one occasion when he phoned me, he said 'we' when he mentioned a walk in Hyde Park. 'We', of course, is a word that couples get used to. They say it almost without thinking.

Eloise is a 'we' too. She got married last month, to a fabulously rich and handsome man; it must have been a very short and passionate engagement. Glamorous photos of their wedding were splashed all over the papers.

In the circumstances, it's probably best that Nathaniel is out of my vicinity. I probably wouldn't be able to fit him into my schedule anyway, because of my new interests in gospel singing and cookery and my torrid affair with the well-known actor Mel Sinclair. This relationship is wonderfully undemanding, since Mel doesn't know I exist. I rent him when I need him.

During Nathaniel's one and only phone call, I managed to

unearth the truth about his unlikely friendship with 'Fabrice'. It turns out he found out Fabrice was DeeDee on the day they first met in Aggie's bedroom. After their visit, he offered her a lift into town and she accepted; and as she was sliding herself cumbersomely towards the passenger seat, Fred grabbed playfully at one of her dangling earrings and pulled off her wig. When the wig was reclaimed, Nathaniel was going to ask Fabrice why she was wearing a wig in the first place – she did, after all, seem to have nicer hair underneath it, and the wig hid large parts of her face – but then he studied her more closely and found himself saying, without thinking, 'DeeDee?'

'Yes?' she said; then she suddenly realised her mistake and frowned. 'Why are you calling me that name?' she added brusquely. 'My name is *Fabrice*, dear.'

'Oh, DeeDee!' Nathaniel flung his arms around her, and that was that, really. He disarmed her, like he seems to disarm all of us. She ended up telling him her story, though of course she swore him to secrecy. He said he had almost told me many times.

'That's why I kept wanting you to know her better,' he explained.

'Where did you go, that time you both flew off someplace?' I asked, feeling as though I was, at long last, finding the missing pieces of an extremely large and unlikely jigsaw.

'London. She was travelling back there anyway, and she wanted me to see Extravaganza and meet Craig. I kept telling her she should be sharing these intimacies with you and the rest of her family, but she seemed more comfortable with a total stranger.'

A Beautiful Stranger, I thought. You do make a very Beautiful Stranger.

'When exactly did you first meet DeeDee?' I found myself asking. 'DeeDee told me you'd been into Extravaganza with a friend and met her quite a while ago,' I commented. 'She said you phoned her when you heard me mention my lost great-aunt.'

'Actually, that was a fib.' Nathaniel sighed. 'We had to

make you believe I knew about DeeDee without implicating Fabrice. She was still very undecided about whether she could face Aggie as her real self; and she thought that, if you knew about her visits, you'd be even more frustrated about her doubts. I'm sorry.'

'Oh, well. I eventually found out the truth.' I smiled. 'I suppose one sometimes has to build up to it gradually.'

'I knew you'd understand.'

'Do you ever see her now?'

'Yes.' Nathaniel laughed. 'In fact, I think I'm addicted to her marble cake. They may have to start a twelve-step programme for it. You should pop over; she'd love to see you again.'

But what about you, Nathaniel? I wanted to ask. *How would you feel about seeing me again?*

'Tell Fred I miss him far more than I should, given that he's a disrespectful, jewel-thieving mongrel,' he added cheerfully. Then he was gone, and I sat down on the sofa and cried for a bit because I missed him. But I quickly dried my eyes and told myself not to be so stupid. How could I have forgotten that I was actually *enjoying* being single? My social life had expanded, and I was eating far fewer biscuits.

Another good thing about Nathaniel's absence is that I get to borrow his dog. Fred needs plenty of entertainment and exercise if he is to be prevented from stealing jewellery (Greta's gold bracelet was eventually located under the hydrangeas when Nathaniel hired a metal detector), so he and I regularly stroll along the shoreline together. Fred is a wonderful aid to slimming, though of course walking makes me hungry and I have to sternly avert my gaze any time I pass an ice-cream pusher, in his van, virtually trying to force a large cone into my mouth.

Greta is immensely grateful to me for helping her to look after 'that mongrel'. She also sometimes insists I sit in her Provençal-style kitchen and says things like, 'So, Sally, have you found someone else?' She's beginning to sound just like April, but for some reason she also looks a bit worried. The other day, to cheer her up, I mentioned that I'd been dating a guy called Brian Mulligan. I made it sound like Brian was a real find. In fact he makes me want to stick my head into a hot towel with boredom, which is why I don't plan to see him any more, but I felt I could spare Greta these unimportant details.

I thought she'd be pleased to hear about Brian, but she actually looked a bit jumpy. 'Take care not to marry on the rebound, dear,' she said sombrely.

I never expected her to take such interest in my personal life. 'Oh, Brian and I would discuss things in great detail before we did anything like that,' I reassured her.

'So you've discussed marriage?' She leaned forward and almost spilt her tea.

I began to wonder whether Greta secretly fancied me. What else could account for her unnatural interest in the men in my life, or the lack of them?

The truth about Brian Mulligan is that I met him at a gallery opening and we got talking and I let him fetch me a glass of wine. He was tall and well built and had a broad, handsome face that I didn't find particularly attractive, but he seemed pleasant enough, so we went out for a pizza afterwards. I don't really remember what we talked about. A few days later we went to a film and I let him kiss me outside the door of my cottage; it was a soft, passionless kiss that slid off me as soon as I got indoors. After that we went on a Sunday-afternoon drive and had tea in a nice café and walked a bit in the countryside. Then, some days later, we went out for a slap-up Italian dinner and Brian brought me back to his flat – a very tidy, high-tech place – and we slept together. Brian seemed to enjoy it, but I was distracted by the tightly patterned wallpaper.

A few days later Brian 'popped by', just like Diarmuid used to, and I told him I didn't think we should date any more because I was trying to get over the ending of my marriage. He was naturally surprised that I hadn't mentioned this marriage earlier, but he didn't seem particularly disappointed, though I sensed he regarded the announcement as mildly inconvenient: he would now have to find someone else, which he seemed to regard as a chore. I watched his departing car with considerable relief and luxuriated in a wonderfully single evening – a long bath, a high-quality convenience dinner, and rubbish telly watched in bed in wonderfully cosy, unflattering clothes. I didn't eat one biscuit.

April calls more often these days. The whole family knows about Al now; apparently the rumour spread discreetly but rapidly at Marie's party, just like Mum must have known it would. April returned to San Francisco with a broad smile on her face and a large Waterford crystal bowl in her hand luggage.

'So have you found someone else yet?' she often asks, in her perky Californian way.

'Yes, Mel Sinclair will be moving in any day now,' I reply. 'I may need to construct a secret entrance for him because of the paparazzi.'

'Aw, come on, Sally,' she protests.

'Look, I like being single,' I tell her. And in many ways that's true. My days are full and I'm not unhappy, and at long last I have sufficient storage space in my kitchen. I gave in to Diarmuid about the cabinet eventually. He kept ringing and asking me if I was really sure I didn't want it, and one day I said I did, just to shut him up. I told him to come on a day when I knew I would be out, learning about curries and spices from some of the people Erika and I teach English to.

I can no longer lump them all together and call them 'Erika's refugees'. They have names now, and stories, and I like some of them more than others. They make me forget the things I feel I should feel sad about; they make me remember that, in the grand scheme of things, I have a great deal to be grateful for. And some of them are excellent cooks. Every so often The Sunday Lunch allows me to write articles about ethnic cuisine, and my students have been providing the recipes. We try them out in a small kitchen down the corridor from the hall where we hold the English classes. I have eaten fruits and vegetables I didn't know existed, and types of meat and grains I would never have considered. When we try out a recipe we cook enough for the whole class, so sometimes our English classes are, basically, large and somewhat boisterous dinner parties. Erika brings along some wine and fruit juice, and people end up talking loudly and opinionatedly about all sorts of matters, with varying levels of expertise. Occasionally there are tears, but there is also plenty of laughter. In the past, the mixed nature of these gatherings would have distressed me – though I claimed to value honesty, I would have felt disappointed by the sobs amidst the smiles – but now it seems to me that this is entirely normal, given the circumstances. And it is also entirely normal that we often stray onto less serious topics.

It was at one of these dinners that Erika announced that she was pregnant with Lionel's baby. I should have known it. Her cats have a maternal look to them these days. They sell far better than they used to, because of Lionel's marketing. She now works part-time at International Holdings. She plans to leave 'any day now', but she's staying on 'for a little while longer' because of the cream puffs at tea break and the wisdom of their hour-and-a-quarter lunchtime; those extra fifteen minutes make all the difference, she says. Actually I think she's grown quite fond of the place and its numerous eccentricities – which, of course, include her own.

Once Erika shared her joyous news, I felt I had to tell everyone about Nathaniel. I had that feeling again, that we were all in a truth club we didn't even know we'd joined. I said I loved a man who didn't love me but who was a wonderful friend, and I added that it was fine because I had completely accepted the situation and had loads of other interests. Everyone was very moved by this announcement, including Katya, who asked me if what I said was really true. 'Is it true in your heart, Sally?' she kept persisting. After all, Sergei had given her very little encouragement, apart from the occasional fried tomato, but somehow she had known he cared for her – and she was right. These days he sometimes wants to give her his entire breakfast.

'I haven't asked my heart about Nathaniel, because he's already answered the question for me,' I told her. 'He isn't even in the country any more.'

'The oak tree and the cypress grow not in each other's shadow,' Erika commented, and I almost fell off my chair, because she had never been able to get that quote right before. I think she just said it to show off, because it was entirely irrelevant; after all, neither of the trees had emigrated. It seems that Fiona has given her a copy of *The Prophet*, so she can check the wording of quotations any time she wants.

Fiona is now back at her job, and Erika and I still love her, even though we should loathe her. Sometimes we try to feel sorry for her because she works in software, only she loves software – and naturally she has managed to negotiate flexible hours and occasionally works at home, so that she can have her coffee breaks with Milly gurgling on her lap. Of course, she frequently complains about being tired and not having enough time to herself and missing things like going to the cinema and lie-ins and long baths. She also looks extremely happy, if a little less well groomed than she used to be; I believe she hasn't had her hair professionally styled for at least a month, and the more casual look actually suits her. She looks more beautiful than ever.

I'm glad Erika and Fiona have found love – or, in Fiona's case, managed to keep it. I don't tell them I have given up any significant dreams of finding it myself. What people don't seem to understand is that it's quite bracing not having a romance, or indeed a partial marriage, to bother about. Love is such a complicated business, and I have so many other passionate interests that I'm not sure I could fit a man into my life at the moment. Gospel singing with Erika, for example, takes up many a Sunday morning; we've found this small church that has a great dramatic choir. A number of the singers are black, and the whole thing is wonderfully soulful and uplifting. I also often go to the stables to ride Blossom, and I even played one game of tennis a few weeks ago.

Everyone has been a bit different since Marie's party. Mum

392

and Dad, for example, are going to have their lawn back. They say it's to cheer up Marie, who is somewhat vigilant with us all these days; it wouldn't surprise her if Dad turned out to be a transvestite and April a lesbian. (She is also the only one of my relatives who has pestered me for details about Diarmuid's mice. She seemed to think he had a mouse fetish; heaven knows what she thought he might be doing with them.) But I think Mum and Dad actually wanted the lawn themselves. They wanted the rhythm of it, the requirements. So now Mum sometimes goes off to the garden centre and comes back with unusual shrubs, which she and Dad discuss in the kitchen over coffee. Sometimes they have heated arguments about the shrubs, actually, but I suppose that's marriage for you. Sometimes Dad storms out of the house, but he comes back later and they eat dinner and watch telly snuggled up on the sofa.

And I even let Diarmuid mend my music box. I also told him I had flung it at the floor. He didn't seem that surprised. I don't know quite what to do with the music box now. Sometimes I put it in a cupboard and think I'll give it away; and sometimes I take it out and look at it and wonder if I should fling it at the floor again, but I don't. Once I even got it to play its tinkling, tinny tune. As the girl in her flouncy pink dress turned round daintily, I found I couldn't hate her. Her young, hopeful face seemed to have an innocence about it that I hadn't noticed before. Even so, she may end up in Help the Aged along with my wedding ring. My wedding dress went to Oxfam.

Since we sold the house, Diarmuid and I don't have much reason to talk to each other. Very occasionally he phones, and I tell him I'm busy and won't be able to talk for long. 'How's Charlene?' I say pointedly, half hoping he'll say she's run off with an Italian waiter, but it seems that she hasn't. He isn't insensitive enough to add that they are very happy, but he doesn't have to; I can hear it in his voice. Sometimes, for moments, I find myself forgetting all the stupid things we did to each other; but when he's gone I feel a sense of relief – and not

393

just because the phone call is over. I'm relieved that he's happy. He is no longer the 'poor Diarmuid' who provoked such guilt. He is what he should have always been to me: a friend. My Tool-Belt Man. The nice guy someone else should marry.

'How is dear Diarmuid?' Aggie occasionally asks. Her mind sometimes wanders these days. On some visits she thinks I'm DeeDee, and on other days she thinks I'm her mother. There are moments when she thinks she is young again and talks about dances and dresses and walks in the mountains. In a way it's OK. I've got used to it. It's as if an old woman can get young again any time she chooses.

Sometimes Aggie mentions men, young men, who make her eyes grow bright. And one day she said suddenly, 'I should have married one of them, dear, not Joseph. Not after what he did to dear DeeDee.'

'But you loved him,' I said, even though I agreed with her.

We didn't talk about it after that. I've begun to understand that knowing when to stay silent is a powerful kindness. It's not always a good thing to push someone into an honesty they may not be able to bear. We sometimes need our white lies and our evasions, our fibs and tender deceits. And it seems to me that the facts are often only part of the story, anyway. There are so many ways of seeing things; so many ways of being in this weird, wondrous world.

One thing I know, though, is that a lot of us get caught up in dreams that aren't our own. We are sold them expertly, hungrily, by those who need us to believe them. We are asked to enter a trance where a new car or sofa or hot-shot job will bring us happiness. We are asked to believe that some people we have never met are our enemies and others are our friends. More than ever, it seems a time for questions, because sometimes they are so much wiser than our answers. So these days, when I feel I know the truth about something, I make space for doubt; I make space for humility. I ask myself if this is just another story I am telling myself, or being told.

Aggie is happier these days. DeeDee comes over about once

a month; it's as if they're trying to make up for lost time. Now Aggie wants to meet Craig. In fact, we all want to meet Craig. Mum says she'll hold a dinner party if he'll attend it, and it looks like he wants to, so there is already much talk of starters and main courses and Marie is wondering if she should make her lemon meringue pie. They want DeeDee to sing her songs from the shows, since she didn't get around to it at Marie's party. I hope to God she sings better than Erika. (Although Erika is actually learning how to play the guitar, from a book called *Guitar Playing Made Simple*. Lionel gave it to her, probably after a number of evenings of tuneless serenading. I admire his courage.)

DeeDee phones me regularly, and she's invited me to spend part of the summer helping her to restore the old walled garden in her Tuscan villa. She wants me to see the olive groves and the orange trees and walk on that dry, wise, sun-baked earth. I like the idea of it. I feel the need to fetch stones and place them carefully in gaps in the old walls, to tend neglected plants, to help things grow and blossom. Afterwards DeeDee and I will sit on the large veranda, sipping wine from the local vineyard. It would be nice to sit in the sun like a lizard, letting it soak into me. I could scour the local shops for tips about Tuscan interior decoration – and, anyway, it's high time I flirted with a dangerously dark-eyed, pert-bottomed Italian waiter.

'Have you seen Nathaniel, dear?' DeeDee keeps asking when she phones.

'No, I've told you he's in London,' I reply.

'Yes, I know, but… but doesn't he come over on visits?' she enquires. 'He said he was going to when I saw him a while ago.'

'He's got a new life now,' I tell her. But what I'm thinking is that he doesn't seem to miss us. He never really belonged here; he was like a beautiful bird that landed for a while, and then just flew away. But I'm glad I met him. I know he sometimes finds life just as strange as I do. I know we share some of the same questions, and that makes me feel less alone and odd. Sometimes just the thought of him makes me smile – his banged-up old car, his crazy exaggerations, that naughty, bright grin of his. His lightness. His wild, playful strength.

Erika says I should go over to London to see him and bring some of her wildflower liqueur with me.

'But I don't even really miss him any more,' I told her last time we spoke. 'I've got a new love now.'

'Look, forget about Mel Sinclair,' she said bossily.

'Oh, not Mel,' I replied. 'Sammy, the young fellow in the delicatessen who gives me extra cheese and huge handfuls of watercress. I don't think he even weighs the hummus.'

I wasn't lying about this. Sammy is an extremely handsome young man with a wild, rebellious look and a passionate glow in his eyes. His fingers look beautifully long and sensuous, particularly when they are plunging into a bowl of olives. I flirt with him and he flirts with me. If he called by for tea and biscuits, I don't think Erika's wildflower liqueur would be needed.

'You can borrow my camper van and run off with Nathaniel for the weekend,' Erika coaxed. She now actually owns a camper van. Lionel gave it to her when she told him about her dreams of travelling around Europe, though so far they've only used it for a trip to the stretch of strand across the road from my cottage. They watched the sunrise and the sunset and slept to the sound of the ocean. And they were reassured by the knowledge that, if the thing wouldn't move in the morning, they could curl up on my sofa and ring a taxi. This is because Erika's camper van is extremely old; Lionel couldn't afford a new one. But Erika says it has a lovely friendly feel to it and second-hand camper vans have much more character than new ones.

So now I'm walking beside the waves with Fred and wondering if Sammy would enjoy a camper-van weekend with me. I doubt we'd have much to talk about – he's obsessed with football – but he'd be an ideal toy boy. And he'd probably be able to bring along quite a few tasty tidbits. He must get discounts.

As I'm thinking this, the seagulls are calling and the wind is blowing mightily, and it looks like it might rain, which is not unusual. 'Fred,' I call. 'Come here. It's time to go home.'

He doesn't seem to hear me.

'Come on, Fred! Food!'

That usually gets him to come back straight away, but this time he runs ahead. He is running towards a man in the distance.

'Come back, Fred!' I shout, as the man draws nearer. I watch the lanky strides, the mixture of looseness and purpose as he walks. Even from here I can see there is something different about him – a lightness; an intensity.

I squint my eyes against the flecks of seawater. And then I stand stock-still. It's Nathaniel, and he's seen me. In a few seconds he will be by my side.

Chapter Forty-Six

HE'S WEARING JEANS AND a thick woollen jumper, which has a hole in the left elbow. 'Greta told me I'd find you here.' He is out of breath. He must have been walking very quickly.

'Oh.' I just look at him. His hair is shorter and he seems taller somehow, and thinner and sadder. That's what I've always known about Nathaniel – that part of him is sad, despite the gleeful smiles and laughter. And I suppose he sees the same thing in me. There are some people you just can't hide from.

'What… what are you doing here?' I stutter.

'Looking for you – and Fred, of course.' Fred is jumping up and down as though he's on a trampoline. Nathaniel bends down and Fred licks his hands.

'Hi, sweet thing,' Nathaniel says, caressing Fred's long untidy ears. 'So you missed me, huh?'

'Yes, he did miss you.' I try not to say it too reproachfully. 'In fact, he missed you a lot.'

'I'm sorry.' Nathaniel gazes at me, and I see that bruised light in his eyes that always goes straight to my heart.

'He tried to bury my keys the other day.'

'You're a delinquent, Fred,' Nathaniel laughs. 'What on earth are we going to do with you?'

I stare out to sea. Why did he have to turn up just when I was getting used to him not being here?

'It's good to see you again, Sally.'

'And likewise,' I say. When did I last say 'likewise'? We fall easily into step beside each other. Why is it always like this with him? Why couldn't it have been like this with Diarmuid?

I begin to feel awkward. I begin to feel I should be saying important things, but I don't know what they are. 'Are… are you over here on holiday?'

'Sort of.'

'What do you mean, "sort of"?'

'Well, I've finished the job I was doing in London, so I

suppose that means I'm sort of on vacation – though Greta will be roping me in to help with her press receptions any minute.'

'I… I thought you'd settled there.' I look up at him.

'Where?'

'In London, of course.' I'm getting irritated.

'No, that wasn't the plan.'

'So what was the plan?'

'To make some money so that I could buy some new shirts.' He smiles at me. Why does he never answer my questions properly?

'You've got a hole in your jumper,' I say pointedly.

'I know,' he replies calmly.

We just keep walking. I don't even know where we're going; we've passed the small road that leads to Greta's house.

'Were… were you in London on your own?' I feel I have to ask it, even though it's somewhat nosy.

'No, I shared the city with millions of others. Far too many people, really. I think some of them should move to Manchester.' I look down at the sand and the tiny pebbles. I'm tired of this game of hide-and-seek he plays with me. I'm tired of his teasing. 'I didn't find love there, if that's what you mean.' He glances at me quickly and then looks away.

I should tell him I love him, I think. *I should get it over with. He'll be understanding and sweet; he won't make me feel rejected. He'll say he values me dearly as a friend, and I'll tell him I can't just be his friend. I don't want to be good old Sally who, unlike the others, wants nothing from him. It's gone way beyond that. It's time he knew the truth.*

I open my mouth to say this, only what emerges is, 'I suppose you've sold your car.'

'No, I'm getting Gloria all done up,' he says.

'Gloria?'

'Yes. That's what I've decided to call her. She'll be as pretty as a picture. Of course the people in the garage have been trying to frighten me with talk of sprockets and valves and suchlike, but I've told them I'm not intimidated and I've studied karate.'

399

'Have you?'

'Of course not. I tried tai chi once, only I couldn't remember any of the movements afterwards.'

I look at a yacht in the distance. How can we be so alike and yet so different? It doesn't seem fair. The pebbles are crunching beneath our feet, and every so often I stumble slightly. The wind is stinging my cheeks. It really is time I headed home. I have a long article to write about vases.

'So what about you, Sally? Have you found love again?' Nathaniel suddenly asks, apparently casually.

For some reason I think of the time Diarmuid found us together on my sofa. I recall Nathaniel's horrified expression, his embarrassment, how eager he was to reassure Diarmuid that nothing had happened between us. Even when I told him Diarmuid had gone off with Charlene, he still acted as though I was firmly married. He just doesn't fancy me; that's the truth of it. He seems to, sometimes, but that's just because he's so good at intimacy. He's expert at making people feel special.

I decide not to answer his question. I want to be a woman of mystery for a change. I stare moodily out at the sea and leave him wondering.

'Greta tells me you've been dating a very rich, dark and handsome man called Brian.'

So Greta has been gossiping behind my back, and making Brian sound much more desirable than he actually is. I find that I'm grateful, if baffled.

'Yes, I've been dating a man called Brian,' I say. 'I think I'll head home now. It's really getting rather late.'

Nathaniel suddenly reaches out and brushes a stray hair from my face. His hand briefly touches my cheek. It feels strong and warm. I wish he wouldn't do things like that. All the old glowing feelings are coming back, the pointless, beautiful longings. Fred runs back to us and shakes himself vigorously. We are suddenly covered in droplets of water.

'So you thought I could leave Fred without a backward glance?' Nathaniel says, picking up a flat stone and skimming it

400

across the water. 'You thought I could just completely forget him?'

He hasn't even asked who Brian is or what I feel about him, I think. *Even a friend should show some curiosity.*

'There's also a young man called Sammy,' I find myself adding, wanting to prove to Nathaniel that he's not the only person who can have a number of admirers. 'We... we're getting quite close, actually. He gives me wonderful advice about cheese.'

'What?' Nathaniel frowns.

'He works in the local deli.'

'I see.' Nathaniel looks worriedly at an approaching terrier, who is growling. 'Come here, Fred,' he shouts. Fred returns obediently. He doesn't do that for me.

The wind is stronger now and the waves are larger. I move away from them, onto the stretch of sand that is covered in seashells and stray bits of wood and seaweed. It's utterly pointless trying to make Nathaniel feel jealous.

'What were you actually doing in London?' I finally ask. We are heading back towards Greta's house and my cottage.

'I was a social worker. It was just for five months. The guy I was replacing needed some time off to finish his PhD. Now I plan to see if I can get a social-work position here. If I can't, Greta thinks I could make a good flower-arranger. I'd enjoy getting big displays ready for VIP parties, and helping famous people choose orchids. I'd love bossing people around.'

I look at him wearily. 'No, you wouldn't.'

'All right, then, I wouldn't. I want to be a social worker again. It's kind of interesting... and it's better than working for Greta. She's very bossy.'

I pick up a stick and throw it. Fred runs after it and carries it into the sea.

'So how have you been, Sally?'

'Oh, you know... busy,' I say brightly. 'I'm involved with refugees and ethnic recipes, and I've got the columns. And Erika's pregnant now, so she likes being fussed over. My parents are getting a new lawn, and...'

'No, I mean how have you *really* been?'

I pick up a small white seashell. 'I've just told you.'

'No, you haven't.'

I consider walking away from him, onto the nearby road with its cars and its traffic lights and its crowded buses. Instead I just walk more quickly, trying to put some distance between us. He catches up with me easily.

'Do you fancy a Chinese takeaway?'

'No.' It's getting darker; the orange and pink sunset is marbling the sky.

'Burger and chips?'

I shake my head.

'Chocolate cake and tea?'

I hesitate. 'No. I'm not really hungry.'

I start to walk again; in fact, I'm almost running. I can't bear this any longer. I keep wanting to reach out and touch his cheek, bury my face in his shabby jumper. I keep wanting him, but I mustn't. I enjoy being single. I don't need him. What I really need is a very long bath.

'Stop running away from me.' He grabs my arm roughly, and I flinch.

'I'm not running away from you.'

'Yes, you are…' He sighs. 'And I might as well admit it.'

'Admit *what*?' I snap.

'You're shouting at me.'

'Yes, I know I am. And that's because you can sometimes be extremely irritating, Nathaniel. Extremely annoying, and… and quite uncaring, actually.'

And then Nathaniel leans forward and kisses my lips for the briefest of moments. 'Shut up, Sally,' he says softly. 'Please just shut up and let me speak.'

I'm so dumbfounded that I just stare at him.

'What I was going to admit,' he begins slowly, 'is that I suppose I've been running away from you, too.'

My breath catches in my throat.

He places his hands firmly on my shoulders and looks steadily into my eyes, unblinking. 'Let's face it, Sally: we scare each other shitless. Because if we get into this – this weird thing we have, it's going to be really hard to get out of it.'

There are butterflies doing the rumba in my stomach.

'In fact, we may never want to get out of it,' he continues. 'We may be stuck with each other.'

'But… but why haven't you said this before?' I gasp.

'I've given you countless hints that I care for you, but you've perversely ignored them.'

'What hints?' I demand defensively.

'I have scoured Dublin for Chinese takeaways for you. I have helped you find *two* lost great-aunts and a wedding ring. I saved you from having your bottom spanked at that reception, and stopped you from flying off to California, and –'

'I wouldn't have allowed him to spank my bottom!' I declare indignantly.

'Look at you now, Sally! I'm telling you I love you, and you're turning it into some kind of argument.'

'You *love* me?' I almost fall over onto a large, wet bit of seaweed.

'Yes. So now you can go off to Brian, or Sammy, or whoever your latest beau is, and forget about me. But at least I've *said* it.' His eyes are blazing with emotion.

I don't know what to say. I'm pretty sure I'm dreaming. He can't love me. A man like Nathaniel wouldn't love me. Men like Diarmuid love me – or think they do for a while. This kind of thing doesn't happen to me. Or maybe it does…

Suddenly I feel absolutely terrified. I am actually shaking. 'It's not true. You're making it up.'

His blue eyes suddenly soften. He reaches out and enfolds me tenderly in his arms. 'I know,' he whispers into my hair. 'It's kind of awful in a way, isn't it? Kind of scary and sweet, all at the same time.'

'Yes,' I whisper back.

His lips brush the nape of my neck. He pulls back and looks at me quizzically; then he kisses the tip of my nose.

'But what about the others?' I press my face into his jumper. 'Greta told me all about them,' I continue, though my voice is slightly muffled. 'She made it sound as if you were besieged with female admirers.'

'Of course there aren't hordes of women chasing me, Sally. If there were, I'm sure I would have noticed.'

'But –'

'I suppose there are some women who *like* me,' he continues, running a hand gently across my back. 'But nothing like as many as Greta suggested. She decided to talk me up, like she talks up her PR clients. I think she thought you'd be impressed.'

'But... but why would she bother to do that?' I frown.

'Because she knew how I felt about you. She wanted to be a matchmaker. She confessed on the phone yesterday... and then she went on about this Brian Mulligan fellow. Who is he?'

'No one you need to worry about.' I smile, and hold him more tightly.

'That's why I rushed over. I wanted to prise you from Brian's clutches.'

'I was never really *in* his clutches at all.'

'Good.' Nathaniel hugs me so tightly I gasp for breath.

'I wish all this had happened a bit earlier,' I say. He takes my hand and we walk towards my cottage.

'Yes, so do I,' he sighs, pressing me snugly to his side. 'But I backed off because of Diarmuid. I really felt that, if you could make your marriage work, I should let you. And then Diarmuid went off with...'

'Charlene,' I supply.

'Yes, Charlene. And I thought I should wait for a while. Your marriage was so on and off, I thought it might start up again. I didn't want to pounce on you.'

'Oh, dear... I wish you had.' I kiss him again. I want to kiss him all over.

'And then I had a secret I couldn't tell you, about DeeDee,' he continues. 'And you suddenly got all distant and haughty –'

'Only because I thought women were virtually throwing their knickers at you in Grafton Street.'

'Then I decided that you were emotionally vulnerable and I

shouldn't exploit the situation, so I took the job offer in London to see if I could forget you.'

'Why?' I frown.

'Well, I think we've both had some sobering romantic experiences recently. I didn't want us to end up together on the rebound... and you didn't seem that interested in me, anyway.'

'I must be almost as good an actress as DeeDee,' I say.

'But I think I made my own feelings pretty obvious, as I said earlier.'

'No, you didn't,' I protest. 'You behaved as though you saw me as a friend.'

'I probably thought about it all far too much. I'm sorry.' He smiles at me sheepishly. 'My head was buzzing with complications. And then DeeDee told me to calm down and listen to my heart instead. It worked. I suddenly knew that I had to see you.'

'DeeDee?'

'Yes, I went to talk to her about all this yesterday.'

'Oh.' I can't quite take it all in. I feel quite giddy with disbelief and relief, and joy. I need to be somewhere warm. I need to let all this sink in, with Nathaniel beside me – and Fred, of course. He has been watching us very quietly, almost hopefully.

'I think you mentioned something about chocolate cake and tea,' I find myself saying. 'There's a nice café off that side-street. If we hurry, it might still be open.'

'Can I come back to your cottage afterwards?' Nathaniel's eyes have darkened; he grips me more tightly.

'No.'

I can feel his disappointment.

'We're going to Bull Island in Erika's camper van.'

'What?'

'Don't worry,' I giggle. 'I'll explain over a large slice of Black Forest gâteau.'

'I'm not sure if this was such a good idea,' I say, much later.

'Yes, why *did* you suggest this, Sally?' Nathaniel grins at me. 'This van isn't particularly comfortable.'

'I... I think I wanted to show I could be as impetuous as you are. It was stupid.'

'Yes, very stupid... but kind of nice.'

'At least it got us here,' I say. 'I wasn't sure it would. Erika was very surprised, wasn't she?'

'Yes, and grinning from ear to ear.'

'It's lovely to be so close to the sea, though. God, is that a flea?'

'Maybe. Come here.' He grins dangerously.

'But –'

I don't complete the sentence because his lips are on mine. My head is bent back with the force of his kiss. His tongue is searching my mouth. He is holding me with such passion, such longing. I want him to ravish me, see all of me, search me out. The thing is, I'm not sure either of us can wait to get undressed.

'Take off your blouse,' he orders.

'Only if you take off your shirt,' I order back.

We disrobe silently, determinedly, staring at each other. It's like an exquisite striptease. As each layer goes, I feel more desperate to have him close, so close that he is part of me, in me and around me – no escape, just him kissing my eyebrows, the back of my shoulder, the little wrinkled spot on my elbow. Not just going for the obvious. Taking care.

'Now,' I say. 'Please, now!'

I gasp at the force of him, the hard, impatient passion; the depth of it. No one has ever reached that far. That far into my heart.

The camper van rocks. There is nothing I want to hide from him. Glorious sensations are rippling through every molecule of me, and I feel them building until a flood of ecstasy fills me. I let go, and he does too.

For a moment we are too dazed even to register where we are or what has just happened. Then we look at each other and laugh.

Half an hour later we are sitting up in bed, cosily eating

chocolate biscuits. Nathaniel bought them on our way here. As I eat them, I decide I'm going to take up DeeDee's offer. She wants to open an Extravaganza in Dublin – she has enough savings to fund the enterprise for a year, to see if it takes off – and she's asked me to be the manager. I've told her that I'd like the emphasis to be on tea rather than coffee, though of course we would offer both – and hats, and Erika's cats, and sofas, and heaven knows what else. It will be our version of the kind of shop they used to have in Ireland, where you could get a pint of beer and a new shirt and a bag of coal to keep you warm. We need more warmth, in this strange new world with its reality TV and loneliness, where we know more about eight people locked in a house for a month than we do about our own neighbours; where we can hardly summon up the courage to look a stranger in the eye. We need more contact, more connection. We need more beautiful strangers.

Nathaniel is sleeping like a little boy now. Tears of amazement and relief prick my eyes. Nathaniel, my Nathaniel, the most beautiful stranger I have ever met, is lying right here beside me. We are covered in love and chocolate biscuits. I wipe a cascade of crumbs from the pillow and softly kiss his cheek.

Also by Grace Wynne-Jones:-

Ordinary Miracles   1905170647   **£6.99**

Praise for Ordinary Miracles

'Ordinary Miracles has that rare combination of depth, honesty and wit…and all of this backed by a deliciously soft, gentle and loving humour…If you try one new author, try Grace Wynne-Jones.' - OK! MAGAZINE

'Ordinary Miracles is about relationships and love and sex and a little bit of guilt. Jasmine is a worried and witty heroine…an engagingly high-spirited and perceptive debut.' - THE IRISH INDEPENDENT

'Wynne-Jones's sense of humour and the self-mockery of her heroine makes it both funny and touching.' - TIMES LITERARY SUPPLEMENT

Wise Follies   **1905170637**   **£6.99**
Why waving goodbye to Mr Wonderful may be the wisest folly of all...

Ready or Not?   **1905170653**   **£6.99**
Sometimes you've got to forgive the person you were to be the person you can be....